MUSIC FROM
BRITISH UNIVERSITIES

edited by

JOHN CALDWELL
OXFORD UNIVERSITY

DUET AND ENSEMBLE IN THE EARLY OPÉRA-COMIQUE

ELISABETH COOK

GARLAND PUBLISHING, INC.
NEW YORK & LONDON / 1995

Library of Congress Cataloging-in-Publication Data

Cook, Elisabeth.
    Duet and ensemble in the early opéra-comique / Elisabeth
Cook.
        p.   cm. — (Outstanding dissertations in music from
British universities)
    Includes bibliographical references (p.   ) and index.
    ISBN 0-8153-1893-6 (alk. paper)
    1. Opera—France—18th century.   I. Title.   II. Series.
ML1950.C66   1995
782.1'0944'09033—dc20   95-14167
                                                    CIP
                                                    MN

Printed on acid-free, 250-year-life paper
Manufactured in the United States of America

to
John and Mollie

Contents

Preface

Several people have contributed to the completion of this book and I would like to record my gratitude first and foremost to Dr. David Charlton, Reader in Music at the University of East Anglia, whose knowledge, acumen, and sense of humor have guided the work through every stage of its production. I also wish to express my appreciation to Michel Noiray of the Centre National de la Recherche Scientifique, Paris, for his guidance and advice over several years, to Patricia Cooke for her time spent typing and correcting my drafts, to Andrew Skirrow of Camden Music, London, for setting the musical examples and preparing the final typescript, and to John Wagstaff of Oxford University for his careful proof-reading of the completed material. Submitting the work in its original Ph.D. form, in 1989, would not have been possible without funding from the British Institute in Paris, which enabled me to carry out important primary research. In preparing the Garland Publishing edition, several changes have been made: some material has been omitted but much has been recast and updated.

The quotations from French language sources that appear throughout this book have been left untranslated and all original spellings have been retained ("sic" being avoided in all but the most necessary cases). Titles of operas and dates of first performances have been taken from *The New Grove Dictionary of Opera*, ed. S. Sadie (London, 1992), as have names of composers, librettists, and other figures mentioned. In the musical examples certain aspects of presentation have been modernized, including the translation of parts originally notated in alto and tenor clefs to treble clef for ease of reading. The system of library sigla adopted follows that used in RISM (Series A) publications.

Elisabeth Cook

Introduction

This book is a study of the duet and ensemble in 18th-century French opera. It focuses on one genre, the *opéra-comique*, during the third quarter of the 18th century—an important phase of expansion and development—but for background purposes investigates ensemble composition in a variety of French and Italian genres prior to 1750: *tragédie en musique, opéra-ballet, comédie-vaudeville; opera seria, opera buffa, intermezzo.* Some consideration is also given to the development of ensembles in French serious opera after 1750, and one work in particular—Philidor's *Ernelinde*—is analyzed in detail.

Use of the term "ensemble" should be understood throughout to indicate a musical movement combining two or more characters individually in song, whether in concerted finales or at intermediate stages within works. In addition to duets, therefore, the study is concerned with trios, quartets, quintets, sextets, and septets, the septet being the largest type of ensemble encountered. Various forms of "mixed" ensemble receive attention in certain chapters. These either contrast combinations of individual characters with a larger choral body (as, for example, in the duet-chorus) or call upon several soloists to form a small chorus. Full-scale chorus movements, in which several voices with no individual identity share the same line of music, are excluded from the context of this study.

Although French writers have long been attracted to the 18th-century *opéra-comique*, it is only in recent decades that studies in the English language have become more numerous. Prior to the 1960s, available literature was limited to Martin Cooper's brief history of the genre, *Opéra-comique* (London, 1949), and to Donald J. Grout's dissertation *The Origins of the Opéra-comique* (Harvard U., 1939), extracts of which subsequently appeared in various journals.[1] Since the 1960s several more dissertations have been devoted to the subject: Clifford Barnes: *The Théâtre de la Foire (Paris, 1697–1762): its Music and Composers* (U. of Southern California, 1965);[2] Frances Harris: *Jean Claude Gillier: Theatre Musician of the Early Eighteenth Century* (U. of

Minnesota, 1975); Kent M. Smith: *Egidio Duni and the Development of the Opéra-Comique from 1753 to 1770* (Cornell U., 1980); James Butler Kopp: *The Drame Lyrique: a Study in the Esthetics of Opéra-Comique, 1762–1791* (U. of Pennsylvania, 1982); and Bruce Alan Brown: *Christoph Willibald Gluck and Opéra-Comique in Vienna, 1754–1764* (U. of California, 1986).[3] *Grétry and the Growth of Opéra-Comique*, by David Charlton (Cambridge, 1986), is the first full-length study in the English language of an 18th-century *opéra-comique* composer; and Robert Isherwood's *Farce and Fantasy: Popular Entertainment in Eighteenth-Century Paris* (Oxford, 1986) updates, and substantially clarifies, the intricacies of early French comic opera for the general reader and specialist alike.[4]

In contrast, studies of the duet and ensemble are scarce. Existing literature most usually treats the subject in the context of a wider study (in which case findings rarely extend beyond a few pages or are scattered throughout the volume), or addresses the topic in shorter articles (which are, of necessity, limited in their scope of enquiry), or takes Mozart as a starting point. This latter stance, indeed, characterizes much of the available literature on the subject.[5] A detailed monograph exploring the operatic ensemble over an extended period of time and in contrasting genres remains to be written. The present work aims to commence this process by clarifying early approaches to ensemble composition and focusing the spotlight on one of the genres undoubtedly influencing the composer most frequently acknowledged as a great exponent of the ensemble: Mozart.

One article dating from the beginning of the present century remains an important piece of research. This is Edward Dent's 'Ensembles and Finales in Eighteenth-century Italian Opera', which appeared in *SIMG*, xi (1909–10) and xii (1910–11). Analyses of duets, trios, and quartets in works by Alessandro Scarlatti, Vinci, Leo, Pergolesi, and Logroscino are provided, illustrated by copious musical examples, and Dent concludes with comments on the development of techniques in operas by Galuppi and Piccinni in the second half of the century. His research leads to the identification of two types of ensemble: one providing an emotional intensification of the stage picture, the other incorporating dramatic action.

Writers appear to have expressed little further interest in the ensemble for several decades. Then, in 1967, Charles Koch attempted a study similar to Dent's, transferring the sphere of his enquiry to the *opéra-comique* of Duni, Monsigny, Philidor, and Grétry, and concentrating specifically on the ensemble finale.[6] Movements were divided into two categories, "expressive" and "dramatic," and examples cited aimed to illustrate Grout's premise that "the French never developed the dramatic ensemble finale to the extent the Italians did."[7] Koch's article embraced only 11 pages (three of which listed the sources consulted), adopted narrow criteria as a basis for the enquiry, assessed finales only cursorily and, strangely, compared French models with the sophisticated creations of Mozart rather than with finales by the Italian contemporaries of the French composers in question.

Only several decades after the appearance of Dent's article were the suggestions for future research it contained comprehensively followed up. Daniel Heartz's excellent study on the development of the *buffo* finale in Italian opera helps fill the lacuna on this subject.[8] He pinpoints the genesis of the *opera buffa* action—or "chain"—finale to *L'Arcadia in Brenta*, a collaboration between the composer Baldassare Galuppi and the playwright Carlo Goldoni staged in 1749. The article then traces the rapid development of this phenomenon over the following decade in other works resulting from this partnership, and points to the considerable influence of Goldoni on later composers such as Piccinni and Mozart.

An article published in 1980 by Heinz Becker, 'Das Duett in der Oper', is unusual in treating one type of ensemble in detail and therefore breaks new ground.[9] However, since it is wide-ranging in its scope, covering operas from Monteverdi to Richard Strauss, it focuses only on one aspect of duet composition, that of vocal textures, charting in particular the development of dialogue and of simultaneous singing. Becker's discussion of the duet in 18th-century opera before Mozart spans three pages (the article comprises 17 overall) and reaches the rather general conclusion that many such pieces from this period were simply *Arie a due*.[10] Scott Balthazar's 'Mayr, Rossini, and the Development of the Opera Seria Duet: Some Preliminary Conclusions' follows Becker's procedure of establishing the duet as a separate field of enquiry.[11] This article investigates the treatment of the duet in the early 19th century and explores antecedents in style and structure from the late 18th century, in the process highlighting the lack of adequate research into the history of the evolution of the duet and the difficulties encountered when Mozartian and post-Mozartian examples are taken as the starting point.

Finally, two monographs on the *opera seria* and the *opera buffa* in the *Analecta musicologica* series have considered, as part of a wider survey, aspects of ensemble composition. Helda Lühning, in *'Titus'-Vertonungen im 18. Jahrhundert: Untersuchungen zur Tradition der Opera Seria von Hasse bis Mozart*, compares the approach of different composers in settings of the same Metastasian libretto at various stages of the 18th century, thereby offering an insight into the gradual expansion in dramatic character and function of concerted movements.[12] Sabine Henze-Döhring, in *Opera seria, opera buffa und Mozarts Don Giovanni*, continues the path traced in Heartz's earlier study by investigating the construction of ensembles and finales in works from Piccinni to Mozart.[13]

The main advantages of a study concentrating exclusively on the ensemble are that a continuous and comprehensive picture of this aspect of operatic composition is allowed to emerge, and that generalized or anachronistic observations are avoided. The present work is structured in three main parts. Chapter I provides the background to the central theme by outlining the diverse approaches to ensemble composition in the first half of the 18th century in France and Italy, and Chapter II steers the study through the *opéra-comique*'s complex transitional period during the 1750s. Chapters III and IV then focus on the continuation, development, and fusion of techniques in the *opéras-comiques* of Duni, Monsigny, and Philidor, separating dramatic and literary experiments and achievements from purely musical ones. To set these important findings in a broader perspective, Chapter V collates evidence from contemporary writings on music and on opera to present a picture of aesthetic thought relating to the 18th-century duet and ensemble, and Chapter VI assesses the relation of theory to practice, also taking into consideration the extent to which public expectations and reactions shaped developments in both spheres.

This work has a twofold aim. Firstly, it intends to show that, from a much earlier stage in the 18th century than has hitherto been recognized, there existed a "basic belief in the ensemble as a modern resource, promoting musico-dramatic realism," upon which later practitioners of opera were able to capitalize considerably.[14] Secondly, it presents the argument that Mozart's achievements in the sphere of ensemble composition, although significant and far-reaching, in fact represented the culmination of many years' experimentation and development by a host of earlier composers and librettists. Mozart and his collaborators had the advantage of building upon a well-established practice. Their contributions, and the innovations they implemented, can only be understood fully in the light of the traditions from which they stemmed.

Notes

1. 'Seventeenth-Century Parodies of French Opera', *MQ*, xxvii (1941); 'The Music of the Italian Theatre at Paris, 1682–1697', *PAMS 1941*; and 'The *Opéra Comique* and the *Théâtre Italien* from 1715 to 1762', *Miscelánea en homenaje a Monseñor Higinio Anglés*, i, (Barcelona, 1958).

2. Extracts were published in *RMFC*, v (1965) and viii (1968).

3. See also Brown's *Gluck and the French Theatre in Vienna* (Oxford, 1991).

4. Sources dealing with the *opéra-comique* from a more literary point of view include A. Iacuzzi's *The European Vogue of Favart: the Diffusion of the Opéra-Comique* (New York, 1932). Articles by Karin Pendle should also be noted. These include: 'The Opéras Comiques of Grétry and Marmontel', *MQ*, lxii (1976); and '*Les philosophes* and *opéra-comique*: the Case of Grétry's *Lucile*', *MR*, xxxviii (1977).

5. Dissertations include: D. Rossell: *The Formal Construction of Mozart's Operatic Ensembles and Finales* (George Peabody College, 1955); L.I. Wade: *The Dramatic Functions of the Ensembles in the Operas of Wolfgang Amadeus Mozart* (Louisiana State U., 1969); and J. Platoff: *Music and Drama in the Opera Buffa Finale: Mozart and his Contemporaries in Vienna, 1781–1790* (U. of Pennsylvania, 1984). Articles include A.O. Lorenz: 'Das Finale in Mozarts Meisteropern', *Die Musik*, xix (1926–7); and H. Engel: 'Die Finali der Mozartschen Opern', *MJb 1954*. Recently, Marita McClymonds has focused on '*La clemenza di Tito* and the Action Ensemble Finale in Opera Seria before 1791', *MJb 1991*.

6. C.E. Koch: 'The Dramatic Ensemble Finale in the Opéra Comique of the Eighteenth Century', *AcM*, xxxix/1–2 (1967).

7. D.J. Grout: *A Short History of Opera* (New York, 1947), p. 257. (Cited by Koch, p. 72.)

8. D. Heartz: 'The Creation of the Buffo Finale in Italian Opera', *PRMA*, civ (1977–8).

9. H. Becker: 'Das Duett in der Oper', *Musik, Edition, Interpretation: Gedenkschrift Günter Henle* (Munich, 1980).

10. "Häufig sind die Duette in der Oper des 18. Jahrhunderts wirklich nichts anderes als *Arie a due*, die sich zumeist ohne Einbuße zur einfachen Arie reduzieren ließen" (p. 87).

11. *I vicini di Mozart*, ed. M.T. Muraro, i (Florence, 1989).

12. *AnMc*, no. 20 (1983). See, in particular, pp. 59–67 and pp. 96–108.

13. *AnMc*, no. 24 (1986). The relevant section is entitled "Angleichung der caratteri und Ausbau der Ensemble- und Finaltechnik" (pp. 85–104).

14. D. Charlton: '"L'art dramatico-musical": an Essay', *Music and Theatre: Essays in Honour of Winton Dean* (Cambridge, 1987), p. 246.

List of Musical Examples

List of Abbreviations

A	alto, contralto (voice)
AcM	*Acta musicologica*
AnMc	*Analecta musicologica*
Aug.	August
B	bass (voice)
BSIM	*Bulletin français de la Société Internationale de Musique*
CI	Comédie-Italienne
CMc	*Current Musicology*
COJ	*Cambridge Opera Journal*
diss.	dissertation
ed(s).	editor(s), edited by
facs.	facsimile
ff	following pages
fl	floruit
Font.	Fontainebleau
F-Pc	Paris, Fonds du Conservatoire National de Musique [in *F-Pn*]
F-Pn	Paris, Bibliothèque Nationale
F-Po	Paris, Bibliothèque-Musée de l'Opéra
FSG	Foire Saint Germain
FSL	Foire Saint Laurent
GB-Lam	London, Royal Academy of Music
GB-Lbl	London, British Library
GB-Lcm	London, Royal College of Music
IMSCR	*International Musicological Society Congress Report*
JAMS	*Journal of the American Musicological Society*
m(m).	measure(s)
M.	Monsieur
Mme	Madame
MR	*The Music Review*

MS	manuscript
MT	*The Musical Times*
n.d.	no date (of publication)
No(s).	number(s)
NOHM	The New Oxford History of Music
p(p).	page(s)
PRMA	*Proceedings of the Royal Musical Association*
priv.	private performance
pubd	published
R	editorial revision or reprint
rev.	revision; revised (by/for)
RdM	*Revue de musicologie*
RMFC	*Recherches sur la musique française classique*
S	soprano (voice)
s.l.	sans lieu (no given place of publication)
sc.	scene
SIMG	*Sammelbände der Internationalen Musik-Gesellschaft*
suppl(s)	supplement(s)
T	tenor (voice)
U.	University
Vers.	Versailles
Vve	Veuve
wk(s)	work(s)
ZIMG	*Zeitschrift der Internationalen Musik-Gesellschaft*
Ii (etc)	Act I, scene i

Duet and Ensemble in the Early Opéra-Comique

Chapter I

France and Italy: Early Approaches
to the Ensemble

Until around the middle of the 18th century, the integration of the duet and ensemble in opera might, in the case of a great many composers and librettists, be deemed conservative. Early French opera was modelled closely on the spoken *tragédie* and was considered as much a poetic as a musical form of expression. The emphasis placed on poetry was reflected in the generic description *tragédie en musique*, and this led contemporary critics to judge such works not, at first, on their own grounds but by the standards that had been set for French classical drama. Little wonder, therefore, that French composers limited the occasions for combining characters in simultaneous song, when *littérateurs* such as Saint-Evremond were castigating continuous lyrical declamation as a wholly unnatural phenomenon: words were poorly understood when sung even by one character.[1] Italian opera, though shaped by different traditions and conventions, was no less averse to the inclusion of vocal ensembles. By the early 18th century the pre-eminent genre, the *opera seria*, had developed into a singers' opera in which the solo aria assumed a position of unrivalled prominence. Arias were distributed carefully, in accordance with the singers' rank and importance within the opera, and the dictatorial nature of many virtuosi would often militate against the composition—or at least inclusion—of ensembles.[2] In contrast, however, the *opera buffa* and *intermezzo* would experiment with new ideas and techniques, allowing the inclusion of a greater number and variety of concerted movements. The *vaudeville-comédies* and embryonic *opéras-comiques* staged at various locations in Paris during the first half of the 18th century, while much less sophisticated than their comic counterparts in Italy, likewise established certain quite similar patterns and characteristics.

By the middle of the 18th century conventions regarding the musical and dramatic treatment of duet and ensemble had emerged. The occasional innovation is also apparent. Tracing the evolution of these conventions in the French and Italian genres mentioned above forms a basis for recognizing unusual or daring exceptions to the norm and for understanding developments that took place in ensuing decades.

The Tragédie en Musique and Related Genres

Appendix I (pp. 299–302) lists those works staged between 1673 and 1751 at the Académie Royale de Musique (the Paris Opéra) on which findings are based. Its purpose is to clarify the scope of the discussion below and to show that observations concerning the treatment of ensembles are drawn from a wide and varied repertory. Included in the Appendix are *tragédies en musique*, *opéras-ballets*, *ballets-héroïques*, and an assortment of other genres including *pastorales-héroïques*, *comédies-ballets*, and *divertissements*.[3] Studying ensembles from this varied repertory throws up the initial problem of establishing what should or should not constitute an ensemble: the formal construction of the early *tragédie en musique* was such that many individual scenes fluctuated between recitative, short *airs*, arioso, and moments of ensemble, with blurred lines of demarcation between each. In Lully's works, three types of concerted movement are present: fragmentary ensemble exclamations (anything up to 10 bars in length but often only one or two); *ensembles en scène* (semi-structured ensembles closely integrated with surrounding music); and individual movements in closed forms (binary, ternary, rondo). Very short ensemble fragments in works from the Appendix have been omitted; however, distinguishing between fragments and *ensembles en scène* can be difficult and the decision to omit or include is based on whether the sentiments expressed are merely interjectory or relevant to the drama. From the *préramiste* period onwards, *ensembles en scène* become less common, and the distinction between fragmentary ensembles and larger-scale ensembles is consequently more marked.

Problems of identification are also encountered. Prologues and *divertissements* abound with ensembles for anonymous characters drawn, in all probability, from the chorus. Those written for two voices have been classed as duets, but those for three or more are excluded since their predominantly homophonic textures suggest that the characters functioned more as a *petit choeur* than as individuals.[4] Such hybrid movements, common in Lully's operas, feature less prominently in the works of his successors (with the exception of Rameau), partly because they were more a phenomenon of the *tragédie en musique* than of the increasingly popular *opéra-ballet* and its related genres.

Ensembles combining soloists with the chorus (again common in prologues and *divertissements*) create further problems of classification and are included if the ensemble portions for individual characters are substantial and distinct from the chorus. One pattern which has been included is the "duet-chorus," where the chorus repeats material previously sung by two soloists. This was used frequently by Lully and remained popular with composers throughout the first half of the 18th century. Less common, however, and excluded from present consideration, were "mixed" ensembles in which the soloists' material either alternated intermittently with, or is superimposed over, choral utterances. Rameau was the first composer to include such ensembles consistently in his works, a tendency that became more apparent as his dramatic career progressed, by contrast with his contemporaries who were generally less experimental.[5]

The first part of this chapter therefore considers ensembles cast in closed musical forms, a range of *ensembles en scène* from the early period of the *tragédie en musique*, hybrid movements in which unnamed participants function as individuals rather than as a collective group, and mixed ensembles where the soloists' sections are clearly separated from those sung by the chorus. These movements established patterns of ensemble composition in the mainstream of French opera and, since the results were a creative collaboration between composer and librettist, the emergence of these patterns needs to be considered first from a literary, then from a musical, perspective.

Ensemble Texts: the Librettists' Approach

Librettists were responsible for choosing which type of ensemble to include, their placement within scenes, the structure of the text, and the nature of the sentiments expressed.[6] Inevitably, they came to fashion certain expressive types of ensemble from standard dramatic situations.

The duet was by far the most commonly encountered ensemble in librettos, comprising 80% of the concerted numbers set by Lully and 90% of those set by the *préramistes*, by Rameau, and by his contemporaries. Trios made up much of the remainder since the inclusion of quartets and larger ensembles was rare.[7]

The popularity of the duet did not—at least in the late 17th century—limit its dramatic scope, although a move towards standardizing its role is evident in the following century. Many duets were written for the two main lovers who might voice their mutual love or a common anguish, argue playfully, or be locked in more violent dispute. Duets for different pairings included lovers with their confidant(e)s or with a thwarted suitor. Those rejected by both hero and heroine might also sing together as, occasionally, would two male characters vying for the attentions of the heroine. Table 1 indicates that the wide range of dramatic situations portrayed in duets set by Lully (less than one-third for lovers and nearly one-quarter for diverse pairings of secondary characters) developed with time into an increasingly pronounced preference for combining happy lovers in song.

Table 1: Expressive Types of Ensemble

Type of Duet		Lully	Préramistes	Rameau	Contemps
Lovers:	unification	17%	24%	44%	45%
	confrontation	1%	3%	1%	3%
	supplication	7%	11%	8%	5%
	parting	4%	4%	2%	2%
		29%	42%	55%	55%
vengeance		7%	12%	1%	3%
rejection		2%	5%	1%	4%
lover with confidant(e)		5%	3%	---	4%
male confrontation		3%	1%	1%	2%
secondary characters (i.e. various situations)		24%	13%	8%	13%
		41%	34%	11%	26%
prologue/divertissement		30%	24%	34%	19%

Trios during this period combined the hero and heroine with either a sympathetic third party (a parent or deity) or a character in opposition (a rejected suitor). Those in prologues and *divertissements* offered more varied groupings of pastoral figures in which joyful, celebratory sentiments might be voiced.[8]

Ensemble texts in librettos set by Lully were diverse in both syntax and versification; the only consistent features were that prologue and *divertissement* texts tended to have fewer syllables per line but longer strophes (often presented in pairs). During the *préramiste* period patterns became more pronounced: some 40% of ensembles in *tragédies* were based on quatrains, rising to 60% in the *opéra-ballet* and related genres. The design of ensemble texts was such that characters most frequently shared the same (or closely identical) words, a procedure that still allowed them to voice opposing sentiments since the alteration of a salient word here and there—"Il faut *aimer/changer* toujours"—was sufficient to delineate confrontation.[9] These *unanime* texts ensured clarity, an important requisite in French opera, and provided a model from which Quinault and his immediate predecessors rarely deviated.[10] Exceptions to this rule are worth pointing out since they anticipate techniques that became commonplace in the second half of the 18th century. These included the interleaving of related texts, the use of sung dialogue, and the juxtaposition of contrasting blocks of text.

In IIvi of *Bradamante* (1707) Roy has the two lovers express different ideas (though they are essentially in accord) through the interleaving of two quatrains, partially repeated, with the first line identical and the rest employing the same meter and rhyme scheme:

ENSEMBLE
Je periray plûtôt moy-même,
ROGER   Que de hasarder vos jours.
BRADAMANTE   Que de trahir nos amours.
ROGER   C'est un trop cruel secours.
BRADAMANTE   Heureux, heureux le secours,
ROGER   Que d'exposer ce qu'on aime.
BRADAMANTE   Qui peut sauver ce qu'on aime.
ENSEMBLE
Je periray plûtôt moy-même,
ROGER   Que de hasarder vos jours.
BRADAMANTE   Que de trahir vos jours.[11]

This procedure extends the technique of altering only a few words in a *unanime* text, and achieves most effective results in situations where the characters are essentially in sympathy yet express their feelings in different ways. In Roy's setting Roger voices his distress at the prospect of harming his beloved in combat while *Bradamante* desperately hopes for an answer to the problem, sentiments that are reinforced by protestations of mutual self-sacrifice.

The use of dialogue as a means of tempering monologues and drawing characters together in more direct discourse, can be traced back to antiquity, but while (as will presently be shown) Italian duet texts in the early 18th century favored this device almost exclusively, ensemble texts in the *tragédie en musique* and related genres were based only infrequently on dialogue. Where this occurred, the voices generally alternated line by line and merged at the close, as in the following example by Lamotte from the prologue of *Sémélé* (1709):

LE PRESTRE
Chantons ses glorieux exploits.
LA PRESTRESSE
Chantons sa jeunesse & ses charmes.
LE PRESTRE
Il mit l'Orient sous ses loix.
LA PRESTRESSE
D'Ariane trahie, il essuya les larmes.
Qu'il charme,
LE PRESTRE
Qu'il triomphe,
ENSEMBLE
Et qu'il goûte à la fois
La douceur des plaisirs, & la gloire des Armes.[12]

Sometimes short portions of ensemble texts might be amalgamated with preceding material to create a more substantial movement with a predominantly dialogued text. Lully occasionally made use of this technique, but it was exploited extensively by *préramiste* composers as a means of creating longer, more unified ensembles. One of many examples is found in IViii of Danchet's *Alcine* (1705). Ensembles based on some degree of dialogue could, in other words, be the result of a composer's modification of the text rather than a feature initially suggested by the librettist.

Rameau's librettists occasionally carried the notion of divergent expression in ensembles a stage further by allowing characters to voice contradictory opinions simultaneously using more strongly contrasting language. Louis Cahusac included this text in Viv of *Zoroastre* (1749):

ZOROASTRE	ABRAMANE
Ciel! Laisse éclater ton courroux	Frapons, les Dieux sont pour nous
Ciel! ô Ciel! C'est trop te suspendre	Frapons, rien ne peut le défendre.
Acheve, ô Ciel! encore un prodige	Il va périr; j'en crois ce prodige
nouveau.	nouveau.
Qu'un éclat de Tonnerre,	Qu'un éclat de Tonnerre,
Sous leurs pas entr'ouvre la terre,	Sous ses pas entr'ouvre la terre,
Et creuse leur tombeau.	Et creuse leur tombeau.[13]

The verses for Zoroastre (God of Light) and Abramane (Spirit of Darkness) are sharply differentiated at the outset, although by the end of the third line the two adversaries share very similar words. A more sustained divergent text was provided by Voltaire in the *divertissement* (IIxi) of *La princesse de Navarre* (1745). Rameau, however, omitted this from his score (having also omitted a *divertissement* duet from the first act of the same work):

UNE BERGERE	UN BERGER
J'aime, & je crains ma flâme.	Ah le refus, la feinte,
Je crains le repentir.	Ont des charmes puissants;
Tendre desir,	Desirs naissants,
Premier plaisir,	Combats charmants,
Dieu de mon ame,	Tendre contrainte,
Fais moi moins gémir.	Tout sert les Amants.[14]

Other divergent ensemble texts were written for Rameau by Fuzelier (a trio in *Les Indes galantes*, IIvii) and by Autreau and Le Valois d'Orville (a duet in *Platée*, IIIvii). Few comparable examples are found in librettos set by Rameau's contemporaries. Duclos provided Bury with a divergent duet in scene ii of the prologue to *Les caractères de la Folie* (1743), but the composer responded with a setting only eight bars in length. Niel composed a longer duet to a divergent text by Fuzelier in IIIiii of *L'école des amants* the following year, but this was divergent only in that one character sang in French and the other in Italian.[15] During the same period librettists structured some duets in dialogue form: Roy, in the final scene of Rebel and Francoeur's *Le ballet de la Paix* (1738), and Fuzelier in Iii of Mondonville's *Le carnaval du Parnasse* (1749). Fuzelier's penchant for dialogue and divergent ensemble texts (examples from three operas have just been cited) may well have been the result of his association with the fair theatres whose plays contained many such ensembles, based on vaudevilles.[16]

Ensembles were sited at various stages in individual scenes: at the beginning, *en scène*, near the end (in which case a brief portion of recitative linked that scene to the next), or to conclude scenes. More substantial ensembles sometimes comprised entire scenes.[17] Those within prologues and *divertissements* were always allocated an intermediate position since such festivities concluded with choruses or dances. Essentially, the dramatic function of ensembles was to summarize and substantiate what had previously occurred; they did not in themselves further the action. This appears to have been common in ensemble composition in all genres throughout the first half of the 18th century.

The Musical Characteristics of Ensembles

Ensembles in Lully's *tragédies* were neither lengthy nor of strong formal design. They were between 20 and 40 bars in length (those in prologues and *divertissements* tended to be longer, while *ensembles en scène* were shorter). Longer movements might be cast in binary, ternary or rondo forms, although these designs accounted for only 50% of ensembles placed outside prologues and *divertissements*. As the 18th century progressed, individual movements sited within the main action of the *tragédie* achieved greater cohesion through harmonic organization, and binary form superseded others in popularity. Prologue and *divertissement* ensembles, however, were just as readily cast in rondo form, and from around 1698 ternary structures (da capo, dal segno) were imported from Italy.[18]

Rameau's ensembles showed no significant increase in length: only a few extended beyond 60 bars.[19] Their brevity can be explained by the fact that they were often conceived as part of a larger design and achieved substance through being integrated into larger musical contexts. Since, as noted earlier, his contemporaries avoided such constructions, their individual ensembles were often longer, several extending to 60 or 70 bars. Binary form maintained its popularity, with 58% of the ensembles examined using this pattern.

Closely allied to the predominantly *unanime* texts of this period were the homophonic vocal textures around which many duets were patterned. (Trios and quartets favored these too: their textures are considered separately.) It was usual for both voices to combine in parallel sixths and/or thirds, but delayed entries and sustained imitative writing could add variety to this design. Significantly, some 20% of duets from the *préramiste* period experimented with more contrapuntal vocal textures, this figure rising to 27% with the advent of Rameau and his contemporaries. Thus, although a homophonic texture is one typically

Example 1.1 "Voyez couler mes larmes / Ecoutez mes soupirs" *Proserpine* IViv (Lully, 1680)

encountered, examples of more innovative patterns do exist and are worth examining.[20]

Example 1.2 "O sort heureux, aimable jour" *Hypermnestre* IIv (Gervais, 1716)

Only about one-third of Lully's duets had the voices moving in parallel sixths or thirds throughout (i.e. an entirely homophonic texture). While a further half of his duets had predominantly homophonic textures, the means of varying this style were not as narrow as previous writers have suggested. Imitation might be sustained over several bars (as in the duet "Non, non, rien n'est comparable" from IIIiii of *Phaëton*). Another common device was for one voice to embellish words (such as "volez", "gloire", "chaîne") while another sustained a long note. The remaining one-sixth of Lully's duets varied note-against-note writing with freer techniques, the duet from IViv of *Proserpine* (Example 1.1) being a good case in point. Here, alternating passages in dialogue give way to quasi-imitative counterpoint at the words "Ma douleur mortelle/Mon amour fidelle," the voices cadencing briefly ("Ne touche point vostre coeur") before pursuing different melodic and rhythmic ideas (bars 12–28), the result initially of suspensions and then of Pluton's slower moving line. Only in the penultimate bar do the voices reach agreement as they prepare the cadence.

During the *préramiste* period duets with contrapuntal elements (as mentioned above, 20%) were found most often in the main action of the *tragédie*. Examples 1.2 and 1.3 illustrate this point. "O sort heureux" from IIv of *Hypermnestre* (1716) and "Une flâme vive et constante" from Iii of *Tarsis et Zélie* (1728) are both relatively contrapuntal and have the characters singing different lines of text quite persistently. This is certainly unusual given that both are unification duets for the main lovers, a dramatic context in which one would normally expect homophonic, *unanime* singing. Moreover, the minor key of Example 1.3, again surprising given the context, is in keeping with the *préramistes'* preference for ensembles in the minor key.[21]

Example 1.3 "Une flâme vive et constante" *Tarsis et Zélie* Iii (Rebel/Francoeur, 1728)

Duets with contrapuntal textures in which characters also express opposing sentiments, although few in number, are of interest as prototypes of the divergent duet. James Anthony describes Louis Bourgeois as "one of the few préramiste composers to write genuine 'divergent' duos" and uses the duet from IIii of *Les plaisirs de la paix* (1715) as an illustration (Example 1.4).[22] Other examples, both by Mouret and the first predating the Bourgeois duet, can be added here in order to emphasize that such

Example 1.4 "Cesse d'aimer/Cesse de boire" *Les plaisirs de la paix* IIii (Bourgeois, 1715)

experiments were not isolated ones. In Example 1.5, "Quand on fuit les (cède aux) tendres Amours" from IIiii of *Les fêtes de Thalie* (1714), two female characters take up opposing views on falling in love in a duet whose texture is first imitative (bars 1–10), then more persistently contrapuntal and lacking in obvious thematic accord at cadences. Example 1.6, "Ah! devroit-on deux fois se rendre" from IViii of *Les amours des dieux* (1727), features Ariane and Bacchus in confrontation, the former resisting the latter's advances. While the voices cadence more uniformly (bar 10, bar 14) than in the previous example, the characters' texts bear much less initial resemblance. In both examples the singers' melodies and rhythms are quite clearly distinguished and a contrapuntal vocal texture maintained against conflicting lines of text. Mouret, like Bourgeois, was certainly going against convention in these duets.

Example 1.5 "Quand on fuit/cède les tendres Amours" *Les fêtes de Thalie* IIiii (Mouret, 1714)

Stage works by Rameau and his contemporaries contained fewer duets written in an entirely homophonic style and tended to incorporate more contrapuntal elements. Additionally, duets with dialogue textures and those with divergent texts set to contrapuntal textures are found, but principally in works by Rameau: dialogue duets, for example, in Viii of *Dardanus* and IIIvii of *Platée* (Example 1.7), and divergent duets in IIi of *Hippolyte et Aricie* (Example 1.8) and Viv of the 1749 version of *Zoroastre*.

Example 1.6 "Ah! devroit-on deux fois se rendre" *Les amours des dieux* IViii (Mouret, 1727)

Patterns of vocal textures in larger ensembles did not differ significantly from those of duets. Some made use of contrapuntal features in a manner ahead of their time, for example trios in the prologue of Campra's *Le carnaval de Venise* (this for three bass voices), in IIIii of Gervais' *Hypermnestre*, and in Iv of Lacoste's *Télégone*. Example 1.9 is a somewhat unusual quartet from IVviii of Montéclair's *Les festes de l'été*, which eschews the usual practice of ranging the characters in a double duet formation and has them enter instead in imitative fashion and maintain some degree of contrapuntal activity (although Belise and Valère

Example 1.7 "Que toi, Qui moi!" *Platée* IIIvii (Rameau, 1745)

sing very much in agreement) before cadencing with the text "Ne contraignons plus nos desirs."[23]

Rameau often treated larger ensembles in an adventurous manner. Some trios, for example, experimented with mixed textures (homophonic utterance interlaced with contrapuntal activity) and had characters voice contrasting sentiments. Of particular note is "Plaignons-nous à l'Amour" from IIiii of *Castor et Pollux*, in which Phébé despairs of winning Pollux while he laments the death of his brother and is encouraged by Telaïre to rescue him from Hades (Example 1.10). A second trio for the same characters in the following scene portrays Pollux supported by Telaïre but opposed by Phébé, for having decided to rescue his brother. The quartet in IIIvii of *Les Indes galantes* (omitted from later revisions) is one of Rameau's most adventurous larger ensembles, sustaining a contrapuntal texture throughout, even though it presents happy, paired lovers at the close of the work.

Example 1.8 "Contente-toi d'une victime" *Hippolyte et Aricie* IIi (Rameau, 1733)

Even given the small number of trios and quartets in works by Rameau's contemporaries, textures were often innovative. The trio in Iiii of *Nitétis* (1741) allowed the three voices to pursue separate melodic and

Example 1.9 "Pour former les plus douces chaînes" *Les festes de l'été* IVviii (Montéclair, 1716)

rhythmic ideas, and a quartet closing *Zaïde* (1739) concentrated on
dialogue singing. A unique quintet, from *Don Quichote chez la*

Example 1.10 "Je reverrai donc/Je ne verrais plus" *Castor et Pollux* IIIiii (Rameau, 1737)

duchesse (1743), focused on a single character and had the remaining four sing in double duet formation.

The voice types combined in concerted movements were the result of the characters involved and the conventional types of ensemble that evolved. Female singers took the soprano range and the *haute-contre* was used for many male roles. Thus lovers' duets characteristically paired soprano and *haute-contre* voices while duets of rejection or vengeance were written for soprano and bass. Over half of Lully's duets used a male-female pairing, generally soprano/bass but also soprano/*haute-contre* and occasionally soprano/tenor, this variety reflecting the range of dramatic situations expressed in duets during this short period. Duets in prologues and *divertissements* were more frequently written for two male or for two female voices, the former thus using diverse vocal groupings. Trios generally mixed male and female voices although some for three men (never three women) are found.

During the *préramiste* period a male-female pairing remained the norm. 80% of duets forming part of the main action in the *tragédie en musique* were of this complexion, the remainder being divided equally between combinations of two men or two women. In prologues and *divertissements*, however, this ratio dropped to 45% while duets for female characters rose to 40% of the total, far in excess of the 15% allocated to male characters. Ballet genres steered a middle course, resulting in an overall distribution of: male-female (71%), two females (19%), two males (10%). Popular combinations in all works were soprano/bass (40%), soprano/*haute-contre* (30%), two sopranos (20%), the remainder using other pairings. Trios mixed male and female voices rather than characters of the same sex (for example two sopranos/bass or soprano/*haute-contre*/bass), and quartets always balanced the sexes, a common combination that of two sopranos, *haute-contre*, and bass.

Rameau's vocal distributions reveal some suprising changes, these linked to the standardization of duet situations at this time. A high proportion of all his duets (80%) involved a male-female pairing, and in over half of these Rameau reversed preferences of the preceding period by combining soprano with *haute-contre* rather than with bass; this practice was maintained by his contemporaries. The remaining 20% of his duets favored pairings of male rather than female characters, which reversed patterns established by his predecessors (although these movements retained the usual vocal pairings). In works by his contemporaries, however, pairings of two sopranos rose to comprise 15% of the duets examined while those for male characters fell to a little over 10%. Larger ensembles by Rameau and others retained combinations of characters and voice distributions familiar from earlier in the century.

Vocal ensembles in Lully's *tragédies* were, almost without exception, accompanied by a *basse-continue*. If the movement included *ritournelles*, the bass line was temporarily reinforced with stringed instruments, but only two concerted movements in Lully's entire operatic output made use of a five-part string accompaniment throughout.[24] During the early years of the 18th century, *préramiste* composers began to thicken string textures and add various woodwind instruments (flutes, oboes, bassoons). Marais' dialogue duet from the prologue of *Sémélé* (1709) was unusual in using continuo, flutes, trumpets, and "4 violons et le petit choeur," these additional instruments offering a discreet accompaniment, doubling one or other of the vocal lines and occasionally lending extra color and texture to the ensemble. Destouches' vengeance duet "Tonnez, Dieux immortels" in IIIii of *Sémiramis* (1718) used violins to accentuate the passionate outbursts of the singers. Indeed, from Lully to Rameau and beyond, vengeance ensembles were invariably characterized by frantic string accompaniments. Ensembles as a whole by Rameau and his contemporaries continued to be supported by continuo alone, although the addition of unison violins was not uncommon.[25] The autonomy of the accompaniment was sometimes highlighted, although clarity of text was an ideal to which composers still adhered.

Major and minor tonalities were used in equal proportion by Lully in his ensembles although *préramistes* favored minor keys. Time signatures might fluctuate in individual numbers between common and triple time in order to accommodate the lack of tonic accent in the French language, but these changes occurred less frequently as the 18th century progressed and many ensembles came to be cast in triple time, especially those in prologues and *divertissements*. Indications of tempo remained rare. Completely absent in Lully's scores, markings such as *vite*, *vif*, or *vivement* were gradually incorporated, especially for vengeance ensembles, and lovers' duets were generally marked *gai*, *tendrement*, or *légèrement*.

Italian Genres

Appendix II (pp. 303–306) lists the sources consulted for preparing the following analysis of ensemble composition in Italian serious and comic genres to about 1750. Only complete operas or extant individual acts have been included.[26] For ease, three chronological categories have been created: (i) all genres of opera composed before 1720 (a year established as a watershed between Baroque and pre-Classical styles by previous writers);[27] *opere serie* written between 1720 and 1750; and (iii) comic works from the same period (extended a little beyond 1750 to increase the number of available sources). These works, however, represent only the tip of the iceberg since 18th-century composers wrote—and revised—operas with astonishing speed. There are undoubtedly omissions;[28] and since this study is concerned with a great many composers' and librettists' treatment of a single aspect of operatic composition the problems arising from the practice of *rifacimento* do not receive any detailed consideration. Nonetheless, the number of ensembles encountered still provides a good cross-section of material, allowing detailed observations concerning conventional and innovative approaches to emerge.

Ensemble Texts: the Librettists' Approach

Among the many librettists active in Italy during the first half of the 18th century, the most prominent in the *opera seria* alongside Pietro Metastasio were Apostolo Zeno, Silvio Stampiglia, Antonio Salvi, and Giovanni Pasquini. During the first two decades of the 18th century these poets effected a series of reforms aimed at greater dramatic coherence through plot simplification. The profusion of separate actions and events was reduced by limiting the number of scenes, characters, and arias, and by gradually excluding comic elements. These changes affected the treatment of ensembles considerably. Poets active in the comic sphere included Gennaro Federico and, later, Carlo Goldoni. They, in turn, transformed the character of the *opera buffa* from farce to sophisticated intrigue, so that eventually it came to rival the *opera seria* in dramatic stature.

Before 1720, Italian librettos seem to have varied greatly in their provision of ensemble texts. Some contained as many as 10 or more, others around five, several only two or three. Only three of the 33 works examined contained none at all. Duets accounted for 88% of all concerted texts, quartets 8%, and trios 3%.[29] In the *opera seria* after 1720, numbers decreased sharply: 29% of the works consulted contained no ensembles, 45% included one, and 20% two.[30] This trend was formalized in Metastasian librettos which, on average, contained one ensemble (or less) apiece. Metastasio was opposed to the simultaneous expression of emotions and recorded his dislike of concerted movements on several occasions.[31] The near-elimination of ensembles from serious librettos was at the expense of larger concerted movements: in the pre-classical *opera seria* the duet was the most common type of ensemble composed.

Not so in comic librettos. An *opera buffa* would provide for at least three concerted movements, often four or five and occasionally more.[32] Duets accounted for only half of the ensembles featured, since trios and quartets became commonplace and movements for even more voices less unusual.[33] The shorter *intermezzi* incorporated fewer concerted numbers and these, like the genre itself, required only two characters; however expansion of the form in the 1740s led to larger casts and, correspondingly, to the inclusion of more complicated ensembles.[34]

The texts of ensembles in serious and comic genres were invariably modelled upon dialogue patterns, although the nature of the dialogue in each case was very different. Those from the *opera seria* were skilfully streamlined so that the singers were balanced in alternating verses or couplets, joining with one another at the close of sections. Their conversation had a very orderly appearance and texts were often distributed in a symmetrical fashion. Comic texts were less formally expressed, their characters conversing in more rapidly alternating dialogue. Many were based on irregular line-by-line utterances, these developing momentum as the participants interrupted one another, exchanged shorter, disjunct phrases, and occasionally merged in unison. This technique was particularly applied to texts of larger ensembles which required a clear yet adroit distribution of material among the requisite number of characters.

In *opera seria* texts, characters expressed identical or near-identical sentiments. Short dialogued stanzas and couplets allowed them to articulate their feelings individually, but these followed on from each other in a balanced and orderly manner, and gradually gave way to *unanime* singing. On the rare occasions that divergent sentiments were expressed, only salient words were altered to produce antithetical meanings (a device employed, as seen earlier, in French librettos). Meter and rhyme schemes remained the same and lines were blended, where possible, through assonance and alliteration, the text thus retaining a cohesive, symmetrical appearance. Comic ensemble texts, by contrast, were subject to far fewer restraints of language. Characters were generally at variance, expressing opposing sentiments which were easily incorporated into the freer framework of their texts. There was little sense of symmetry in this dialogue, and when voices merged different lines were often juxtaposed, this simultaneous divergent expression enhancing the chaotic character of such pieces.

The profusion of ensembles in late-17th and early-18th-century librettos had resulted in their siting at many different points in individual scenes. From around 1720 onwards, in the *opera seria*, the convention of the exit aria came to dictate that ensembles (like arias) be placed at the end of a scene. On a broader scale, about one-third of ensembles from this later period were placed at the end of internal acts, and many of those remaining were incorporated within the final act. Librettists subscribed to the notion that a concerted movement intensified the drama in preparation for the curtain or the dénouement. Comic genres articulated this principle more pervasively. Ensemble finales to each act of an *intermezzo* had long been traditional (indeed, this was their only possible siting until the expansion of the genre in the 1740s admitted more characters and facilitated the composition of internal ensembles). Concerted finales in the *opera buffa* also became the rule and, in addition, internal ensembles tended to gravitate towards the closing stages of an act, thus accelerating the pace in the build-up to the curtain. The expression of dramatic climax through the ensemble was thus more characteristic of comic than serious genres, and is a subject of significance in our subsequent chapters.

Early-18th-century reforms in the *opera seria* libretto led not simply to a decline in the number of ensembles included in a work, but to a considerable stereotyping of their dramatic context. From 1720 onwards it became customary to combine *primo uomo* and *prima donna* at some point in a duet, and these ensembles accounted for over two-thirds of the corpus examined.[35] Lovers' duets depicted scenarios similar to those found in contemporary serious genres in France, as did the situations making use of trios and quartets, although some quartets successfully depicted moments of complexity at the height of the dramatic action.[36]

The two characters of the *intermezzo* were (or eventually became) partners: initially a lascivious *vecchia* played by a man and an innocent youth sung by a female, the roles reversed gradually to a middle-aged bachelor and a wily young maiden. Plots always ended in marriage or reconciliation, but before this outcome the pair were embroiled in a series of arguments, misunderstandings, and ruses. Duets were spirited encounters quite distinct from those sung by lovers in *opera seria*. Full-scale comic works provided by far the greatest opportunity for librettists to develop the importance of ensembles. Characters were not bound by the system of ranking so rigidly maintained in the serious genre and could therefore participate in this type of movement more freely. However, since the *opera buffa* mixed comic and serious characters and included those midway between the two (*mezzi caratteri*), a wide variety of ensemble types was nurtured. Duets were written in both *buffa* and *seria* styles, and larger ensembles portrayed characters in a number of situations. Since these were largely dictated by the circumstances of individual plots it is difficult to describe typical scenarios, but they generally emphasized the complex and confusing. Their participants were invariably at odds with one another and the simultaneous expression of diverse, contradictory opinions was their hallmark.[37]

The process of setting texts to music required the composer to adopt several different methods: repetition, fragmentation, interruption, omission, addition, and transference of lines. Although these will not be described in detail, one point should be stressed: composers manipulated serious texts far less frequently than comic ones. In the former it was customary for introductory verses to be set once through before being subjected to any of the above treatment. Comic ensemble texts, in contrast, were often set in a more random and disjointed manner before the whole had been articulated clearly. Musical and poetic expression in the *opera seria* aimed at order and clarity. That in comic genres was deliberately more disjointed.

There is also evidence of manipulation of ensemble texts on a wider scale. This is surprising given the control and influence of the most popular poet of the pre-classical period, Metastasio, and his dislike of concerted pieces (which, he felt, diluted the effect of individual emotions).[38] That composers did not always abide by his dictates is evident from the addition of a duet in Porpora's setting of *Didone abbandonata* (1725) and of a trio in Jommelli's *Ezio* (1741). The trend towards adding more ensembles, in particular larger ensembles, became even more pronounced towards the end of the 1740s, especially in Metastasian librettos set by Galuppi. His *Semiramide riconosciuta* (1749) included a trio in addition to the poet's original duet. (This duet, incidentally, was omitted in settings by Porpora (1729), Jommelli (1741), Hasse (1744), Gluck (1748), and Perez (1750), proof of the process working in reverse.) Even more enterprising was Galuppi's addition of a quartet finale in the first act of *Artaserse* (also 1749) which ambitiously replaced the series of solo arias concluding that act. (Graun had tried a similar experiment in his 1743 setting of the same libretto.) Galuppi's new quartet produced a movement of considerable power:

> "One of the most expressive effects of this quartet is the way the music enhances the tragic isolation and moral strength of the hero. Arbace controls most of the modulation, confirms the tonal arrivals, and stands out, alone, vocally, for the most part, against the others. . . . Dramatic quartets like this are scarce in the 18th century, whether in the first half or the second."[39]

This innovative move was not approved by Metastasio, who favored the castrato Carlo Farinelli with his opinion of Galuppi, concluding that he was:

> "... a very bad workman for poets. He thinks as much about the words when he is setting them, as you do of being elected Pope. . . . In short, he is not my Apostle. I speak with sincerity to my dear Gemello, but in public, I leave him in that state of credit in which he is held by those who judge with the ear, and not the understanding."[40]

Significantly, Galuppi's quartet was not included in performances of the opera in Padua two years later, although this had probably less to do with Metastasio's opinions than with those of the virtuosi singers, who were anxious that their rights should not be undermined by composers telescoping individual arias to create ensemble movements. Metastasio, even well beyond this date, continued to disapprove of elaborate concerted numbers. Correspondence 20 years later with Saverio Mattei (who had just refashioned *Ezio* for Sacchini) records his view of a quartet added to the second act:

> "The *Quartetto* which you have written is decent, convenient, and happy; and if it is well treated by the composer and performers, I believe it will have a good effect in the representation. Indeed it will render the second act somewhat barren of airs, in which the two principal personages will have but one song

a-piece: which would have been thought sacrilege, when I wrote the opera ... it is a false supposition that I ever wrote a *Quartet* for *Ezio*, or that I ever requested one."[41]

That the role of the ensemble was slowly changing is evident in these mid-century experiments exploring new dramatic devices offered by the immediacy and economy of simultaneous expression and by the ability of concerted movements to telescope dramatic situations more eloquently and concisely than a succession of solo arias.

Musical Characteristics of Ensemble Composition

One consequence of the "exit aria" convention was an increase in the average length of movements. From comprising fewer than 50 bars before 1720, ensembles composed after this date could be in excess of 100 bars, and several approached 200 in length. Pre-Classical *opera seria* made considerable use of the da capo pattern to the extent that 85% of its ensembles were cast in this mould. By around 1720 the original ABA structure had expanded into a five-part form in which the A section was bipartite.[42] Longer middle sections were introduced during the 1740s which led to the composition of some extremely extensive movements.[43] Changes in meter, pulse or tonality, perhaps combined in various ways, afforded other opportunities for contrast, as did various dal segni patterns and the use of *ritornelli* to punctuate the different sections. Shorter movements in single sections (after which characters would remain on stage) are found quite frequently. Less common are examples of binary form;[44] so, too, are through-composed movements in contrasting sections, Jommelli's 1743 setting of *Demofoonte* containing two such examples which, concluding Acts I and II respectively, have the musical appearance (though not the dramatic action) of embryonic chain finales.[45]

The formal structure of ensembles in comic genres was far more diverse. These ensembles needed a musical framework to match their texts and the dramatic situations they portrayed; they were thus more freely shaped to suit the action. While da capo and dal segno patterns were still employed, mainly for *intermezzo* finales and for internal ensembles of the *opera buffa*, a good many other movements were cast in binary form, chain form, were through-composed or were short, single section pieces. Simple AA[1] or AB binary structures gave way to AA[1]BB[1] designs and to the two-tempo form.[46] Through-composed movements and chain structures were located from the 1730s onwards as both internal ensembles and finales, the earliest example from the repertory studied occurring in Hasse's *intermezzo Lucilla e Pandolfo* (1730). This was a duet finale in four sections spanning 91 bars: $\frac{4}{4}$ *Andante ma poco*, $\frac{3}{8}$ *a tempo giusto*, $\frac{4}{4}$ *Allegro*, $\frac{3}{8}$ *tempo giusto*. In this example—as in those examples in chain form from the *opera seria* cited earlier—one vital ingredient was missing to make these innovations *par excellence*: stage action. This was achieved, as Daniel Heartz has highlighted, in the quartet closing Act II of Goldoni and Galuppi's dramma giocoso *L'Arcadia in Brenta*.[47] Here, the ensemble becomes a vehicle for dramatic action, and the implications of this achievement are tremendous.

As the 18th century progressed, *opera seria* composers grew to favor vocal textures cast in dialogue and, by the 1720s, a standard pattern had emerged that was to be retained for several decades. First established in duets—from which stems the term "dialogue duet" used by writers from that century onwards—the technique was quickly transferred to larger ensembles.

The Italian dialogue duet was based on the principle of opening, imitative solos building up through shorter alternating and eventually overlapping phrases, culminating in simultaneous singing and cadential agreement. The first manifestations of this pattern were apparent in the years leading up to 1720;[48] during the following decade, when the pattern was applied specifically to the five-part da capo form, dialogue textures in duets were constructed upon these lines:

A: opened with lengthy, imitative solos followed by shorter phrases and motives, briefly overlapping or combining the voices and concluding with cadential homophony.

A[I]: concentrated on the interplay of shorter phrases and motives built around a series of *à2* climaxes and retractions, likewise culminating in cadential agreement.

B: was far more varied in appearance with textures ranging from solos or simple dialogue to contrapuntal interplay between voices, and not necessarily ending with homophony.

Although subtle modifications and alterations were made to this basic plan, the overall contour of the vocal texture in the individual sections from simple to dense provided a framework to which composers

Example 1.11 "Tu vuoi ch'io viva o cara" *Artaserse* IIIvi (Vinci, 1730)

Example 1.11 *(cont.)*

generally adhered. Example 1.11, from Vinci's *Artaserse* (1730), is a typical Italian dialogue duet from this period.

Ensembles cast in single sections and in binary form likewise progressed from solos to cadential homophony via overlapping and juxtaposition of parts, while the very few in free form would blend the vocal parts more haphazardly in a disparate mix of dialogue, counterpoint, and homophony. Like duets, larger ensembles relied greatly on dialogue patterns, opening with thin textures and gradually acquiring more complexity. A greater number of voices offered more opportunity to experiment with counterpoint, and composers at times achieved an intricate blending of voices over sustained periods.[49]

Comic ensembles incorporated a more accelerated style of dialogue, made greater use of contrapuntal elements and, above all, avoided standard patterns such as those typical of the dialogue duet, although the progression from simple to complex texture and the notion of interim ensemble points still served as a framework. A general distinction between serious and comic opera is that the music of the former was conceived in terms of its broad effect while the latter's reflected minute changes in the action and sense of the words.[50] This is particularly true of vocal textures in comic ensembles, which are much less predictable than their serious counterparts.

Vocal tessituras in 17th- and 18th-century Italian opera were characterized by a preponderance of high voices, since this was the heyday of the castrato singer. Castrati had, like female voices, a soprano or alto range and they took the role of the heroic lover. Roles allocated to tenors and basses were secondary in status and importance. Sopranos and altos were associated with youth and innocence, tenors and basses with age and experience.[51]

With the general streamlining of ensembles in the *opera seria* during the early years of the 18th century and the customary meeting of the leading couple in a concerted movement, the majority of duets written after 1720 were for castrato soprano and female soprano. Only a few exceptions to this pattern exist: one is the single duet in Feo's *Andromaco* (1730) pairing the *prima donna* (soprano) with an ancillary male character (tenor). Duets rarely combined characters of the same sex. The notion of ranking to which singers so rigorously adhered could barely concede that two principals meet in an ensemble, let alone that a principal should sing with others of the same sex (i.e. with a lower ranking character).[52]

Given the small number of larger ensembles in the *opera seria*, vocal groupings were far less consistent than in duets. Some trios and quartets continued to favor a combination of high voices while others opted for a wider distribution of tessituras involving natural male voices.

The interaction of *parti serie* and *parti buffi* in the *opera buffa* led to a variety of combinations, including the soprano/castrato soprano pairing from the *opera seria* but, more commonly, that of soprano (or contralto)/bass from the *intermezzo*. Characters of the same sex were brought together without reserve, the combination of two bass voices proving particularly popular. Vocal groupings in larger ensembles emphasized the greater freedom of concerted writing in the comic sphere. Various permutations were used in trios; quartets and quintets tended to polarize sopranos with natural male voices, the latter often outnumbering the former.

Instrumental accompaniments to ensembles at the turn of the century comprised either two-part string textures (violin and continuo) or the continuo line by itself. Gradually separate viola parts and divisi violins were introduced to create a four-part string texture, but only a very small number of ensembles added extra instruments (such as flutes, oboes, bassoons, and horns). Some innovative experiments with timbres and textures are, however, found. Scarlatti's duet in IIix of *Il prigioniero fortunato* (1698) comprised antiphonal groupings of cellos, lutes, and continuo; and in a later opera, *Telemaco* (1718), he included a duet in the opening scene whose orchestration extended to 15 staves.

After 1720, *opera seria* ensembles continued to make use of stringed instuments, textures fluctuating between two, three, and four parts. Extra woodwind instruments were rarely called upon: given the prevailing preference for beautiful melody, instrumental writing was secondary to the vocal interest. String parts would double vocal lines, embellishing them on occasion, but more often providing padding in between phrases, at heightened moments such as main cadences, and during the *ritornelli*.

Comic ensembles favored even thinner, unencumbered orchestral textures that allowed for textual clarity and flexibility of tempo, both vital ingredients for an effective performance. Instrumental writing was of a more interjectory and sporadic character and frequently incorporated independent motives of great rhythmic vitality. Indeed, the more disjunct vocal textures of comic ensembles offered greater scope for the accompanying forces to exert themselves, and this could give rise to a lively interplay which enhanced the momentum of the piece and ensured musical continuity. In large ensemble finales, woodwind and brass instruments might be added to lend grandeur to the occasion and provide a fitting conclusion to the work.

Ensemble movements in works composed up to 1720 used major keys twice as often as minor keys. Common-time signatures were far more usual than meters in triple time (when $\frac{3}{8}$ rather than $\frac{3}{4}$ was preferred). While a quarter of the ensembles studied carried no tempo indication, around 40% bore markings of *Allegro* and its variants, and 30% *Andante* or descriptions of similar intent such as *amoroso* and *grazioso*. Some 5% were headed *Vivace* or *Presto*. After 1720 there was a noticeable rise in the use of major keys: only 20% of *opera seria* ensembles were cast in a minor key, this figure decreasing to a mere 10% in comic works. Tempo markings in serious ensembles were spread evenly between *Allegro* (and variants), *Andante*, and slower pulses (*Largo, Lento, Adagio*). Comic movements, in contrast, employed a narrower range of tempos, concentrating on *Allegro* or *Andante*. *Presto* and *Vivace* markings were less common than one might expect, and slower pulses were extremely rare. However, ensembles in comic genres, and in the *intermezzo* in particular, specialized in fluctuating styles and tempos which:

> "... seem to result from the composer's genuine effort to reflect changing moods of the text. In contrast to set pieces in contemporary *opera seria* where the ideal, at least, was to establish and maintain a single affect throughout an aria, composers of *intermezzi* seem to have felt no compunction whatsoever about introducing drastic changes of style and tempo within a given number when such changes were suggested by the text."[53]

The same commentator also observes that in changing tempos and time signatures so frequently, composers were merely writing into their scores a performance practice already established by singers themselves.

Vaudeville Comedy and the Emergence of the *Opéra-Comique*

This is not the place to give a detailed account of the development of the *opéra-comique* as an institution and a genre, or of the theatrical legislation and vicissitudes influencing the evolution of a genuinely

French style of comic opera during the first half of the 18th century.[54] Rather, the task is to consider the repertories of those institutions staging works that can be gathered loosely under the general term *opéra-comique*, and to investigate the character and significance of ensemble numbers therein. Musical comedy had spread its roots widely in France during the 17th century such that, in works subsequently presented by the Comédie-Italienne and the Comédie-Française, music played a prominent role. However, comedians at the Foire Saint Germain and the Foire Saint Laurent—the two most important Parisian fairs—who specialized in loosely compiled *comédies* mingling spoken dialogue with song, dance, and acrobatic display, were foremost in cultivating a style of musical comedy that eventually developed into the *opéra-comique*. It was not uncommon for playwrights and composers to be employed by more than one establishment during the course of their careers.

A conservative estimate suggests that the two fair theaters alone produced over 1000 original plays during the first half of the 18th century. The Comédie-Italienne presented 648 new pieces between 1716 (the year of its re-establishment) and the arrival of the Bouffons in August 1752, while the repertory of the Comédie-Française included 776 new works for the period April 1701 to March 1774.[55] Not all these compositions are, of course, relevant to the development of the *opéra-comique* and one question worth posing at this point is: were these works simply plays with music or embryonic music dramas?

Sources for resolving this question are plenteous.[56] They show that comedy was enhanced by music through the use of vaudevilles (popular songs), *chansons*, French *airs* and Italian *ariettes* (i.e. borrowed music), instrumental numbers and, occasionally, specially composed pieces. Initially, the bulk of this music appears to have been confined to *divertissement* interludes, although in the fair theater repertory and in many works given by the Comédie-Italienne scenes forming part of the main intrigue were increasingly interlaced with vaudevilles, the design of whose texts was required to correspond closely to the musical syntax of the chosen vaudeville. This practice made few demands on composers but did call for considerable dramatic acumen on the part of playwrights. More importantly, it shows music appropriating the function of words, and when this practice is extensive, the point is reached where music becomes essential to the drama: the poetic text cannot stand on its own. Given the increase in the amount of specially composed music incorporated into the *opéra-comique* in the decades leading up to 1750, the popularity of music borrowed from mainstream operas and, above all, the widespread integration of vaudevilles, one can conclude that by 1750 the *opéra-comique* had almost managed the transition from play with music to cohesive musical drama and was poised to enter the mainstream of operatic history.

The Vocal Ensembles

Ensemble movements in the repertories of the theaters in question fall into three categories: those based on vaudevilles; ensembles parodied (borrowed) from contemporary sources such as the *tragédie en musique*; and original compositions. Each has different musical characteristics as well as differing dramatic functions and implications.

Ensembles based on vaudevilles are the most commonly encountered and these, in turn, divide into different groups: vaudevilles concerted fully throughout; those concerted only partially; and dialogued vaudevilles. Vaudevilles with texts shared by several characters were a traditional means of combining actors in song, but how these pieces were performed is still a matter of speculation. Many may simply have been sung in unison, others were written in parts. "Quel plaisir de boire du vin" and "Vuidons les pots et la bouteille", for example, were both based on two-part *airs à boire* and "Ah! Mme Anroux" originated as an *air à boire* for three voices. The task of reconstructing the character of these embryonic ensembles is difficult. As vaudevilles were so well known they were not included in musical supplements. Moreover, comedians performing these ensembles were actors, rather than trained singers, and were very likely to improvise at will. The following passage, from scene vii of *Le temple de l'ennui* (Le Sage and Fuzelier, FSG, 1716) shows how they appeared in print:

Pendant qu'on jouë l'Air des Rats, *Arlequin, Mezzetin, Pierrot & Colombine dansent; & sitôt que Momus paroît en l'air dans son char, ils chantent:*

TOUS, *ensemble*

AIR 62. (*Les Rats.*)

Vien, Momus; garotte
Les ennuis fâcheux;
Et que ta marotte
Regne dans nos jeux.

(les violons reprennent l'Air.)

Momus, que tes Rats
Se rassemblent tous à la Foire.
Momus, que tes Rats
Nous prétent de nouveau appas.

(Momus descend de son char.)[57]

Sometimes only parts of vaudevilles were concerted and these, very commonly, were solo *airs* concluding with short ensemble refrains. Among the most popular *timbres* (the vaudeville incipit or refrain) treated in this manner were "Allons gay", "Talalerire", and "Et vogue et galere":

AMINE

AIR 20. (*Allons, gay*)

Ne parlons plus de peines;
Oublions nos douleurs:
Par d'éternelles chaînes
Lions nos tendres coeurs.

TOUS QUATRE

Allons gay,
D'un air gay, &c.[58]

It was also common for a vaudeville to be divided between singers. The pace of this dialogue varied considerably: characters might alternate stanza by stanza, couplet by couplet, line by line, or interrupt one another in mid-line. Their dialogue sometimes lasted for one or two vaudevilles or might be sustained over several. In scene xvi of *Pigmalion* (Panard and L'Affichard, FSG, 1735), for example, a lively dialogue for three characters extended over eight successive vaudevilles. Brief moments of ensemble often punctuated the ebb and flow of the dialogue, as in this extract, from scene xi of *Le rappel de la foire à la vie* (Le Sage, Fuzelier, and d'Orneval, FSL, 1721):

M. VAUDEVILLE.

AIR 140. (*Ma Comére, quand je danse*)

Paris reverra la Foire,
En dépit des Envieux.
La FOIRE.
Mettons toute notre gloire
A faire de notre mieux.

Ensemble.
Que dans nos Jeux
Rien ne soit vieux.
La FOIRE.
Rien sérieux.
M. VAUDEVILLE.
Rien ennuyeux.
La FOIRE.
Rien ne soit vieux,
Sérieux,
Ennuyeux.
Ensemble.
Paris reverra la Foire,
En dépit des Envieux.[59]

Given these basic designs, playwrights proceded to elaborate freely and produced many variations. Some results were extremely unusual and enterprising. In Ivii of *Les chimeres* (Piron, FSG, 1725) conflicting texts were distributed among three characters to the *timbre* "J'aime le vin, et moi l'oignon, et moi la belle Janneton," which were all then sung in canon. A dialogue vaudeville of similar intricacy, from Iii of *La princesse de Carizme* (Le Sage, FSL, 1718), has been described thus:

> "The Prince and Arlequin are conversing in front of an insane asylum, and their dialogue is set to the *timbre* 'Comme un Coucou que l'amour presse.' Their conversation is interrupted by three inmates of the asylum, whose voices are heard from offstage, each singing to a different *timbre*. Gilliers [sic], who helped Lesage with the music of this play, undoubtedly played an important part in arranging the melodic and harmonic structure of this scene."[60]

A third example closed the prologue to *Arlequin Endymion* (Le Sage, Fuzelier, and d'Orneval, FSG, 1721). The situation was amusing and highly topical: three characters discussing the precarious situation of the fair theaters. Each character suggested a different solution to help them. La Comtesse argued that the actors should continue to sing, Le Marquis that they perform only spoken *comédies*, and Le Chevalier that they present *pièces en écriteaux* (plays using placards rather than the spoken word). After a cry of "Tous trois ensemble," La Comtesse sang a vaudeville, Le Marquis started a monologue, and Le Chevalier encouraged the crowd ("plusieurs voix à la fois") to sing from placards. The stage directions implied that these activities were simultaneous, since a fourth character appeared on stage "Comme ils font ce Trio." This example emphasizes how bizarre the juxtaposition of characters and music could sometimes be in the early *opéra-comique*, how freely playwrights were able to experiment, and how few rules there were to constrain them.

The freedom to experiment and introduce innovative techniques in concerted vaudeville writing must have served the twofold purpose of preparing the ground for a wealth of further experiments in ensemble composition in the first flowering of the *opéra-comique* from the late 1750s onwards, and of emancipating attitudes towards the ensemble. Obviously the structure of individual plays dictated the extent to which the various vaudevilles described above were integrated into the musical *comédies* of the repertories in question, but that vaudevilles were the stock-in-trade of the fair theaters and, to a lesser extent, the Comédie-Italienne, is evident from their play texts. Two conventions were clearly established. First was the importance and use of dialogue in ensemble composition as representative of flexible communication between characters, offering scope to the drama to change its course and pace rather than remain fixed, and scope for a rudimentary style of musical ensemble to be responsible for this. Second was the move towards rounding off works with a concerted vaudeville, which established the tradition of a final vaudeville sequence that was to characterize the fully-fledged *opéra-comique* in the later 18th century. These, in a much less sophisticated way, paralleled contemporary developments in Italian comic opera.

Just as composers were at hand to arrange vaudevilles, so they were available to rearrange music borrowed from contemporary operas. Alongside parodied *airs* and instrumental numbers are found one dozen ensembles, all but one occurring in fair theater productions, and all but three being parodied duets (the rest were trios).[61] Lully was the composer mainly plundered for parody ensembles, seven being lifted from his *tragédies* (including *Alceste* and *Persée*); Campra proved quite popular, with three (from *Les fêtes vénitiennes* and *Tancrède*), and there was one apiece from Collasse and Destouches. Transferring a well-known piece of music from a serious to comic milieu could produce an immediate and profound impression on audiences, one that was at once humorous and bathetic, capturing a given situation more concisely and effectively than ordinary speech. For example, in *La querelle des théâtres* (Le Sage, FSL, 1718), a play performed shortly before official powers forced the fair theaters to close, two parody duets were sung by the characters La Comédie Française and La Comédie Italienne in imitation of the vengeful

Gorgons from Lully's *Persée*. For contemporary audiences this would have captured more beautifully than words the prevalent spirit of theatrical warfare: try as they may, the official companies could not, through legal means, dampen the enthusiasm or success of the humble fair theaters.

Parody ensembles portrayed a whole gamut of scenarios—lovers' lamentations, reconciliations, various arguments, and confrontations— and had other atypical features, for example vocal textures based mainly on dialogue and imitation, and the mixing of contrapuntal and homophonic elements. They must have played some role in accustoming audiences to more sophisticated concerted movements and, undoubtedly, their characteristics served as models to be emulated by composers writing original ensembles. Indeed, after around 1730, parody ensembles were gradually replaced, in fair theater productions at least, by specially composed ones.

This final category of ensemble is found in the repertories of the Comédie-Française, the Comédie-Italienne, and the fair theaters from the earliest years of the 18th century. Source materials provide music for 32 duets and one trio at the Comédie-Française, 14 duets at the Comédie-Italienne, and nine duets and three trios at the fair theaters. These may not, of course, represent the full picture but they offer an idea of the general characteristics of original ensembles and the influences upon which they drew.

That works performed at the Comédie-Française should contain the largest number of extant ensembles stresses the importance of music at this establishment.[62] These compositions owe much to the Lullian style in the preponderance of duets, their emphasis on homophonic textures, and their *unanime* texts. Binary and ternary were the preferred forms, and one-third of the corpus examined achieved a length in excess of 30 bars. Significantly, 10 of the 32 duets made use of dialogue texts and textures (six of the duets were actually termed "Dialogue"). These were presented as simple, natural conversations with cadential homophony in places, if at all. While, musically, many of these ensembles were evidently conceived as individual pieces, dramatically they were placed almost without exception in *divertissement* scenes in which their function was purely decorative.

The 14 original ensembles from the repertory of the Comédie-Italienne were all duets composed by Mouret between 1718 and 1730 and survive in his *Recueils des divertissements du Nouveau Théâtre*

Italien. They follow on chronologically from the ensembles discussed in the preceding paragraph and bear many similar features. They, too, are confined to *divertissements*; 13 of the 14 are written to *unanime* texts, and 11 have homophonic textures. Mouret evidently simplified his approach for the Comédie-Italienne which, after all, had less experienced singers and musicians than the Opéra. He did, however, carry out an unusual experiment with the playwright Lisle de la Drevetière in the comédie *Le faucon* (1725), setting a duet with a bilingual text. One character sang in French, the other in Italian, and Mouret capitalized on this by creating a texture involving much juxtaposition of the two lines. Example 1.12 reproduces the opening of this duet.

Example 1.12 "Bambino e l'amore" *Le faucon* (Mouret, 1725)

The 12 original ensembles from works performed at the fair theaters (see Table II) divide into two groups: those composed during the 1720s by Jean-Claude Gillier and his son (Nos. 1–5) and those written by a new

Table II: Original Ensembles in *Opéras-Comiques* before 1750

1.	TRIO (1721) "Heureuse intelligence" *Le rappel de la foire* (Le Sage, Fuzelier, & d'Orneval)	*Théâtre de la foire*, iii	Gillier
2.	DUET (1728) "Honneur cent et cent fois" *La Pénélope moderne* (Le Sage, Fuzelier, & d'Orneval)	*Théâtre de la foire*, vii	Gillier
3.	DUET (1729) "Grands Dieux" *L'impromptu du Pont-Neuf* (Panard)	*Théâtre de la foire*, vii	Gillier
4.	DUET (1730) "Chantons, chantons" *L'espérance* (Le Sage, Fuzelier, & d'Orneval)	*Théâtre de la foire*, viii	Gillier
5.	DUET (1730) "L'homme au fond" *Les deux suivants* (Panard & Pontau)	*Théâtre de M. Panard,* ii	Gillier *fils*
6.	DUET (1734) "Celebrons en ces lieux" *Les audiences de Thalie* (Fuzelier)	*IIe Recueil de l'opéra-comique* (Paris, *c*1734)	Corrette
7.	DUET (1738) "Marions Julie" *Le bal bourgeois* (Favart)	*Théâtre de M. Favart*, viii	?
8.	DUET (1740) "Le Tic-Tac" *La servante justifiée* (Favart)	*Théâtre de M. Favart*, vi	?
9.	DUET (1743) "Cruelle Sévérine" *Les nymphes de Diane* (Favart)	*Vaudevilles et ariettes de l'opéra-comique* (Paris, *c*1750)	Corrette
10.	TRIO (1744) "Chantons, que notre voix éclate" *Acajou* (Favart)	*Théâtre de M. Favart*, vii	? Blaise
11.	TRIO (1744) "Les cinq voyelles" *Acajou* (Favart)	*Théâtre de M. Favart*, vii	Blaise
12.	DUET (1744) "Amour à nos tristes soupirs" *Acajou* (Favart)	*Théâtre de M. Favart*, vii	?

generation of composers, including Michel Corrette and Adolphe Blaise, during the next two decades (Nos. 6–12). They embody, therefore, the conventions and innovations of the period.

The first five were all placed in *divertissement* scenes and, structurally, formed part of larger movements (except No. 1, a short, independent piece of 16 bars): Nos. 2 and 5 served as refrains in rondo forms; No. 3 comprised three stanzas, the last sung in ensemble; and No. 4 sandwiched extensive solo singing between opening and closing ensemble sections. The first three pieces were all based on *unanime* texts

Example 1.13 "Le Tic-Tac" *La servante justifiée* (1740)

Example 1.14 "Cruelle Sévérine" *Les nymphes de Diane* (Corrette, 1743)

and were homophonic in texture (although No. 3 followed popular French practice in setting the word *enchaîne* to lengthy vocal melismas). Nos. 4 and 5, composed in 1730, included some less typical features: the closing ensemble section in No. 4 incorporated some neat dialogue interchanges and No. 5, admittedly only a seven-bar rondo refrain, avoided a homophonic setting of its divergent text.

From 1734 (No. 6) onwards, each ensemble except the last explored one or more new ideas. No. 6 used the italianate da capo form. No. 7 was a fine dialogue duet and actually bore this description in the text; moreover, it opened the play, thus introducing the action, a device favored greatly in the *opéra-comique* of the 1760s. In *Le bal bourgeois* the plot is set in motion as tutor and aunt of the heroine agree that their ward should be married as soon as possible.[63]

Nos. 8 and 9 each had divergent and extremely florid vocal textures. The former, entitled "Le Tic-Tac," was included as an *air nôté* in the musical supplement to Favart's play, although its text did not feature in the libretto itself. (It would appear to close the final scene of *La servante justifiée*.) An extensive movement, 88 bars in length, it divided into several sections—some solo, some ensemble—forming an overall structure of AABABCDEF. The final section, transcribed in Example 1.13, contains some sprightly duet writing. No. 9, likewise not located in the printed version of Favart's play, exists in Corrette's collection of *Vaudevilles et ariettes de l'opéra comique*. Another extensive ensemble movement, it opens with a 17-bar solo in $\frac{6}{4}$ for Le Satire followed by a shorter nine-bar solo in $\frac{3}{4}$ for Sévérine, concluding with 50 bars of duet in $\frac{2}{4}$. This closing section, which appears as Example 1.14, has some highly virtuosic vocal writing, particularly for Le Satire who is required to sing long melismas in semiquaver and demisemiquaver rhythms, in obvious parody of the Italian *bravura* style.

Nos. 10 and 11 were both trios. The composer of the first is unknown but the latter was written by Blaise and, as both ensembles are found in the same scene of the same play, it is possible that Blaise also composed the former (although both have very different musical characteristics). The homophonic texture of No. 10 is reminiscent of trio and *petit choeur* writing in the *tragédie en musique*; however, the movement is in da capo form. No. 11, reproduced as Example 1.15, boasts a melismatic and contrapuntal texture, a deliberate—and satirical—imitation of Italian practice and of vowel sounds in this

Example 1.15 "Les cinq voyelles" *Acajou,* Iv (Blaise, 1744)

language since one of the characters, in his speech introducing the trio, remarks:

> Mon cerveau a produit cette saillie;
> Je fais honte à l'Italie,
> Par un chant d'un goût nouveau.[64]

Another unusual feature of both trios was their siting so close together and within a scene forming not a *divertissement*, but part of the main action. This is quite unprecedented in the *opéra-comique* of this period.

The last ensemble—a duet—was drawn, like Nos. 10 and 11, from *Acajou*, emphasizing the importance of original concerted movements in this *opéra-comique*. No. 12, however, is conservative in musical and dramatic appearance. Written for the main lovers and sung in the closing *divertissement*, it is a short movement of 22 bars, in binary form and with a homophonic texture. Whether Blaise composed this as well cannot be ascertained; its features are entirely analagous to the style of ensemble composition in the contemporary *tragédie en musique*.

By the middle of the 18th century serious and comic operatic genres in France and Italy had articulated clearly formed approaches vis-à-vis the place and scope of duet and ensemble in their overall dramatic organization. Composers of the *tragédie en musique* and the *opera seria* preferred a more standardized, less adventurous approach based on defined conventions, whereas *opera buffa*, *intermezzo*, and *opéra-comique* were more inclined to experiment beyond these boundaries in response to their dramatic needs and in pursuit of new dramatic functions for ensembles.

Ensembles in serious genres were predominantly duets for the two main lovers, communicating one dominant emotion and, dramatically, simply reinforcing the stage scenario. Musically this was translated into set patterns: in Italy the da capo format and dialogue duet, in France predominantly homophonic textures and *unanime* texts. Exceptions and experiments were to be found, features this chapter has aimed to outline. In the *opera seria*, for example, there were interesting experiments with the formal structure of ensembles during the 1740s and, at the same time, conscious manipulation by some composers of oft-set librettos in telescoping scenes to create more opportunities for ensembles, usually larger ones. The *tragédie en musique* sought, on occasion, a form of expression enabling homophonic, *unanime* utterance to be replaced with poetically divergent texts and with dialogue textures or contrapuntal interplay of voices. It should also be remembered that the *tragédie*, less bound than the *opera seria* by the system of ranking and the prerogatives of individual singers, included more ensembles.

Ensembles were an essential feature of comic genres, "the more the merrier" becoming something of a maxim both in terms of the frequency with which they occurred and the number of characters they deployed. In the more sophisticated Italian genres the most important developments included: establishing freer and more expansive formal frameworks for ensembles and developing the concerted movement as an exciting expression of dramatic climax; developing quite complex vocal textures which, in larger ensembles, prepared the way for intricate ensembles of perplexity in the second half of the century; and incorporating, slowly at first, stage action so that the ensemble could assume responsibility for articulating developments in the plot rather than serving as a "set piece" for a predictable combination of characters. This, above all, was the most exciting breakthrough achieved by the mid-point of the century.

The *opéra-comique* undoubtedly had the same ends in sight but lacked the resources and compositional expertise to articulate these in as refined a manner as described above. Italian artists were to give French playwrights and composers the lead when, in the summer of 1752, the Bouffon troupe under the direction of Eustachio Bambini arrived on the Parisian scene. The history of the *opéra-comique* in the decades immediately following this artistic explosion saw the assimilation of Italian techniques to create, in ensemble composition as much as in all other aspects of operatic craft, a sophisticated, indigenous style of comic opera with a coherent musical and dramatic rationale.

Notes

1. 'Sur les opera (sic) à Monsieur le Duc de Buckingham', *Oeuvres mêlées*, ii (London, 1709), pp. 214–222.

2. See W. Dean: *Handel and the Opera Seria* (Berkeley, 1969), p. 31 and D. Libby: 'Italy: Two Opera Centres', *Man and Music: the Classical Era*, ed. N. Zaslaw (London, 1989), pp. 29–30 for details of competitiveness in ensemble singing in the 18th-century *opera seria*.

3. "The generic and elusive term 'opera' is at no other time or place more difficult to elucidate than in France during the period under consideration." G. Barksdale: *The Chorus in French Baroque Opera* (diss., U. of Utah, 1973), p. 9.

4. Examples include the "Trio des Parques", a combination found in Lully's *Isis* (IVvii) and Rameau's *Hippolyte et Aricie* (IIiii and IIv); and the "Trio des Furies" in Lully's *Psyché* (IVii) and his *Proserpine* (Vii). Similar pieces are written for *pastres*, *amans*, *matelots*, *sacrificateurs*, and *captifs*.

5. *Les fêtes d'Hébé* (1739) contains two intermittent duets with chorus (duet portions alternating with choral singing). The first version of *Zoroastre* (1749) includes three intermittent duets with chorus, a superimposed trio with chorus, and a quartet of similar appearance.

6. It was by no means unusual, however, for a composer to change elements of his librettist's plan. See also p. 8 and notes 7 and 8.

7. Lully and Philippe Quinault constructed only one quartet, "Venez-vous livrer au supplice," in Vii of *Atys*. This was not an ensemble with four independent parts but a double duet in which two pairs of voices alternated. (For a contemporary critique of this quartet, see pp. 223–224 below.) Rameau set two quartets whose texts were adapted out of other material: "Tendre amour" (IIIvii, *Les Indes galantes*) from a couplet headed "Tous", and "Courez aux armes" (IVvii, 1749 version of *Zoroastre*) from a trio. (Both support the point made in note 6 above.) A third, but very brief, quartet of nine bars is found in Iiv of *Platée*. Only one quintet, in Favart and Boismortier's *Don Quichote chez la duchesse* (1743), was encountered (a feature of the manuscript score alone and not of the printed libretto or the 1971 score).

8. Exceptions to these situations are found in *Les amours de Ragonde* (1742), which includes two short trios for different permutations of characters placed in comic situations. An unusual trio, in which three characters seek vengeance on the unfortunate lovers, is also found in IVvii of Cahusac's libretto to *Zoroastre* (1749). Rameau reshaped this text into an intermittent quartet and chorus in IVv of his first setting and the movement became a general chorus in the 1756 revision.

9. This example is from Iiv of Lully and Quinault's *Alceste*, and is a duet sung by Straton and Céphise.

10. 80% of concerted movements in Rameau's operas had essentially *unanime* texts, a figure which rises to 90% in works set by his contemporaries between 1733 and 1752.

11. Printed libretto in *Recueil general des opera représentez par l'Académie Royale de Musique*, x (Paris, 1710), p. 256.

12. Printed libretto: Paris (Ballard), 1709, p. vi.

13. Printed libretto: Paris (V. Delormel & *fils*), 1749, pp. 69–70. This was one of eight duets in the 1749 version (in addition to the trio turned into a quartet: see note 7 above). The 1756 libretto includes only seven duets, reduced still further in the score to five. The divergent duet quoted here numbers among these omissions. Possibly Rameau's more cautious approach to the ensemble in his later version was the result of adverse reactions to earlier experiments.

14. Printed libretto: Paris (Ballard), 1745, p. 71. Ensemble texts created by librettists were not always used by composers; conversely, composers would occasionally include extra ensembles. Since librettos were printed in advance of scores (in time for the work's première), sources do not always coincide precisely in all points of detail. See M.E.C. Bartlet: *Etienne Nicolas Méhul and Opera During the French Revolution, Consulate, and Empire: a Source, Archival, and Stylistic Study* (diss., U. of Chicago, 1982), p. 64.

15. This may have influenced Voltaire, the following year, when writing *La princesse de Navarre*. The final *divertissement* in this work contains a duet ("Charmante Hymen") in which one character sings in French and the other in Spanish. However, the earliest example of a bilingual duet found in the present study is in *Le faucon, ou Les oyes de Bocace*, a play performed at the Comédie-Italienne in 1725, libretto by Lisle de la Drevetière, music by Mouret. (See p. 41, Example 1.12).

16. See p. 36ff. 20th-century writers make reference to the "divergent duet" and "dialogue duet" in 18th-century opera. No definition of these duets is given at this stage since the format of ensemble texts did not dictate, but only suggest, to a composer the musical form it should assume. Divergent texts could be set simultaneously, dialogue texts juxtaposed, and *unanime* verses treated in a far from straightforward manner. Definitions of these terms therefore need to take into account musical characteristics: patterns of vocal textures, the relation of text to texture and, if changes to the librettist's text have been made, the process of text manipulation. As different styles of ensemble in a range of 18th-century genres are analyzed, the use of such terms and their scope of reference become clearer.

17. See *Alceste* Iii and *Bellérophon* IViii for the Lully period, and *Sémiramis* IViv (Destouches, 1718) for the *préramiste* period. No examples for the period 1733–52 were located.

18. The first da capo ensembles located in this study date from 1698 and are found in Desmarets' ballet, *Les festes galantes* (IIii and IIIii). Both are duets. Campra wrote a "Trio Italien" in dal segno form the following year, in IIv of *Le carnaval de Venise*.

19. "Manes plaintifs", in Iiii of *Dardanus* (1739), was Rameau's most extensive solo ensemble. It was 97 bars long.

20. The manner in which the separate voice parts combined in ensembles in the *tragédie* (and related genres) has been the focus of some attention during the present century. James Anthony, for example, has written in rather general terms of Lully's duet textures: "Most are strictly homophonic with the points of imitation found often at the beginning of phrases—a type of sham polyphony that by the second measure has already stabilized into a note-against-note style. This lack of polyphony is consistent with a 'word-born' style and predictably dominates all ensemble writing in Lully's operas." *French Baroque Music from Beaujoyeulx to Rameau* (London, 1973, rev. 2/1978), p. 88. See also L.E. Brown: 'Departures from the Lullian Convention', *RMFC*, xxii (1984), pp. 66–69 and P.-M. Masson: *L'opéra de Rameau* (Paris, 1930), pp. 263–287.

21. See p. 22.

22. *The Opera-Ballets of André Campra: a Study of the First Period French Opera-Ballet* (diss., U. of South Carolina, 1964), p. 538.

23. Montéclair may have transferred techniques of choral writing in his motets and cantatas to this operatic quartet.

24. The vengeance duet "Esprits de haine" in IIii of *Armide*, and "Ah! j'entends un bruit qui nous presse" from the prologue to *Amadis*.

25. Textures may have been even fuller: Graham Sadler notes that many works were issued in reduced scores which omitted the inner parts of the orchestra and chorus. See 'The Role of the Keyboard Continuo in French Opera, 1673–1776', *Early Music*, viii (1980), p. 155.

26. Popular editions of *Favourite Songs* published throughout the 18th century are excluded as they do not provide important details concerning placement and dramatic context.

27. See E.O. Downes: *The Operas of Johann Christian Bach as a Reflection of the Dominant Trends in Opera Seria 1750–1780* (diss., Harvard U., 1958), and G. Lazarevich: *The Role of the Neapolitan Intermezzo in the Evolution of Eighteenth-Century Musical Style* (diss., Columbia U., 1970).

28. One deliberate omission is Handel, a study of whose ensembles is best treated as a topic in its own right (besides having no relevance to the formal history of the *opéra-comique*). See W. Dean: *Handel and the Opera Seria* (Berkeley, 1969) and W. Dean and J. Merrill Knapp: *Handel's Operas, 1704–1726* (Oxford, 1987) which discuss various ensembles from Handel's works.

29. Capece included one quintet in *Telemaco* (1718) and Stampiglia a septet in *Eraclea* (1700).

30. Only five of the 81 works examined contained more than two ensembles. With the exception of *Spartaco* (1726), which archaically retained the *intermezzo* within the context of the main *opera seria* (this accounting for three of the five ensembles), these were all librettos written by Paolo Rolli for a series of operas staged in London by Nicola Porpora.

31. See p. 26–28.

32. Latilla's *Angelica ed Orlando* (1735) included a total of eight ensembles: four duets, one trio, and three quartets.

33. Quintets, for example, appeared in *Li zite 'ngalera* (1722), *Lo frate 'nnamorato* (1732), and *Il governatore* (1747); *L'ambizione delusa* (1742) contained a septet.

34. *Don Chichibio* (1742), written for four characters, included a trio and a quartet in addition to a duet. *Don Trastullo* (1749) included two trios and a duet.

35. Exceptions include duets for the *seconda* pair in two operas by Porpora (*Didone abbandonata* and *Ifigenia in Aulide*), and combinations of first with second—or third—ranking male characters in Vinci's *Elpidia* and Porpora's *Ifigenia in Aulide* (otherwise, duets for characters of the same sex were rare).

36. See p. 27 for a description of Galuppi's quartet in *Artaserse* (1749), and M. Robinson: 'Porpora's Operas for London, 1733–1736', *Soundings*, ii (1971–2), p. 76, for a detailed commentary on Feo's excellent quartet from IIIiv of *Andromaco*.

37. The ensemble of perplexity and its dramatic importance is discussed in detail in Chapter III.

38. Metastasio's control, as a stage director, of productions of his operas is outlined in D. Heartz: 'The Poet as Stage Director: Metastasio, Goldoni, and Da Ponte', *Mozart's Operas*, ed. T. Bauman (Berkeley, 1990).

39. D. Heartz: 'Hasse, Galuppi and Metastasio', *Venezia e il melodramma nel settecento: Studi di musica veneta*, vi (Florence, 1978), pp. 326–331. H. Lühning: *'Titus'-Vertonungen im 18. Jahrhundert: Untersuchungen zur Tradition der Opera Seria von Hasse bis Mozart*, AnMc, no. 20 (1983) [whole issue] also considers how Metastasian librettos were adapted to accommodate more ensembles in the second half of the 18th century (see pp. 59–67 and pp. 96–108 in particular).

40. C. Burney: *Memoirs of the Life and Writings of the Abate Metastasio*, i (London, 1796), p. 297. (Letter dated 27 December, 1749.)

41. *Ibid.*, iii, pp. 117–118. (Letter dated 18 September, 1771.) Lühning's study (see note 39 above) explores in some depth the issue of ensembles replacing arias and condensing the action in later settings of Metastasian librettos.

42. Downes: *Op. cit.*, pp. 15–16. This was established first in solo arias and thereafter in ensembles. See also pp. 398ff. of Downes' study for a more detailed discussion of the expansion of da capo form during this period.

43. The second act finale to *Ezio* (Jommelli, 1741) extended to 286 bars, and a duet in IIIvi of *Artaserse* (Galuppi, 1749) was 220 bars in length.

44. Two examples, both from towards the end of the period in question, were located: a duet by Perez in *Artaserse* (1748) and a trio by Galuppi in *Semiramide riconosciuta* (1749).

45. The trio concluding Act I, 170 bars in length, is composed in three contrasting sections, each set to different text and interspersed with recitative. The duet closing Act II spans five sections: *Andantino*, $\frac{4}{4}$, B♭ major (43 bars); *Allegro ma non presto*, $\frac{3}{4}$, C major (83 bars); a five-bar transition in *Larghetto* tempo; *Come prima* (31 bars); and *Allegro spirituoso*, $\frac{2}{4}$, (73 bars).

46. The first example of two-tempo form encountered in this study was the trio finale to Act I of *Don Trastullo* (Jommelli, 1749). However, H.C. Wolff has noted that a 1727 comic opera by Leo, *Lo matrimonio annascuso*, used a similar structure ('Italian Opera 1700–1750', *Opera and Church Music, 1630–1750*, NOHM, v (London, 1975), p. 114).

47. D. Heartz: 'The Creation of the Buffo Finale in Italian Opera', *PRMA*, civ (1977–8), pp. 70–71.

48. See, for example, duets by Scarlatti in IIi of *Telemaco* (1718) and IIviii of *Marco Attilio Regolo* (1719).

49. As, for example, in trios in IIIvi of *Polifemo* (Porpora, 1735) and Ixii of *Demofoonte* (Jommelli, 1743); and the quartet in IIIi of *Enea nel Lazio* (Porpora, 1734).

50. M. Robinson: *Naples and Neapolitan Opera* (Oxford, 1972), p. 226.

51. Dean: *Handel and the Opera Seria*, p. 16.

52. *Elpidia* (Vinci, 1725) was unusual in pairing a castrato soprano with a castrato alto, rivals in love, in Iiii. Porpora's *Ifigenia in Aulide* (1735) also brought together two male characters (a castrato soprano and bass) in IIvi, this being a seemingly rare appearance for a bass voice in an *opera seria* ensemble.

53. C. Troy: *The Comic Intermezzo* (Ann Arbor, 1979), p. 100.

54. Of the abundant literature that exists on these subjects, the most concise and easily available English language sources include R. Isherwood: *Farce and Fantasy: Popular Entertainment in Eighteenth-Century Paris* (Oxford, 1986) and an article by O. Brockett: 'The Fair Theatres of Paris in the Eighteenth Century: the Undermining of the Classical Ideal', *Classical Drama and its Influence: Essays Presented to H.D.F. Kitto* (London, 1965). Two dissertations cover the subject amply: D.J. Grout: *The Origins of the Opéra-Comique* (diss., Harvard U., 1939) and C. Barnes: *The Théâtre de la Foire (Paris, 1697–1762): its Music and Composers* (diss., U. of South California, 1965). Georges Cucuel's *Les créateurs de l'opéra-comique français* (Paris, 1914) remains an important source and Emile Campardon's *Les spectacles de la foire* (Paris, 1877) contains much essential archival information.

55. These figures are derived from: F. Carmody: 'Le répertoire de l'opéra-comique en vaudevilles de 1708 à 1764', *University of California Publications in Modern Philology*, xvi (1933); C.D. Brenner: *A Bibliographical List of Plays in the French Language, 1700–1789* (Berkeley, 1947, rev. 2/1979)

and his *The Théâtre Italien: its Repertory 1716–1793* (Berkeley, 1961); and H. Carrington-Lancaster: 'The Comédie Française, 1701–1774', *Transactions of the American Philosophical Society*, xli (1951).

56. They include: (i) for the fair theaters: *Le théâtre de la foire* (Paris, 1721–37), a 10-volume collection of plays by Le Sage, Fuzelier, and d'Orneval; collected works of other authors (Favart, Piron, Panard, Fagan, Vadé); printed music composed by Michel Corrette (see Table II, p. 42, for details); (ii) for the Comédie-Italienne: *Les parodies du nouveau théâtre italien* (Paris, 1738); *Le nouveau théâtre italien* (Paris, 1753) and its *Supplément* (Paris, 1765); *Théâtre de M. et Mme Favart* (Paris, 1763–72); the *Recueils des divertissements du Nouveau Théâtre Italien* (Paris, c1737), a six-volume collection of *divertissements* for 71 plays composed by J.-J. Mouret; (iii) for the Comédie-Française: *Airs de la Comédie-Française* (Paris, 1705), containing music to over 20 productions; *Le théâtre de M. Dancourt* (Paris, 1760), including vocal parts to J.-C. Gillier's music for Dancourt's plays; see also J.S. Powell: 'The Musical Sources of the Bibliothèque-Musée de la Comédie-Française', *CMc*, xli (1986).

57. *Le théâtre de la foire*, ii (Paris, 1721), p. 274.

58. *Ibid.*, iv (Paris, 1724), pp. 10–11.

59. *Ibid.*, iii (Paris, 1721), pp. 436–437.

60. Barnes: *Op. cit.*, p. 163.

61. The twelfth parody ensemble was from a work given at the Comédie-Italienne. That so few ensembles of this nature were located in this repertory may be due to the lack of sufficient indications in printed librettos.

62. Musical sources are listed in note 56(iii) above, although these cover only a limited period up to 1714.

63. See Chapter III, in particular the sections on the "expository" ensemble, p. 106 and pp. 129–131.

64. *Théâtre de M. et Mme Favart*, vii (Paris, 1763–72), p. 31.

Chapter II

Transition and Change:
Duet and Ensemble in the 1750s

On the first day of August 1752 *La serva padrona*, an *intermezzo* by Giovanni Battista Pergolesi, was staged at the Académie Royale de Musique. This event was to cause great controversy among the musical *literati* of Paris and had, moreover, a significant impact on the development of the French *opéra-comique* during the second half of the 18th century. Pergolesi's work was performed by a troupe of Italian comedians who had woven an interesting route to the French capital. They had originally been engaged to appear in Rouen; a contract with Jean-Baptiste Rousselet, the resident director of public entertainments in that city, was dated 24 May 1752 and covered the period from 1 November 1752 until Ash Wednesday the following year. When, shortly afterwards, the Académie discovered their monopoly had been infringed, the Bouffons were obliged to cancel their agreement with Rousselet, and were called from Strasbourg (where they were at this time based) to the French capital itself.

The Bouffon troupe was led by Eustachio Bambini and comprised, initially, three singers: Bambini's wife Anna Tonelli, Pietro Manelli, and Giuseppe Cosimi. Judging from comments in the contemporary press, it appears that the Académie intended to engage the Bouffons for a short period only, and that they were expected to perform a small number of *intermezzi*. However, after the success of their first three productions, the troupe's sojourn in Paris was extended and extra singers were engaged: Giovanna Rossi, Francesco Guerrieri, and the Lazzaris, a husband and wife combination. In June 1753 Caterina Tonelli, younger sister of Anna, made her first appearance; she was followed, in September, by Dionisia

Lepri. They appear, from cast lists, to have replaced Giovanna Rossi and Mme Lazzari.

The Bouffons were to remain in Paris for a full 20 months, a far longer period than either they or anyone else had initially envisaged, and during this time they gave over 150 performances of 13 different works (listed in Table III), their last appearance taking place on 7 March 1754.

Table III: The Bouffon Repertory

Work Performed/No. of Acts	Composer	Date
La serva padrona (2)	G. B. Pergolesi	1 August 1752
Il giocatore (3)	G. M. Orlandini	22 August 1752[1]
Il maestro di musica (2)	P. Auletta	19 September 1752
La finta cameriera (2)	G. Latilla	1 December 1752[1]
La donna superba (2)	Rinaldo di Capua	19 December 1752[1]
La scaltra governatrice (3)	G. Cocchi	25 January 1753[1]
Tracollo (2)	G. B. Pergolesi	1 May 1753
Il cinese rimpatriato (1)	G. Selletti	19 June 1753
La zingara (2)	Rinaldo di Capua	19 June 1753
Gli artigiani arricchiti (2)	G. Latilla	23 September 1753
Il paratajo (2)	N. Jommelli	23 September 1753
Bertoldo in corte (2)	V. Ciampi	9 November 1753
I viaggiatori (3)	L. Leo	12 February 1754

1.   Conflicting dates of 12 August 1752, 30 November 1752, 29 December 1752, and 23 March 1753 respectively are given by L. de La Laurencie: 'La grande saison italienne de 1752: les Bouffons', *BSIM*, viii (1912) and are often cited in later literature. The dates in Table III are taken from the *Journal de l'Opéra*, housed at *F-Po*, and ratified by evidence in the *Mercure de France* and by archival documents from the series AJ[13] (held at the Archives Nationales, Paris). From this latter source, however, it should be noted that the date for the first performance of *La finta cameriera* is given as 30 November.

(Note: On 1 March 1753 the Bouffons also gave the first performance of *Le jaloux corrigé*, an *opéra bouffe* by the French composer Michel Blavet. They sang in French, not in Italian, and to mixed reviews.)

The various additions and changes in personnel described above suggest that the Bouffons were not an integrated troupe, and retracing the careers of the individual singers prior to their arrival in the French capital reveals that none—with the possible exception of Anna Tonelli—had enjoyed particular success in Italy or elsewhere. In reality they were a group of minor actors, few of whom had performed together before meeting in Strasbourg, operating on the periphery of the Italian operatic world. That they took Paris by storm and created an overnight sensation with *La serva padrona* is a myth. The level of publicity and success they eventually enjoyed was due to the fact that they involuntarily served as a symbol of liberalism within a complex and highly-charged constitutional debate of which the literary controversy—the Querelle des Bouffons—was but one manifestation. Religious and political factors, alongside philosophical agitation, accounted for the success of the Bouffons in winning over Parisian audiences to Italian opera where previous efforts by their compatriots in 1729 (*Baïocco e Serpilla* and *Don Micco e Lesbina* at the Académie) and 1746 (*La serva padrona* at the Comédie-Italienne) had failed.[1]

In addition to inspiring wide-reaching debate of a non-musical nature, the Bouffon troupe and their repertory exerted a considerable influence over the subsequent evolution of the *opéra-comique*. Therefore, the works heard in Paris need to be considered in some detail, in particular the ensembles they contain, as these did much to enhance the importance of concerted movements in the *opéra-comique* of the 1750s.

The Bouffons' Legacy

Of the 13 works performed by the Bouffons, only two—*La serva padrona* and *Il giocatore*—were traditional *intermezzi* (if one excludes the *personnage muet* in the former). *Il maestro di musica, Tracollo, Il cinese rimpatriato,* and *La zingara* were written for three singing actors, and *Il paratajo* and *Gli artigiani arricchiti* involved four and five characters respectively. The remaining five works all called for six roles, *La scaltra governatrice* including in addition *une esclave muette*. The troupe's repertory thus comprised a mixture of short *intermezzi* and longer *opere buffe*.

Sources include all 13 librettos (printed between 1752 and 1754 by Vve Delormel & *fils* in Paris) but far less musical material: five printed scores all published in Paris during the early 1750s (*La serva padrona, Il giocatore, Il maestro di musica, Tracollo, La zingara*), two manuscript scores housed at *F-Po* (*Il paratajo* and *Bertoldo in corte*, the latter incomplete), and various fragments (a duet from *La finta cameriera* at *F-Pn*, one duet and one trio from *La donna superba*, also at *F-Pn*, and duets from *Il cinese rimpatriato* at *F-Po*). It is probable that librettos were published to coincide with the opening performance of a new work, given dated *approbations* and the appearance of complete French translations alongside the Italian original for the audience to follow. Printed scores did not apparently leave the presses so promptly.

Tracing the performance histories of these works prior to their staging in Paris highlights the extent to which they had been subjected to change and modification. *La finta cameriera*, encountered in its 1743 version in the preceding chapter (this itself a revival six years after the original), illustrates this *rifacimento* process well. The three acts of the 1743 manuscript comprised a total of 45 scenes, 27 arias, three ensembles (two duets and one trio), and a closing *coro* movement. Performances in Paris, according to the libretto, offered a curtailed version in two acts, reducing the number of scenes to 15 and including only 13 arias, two duets (one of which was a substitute), and the closing *coro*.[2]

Discrepancies between librettos and extant musical sources, alongside comments in the contemporary press, show that alterations to individual movements were made by the Bouffons between performances of the same work in Paris. These emphasize two vital points about their

Table IV: Ensembles in the Bouffon Repertory

Work Performed/No. of Acts	Duets	Trios	Quartets
La serva padrona (2)	2	-	-
Il giocatore (3)	3	-	-
Il maestro di musica (2)	1	2	-
La finta cameriera (2)	2	-	-
La donna superba (2)	1	1	1
La scaltra governatrice (3)	-	2	2
Tracollo (2)	2	-	-
Il cinese rimpatriato (1)	2	-	-
La zingara (2)	2	1	-
Gli artigiani arricchiti (2)	1	-	-
Il paratajo (2)	1	-	1
Bertoldo in corte (2)	1	1	1
I viaggiatori (3)	1	1	2
Total	19	8	7
Proportion of ensembles as a whole	(56%)	(23.5%)	(20.5%)

repertory: first, that it did not always prove popular with the Parisian public; and second, that the success of the Italian comedians was in no small measure attributable to their knowledge of how to satisfy their critics and accommodate productions to prevalent taste. They capitalized on popular numbers and dispensed with those that were less well received.

The Ensembles

The operas from the Bouffons' repertory are rich in ensembles and Table IV lists the types found in each work. Table V provides an incipit for each ensemble and indicates whether the music is extant. Of the 36

Table V: Details of Individual Ensembles

* = duets † = trio ‡ = quartet
Bold text indicates an extant musical source. Incipits taken from printed librettos.

La serva padrona
    * **"Lo conosco a quegli occhietti"**
    * **"Per te mi sento al Core"**[1]
Il giocatore
    * **"Serpilla diletta"**
    * **"Quest'è quel uomo?"**
    * **"Ogni trista memoria"** (libretto)[2]
    or   *"Pace, pace" (score)
Il maestro di musica
    † **"Come chi gioca alle palle"**
    * **"Qual doppo insano"**
    † **"Caro Signor maestro"**
La finta cameriera
    * **"Quando senti la campana"**
    * **"Per te o' io nel core"**
La donna superba
    † **"Mio Padrone con le buone"**
    * **"Che freddo! . . . che caldo!"**
    ‡ "In virtù dell'esser vostro"
La scaltra governatrice
    ‡ "O Cosi, cosi vi voglio"
    †"Bella mano or che ti stringo"
    ‡ "Cara Drusilla"
    †"Scellerata a me rispondi?"

Tracollo
    * **"Vado a morte ed avrai core"**
    * **"A quella che t'adora"**
Il cinese rimpatriato
    * **"Mi stà d'incanto"**
    * **"Sei compito, è sei bellino"**
La zingara
    * "Colla speme di goder"
    * "Amore, o che diletto"
    † "Ogni tromba, ogni tamburo"
Gli artigiani arricchiti
    * "Non sò frenare il pianto"
Il paratajo
    * **"Nipotina senti mè"**
    ‡ **"Vò pensando col cervello"**
Bertoldo in corte
    † **"Và figura del Calotta"**
    or   † **"Ferma, ferma, non conviene"**
    ‡ "Vuò conoscere quella Marfisa"
    * "Caro morir vogl'io"
I viaggiatori
    ‡ "Signor Padre scusi lei"
    * "Si tu sei l'idolo mio"
    † "Son restato come resta"
    ‡ "Io già sento il fonte e il rio"

	Duets:	Trios:	Quartets:
Total (including alternatives)	20	9	7
Extant Musical Sources	16	6	1

1. The printed score alters the first line of this duet to "Per te io ho nel core." This should not be confused with "Per te o' io nel core" from *La finta cameriera*.
2. Probably "Contento tu sarai," reprinted in *G.B. Pergolesi: Opera omnia*, ed. F. Caffarelli (Rome, 1939–42), xi. See the discussion on p. 60 relating to these duets.

concerted movements encountered, the music to 23 survives: 16 of the 20 duets, six of the nine trios, and one of the seven quartets.

Like all other aspects, ensembles were not immune to *rifacimenti* alterations, which to some degree allow contemporary French attitudes to Italian concerted writing to be gauged. One such change is immediately apparent from Table V: the discrepancy between score and libretto relating to the duet closing Act III of *Il giocatore*.[3] The *Mercure* provides further details:

> "Les deux Acteurs qui avoient ôté à la troisiéme [sic] représentation le duo du troisiéme Acte, pour lui substituter un duo inférieur, ont remis le premier: il est de Pergolese & digne de son Auteur."[4]

However, no reference to either movement by name is made. Since librettos were usually printed to coincide with premières, the first duet, by Pergolesi, was probably "Ogni trista memoria" from the printed libretto; this is supported further by the fact that the text, after the first six lines, is identical to that of another popular Italian duet of the period, "Contento tu sarai," which had originally closed the second act of *La serva padrona* and had been heard in Paris in 1746. "Pace, pace" would appear then to be the "duo inférieur" to which the *Mercure* alludes, although it is unusual that the score, printed some time afterwards, did not take into account alterations to musical numbers that were made during the course of performances.

Further comments in the *Mercure* indicate that ensembles in other works were changed, generally whenever they were judged to have received a poor response from the audience. After unfavorable reactions to the trio originally chosen to conclude Act II of *Il maestro di musica*, for instance, a substitute was offered that met with greater success.[5] In *La finta cameriera* the closing *coro* ensemble was replaced by a solo quartet.[6] The incomplete manuscript of *Bertoldo in corte*, which preserves the music to the first act only, contains two trios, either of which, presumably, might have been chosen to conclude the act. "Và figura del Calotta" is found from folio 73 onwards as well as in the printed libretto. "Ferma, ferma, non conviene," composed for the same three characters, appears from the verso of folio 80 onwards. The *Mercure* makes no reference to any substitution at this point in the work and simply records that the trio closing the first act was extremely well received.[7] Whether "Ferma, ferma" was ever used remains uncertain, but its inclusion in the manuscript score emphasizes the contemporary Italian belief in the interchangeability of musical numbers.

The ensembles from the Bouffons' repertory represent a cross-section of the style of concerted writing discussed in the preceding chapter. Thus, only a brief description of these pieces is offered here. Each work contained on average two or three concerted movements, just over half of which were duets, the remainder comprising trios and quartets. *La scaltra governatrice* was unusual in including four ensembles, as was *I viaggiatori*. *Gli artigiani arricchiti*, on the other hand, contained only one duet: this closed the first *intermezzo* and a *coro* movement was used to conclude the work. Almost three-quarters (74%) of the concerted movements in Table IV were finales, emphasizing the importance in Italian opera of ensemble climaxes.

With two exceptions, the 20 duets were for a male-female pairing.[8] Many were written for lovers, painting either disagreements or reunions, although male/female pairings also portrayed family relationships (brother/sister, uncle/niece). Duets for characters of the same sex were based on more informal subject-matter. In the larger ensembles male voices were heard more frequently: the majority of trios were written for two men and one woman, and two of the seven quartets combined three male voices with only one female voice. The remaining five balanced two singers of either sex. Many different characters were brought together in ensemble movements to delineate complicated and perplexing scenarios at the heart of the action. Larger ensembles would also serve as dénouements.

Thirteen of the 23 ensembles with extant music (just over half) were cast in binary form. Da capo structures were the next most common type encountered: all three duets from *Il giocatore* were written in this form, as were movements from *La finta cameriera* and *La donna superba*. The two ensembles from Jommelli's *Il paratajo* were ambitious chain structures reflecting the progressive nature of this composer's concerted writing.[9] Other formal structures were occasionally encountered: "Come chi gioca" (*Il maestro di musica*) and "Mio Padrone" (*La donna superba*) were written in free form, and "Qual doppo insano" (*Il maestro*) as a single section. The majority of the ensembles in question (about 75%) were over 100 bars in length. Ten of the 23 were more than 150 bars long, and five were in excess of 300. The vocal textures of virtually all the extant ensembles favored the dialogue patterns described in Chapter I. Some, however, adopted a different approach and contained extensive sections written in homophony: for example "Pace, pace" (*Il giocatore*) and "Vò pensando col cervello" (*Il paratajo*). "Colla speme di goder" (*La zingara*) was written in a note-against-note style throughout.

That French and Italian approaches to concerted writing differed greatly has already been shown. The Bouffons therefore exposed Parisian audiences to a completely different style, one where ensembles were a vital ingredient, characterized by a sophisticated verve that resulted in a natural and realistic form of expression. This indeed marked the pieces in the repertory as a whole:

> "elles apportaient de l'inédit, du vivant: les héros en étaient des gens du peuple, des petits bourgeois; le décor en était simple, mais réaliste."[10]

How, then, did audiences and critics react to such change? The most useful source for establishing critical reactions to vocal ensembles at this time is the *Mercure de France*. This monthly journal included detailed reviews of productions staged by the troupe throughout their stay in Paris, and confirms that the Bouffons were not an instant success, and that their works were not always well received by audiences at the Académie. Reporting reveals, moreover, that while the Bouffons remained popular, they lost something of their novelty value, since reviews in the *Mercure* became less and less detailed. Those for *La serva padrona*, *Il giocatore*, and *Il maestro di musica*, three of the most popular works staged, each comprised at least four pages and commented on the style and character of many individual movements. Subsequent commentaries spanned only one or two pages, and at times a paragraph alone.[11] Even the troupe's departure in March 1754 was reported in the briefest of terms:

> "Les Italiens qui depuis environ dix-huit mois occupoient tantôt une, tantôt deux, & quelquefois trois fois la semaine, le théatre de l'Opéra, y jouerent pour la derniere fois, le Jeudi 7 Mars. On a substitué à leurs Intermédes *Platée*, qu'on donne le Mardi & le Jeudi."[12]

Ensembles from the Bouffons' first production, *La serva padrona*, received high praise when it was reviewed in the September issue of the *Mercure*. Referring to the duets closing each act, it was reported that:

> "le dialogue & le sentiment y sont exprimés avec une justesse & une finesse qui sont au dessus de tous les éloges."[13]

Those from *Il giocatore* received similar commendation. The first duet, closing Act I, was felt to emanate

> "la plus grande vérité, le Dialogue en est vif & bien entendu, & la déclamation très-naturelle"

and the second, placed at the end of the next act, was

> "encore supérieur à celui du premier Acte. Le Musicien y a si bien sçu tirer parti de la difference des voix, que le Dialogue y est singulierement contrasté, quoique le chant des deux parties soit à peu près le même."[14]

Of the singers the review added:

> "on a sur tout [sic] été très content de la maniere dont ils ont exécuté les duo."[15]

Three major points arise from these extracts. The first concerns the musical texture of the duets, all of which were composed in dialogue style, with solos progressing to overlapping and juxtaposed phrases and then to homophonic cadential agreement. Judging from the *Mercure*, French audiences immediately responded to dialogue textures in ensemble composition. They were felt to lend truth and precision (*justesse*) to the drama and translated the poetic text clearly. They had, moreover, style (*finesse*), great naturalness, and an appealing vivacity. These qualities facilitated the expression of contrasting sentiments much more than the homophonic textures of ensembles in the *tragédie en musique*, and the reaction to the second duet in *Il giocatore* in particular emphasizes this point. Divergent duets were still a relatively rare phenomenon in French serious opera. That such pieces from the Italian repertory could successfully preserve their clarity and musical appeal obviously impressed contemporary listeners.

A second concern appears to have been the striking musical and dramatic *vérité* of the ensembles in question, their aptness and immediacy of expression, and their matching of music to the situation on stage. *Vraisemblance* in concerted writing, as will later be explained, was a crucial concept in France, and expression at all times was required to be clear, lucid, and plausible.[16] The *Mercure* obviously considered that the character of these ensembles—spirited, realistic, and full of comic verve—painted the situation on stage with perfect naturalness.

Finally, the singers' skilful rendition of these ensembles (all were marked *Allegro*, or fluctuated haphazardly between *Allegro* and slower tempos) was another reason for their successful reception. Some contemporary evidence points to the fact that performance standards at the Académie often left much to be desired.[17] While this should be balanced against evidence to the contrary—singers such as Marie Fel and

Pierre de Jélyotte enjoyed extremely long and successful careers—reviews in the *Mercure* suggest that Bambini's comedians, although not in the highest class of performer when measured against their peers in Italy, won acclaim in France for their singing and for their realistic style of acting.[18]

Of the five duets in these works, two will be analyzed here in detail.[19] The first is "Lo conosco a quegli occhietti," closing Act I of *La serva padrona*, in which Serpilla forces Uberto into a corner over the issue of marriage. The most striking characteristics of this piece are its rhythmic vitality and the jaunty, enchanting melody, typical of the *esprit* and *énergie* admired in Italian music by many Frenchmen. The vocal texture follows a classically conceived dialogue pattern: each section of the binary structure begins with long solos and builds up through shorter, alternating phrases to juxtaposition and eventual cadential agreement. The second section, following the usual pattern of Italian dialogue duets, is more complex than the first in its blending of the two voices.

Other characteristics of Italian music also admired—*finesse*, *vérité*, *sentiment*, and *expression*—are found in abundance in the way individual phrases of this duet are set to music. In bars 10–11 and elsewhere, decisive octave leaps emphasize salient words such as "furbi","ladri", and "troppo". Serpilla's conniving ways are reflected through subtle changes in melodic motives; her deliberate and tantalizing sequences falling a diminished fifth (bars 28–29), for example, contrast with earlier solos marked *con spirito*. Uberto's rising chromatic phrase (bars 40–42) portrays his dilemma; Serpilla's answer to this, which imitates the opening *con spirito* idea, emphasizes her insistence and her determination to triumph over her master. The words "graziosa" and "spiritosa" are set, in bars 72–73, in an apt manner (a slurred upward fourth motif), while Uberto's "laralà" exclamations (bars 83–84) have a hollow ring with their minor tonality. Rousseau described this duet as "un modèle de chant, d'unité de mélodie, de dialogue et de goût," praise warranted through its close attention to detail and careful matching of text to music.[20]

"Quest'è quel uomo?", closing Act II of *Il giocatore*, predates Pergolesi's duet by some years. There are fewer individual instances of word-painting although the duet masterfully portrays the dramatic situation and the characters involved. Serpilla has sought reparation for her husband's errant ways and has received an alternative offer of conjugal bliss from the judge hearing her case. When Baïocco reveals himself as the self-same judge his wife begs forgiveness while he maintains a show of inflexibility which throws the interest forward to the final act.

The conflict is enhanced by the use of fluctuating tempos and contrasting melodic ideas. The opening 25 bars serve as a prelude; the two characters take stock of one another, Serpilla deliberately ingratiating herself with the "judge" and Baïocco ironically commenting on his wife's uncharacteristic display of piety (she is disguised *en pèlerine*). When Baïocco reveals himself, Serpilla throws herself on his mercy and the music assumes a faster tempo. Quaver motives build up and are tossed between the two, accentuating their conflict, until they finally merge at the close of the section. Serpilla then adopts a new line of defence with the words "Dov'è l'amore," and the music changes correspondingly to a slower meter (bar 124 onwards). She quickly realizes that this is futile and 14 bars later the duet resumes its hectic course. There is one last try at bar 149. A less frenetic pace and a lilting melodic line reinforce Serpilla's pleas for the weakness and fragility of youth to be excused. Baïocco's condemnation of her feigned virtue brings this section to a close and a da capo repeat throws the couple back to the beginning of their hostilities. The seven noticeable changes in tempo are all introduced by the character of Serpilla and effectively portray her agitated self-justification. Such irregular oscillations also paint the volatility of the couple's relationship. Direct and natural expression, energy, and *génie* all characterize this ensemble.

Reviews of the Bouffons' two following productions, *Il maestro di musica* and *La finta cameriera*, reflect a popular acceptance of larger ensembles. The following reaction to the divergent trio closing the first act of *Il maestro di musica*, "Come chi gioca alla palle," is surprising in its ready approval of what was a very unfamiliar style of ensemble composition in France:

> "Le premier Acte est terminé par un trio très-singulier, dans lequel les trois Acteurs expriment le même sentiment avec des nuances differentes, par un chant, dont le dessein est aussi le même pour tous les trois, mais avec des nuances differentes, la naïveté du *netto, netto*, a beaucoup réussi; mais le *fredda, fredda*, dans la partie chantée par Laurette, lui est encore supérieur."[21]

An analysis of this trio helps explain why the movement should have proved so popular. It brings together the three characters of the *intermezzo*: the music master (and *vieillard trompé*) Lamberto; Collagiani, the visiting theatrical entrepreneur who is searching avidly for young and attractive talent; and Lauretta, the demure singing-pupil upon whom both men have designs. Collagiani, who has been left alone with Lauretta, has almost been successful in his attempt to spirit her away with promises of fame and fortune (and of his own hand in marriage). Lamberto, who sees his personal aspirations about to be thwarted, makes a judiciously timed entrance which marks the beginning of the trio. The appeal of this movement obviously lay in its skilful and humorous characterization, as in the way in which the familiar emotional triangle was depicted in music. Each of the three express their sentiments in apt metaphorical terms, Collagiani as a player of *boules* beaten "tout net" (*netto, netto*) by the last throw, Lamberto as a birdcatcher whose prey has flown from the trap, and Lauretta as an unfortunate servant-girl whose water pitcher has been broken: "toute affligée, elle reste froide (*fredda, fredda*) & immobile dans un coin."[22] Musically, the trio was cast in free form and had a spirited *Allegro* tempo (changing to *Vivo* about half-way through) underlining the pent-up frustration of the three characters. Its dialogue texture skilfully blended the disparate images of a common sentiment and gave emphasis, as the *Mercure* points out, to salient adjectives through humorous octave leaps (*netto, netto*) or through touching chromaticisms (*fredda, fredda*). The overall spirit of irrepressible charm and musicality, the humorous backdrop, lively melody, vigorous accompaniment, and the adroit blending of different nuances of the same sentiment all combined to produce a noteworthy ensemble.

As pointed out earlier, the trio originally closing Act II of the same work was replaced after the first performance with one entitled "Caro Signor maestro." Like the trio closing the first act, this too was praised in the *Mercure* as being:

"un trio très-original, très-neuf, d'autant plus heureusement placé qu'il fait le dénouement, & que le Maître de Musique se trouve fort plaisamment éconduit par les deux autres."[23]

A portion of the ensemble (bars 76–94) is reproduced in Example 2.1. At this point the three voices, having each been allocated a lengthy solo, begin to blend together in preparation for the cadence closing the first section of the movement (which is in binary form). The novel and original features to which the *Mercure* alludes were, first and foremost, the persistent juxtaposition of the three voices to produce a fitting interim climax, but also the frivolous and comic text, the catchy rhythms, and the constant repetition of short, playful motives. The *Mercure*'s comments concerning the more judicious dramatic placing of this substitute trio

Example 2.1 "Caro Signor maestro" *Il maestro di musica* Act II finale (Auletta, 1752)

underline the fact that it was not just the specific musical or verbal characteristics of a piece that ensured its success, but also its general theatrical impact. As the review remarks: "C'est un tableau qu'il faut avoir vû pour s'en former l'idée."[24]

A third favorable response to a large ensemble, this time the quartet replacing the closing *coro* in *La finta cameriera*, appeared shortly afterwards in the *Mercure*. This ensemble was found to be "très agréable" but as the music does not survive it is not possible to establish what these pleasing characteristics might have been.[25] However, the fact that the notion of several characters singing together on stage was proving critically acceptable in France was a significant hurdle for concerted composition to have surmounted.

Since reviews in the *Mercure* of later works performed by the Bouffons became less and less comprehensive, individual ensembles were referred to only in passing rather than described in detail: there is little to relate to specific musical and dramatic characteristics. Certain comments show that ensemble movements continued to attract attention and emphasize the qualities of Italian concerted writing that French audiences found appealing. For example, all three ensembles in *La donna superba* were hailed (alongside several solo *ariettes*) as "les morceaux de plus grande distinction."[26] The first of the two duets in *Tracollo* was deemed "admirable," the second extremely successful.[27] Similarly, the duet concluding Act I of *La zingara* "a beaucoup plu" and its trio finale was "plein de gayeté & d'expression."[28]

Reviews in the *Mercure* of works by French composers during the first half of the 18th century rarely discussed individual ensembles at length. Yet over one-half of the ensembles in the Bouffons' repertory were singled out for attention, either in detail or in passing. This reflects a significant increase in interest in such pieces, from which can be adduced the following conclusions.

The general impact of Italian music on the French public during the time the Bouffons spent in Paris was strong. Such music was admired for its *esprit* and *vérité*, as also for its finesse and naturalness. That concerted movements featured so prominently in this repertory was extremely significant for their future role in French opera, and the influence of the ensembles performed by Bambini's troupe cannot be emphasized too greatly. French librettists and their composers began to include an increasing number of ensembles in each opera, some of which were ambitious movements for several characters at once. But the Italian comedians did much more than simply stamp their imprint on a burgeoning French genre. They fostered a spirit of expectancy, a feeling that French opera should now find its own feet and remodel itself using ideas from Italian practice.

The Transitional
Opéra-Comique, 1752–59

Legislation had forced the closure of the fair theaters by a jealous Académie Royale de Musique in 1745, after a series of successful productions by a troupe working under the entrepreneur Jean Monnet and involving the playwright Favart, François Boucher as stage designer, the young dancer Jean-Georges Noverre, and, possibly, Rameau.[29] This decision was reversed in December 1751—audiences in the intervening years had not flocked back to the established theaters to boost revenue—and Monnet was again able to secure the *privilège* of the Opéra-Comique. From 1752 the institution, as indeed the genre, enjoyed a period of great prosperity and outstanding development.[30]

This decade was, for the *opéra-comique*, a time of experimentation and of change. The most significant development was the transition from popular vaudevilles to original music, and with this the increasing importance of the composer and his eventual precedence over the playwright. Music, in the form of *ariettes*, ensembles, choruses, overtures, and other instrumental movements, became the prime element in many works and carried more and more of the dramatic intrigue while spoken dialogue assumed a more complementary role. Elements of change and continuity existed side by side for a period, some traditional features such as the use of vaudevilles being preserved for decades to come. The resulting diversity in style and structure was great. The *opéra-comique* also developed in dramatic scope, widening the sphere of its subject-matter considerably. Earlier, with Favart, comic and farcical elements had given way to a more sentimental, pastoral outlook. Thereafter, contemporary philosophical ideals inspired the genre, particularly through depiction of the ruling classes and the notion of moral responsibility. Critical attention focused increasingly on the *opéra-comique*: some writers were scathing and dismissive, but many were fulsome in their praise:

> "Ce Spectacle contre lequel la décence s'est récrié pendant longtems avec une sorte de raison, devient aujourd'hui un amusement honnête qui attire tout Paris."[31]

The *vaudeville-comédie* of the first half of the 18th century continued in vogue until shortly after the Bouffon troupe had established itself in Paris. After this point it began to borrow many successful musical items from the Italian repertory, at the expense of vaudevilles. This was, in principle, an application of parody techniques used earlier in the century, but in practice, the character and focus of parody were altered considerably. The Bouffons' repertory was popular, their music spirited, attractive, and sophisticated, and it was for this reason that the *vaudeville-comédie* incorporated the better-known italianate *ariettes* and ensembles. The style of parody thus changed from being verbally satirical to musically eulogistic in intent.

Interlacing the *vaudeville-comédie* with Italian music proved a highly practicable approach and led to the transitory genre known as the *pasticcio opéra-comique* which enjoyed much success:

> "it required no composer and allowed librettists such as Favart, Pierre Baurans and Louis Anseaume, none of whom were composers, to produce popular works which enriched, and in some cases totally replaced, the traditional vaudeville timbres with the most popular Italian music of the day."[32]

The first *pasticcio opéra-comique* was *Le jaloux corrigé*, performed at the Académie in March 1753 by the Bouffons themselves, singing in French. The work was an elaborate pot-pourri incorporating items from three different Italian works: *La serva padrona*, *Il giocatore*, and *Il maestro di musica*. However, since the French composer Michel Blavet was called upon to compose an overture, a *divertissement*, a final vaudeville, and to link the parody *ariettes*—according to the printed score (Paris c1753)—with recitative "fait à l'imitation de celuy des Italiens," *Le jaloux corrigé* represented at the same time an enterprising attempt to synthesize Italian compositional procedures with the French style in order to establish an indigenous form of comic opera.

The two most popular *pasticcio opéras-comiques* of the period were *La servante maîtresse* (1754), performed over 150 times during its first year, and *Le maître de musique* (1755). Both were adapted by Baurans and represented the high-point of a genre which prevailed for a remarkably short period only.[33] Playwrights continued, as earlier in the century, to exploit the Académie's repertory for popular subject-matter and musical items to parody, borrowing dramatic outlines more often than music and remaining essentially satirical in character. This practice reached a peak in 1754 and thereafter began a steady decline as playwrights and composers turned increasingly to original scenarios and to new music. The *pasticcio opéra-comique* suffered an identical fate: one of the last such works to be given, *Le charlatan* in late 1756 (modelled on *Tracollo*), in fact contained a good deal of specially-composed music and heralded the final transformation of the *opéra-comique* during the 1750s.

Works set to original music throughout did, in fact, date from the early part of this decade and two obvious examples are *Le devin du village* (Rousseau, 1752) and *Les troqueurs* (Dauvergne, 1753). Neither piece suggested a single line of development for native comic opera, although both did much to encourage the genre. This was particularly true of *Les troqueurs* which, like *Le devin*, contained recitative, a compositional procedure that the burgeoning comic style was quickly denied:

> "The success of *Les troqueurs* at the Opéra Comique … caused the jealous Opéra to forbid recitative at any rival theater. Although it is not clear exactly how long this edict remained in effect, it undoubtedly helped establish the mainstream approach to the *opéra-comique* in which musical numbers of various kinds were connected by spoken verse or prose dialogue."[34]

The double transition of the *opéra-comique* from vaudeville via recitative to spoken dialogue, and from vaudeville via parody *ariettes* to original music, was realized fully towards the end of the decade. One composer at the forefront of these developments, with works such as *Le médecin de l'amour* (1758) and *L'yvrogne corrigé* (1759), was Jean-Louis Laruette. But the *opéras-comiques* of Egidio Duni moved the most rapidly and consistently towards this objective:

> "He approached his apparent goal, an *opéra-comique* in which all the music was original, in his first two Parisian *opéras-comiques*, *Le peintre amoureux de son modèle* (26 July 1757) and *La fille mal gardée* (4 March 1758), and achieved it in his next two works, *Nina et Lindor* (9 September 1758) and *La veuve indécise* (24 September 1759)."[35]

Some 115 works staged principally at the fair theaters and at the Comédie-Italienne during the 1750s were studied in this survey, the majority of them cast in a single act. Only 10 two-act and 11 three-act works were encountered.[36] Still a somewhat lightweight genre, therefore, the *opéra-comique* of this period tended to include between four and seven characters only. As outlined above, a consistent formal approach was lacking until towards the end of the decade. The ways in which its many elements—vaudevilles, parody *ariettes* and ensembles, original compositions, choral movements, instrumental items—were integrated into an overall dramatic structure were varied. Plays at one end of the spectrum were composed almost entirely in verse or in prose and included only occasional musical interludes or closed with a vaudeville or *divertissement.* Others, in contrast, alternated spoken verse or prose dialogue with musical numbers more frequently. Terminology remains something of a minefield. While around 60% of works retained the two most popular pre-1750 designations—*opéra-comique* (32%) and *parodie* (29%)—nearly one-fifth (19%) used terms ranging from *opéra bouffon* and *intermède* to *pastorale*, *comédie-héroïque*, and *divertissement-comique. Comédie* was the description given to a remaining 12%, while 8% used the increasingly favored *comédie mêlée d'ariettes.* Given so many terms, it was impossible for each to define stylistic boundaries; indeed, many were used interchangeably and discrepancies between libretto and printed score (where the latter exists) abound.[37]

Vaudeville and Parody Ensembles

Vaudeville and parody ensembles common to the *vaudeville-comédie* of the early half of the 18th century remained popular in works written during the 1750s. Simple dialogue songs continued to be distributed freely throughout plays, as were vaudevilles concerted partially or fully throughout, or blending dialogue with moments of ensemble. Many fully concerted vaudevilles were duets derived, as earlier in the century, from two-part *airs à boire*.[38] Those with refrains tended to be written for larger groups, as were those blending dialogue with ensemble singing, these affording especial scope for experimentation in the distribution of text and integration of characters. Favart's opéra-comique *Les nymphes de Diane*, performed in Brussels in 1747 and revised for the Foire Saint Laurent in 1755, offers an insight into the increasingly complex treatment of these ensembles during the 1750s. In scene v Églé tells of an unwelcome lover who has invaded Diane's sanctuary. The 1747 version depicts her entry, her news, and the reactions of the other characters to this with simple economy:

SÉVÉRINE

Un Amant!

CYANE

Un Amant!

THEMIRE

Un Amant!

ÉGLÉ

Ouï Prêtresse,

> Et vous m'en voyez hors de moi.
> La Nymphe Gangan dont l'emploi
> Est de veiller sur la jeunesse,
> A gagné le rhume d'effroi.
>
> Comme elle est toujours aux aguets . . .[39]

In the 1755 version, Favart expands the text thus:

LA PRESTRESSE
Un Amant!
CYANE
Un Amant!
THEMIRE
Un Amant!
Sachons pourquoi . . .
CYANE
Voyons comment.
ÉGLÉ
Chose étonnante!
LA PRESTRESSE
Est-il en mon pouvoir?
ÉGLÉ
Il faut savoir . . .
THEMIRE
Courons le voir,
LA PRESTRESSE
Arrêtez, ô Nymphe imprudente!
ÉGLÉ
C'est Gangan
Notre vieille surveillante,
Qui subtilement . . .
Souffrez que je respire un moment.

THEMIRE & CYANE　　　　　　LA PRESTRESSE
Comment, comment a-t-elle fait?　　　Cessez ce vain caquet,
Allons au fait. *bis*　　　*à Églé.* Allons au fait. *bis.*
La Gouvernante?　　　　　　La Gouvernante . . .
Hé bien contez-nous ça,　　　　*à Themire & Cyane*
Contez-nous, contez-nous,　　　Patiti, patita,
Contez-nous ça.　　　　　　Écoutez-la.

ÉGLÉ dit ce qui suit en même-temps; ce qui fait une espece de quatuor.
Voici le fait. *bis*
La Gouvernante . . .
Hélas! je crois qu'elle en moura.

ÉGLÉ
Comme elle est sans cesse aux aguets . . .[40]

In delaying and expanding Églé's explanation, Favart has not only heightened the dramatic situation but has taken the opportunity to create an interesting quartet in which Églé competes with two excited friends and a sterner third (Séverine in the first example). Example 2.2 shows how the vaudeville, while being preserved intact, was arranged in rapid dialogue and sung *à2*, *à3* or *à4* to divergent text as the occasion demanded. In other plays revised during this decade Favart repeated the technique of allowing ensembles to take the place of solo song. His *Hippolyte et Aricie* (1742, revised 1757) retained three vaudeville duets but, in expanding from one to three acts, added a trio (IIv) and a quartet (IIIvii). Since the music to these movements is not extant it is impossible to establish whether they were original compositions or whether they were still based

Example 2.2 "O Dieux! Un Amant!" *Les nymphes de Diane* scene v (1755)

on vaudevilles.[41] However, that playwrights were seeking to incorporate more ensembles into their works, and in particular larger ensembles, was evidence of a growing appreciation of their dramatic value.

With the advent of the *pasticcio opéra-comique*, parody ensembles enjoyed a significant rise in favor, at least until this genre gave way to the *comédie mêlée d'ariettes*. Whereas ensembles fashioned around vaudevilles constituted one-quarter of the total examined, those based upon models from popular contemporary operas accounted for 35%. Of these, three-quarters were duets, 18% quartets, and 7% trios. The proportion of duets to larger ensembles was still high, but should not conceal the gradual trend during the 1750s towards the inclusion of more trios, quartets, and ensembles of even larger dimensions.

Some 60% of the parody ensembles located were taken from the Bouffons' repertory. As pointed out earlier, the dramatic purpose of parody movements had ceased to be entirely satirical, and the models chosen were not distorted by their new setting. They were instead object lessons in familiarizing French librettists and composers with more sophisticated techniques of concerted writing and they facilitated the transition from concerted vaudeville to original composition.

French adaptors did not always transcribe Italian parody models exactly, but instead integrated them subtly and for their own convenience. This is apparent from a comparison of the many ensembles reproduced in musical supplements (or in the plays themselves) with the original examples. Several were truncated, possibly because a full rendition would have created an imbalance between these and the other musical numbers in a particular work. Others were shaped out of solo or choral material, the versions of *Ninette à la cour* providing examples of this procedure. Two parody duets from the first version (1755), "Tout va nous rendre hommage" (Iiv) and "Tu nous perdras, Colas" (Iv), were based on solo *ariettes* from *Il cinese rimpatriato* and *Bertoldo in corte* respectively; and the quartet "Toute mon ame" closing Act II of the 1756 revision used a chorus from *La zingara* as its model.

The remaining 40% of parody ensembles derived mainly from French sources: the *tragédie en musique*, the *opéra-ballet* or, indeed, from the newly-emerging comic repertory, *Le devin du village* proving a popular model in this respect. A few took either French vocal or instrumental music as their source, and an even smaller number were based on so far undiscovered models.

Original Ensembles: General Considerations

Table VI lists 14 works from the period 1752 to 1758 which were found to contain original ensembles. It shows that towards the end of the period in question many *opéras-comiques* incorporated an average of three or four such movements. A noticeable rise in the use of larger ensembles is also apparent: trios and quartets were introduced more liberally and quintets made an occasional appearance. More information concerning the proportion of one type of ensemble to another is provided in Table VII. Another feature apparent from Table VI is the placing of ensembles at the end of individual acts. One-third of the total examined were finales: for the last two years alone this figure rose to almost 40%. These developments were attributable, overall, to a decrease in the use of vaudeville and parody ensembles, to experience gained from parodying ensembles from the Italian repertory and, not least, to a genuine inventiveness on the part of French librettists and composers.

Table VI: Original Ensembles in Opéras-Comiques, 1752–58

* = an ensemble with no known musical source.
Finales in italic print.

1752 Font.	*Le devin du village* (1)	Rousseau	Duet (sc. vi) Duet (sc. vi)
1753 CI	*Baïocco et Serpilla* (3)	Favart / Sodi	Duet (Iii) *Duet (finale, Act I)* *Duet (finale, Act II)* *Duet (finale, Act III)*
1753 FSL	*Les troqueurs* (1)	Vadé / Dauvergne	Duet (sc. ii) Quartet (sc. iii) Quartet (sc. iii) *Quartet (finale)*
1753 Font.	*La coquette trompée* (1)	Favart / Dauvergne	Duet (sc. iii) Duet (sc. iii) Trio (sc. iv)
1756 CI	*Le charlatan* (2)	Lacombe / Sodi	* Duet (Iii) * Duet (Iviii) Duet (Iviii)[1] * *Trio (finale, Act I)* * Quartet (IIi) Duet (IIvii) * *Quartet (finale, Act II)*[2]
1757 CI	*La capricieuse* (1)	Mailhol / Talon	* Duet (sc. iii) * Trio (sc. iv) * Duet (sc. viii) * *Duet (finale)*

1757 FSG	*La fausse aventurière* (2)	Anseaume-Marcouville/ Laruette	* Duet (Iiv) * *Quartet (finale, Act II)*
1757 FSL	*Le peintre amoureux* (2)[3]	Anseaume / Duni	*Quartet (finale, Act I)* *Quartet (finale, Act II)*
1758 FSG	*Le docteur Sangrado* (1)	Anseaume / Laruette-Duni	Trio (sc. xi)
1758 FSG	*Gilles, garçon peintre* (1)	Poinsinet / La Borde[4]	Duet (sc. ii) Quartet (sc. vi) *Quartet (finale)*
1758 CI	*La fille mal gardée* (1)	Favart-Mme Favart/ Duni	Duet/Trio (sc. v/vi/vii) Trio (sc. xi) *Quartet (finale)*
1758 FSL	*L'heureux déguisement* (2)	Marcouville / Laruette	* *Trio (finale, Act I)* * *Quintet (IIx)* * *Quintet (finale, Act II)*
1758 FSL	*Nina et Lindor* (2)	[Richelet] / Duni	Duet (IIiii) Duet (IIiv) (IIv in libretto) *Quartet (finale, Act II)*
1758 FSL	*Le médecin de l'amour* (1)	Anseaume / Laruette	Duet (sc. ix) Trio (sc. x)

1. Both extant ensembles from *Le charlatan* are reprinted in J. Dubreuil: *Dictionnaire lyrique portatif* (Paris, 1764).
2. "Vive l'allégresse," possibly a parody of the chorus "Plein d'allégresse" (*Le diable à quatre*), in turn a parody of "Quasi fatica" (*Bertoldo*).
3. For the revision of *Le peintre* at the Foire Saint Germain in February 1753 one duet and two trios were added.
4. La Borde omitted a duet in scene vii. (The printed score to this work dates from 1765.)

Table VII: Proportion of Duets to Other Types of Ensemble, 1752–58

Period	Total	Duets	Trios	Quartets	Quintets
Overall:	47 (100%)	23 (49%)	9 (19%)	13 (28%)	2 (4%)
1752–55:	13 (28%)	9 (69%)	1 (8%)	3 (23%)	---
1756–58:	34 (72%)	14 (41%)	8 (24%)	10 (29%)	2 (6%)

The creation of ensembles was a two-way process. Texts written by librettists established the essential characteristics which were developed or modified by the composer when set to music. Chapter I alluded briefly to the librettists' major responsibilities: choosing the different types of concerted movement, how frequently to include them, where to site them, and the dramatic function they were to assume within individual scenes and acts. Thereafter followed decisions concerning the structure and length of texts and whether characters were to express identical or opposing sentiments. Such basic elements suggested characteristics which composers could then explore further in their choice of form, length, vocal texture, instrumental accompaniments, tempos, and in the general style of their musical language.

Composers could, however, override a librettist's initial design in a variety of ways. They might alter the type of ensemble by adding or excluding singers, or change the position of movements within scenes (or from scene to scene), thereby increasing or diluting the dramatic effect of the ensemble. This could also be achieved by extending a short text or reducing a long text. Furthermore, original texts could be omitted or fresh ones commissioned, either in their place or as extra numbers. Finally, the poetry could be manipulated in many different ways: by reallocating lines or phrases, changing the order in which they were to be sung, emphasizing certain aspects through repetition or rendering the text more complex through segmentation.

The manner in which poet and musician collaborated in the creation of ensemble movements is best understood through considering the way in which the partnership operated in general: much depended on the character and experience of individual artists. In some cases librettists were little more than servants; in others, composers relied more substantially on their poets. The most fruitful collaborations were those in which both parties were interdependent, the experience of each being used to mutual advantage; and the most talented and sensitive librettists were those who realized that their work was only complete once the music had been added.[42]

Of the librettists listed in Table VI, the most noted were: Charles-Simon Favart, Louis Anseaume, Pierre-Augustin Lefèvre de Marcouville, and Antoine-Alexandre-Henri Poinsinet. With the exception of Favart, whose career began during the period of the *vaudeville-comédie*, all emerged as playwrights in the 1750s and thereafter collaborated with Duni, Monsigny, Philidor, and other composers of the same generation.

Favart was a seminal figure in the development of the *opéra-comique*, his career spanning three stylistic periods: that of the *vaudeville-comédie*, the transitional years currently under discussion, and the major flowering of the genre during the 1760s and 1770s. He therefore witnessed important changes in the relationship between playwright and musician, and although he collaborated successfully with several composers in the latter stages of his career, he continued to write comedies which retained their emphasis on literary, as opposed to musical, elements. His interest in the ensemble was evident even in early works, Table II (p. 42) in the preceding chapter illustrating that half of the original ensembles encountered in the *vaudeville-comédie* to 1750 were included in plays by Favart. Subsequent revisions, as noted in *Les nymphes de Diane* above, testify to a heightened awareness of the potential of concerted movements. The three works to original scores listed in Table VI continued to focus on the ensemble. *Baïocco et Serpilla*, a *parodie* for two characters, contained four duets, *La coquette trompée* two duets and a trio, and *La fille mal gardée*, responding to recent developments, a duet (which became a trio), one trio, and a quartet finale. Collaborations during the 1760s and beyond with composers such as Duni, Monsigny, Philidor, Grétry, La Borde, and Martini, continued to explore new dramatic possibilities in the design of ensembles; however Favart was inclined to be less innovative and experimental than some of his younger contemporaries.

The career of Louis Anseaume was intimately connected with the development of the new genre. He held various posts at the Opéra-Comique and turned to dramatic composition in the early 1750s when new ideas and techniques were beginning to circulate. His earliest works included the *pasticcio opéras-comiques Bertholde à la ville* and *Le chinois poli en France*; these were followed by collaborations with Laruette and Duni, the two composers most influential in the transition to the *comédie mêlée d'ariettes*. His career extended well into the third quarter of the 18th century; he became Duni's principal collaborator and worked also with Philidor, Grétry, and Gluck. As the following chapter will emphasize, Anseaume was an ardent disciple of Denis Diderot and used his librettos to implement many of the dramatic reforms championed by this philosopher.

Marcouville began writing for the theater around 1750. Although an early venture, the one-act *comédie Le réveil de Thalie*, was entirely his own work, he thereafter wrote mainly in partnership, first with Favart and then with Anseaume (who became his principal collaborator). Several of Anseaume's achievements must also be credited to Marcouville: the design of the *pasticcio opéra-comique* and the fruitful collaborations with Laruette and Duni. In *L'heureux déguisement*, however, Marcouville proved a competent playwright in his own right. Unlike Anseaume, his career did not expand considerably beyond the 1750s, a matter for regret since certain of his experiments—in particular the introduction of quintets in *L'heureux déguisement* and, later, a sextet in Duni's *L'isle des foux* (1761)—were significant in the development of the ensemble.

Poinsinet died at the age of 34, but during his brief career collaborated with several distinguished musicians, most frequently with Philidor. He began with various one-act compositions, including *Les fra-maçonnes* (1754) and *Le faux dervis* (1757), before embarking on his first major work, *Gilles, garçon peintre*, set to music by La Borde in 1758. The complexity of the concerted movements in this *parodie* is all the more striking since Poinsinet had attempted no similar experiments in earlier plays. Subsequent works, however, continued this trend, and collaborations during the 1760s show him to have been an ardent disciple of Italian music (he had visited Italy in 1760). Poinsinet's literary and dramatic talents were often criticized, perhaps rightly, since two of his librettos for Philidor, *Tom Jones* and the *tragédie-lyrique Ernelinde*, were later revised by Sedaine. However, his attitude towards ensembles shows that he was very much alive to developments in this sphere, and willing to experiment.

The remaining librettists mentioned in Table VI—Joseph Vadé, Jean-Jacques Rousseau, Jacques Lacombe, and Gabriel Mailhol—each wrote only one work containing original ensemble texts during this period, and therefore contributed to developments to a much lesser extent than other figures.[43] Vadé achieved early fame as a *chansonnier* and began writing plays in the much maligned *genre poissard* during the 1740s. In these, and in the *opéras-comiques* he produced during the early 1750s, there was very little emphasis on concerted movements and, therefore, little preparation for what he produced in 1753 with *Les troqueurs*: one duet and three quartets. That this work was conceived as a deliberate imitation of Italian music explains the unusual emphasis on the ensemble, along with the absence of vaudevilles and the use of recitative in place of spoken dialogue. Vadé never again collaborated with a composer of Dauvergne's stature, and although in the years following *Les troqueurs* up to his death in 1757 he wrote several *opéras-comiques*, none ventured to substantiate the innovative style of concerted writing in his masterpiece. Some, indeed, contained no ensembles. Only in *Le troc* (1756) were similar pieces found, this due to the fact that the work was itself a parody of *Les troqueurs*.

Rousseau's major claim to fame in *Le devin du village* was in creating both the poem and an original score. He had attempted similar experiments before with the *tragédies-lyriques Iphis et Anaxorète* (c1739–40) and *La découverte du nouveau monde* (1742), but neither had been successful. *Le devin* was a less ambitious work in two acts, containing two duets, but it proved instantly popular.

Lacombe was a man of many talents who dabbled in dramatic composition during the 1750s and produced a one-act *comédie*, *Les amours de Mathurine*, in 1756 before writing *Le charlatan*, a work rich in ensembles. This remained very much an isolated experiment since Lacombe turned thereafter to editing and theoretical writing, and did not repeat what he had achieved in *Le charlatan*.[44] Mailhol also wrote few librettos during this period, and only *La capricieuse* included a significant number of ensembles. His dramatic career, like Lacombe's, did not apparently extend into the next decade.

Developments in Ensemble Texts

The most striking development in concerted writing during the 1750s was undoubtedly the realization that such pieces could contribute actively towards the drama and serve an important role therein. Ensembles had been denied this character in the *tragédie en musique*, and although those in the *vaudeville-comédie* had endeavoured to work towards this objective, the necessary musical means had been lacking in order for it to be reached conclusively. The musical advances of the decade in question, inspired by the imported Italian operas of the Bouffon repertory, allowed a new dramatic identity to be established for the ensemble.

Librettists worked towards this end by designing ensembles to include varied groupings of singers presented in diverse settings. Duets were still written predominantly for lovers, but emulated those from the Bouffon repertory in focusing on quarrels and disagreements. Trios, quartets, and the two quintets, however, explored more unusual and complicated situations. The greater freedom in the interaction of singers rapidly divested concerted movements of their earlier static character and allowed the expression of not one, but a multiplicity of sentiments. Given such contrast within ensembles, it was not long before various twists and developments were included which contributed effectively to the unfolding of the drama.

Vadé's quartet concluding Les *troqueurs*, which in fact comprised the whole of the closing scene, was one of the earliest examples of an ensemble designed to further the action of an *opéra-comique*. It opened with the four characters still locked in disagreement, but allowed them to resolve their differences as the music progressed and, finally, to reach an amicable conclusion. This naturally resulted in an extensive movement, 154 bars in length. The experiment was bold, unprecedented, and extremely successful. However, it was not directly imitated for some years. Instead, librettists concentrated on developing another type of concerted movement, the ensemble of perplexity. This aimed to present a number of characters locked in a complicated situation and expressing conflicting sentiments simultaneously. Such was the trio in scene xi of Anseaume's *Le docteur Sangrado*, which depicted a lively quarrel between the two lovers (Blaise and Jacqueline) and the latter's aunt, arising from the fact that Jacqueline's hand has already been promised to an elderly suitor of her aunt's choosing. Another ensemble of perplexity was the quartet in scene vi of *Gilles, garçon peintre*, designed by Poinsinet, in which Cassandre and Gilles vied with one another for the attention of Isabelle, who claimed that their ungentlemanly behaviour demeaned her, while Colombine, the duenna, sought to placate everyone.

Having explored new ground with the ensemble of perplexity, librettists then returned to the idea of the "progressive" ensemble, as established by Vadé in *Les troqueurs*.[45] The two further examples of this type encountered both date from the year 1758 and emphasize that only towards the end of the decade did such movements began to feature on a more regular basis in the *opéra-comique*. Both were, in different ways, innovative. The first, from *La fille mal gardée* by Favart, spanned three scenes (v, vi, and vii) and introduced a new character part-way through, thereby enabling the action to develop in a hitherto unprecedented manner.[46] Shortly after this experiment, Marcouville incorporated a quintet as the dramatic high-point of *L'heureux déguisement* (IIx). This was a bold coup, not only in carrying the action through to the dénouement, but in being possibly the first quintet to feature in any *opéra-comique*. It follows Julie's exposure of her unfaithful lover (Valère) to his new, but reluctant, fiancée (Lucile) and her father (Geronte), the culmination of a scheme that has required Julie to pass as Lucile's governess. Once this disguise is discarded the quintet begins, first painting everyone's immediate reactions to the unexpected turn in events: Valère's astonishment, Lucile's relief, Geronte's disbelief, and the amusement of

Julie's valet (Frontin). Julie then reminds Valère of his earlier promises; Lucile and her father take this opportunity to upbraid him for his deception. Valère repents and agrees to become Julie's husband, leaving Lucile free to marry the man she really loves. With this the crisis is resolved, leaving all five characters to comment on the happy outcome. Unfortunately the music to this quintet is not extant; the text in the libretto, however, spans almost two pages and is cast in dialogue. This is a reflection of other developments implemented by librettists during the 1750s: the considerable expansion of ensemble texts and the greater prevalence of dialogue over *unanime* expression.

The expansion of poetic texts accorded concerted movements more dramatic significance within the overall structure of works and enabled the expression of more complicated and divergent sentiments. Librettists used three means in particular to create longer, more substantial ensembles. The first was a dialogue framework based not on the haphazard structures of earlier vaudeville dialogues, but on more streamlined patterns appropriated from the Italian repertory. *Baïocco et Serpilla* was one of the first plays to use dialogue texts of this nature consistently, and the following example transcribes the opening part of the duet closing the second act. Virtually every other *opéra-comique* listed in Table VI thereafter included at least one text of similar design, and very often more.

DUO

SERPILLA: Quoi! Voilà donc ce tendre Epoux,
Si complaisant, si bon, si doux?
BAÏOCCO: Voilà donc cette brave femme,
Voilà donc cette honnête Dame.

SERPILLA

Ah, ah, la bonne ame!
Où donc est la charité?

DUO

Avec ta fidelité

BAÏOCCO	Je n'ai point de pitié.
SERPILLA	Quoi, sans pitié!
BAÏOCCO	Je n'ai point d'amitié.
SERPILLA	Pour ta moitié.
BAÏOCCO	Je n'ai plus d'amitié.[47]

Secondly, librettists developed the idea of communicating divergent expression more boldly through juxtaposing contrasting verses. Works from the early part of the period in question, such as *Baïocco et Serpilla*, *Le charlatan*, and *La capricieuse*, still relied on the process of interleaving only mildly contrasting stanzas. The following example, a duet from Iiv of *La fausse aventurière* (Anseaume and Marcouville), expanded these methods a little further:

AGATHE	VALÈRE
Oui, je vous aime	Bonheur extrême!
Ah! croyez que mon coeur	Pour vous mon coeur,
Ressent la plus vive ardeur.	Ressent la plus vive ardeur.
De ma tendresse,	O douce yvresse,
Soyez sur à jamais:	Dure à jamais:
Nos plaisirs seront parfaits.	Nos plaisirs seront parfaits,
Fortune inconstante,	A la rappeller
En vain on te vante;	Si je m'empresse encore,
Quand on s'aime bien,	C'est pour en combler
Tout le reste n'est rien.	L'Epouse que j'adore.
Oui, je vous aime, &c.	Bonheur extrême! &c.[48]

Later texts blended disparate language far more freely, as this duet from scene ii of Poinsinet's *Gilles, garçon peintre* illustrates:

CASSANDRE	GILLES
Ah! c'en est trop,	
Fras-tu silence?	Quoi, vieux magot.
Queux insolence!	
Tu te tairas.	Non pas, non pas,
Tais-toi, croi-moi,	Nenni ma foi,
J' suis t'en colere;	Que veux-tu faire?
De ce bàton,	Ose-le donc,
De ce bàton,	Vieux rogaton.
C'est z'avoir trop d'audace.	Quand tu fras la grimace.

à part.   *à part.*

Je pense qu'il a peur:	Il est blanc de paleur.
Comment, zon m'injurie,	
Attend, attend,	
Pan, pan, pan, pan.	

     Il le bat.

	V'là qui m'met zen furie,
	Me frapper moi présent!
	Il le barbouille avec un gros pinceau.
Comment, comment, za moi!	Tien, tien, voilà pour toi.
Comment, za moi!	Voilà pour toi,
Attend, voleur.	Vieux radoteur.

       Ils se battent.

Pan, pan,	Pan, pan,
Es-tu content?	Es-tu content?

  Le perruque de Cassandre & le chapeau de Gilles tombent.[49]

A third technique, which developed directly from the second, was to present texts in columns. This, as the preceding examples show, was exploited initially in duets. However, the more characters involved, the more intricate the results became, and in trios and quartets this layout provided librettists with the means to present increasingly complex material. One of the earliest examples, by Anseaume and Marcouville in *La fausse aventurière*, is the quartet closing the second act. Here the text is divided into two columns; one pair of characters is offset against another and, to add variety, dialogue also operates within each column:

CHRISANTE, JULIEN	AGATHE, VALÈRE
Au doux plaisir livrez votre ame,	Ah! quel plaisir saisit mon ame!

JUL: Rien ne s'oppose à votre flâme:	AG: Rien ne s'oppose à notre flâme
CHR: J'approuve votre flâme	VAL:Mon Pere approuve notre flâme

Formez les noeuds	Formons les noeuds
Les plus heureux.	Les plus heureux.
Fin.	*Fin.*

CHRISANTE
Je vous pardonne.
JULIEN
Ah! quel effort!   Quel heureux sort!
CHRISANTE *à Valère.*
Je te le donne.
JULIEN
Ah! quel effort!   Quel heureux sort!
Votre folie,
Les justifie.
CHRISANTE
Oui, sa beauté m'avoit surpris.
JULIEN
Mais à votre âge
C'est trop d'ouvrage:
En homme sage,
Cédez la place à votre fils.

On reprend le Rondeau jusqu'au mot Fin.[50]

The librettist of Duni's *Nina et Lindor* attempted a more ambitious quartet as the finale to this work. Here the text is divided into three columns and concludes with an ensemble tercet:

ZERBIN	LA BOHEMIENNE	NINA ET LINDOR
Le mariage est pourtant bon.	L'un dit oui, l'autre non,	
	C'est selon.	
	Qu'un barbon	
	Prenne un tendron.	
Non, non, non.	Le mariage est-il bon?	
Ah, si donc.		
Le mariage est pourtant bon.	C'est selon	L'amour & la raison
		M'ont fait le plus aimable don,
Ah! très-bon,	Ah! très-bon,	Le mariage est-il bon?
Mais très-bon.	Mais très-bon.	

ENSEMBLE

Quand deux coeurs sont à l'unisson,
L'hymen fait un doux carillon;
Alors le mariage est bon.[51]

Presenting texts in columns, as the following chapter will emphasize, rapidly became a favorite device among librettists, especially as they came to include large, complex ensembles for five and more characters in their works. This style of text had significant repercussions for concerted writing in that it allowed the composer much greater scope and freedom in his musical setting. There was ample room for manipulation, for using the poetry to advantage, thereby achieving a closer match between words and music. More importantly, texts designed in this way reflected the changing balance of words and music within the *opéra-comique*. They were not literary entities in their own right: they were dependent on music and only gained coherence through their musical setting.

These advances prepared the ground for important musical developments. The greater dramatic significance of concerted texts and their increasing complexity called for more substantial musical movements exploring new possibilities in form and harmonic structure, vocal textures, instrumental accompaniments, and changes in tempo and tonality. These, however, were developments of the 1760s and beyond: composers creating original ensembles during the 1750s were more concerned with securing the transition from parody to original composition. Of the 43 ensembles listed in Table VI, 29 have extant musical sources. From these it is possible to establish: how much composers drew upon the experience of parodying Italian ensembles; the extent to which native traditions were retained and absorbed into a new idiom; whether any fusion of the two approaches was attempted; and the degree to which composers advanced ideas of a more individual and enterprising nature. What is apparent is that each composer tried something different. Their methods were linked closely to their backgrounds and personal experiences as musicians.

Musical Characteristics of Original Ensembles

Five of the seven composers mentioned in Table VI are discussed below: Rousseau, Charles Sodi, Antoine Dauvergne, Jean-Louis Laruette, and Jean-Benjamin de La Borde. Those omitted are Pierre Talon, whose music to *La capricieuse* does not survive, and Duni, whose first three Parisian *opéras-comiques*, although composed during the last two years of the transition period in question, are considered with his other works in Chapter IV.

Rousseau's *intermède, Le devin du village*, composed during the early part of 1752, was not performed until October of that year, at Fontainebleau, three months after the arrival of the Bouffons. Rousseau was, by the early 1750s, an ardent disciple of Italian music but, ironically, his beliefs at times were at odds with what he actually composed, and the style of *Le devin* owes more to French traditions than to the italianate methods its composer so vociferously advocated.[52]

The *intermède*, in one act and for three characters, had a pastoral setting. The music consisted of an overture, several solo *airs* with simple continuo accompaniment, two duets, various instrumental interludes, and an extensive final *divertissement*. The two duets were for the lovers Colette (soprano) and Colin (*haute-contre*). Both presented familiar dramatic situations, the first a duet of renunciation and the second one of reconciliation. That placed in the early part of scene vi, "Tant qu'à mon Colin j'ai su plaire," was based on a dialogue text culminating in a *unanime* quatrain. The dialogue was set as a musical conversation, not subjected to any manipulation, and the two voices then merged in homophony for the ensemble quatrain at the close and repeated this several times. Thus, both the structure of the text and the musical pattern it followed coincided closely with ideas concerning duet composition Rousseau had recently articulated, which took Italian dialogue duets as their model.[53] Whereas the first duet was a short movement, extending only to 49 bars, cast in single paragraph form and accompanied by a continuo line alone, the second duet, "A jamais Colin l'engage," occurring at the end of the same scene (vi), was a more complex and substantial piece nearly 200 bars long and set in dal segno form. In spite of its italianate structure, this movement owed much less to imported ideas than did the first duet. The text was not based on dialogue, and bore more resemblance to those from contemporary *tragédies*, comprising a *unanime* quatrain followed by a *unanime* couplet and a repeat of the first quatrain. Moreover, the dal segno did not follow the usual five-part form of AA^{I}BAA^I. Instead, it moulded the first section in a tri-partite AA^{I}A^{II} pattern, and presented the middle section as a short transition which returned to a point mid-way through the initial A part of the AA^{I}A^{II} design. Rousseau's setting of the text, however, aimed to achieve some degree of musical dialogue. Each A portion of the first section was based on the opening *unanime* quatrain, initially distributing the lines clearly between the two characters, then juxtaposing this text briefly before allowing the voices to repeat their lines once again in homophony at cadence points. The B "transition" repeated the *unanime* couplet twice, set to a mixture of solos, note-against-note singing and alternating phrases. As a result the overall texture displayed none of the regularity of Italian dialogue patterns, nor yet the typical features of French homophonic writing.

Rousseau's approach to duet composition amalgamates several disparate factors. In the first duet he favored a dialogue text, in the second a *unanime* text. He sometimes opted for a dialogue texture to match his poetry, but then also composed extensive sections in homophony. His choice of dramatic context and soprano/*haute-contre* pairing certainly derived from the *tragédie*. In addition, the character of the first duet looked back to the musical style of the first half of the 18th century. Yet that of the second incorporated rhythmic and melodic figurations that were *galant* in character. Example 2.3 reproduces the opening bars of each duet.[54]

Charles Sodi (*c*1715–88), an Italian by birth who probably arrived in France during the 1740s, obtained a position as violinist in the orchestra of the Comédie-Italienne and became music master to Mme Favart. He wrote two *parodies* for the Comédie-Italienne during the 1750s, *Baïocco et Serpilla* and *Le charlatan*, both rich in original ensembles. The four duets in *Baïocco* are preserved in a printed score but only two duets of the seven concerted numbers in *Le charlatan* survive.

All six duets were distinctly Italian in style. Although the structure of their texts was varied, including solo or *unanime* stanzas and interleaved verses as well as dialogue, Sodi mainly chose to set these to dialogue textures. Four of the six were modelled around the pattern of the Italian dialogue duet. The duet closing the first act of *Baïocco* was, in contrast, entirely homophonic, and the finale concluding this work was composed

Example 2.3(i) "Tant qu'a mon Colin" *Le devin du village* scene vi (Rousseau, 1752)

Example 2.3(ii) "A jamais Colin t'engage" *Le devin du village* scene vi (Rousseau, 1752)

mainly in a note-against-note style. Five of the six duets were written for the soprano/bass pairing common to the *intermezzo* and involved the characters either in humorous altercation or in patching up their differences. (The sixth, in IIvii of *Le charlatan*, was of a more pastoral and amatory tone and was written for soprano and tenor.) With the exception of a short duet (23 bars) in Iii of *Baïocco*, all the movements were cast in binary form and ranged in length from 49 to 120 bars. Those from *Baïocco* were accompanied by an italianate three-part string texture (divisi violins and bass). In common with works from the Bouffons' repertory, Sodi's musical style was *galant* and melodious. That such music was designed around French texts, however, was particularly influential in shaping the character of a native style of comic opera in France. As the title page to *Baïocco* recorded: "Les Paroles de cet Intermède ont été faites sur la Musique." This represented an important break with the tradition of the *vaudeville-comédie*.

Antoine Dauvergne was primarily a composer of serious operas for the Académie, where he also held various administrative posts, but his two ventures into the comic sphere during the 1750s show that he was equally

skilled in both fields. *Les troqueurs* was staged at the Foire Saint Laurent
in July 1753 and *La coquette trompée* at Fontainebleau some months later
(it then became the final *entrée* of the *ballet Les fêtes d'Euterpe*, performed
at the Académie in 1758).

    Les troqueurs contained one duet and three quartets, *La coquette
trompée* two duets and a trio. Dauvergne was at his most italianate in the
three quartets from the first work. Two were based on dialogue texts, the
third on a short couplet; all were cast in dialogue textures in which the
voices alternated rapidly and then merged in cadential homophony. They
were scored for the italianate combination of two sopranos and two basses,
and were supported by a four-part string accompaniment rather than by a
simple continuo line. Two quartets were placed in the same scene (sc. iii),
both as ensembles of perplexity to contribute ever more effectively to the
dramatic intrigue. They were cast in binary form and were 88 and 46 bars
long respectively. That closing the work was through-composed and even
more substantial, extending over 154 bars. It was described above (p. 82)
as a progressive ensemble resolving the final threads of the action.

    The four remaining ensembles blended French and Italian traits
more haphazardly and, overall, achieved no consistent stylistic synthesis.
The duet in scene ii of *Les troqueurs*, "Trocquons, trocquons," was written
for the unusual combination of two bass voices and portrayed two men
agreeing to exchange their fiancées. The text comprised a *unanime*
nine-line stanza, set initially, as Example 2.4 illustrates, in an imitative
fashion before the voices then merged in homophony and continued in
this manner throughout much of the movement. Thus text and texture were
rooted in French practice, although the manner in which the former was
manipulated—its lines were scrambled and juxtaposed—suggested an
italianate approach. (The French, as observed in the opening chapter,
prized clarity and order in the musical setting of poetic texts.) This duet
was 67 bars long, cast in binary form, and accompanied by a four-part
string orchestra.

    The two duets from *La coquette trompée* both featured in the same
scene (sc. iii) which, like the quartets from the corresponding scene in *Les
troqueurs*, accentuated their dramatic effect. The first, "Je veux me venger
d'un rival," was a spirited dialogue duet based on an extensive dialogue
text that comprised three pages in the printed libretto and was therefore
set without manipulation.[55] The musical setting extended to 100 bars and
was through-composed. In contrast to the italianate text and texture, the
pairing of soprano and *haute-contre* was derived from the *tragédie*, and

Example 2.4 "Trocquons, trocquons" *Les troqueurs* scene ii (Dauvergne, 1753)

the two-part string accompaniment was reminiscent of those characterizing vengeance duets in serious French opera.[56] The duet concluding scene iii was entirely French in style. In this, the soprano/*haute-contre* lovers were temporarily reconciled and sang a *unanime* sestet cast in a predominantly homophonic texture. The movement was in binary form, 58 bars long, and accompanied by three-part strings. The final trio drew on similar influences. Here, the happy lovers were joined by a capricious, but sympathetic, third party which resulted in a typically French combination of two sopranos and *haute-contre*. The trio, 98 bars long, was cast in ternary form, the first section set to two interleaved stanzas, this resulting in some contrapuntal interplay between the voices, the second sung as a solo and the third repeating the first.

Jean-Louis Laruette was a figure of prime importance in the development of the *opéra-comique* during the third quarter of the 18th century. He is remembered not simply for his stage works, which nursed the *opéra-comique* from parody composition to the autonomous *comédie mêlée d'ariettes*, but as a popular actor-singer who created many roles in works by the generation of composers following in his footsteps.[57] Four of the pieces listed in Table VI include original music by Laruette: *La fausse aventurière* (a *pasticcio* also using vaudevilles and parody numbers); *Le docteur Sangrado* (likewise a *pasticcio* written in collaboration with Duni); *L'heureux déguisement* and *Le médecin de l'amour* (both of which mixed vaudevilles, but far fewer parody numbers, with increasing amounts of original music). Of the eight original ensembles contained in these works, three are extant: a trio in *Le docteur Sangrado*, and a duet and trio in *Le médecin de l'amour*. To add to this small body of concerted movements, those from another work by Laruette will be taken into consideration. This is *L'yvrogne corrigé*, performed at the Foire Saint Laurent in July 1759, which included one duet, two trios, and a quartet.

The most striking feature of this collection of ensembles is their extensive use of dialogue textures in direct imitation of Italian models. These were reproduced in their simplest terms so that the characters began by singing solos and then joined in homophony. Juxtaposition of contrasting rhythmic and melodic ideas, characteristic of more complex Italian dialogue duets prior to major cadences, was kept to a minimum. Such was Laruette's preference for dialogue textures that he subjected all texts to this treatment regardless of their structure. Indeed, only two trio texts (in *Le docteur Sangrado* and *L'yvrogne corrigé*, IIv) were written in dialogue; the rest were based upon interleaved stanzas or set in columns.

Another interesting feature of these ensembles is that as they included more characters they became longer. The duets were short movements of 68 and 74 bars respectively. The four trios were all in excess of 100 bars (that from Iii of *L'yvrogne corrigé* was 220 bars long), while the quartet extended to 250 bars. Laruette used a variety of formal structures. Three ensembles were cast in binary form and two in ternary; the trio from *Le médecin de l'amour* was through-composed and the lengthy quartet in *L'yvrogne corrigé* was set in da capo form.

Both duets retained the traditional soprano/*haute-contre* pairing of serious French opera and allowed unhappy lovers to vent their despair. The four trios were more diverse in the situations they portrayed. Two combined the lovers with a benevolent third party, a permutation then common in French and Italian serious opera. That in IIv of *L'yvrogne corrigé* was more unusual: its three characters were united in pleading for the release of the hero from the underworld. The fourth trio (in Iii of the same work) also aimed at comic effect, but was based upon a more perplexing situation: a spirited argument between two drunkards and a long-suffering spouse. Vocal groupings in all four trios varied.[58] The quartet was more traditional, designed as a double duet at the close of *L'yvrogne corrigé*, and written for two sopranos, tenor, and bass. All accompaniments in Laruette's ensembles were scored for three- or four-part strings, and four of the seven added extra instruments such as oboes, bassoons, and horns.

Gilles, garçon peintre, a parody of Duni's *Le peintre amoureux de son modèle*, was Jean-Benjamin La Borde's first major *opéra-comique* and one of several works he composed in this genre over the following 20 years.[59] A short one-act composition for a small cast of four characters, it was designed and written with skill and showed the composer's sound technique to advantage. *Gilles* contained one duet and two quartets. These ensembles were less substantial than those found in 's works, but they continued to emphasize the value of larger ensembles and used dialogue textures more ambitiously. The duet was the most extensive movement of the three, 138 bars long and cast in ternary form. It portrayed a heated argument between the painter and his apprentice (bass and *haute-contre*) set to a divergent text.[60] Example 2.5 reproduces the opening 21 bars in which the voices alternate rapidly, are juxtaposed, and then blend, but to conflicting texts; they do not simply progress from solos to cadential agreement as in 's ensembles.

The texture of the quartet in scene vi was of a similar design and had, likewise, a divergent text; this resulted in an impressive through-composed ensemble of perplexity, 95 bars long, in which all four characters gave voice to sharply contrasting emotions. The quartet closing the play was, inevitably, a less ambitious movement since it served as the dénouement. It was 61 bars in length, set to a *unanime* text (since all the characters were in agreement), but achieved, nevertheless, variety in the design of its vocal texture, blending solos with more contrapuntal juxtaposition and with *à2*, *à3* or *à4* singing.

Example 2.5 "Ah! c'en est trop" *Gilles, garçon peintre* scene ii (La Borde, 1758)

* **Note:** The role of Gilles was originally notated in the alto clef.

During periods of transition, change and tradition exist side by side until a new style is completely formed and allowed, in turn, to assert its own conventionality. Composers writing original *opéra-comique* scores during the 1750s relied to varying degrees on new ideas while retaining aspects of earlier practice. Undoubtedly, Italian influences shaped the decade's advances in ensemble composition: the move away from unanimity of expression, the gradual creation of longer, more intricate texts, the presentation of complicated scenarios, and the recognition of new dramatic possibilities cultivated the ensemble as an expression of climax and confusion or as a means of developing stage action.

The Bouffon repertory had shown not only the dramatic means forward, but the musical means as well and, moreover, how closely the two were interlinked. On a dramatic level, Italian works incorporated ensembles into the dramatic intrigue with more flexibility, structuring texts around dialogue patterns which allowed for both diversity and development in expression. Librettists working in the *opéra-comique* during the later 1750s adopted this framework, and then used it as a means to create more complex texts based on divergent verses which were often presented in columns. As a result, ensembles evolved new dramatic functions and these were enhanced as more characters were integrated into concerted movements. Quartets were the largest type of ensemble encountered in the Bouffon repertory. During the years of transition in question, experiments were made in the *opéra-comique* with quintets which were to continue in the following decade in concerted movements designed for six and seven characters. The concentration of so many characters within a single movement eventually became a central dramatic focus of operatic works.

Musically, composers responded to dialogue texts by structuring the textures of their ensembles in dialogue. This represented one of the most important musical developments during the period in question, and was copied directly from Italian practice. However, the tradition of composing ensembles in a note-against-note style was still retained by some composers, as certain examples by Dauvergne and Rousseau considered above illustrate. Also inherited from the *tragédie* was the continued use of the *haute-contre*, although several concerted movements made more extensive use of tenor and bass voices. Ensembles became longer, a direct result of the more substantial and complicated texts with which composers were presented. Another related development was the introduction of fuller accompaniments.

Having recognized the potential of the ensemble, and various ways in which such movements could enrich dramatic composition, librettists and composers needed little encouragement to be guided by their own musical and dramatic instincts. They drew on what was useful from the past but, at the same time, extended the boundaries of conventional practice and developed new methods from old. Their ideas and experiments were carried through to the following decade, and expanded considerably in the works of the first major generation of *opéra-comique* composers: Duni, Monsigny, and Philidor. Their contributions, and those of the poets with whom they collaborated, are examined in Chapters III and IV.

Notes

1. New perspectives on the Querelle des Bouffons are discussed in E. Cook: 'Querelle des Bouffons', *The New Grove Dictionary of Opera*, ed. S. Sadie (London, 1992). The political dimension to the controversy was expanded in a paper read to the Royal Musical Association at King's College, London, in November 1993.

2. Reviews of *La finta cameriera* in the *Mercure de France* indicate that such restyling did not go unnoticed: "le sort ne fut pas heureux. Il y avoit dans cet Ouvrage tant de recitatif pour des oreilles qui n'y sont pas encore faites; on y avoit mêlé un si grand nombre d'airs qui ne sont pas du genre; il finissoit si mal . . . que sa chûte n'étonna personne." December, ii (1752), p. 138. *La scaltra governatrice* was subjected to similar treatment and likewise attracted criticism focusing on the imbalance between recitative and arias and the repetitive character of the latter (see the March issue of 1753, pp. 154–155).

3. *Il giocatore* was certainly one of the most complicated *pasticcios* performed by the Bouffon troupe. Oscar Sonneck has discussed the problems of attributing its music in: *Catalogue of Opera Librettos Printed before 1800* (Washington, 1914), pp. 732–734.

4. October (1752), p. 166.

5. November (1752), pp. 168–169.

6. December, ii (1752), p. 138. In both instances the *Mercure* makes no reference to the titles of the ensembles substituted.

7. ". . . le trio du premier Acte & le quatuor du second ont aussi été extrêment applaudis." December, i (1753), p. 174.

8. These exceptions were "Qual doppo insano" in *Il maestro di musica* (scored for two sopranos) and "Quando senti la campana" in *La finta cameriera* (for two male characters, although one is a breeches part and results in the familiar combination of soprano/bass). Most of the extant duets were written for soprano and bass voices. Exceptions to this combination include the three duets from *Il giocatore*, which were for a contralto/bass pairing, and the duet opening *La zingara*, which was written for soprano/*haute-contre*.

9. See Chapter I above, p. 28.

10. E. Borrel: 'La Querelle des Bouffons', *Histoire de la musique (Encyclopédie de la Pléiade)*, ii (Paris, 1963), p. 29.

11. Reporting on *Gli artigiani arricchiti* and *Il paratajo* in the October issue of 1753, for example, the *Mercure* wrote simply that it was suspending further coverage until the following month, a promise that was not kept. The only comment in the November issue was to the effect that since *Il paratajo* had not been successful, it had been replaced with a more popular work.

12. April (1754), p. 179.

13. September (1752), p. 168.

14. October (1752), pp. 164–165.

15. *Ibid.*, p. 166.

16. This is discussed in Chapter V below, pp. 215ff.

17. Rousseau was one of the most articulate critics in this respect: "no less than four of his articles [in the *Encyclopédie*] treat this item exclusively. (Rousseau: 'Chanter', 'Crier', 'Forcer la Voix', 'Fort.')" A.R. Oliver: *The Encyclopedists as Critics of Music* (New York, 1947), p. 59. Others included C.C. de Ruhlière: "Les autres nations ont eu aisément de bons Chanteurs Italiens, c'est pourquoi elles ont adopté leur Musique plutôt que la nôtre. A peine en avons nous de bons pour nous-même. M. Jeliotte est peut-être le seul aujourd'hui sur notre Théâtre qui ait l'art de rendre le véritable esprit de la Musique Françoise." *Jugement de l'orchestre de l'Opéra* (Paris, 1753), p. 3. Even Mozart, some decades later, was moved to comment: 'And then the men and women singers! Indeed they hardly deserve the name, for they don't sing—they yell—howl—and that too with all their might, through their noses and throats.' E. Anderson, ed.: *The Letters of Mozart and his Family* (New York, 1966), p. 564.

18. Realism in acting became an important component of French drama, particularly in the *opéra-comique* during the 1750s and beyond. It is one aspect considered in Chapter III.

19. The music to both is available in modern editions: several piano reductions of *La serva padrona* have appeared in print this century, and a facsimile reprint (New York, 1984) of *Il giocatore* appears in the series *Italian Opera, 1640–1770*, edited by H.M. Brown. (The version of "Quest'è quel uomo?" heard in Paris is almost identical to that in the Vienna manuscript, from which the bar numbers are taken.)

20. 'Duo', *Encyclopédie, ou Dictionnaire raisonné des sciences, arts et métiers*, ed. J. D'Alembert and D. Diderot, v (Paris, 1755).

21. November (1752), p. 168. The music to this trio is available in volume xxv of *G.B. Pergolesi: Opera omnia*, ed. F. Caffarelli (Rome, 1941). Example 2.1, quoted below, uses this as its source; the spelling Colagianni is preferred in the modern edition.

22. The broken pitcher, later immortalized in François Boucher's painting *La cruche cassée*, was a symbol for the loss of innocence.

23. November (1752), pp. 168–169.

24. *Ibid.*, p. 169.

25. The lack of extant music, in addition to the fact that the quartet was a replacement whose text did not feature in the printed libretto, excludes the movement from mention in Tables IV and V.

26. January (1753), p. 145.

27. June, i (1753), pp. 157–158.

28. July (1753), pp. 170–171.

29. See G. Sadler: 'Rameau, Piron and the Parisian Fair Theatres', *Soundings*, iv (1974).

30. See R. Isherwood: *Farce and Fantasy: Popular Entertainment in Eighteenth-Century Paris* (Oxford, 1986), pp. 101–105 and E. Cook: 'Monnet, Jean', *The New Grove Dictionary of Opera* (London, 1992).

31. F.A. Chevrier: *Observations sur le théâtre* (Paris, 1755), p. 80.

32. K.M. Smith: *Egidio Duni and the Development of the Opéra-Comique from 1753 to 1770* (diss., Cornell U., 1980), p. 51. This technique was heavily censured by Grimm: "La plus cruelle injure qu'on ait faite à cette musique est sans doute celle qu'elle a reçue de certains petits auteurs qui travaillent pour la Comédie-Italienne ou le théâtre de l'Opéra-Comique . . . Ils avaient imaginé de substituer aux paroles italiennes d'un air, des paroles françaises quel-conques." M. Tourneux, ed.: *Correspondance littéraire, philosophique et critique par Grimm, Diderot, Raynal, Meister, etc* (Paris, 1877–82), ii, p. 409.

33. Between 1 March 1753 and 17 November 1756 a total of 12 such pasticcios—those modelled closely upon Italian sources in terms of both plot and music—appear to have been performed. Many other plays borrowed *ariettes* haphazardly from the Bouffons' repertory but used their own scenarios.

34. Smith: *Op. cit.*, pp. 145–146. The Académie had, on many occasions during the first half of the century, forbidden the use of recitative, song, dance, and orchestra.

35. *Ibid.*, pp. 121–122.

36. The *comédie-héroïque Ramir* (Mailhol, CI, 31 January 1757) and the *parodie Les amours de Psiché* (Lourdet de Santerre, FSL, 15 July 1758) were both in four acts; another *parodie*, *Fanfale* (Favart and Marcouville, CI, 8 March 1752), was in five.

37. For example, *Le peintre amoureux de son modèle* (1757) and *La fille mal gardée* (1758) were both termed *parodies* in their respective librettos; yet the score to the former called the work an *opéra-comique*, while that to the latter described the work as a *comédie mêlée d'ariettes*. Unsystematic description was to continue throughout the following decade and, indeed, beyond.

38. Some concerted vaudevilles had derived from popular instrumental pieces, for example "Les Niais de Sologne," a *pièce de clavecin* by Rameau which this composer himself later used as a duet in IIIiii of *Dardanus* (1739).

39. Printed libretto: s.l., 1748, p. 23.

40. Printed libretto: Paris, n.d., pp. 17–18. The music is included as "air no. 3" in the musical supplement, pp. 57–59.

41. The trio is curious in that the text in the manuscript libretto (*F-Pn*: Th[B] 2855) is divided between Thésée and Tisiphone only. Bound with the libretto, however, is a folio of manuscript paper which records separately the words and music that the third character, Mercure, is to sing. Michel Noiray discusses this ensemble in '*Hippolyte* et *Castor* travestis: Rameau à l'opéra-comique', *Jean-Philippe Rameau: Dijon 1983*, pp. 119–120.

42. Grimm criticized Sedaine on the grounds that his poetry did not read well. (See note 35 to Chapter III below.) The question of collaboration between

librettist and composer in the *opéra-comique* from c1760 onwards is explored in detail by David Charlton: ' "L'art dramatico-musical:" an Essay', *Music and Theatre: Essays in Honour of Winton Dean* (Cambridge, 1987), pp. 234ff.

43. Duni's collaborator in *Nina et Lindor* presents a problem. Both C.D. Brenner: *A Bibliographical List of Plays in the French Language, 1700–1789* (Berkeley, 1947, rev. 2/1979) and *The New Grove Dictionary of Opera* identify the poet as César-Pierre Richelet; however, Michaud's *Biographie universelle* (xxxv) records only one César-Pierre Richelet (1631–98), an esteemed grammarian active during the late 17th century.

44. Chapter V (pp. 233–234) outlines Lacombe's theoretical stance vis-à-vis ensemble composition and offers more biographical information.

45. The following chapter defines the "progressive" ensemble as a dramatic type, alongside four others. See below, pp. 106ff

46. See Smith: *Op. cit.*, pp. 123–124 for an analysis and transcription of this ensemble; and Chapter III, pp. 134–135 below.

47. Printed libretto: Bordeaux, 1758, pp. 11–12.

48. Printed libretto: Paris (Duchesne), 1757, p. 16.

49. Printed libretto: Paris (Duchesne), 1758, pp. 14–15. The music to this duet is reproduced in Example 2.5.

50. Printed libretto: Paris (Duchesne), 1757, p. 55.

51. Printed libretto: Avignon, 1759, p. 26.

52. "ce petit Intermède est toujours influencé, dans son ensemble, par les vieux modèles de danse français, alors que les éléments italiens n'y sont qu'artificiellement surajoutés, contrairement à ce qu'avaient écrit Rousseau et Grimm." D. Heartz: 'Diderot et le Théâtre lyrique: "le nouveau stile" proposé par *Le Neveu de Rameau*', *RdM*, lxiv (1978), p. 238.

53. These are discussed extensively in Chapter V.

54. Both examples are from the piano reduction of Louis Alleton (Paris, n.d.).

55. This duet is reproduced as Example 6.7 (see p. 285).

56. See above, p. 22.

57. For a detailed biographical account see P. Letailleur: 'Jean-Louis , chanteur et compositeur: sa vie et son oeuvre', *RMFC*, viii (1968); ix (1969); x (1970).

58. These were: two sopranos and bass; two sopranos and tenor; soprano/*haute-contre*/tenor; and soprano/tenor/bass.

59. In addition to composing over 20 comic works, La Borde had several serious operas performed at the Académie and privately. He later became known as a theorist, publishing his *Essai sur la musique ancienne et moderne* in 1780.

60. See above, p. 84, for a reproduction of the text.

Chapter III

Dramatic and Literary Aspects of Ensemble Composition, 1758–1775

When considered alongside other elements of opera such as recitative, aria, and chorus, ensembles are a relatively new ingredient. They did not become an established or accepted feature of operatic composition for almost a century and a half after the genre was first conceived, in spite of their very unique features.[1] As this chapter investigates the enhanced dramatic role and status of the ensemble in the *opéra-comique* of the 1760s and early 1770s, a useful starting point is to establish how ensemble expression differs from other forms of expression in musical drama. What is achieved by having several characters combine at a particular point in an opera? What special qualities do ensembles possess and what dramaturgical purpose can they serve?

Ensembles are unique in opera in that they allow characters to express their thoughts and emotions concurrently. They differ from choruses in that their participants are motivated as individuals rather than as a corporate body. The sentiments such individuals express may be identical ones or conflicting ones. Unanimity of expression substantiates a particular emotion or situation more powerfully than when communicated by a single character; juxtaposition of contrasting sentiments emphasizes discord, lending greater individuality to the expression of each and heightening the emotional atmosphere, since conflict gives rise to tension. Such effects would otherwise be diluted if communicated in a sequence of solo arias. Ensembles thus allow characters to interact more closely with one another, provide an effective means of offsetting and contrasting different personalities more vividly, and enable all the relevant characters to participate at a greater number of points of action.

Ensembles can result in more rounded characterization and a more intense depiction of various emotional predicaments, but they also affect pace and momentum in the unfolding of a plot. Concerted movements written in place of individual arias, recitative or spoken dialogue can bring together, or telescope, several ideas at once, such compression altering the temporal proportions of a work. Often this feature is actively exploited to maximize dramatic momentum—for example in ensemble finales—and has the effect of propelling expectation forward, increasing interest and tension in the spectator. This ability to compress offers latitude and flexibility in the construction of individual scenes and acts.

Towards the Integration of the Ensemble

Establishing how developments in the construction and general character of ensembles were pioneered is straightforward enough through careful study of libretto texts and—the task of the following chapter—of the music itself. The seminal literary figures of the early *opéra-comique* will shortly be introduced, and their methods and techniques evaluated. Given the central contention of this book, however, that end-of-century examples of concerted writing represent, not an invention, but an evolution of ideas, an equally logical question to consider is not *how*, but *why*? Why, at the mid-point of the 18th century, did artists begin to perceive the ensemble as a viable form of dramatic and musical expression? The explanation offered here is that contemporary philosophical and psychological ideas provided a long-sought rationale for simultaneous expression in opera, and understanding these serves as a springboard for clarifying the new identity and status of the operatic ensemble of this period.

The Doctrine of Association

In a book which eventually concludes with a discussion of ensembles in the comic operas of Mozart, Peter Kivy addresses a wide range of eternal operatic "problems" from the point of view of the philosopher.[2] While his fundamental concern is to resolve the conflict between the demands of musical parameters and the demands placed on music in service of a text, "the transmutation of music into drama while remaining within the bounds of pure musical form,"[3] his system of linking the character of established operatic genres to the reigning psychology of the time is of relevance to the present discussion. Opera is essentially concerned with the representation and expression of emotions, but how each age interpreted and represented human emotions in operatic form varied considerably. Serious opera of the first half of the 18th century (specifically *opera seria*), Kivy claims, mirrors the Cartesian outlook of that period, whereas the dynamic activity of Mozart's comic ensembles reflects the new creed of associationism propounded initially by the British philosopher John Locke at the end of the 17th century and, more pervasively from the middle of the 18th century, by David Hartley.

Associationism supplants Cartesianism in the second half of the 18th century in advocating that emotions are not pre-formed, innate dispositions (Descartes' *esprits animaux* and, indeed, the Baroque *Affektenlehre*) but are instead acquired through the association of ideas relative to individual experiences:

> "each individual who acquires a given emotion will acquire it in a different way ... an emotion is not acquired once and for all, in a fixed, unchanging state, but alters with time as more associations accrue ... Nor are we stocked at birth with a finite collection of emotive possibilities ... The association of ideas is a process whereby emotions are continually acquired as well as continually altered."[4]

Kivy distinguishes between the two camps thus:

> "where the Cartesian [emotions] are hard-edged and discrete, the associationist are blurred and continuous; where the Cartesian are finite and fixed, the associationist are infinite and proliferating; where the Cartesian suggest a static, stable emotive life, the associationist suggest a fluid, evanescent one, of rapid and perhaps violent change."[5]

In likening the appearance of an ensemble amidst the succession of da capo arias in an *opera seria* to "pennies from heaven"[6] and then crediting "the busy emotive hurly-burly of the association of ideas" as the "animating principle of Mozart's dramatic ensembles,"[7] Kivy suggests the significance of the shift from one ideology to another for concerted writing in the second half of the 18th century. Associationism rationalized simultaneous expression and continuous emotive discourse in opera as an alternative to separate emotive poses, features most effectively portrayed in ensembles because these could encompass, in a single movement, the widest range of expressive attitudes and states. In conclusion to his analysis of the third-act sextet to *Figaro* (which heralds the discovery of Figaro's parentage), Kivy observes that "the composer's beliefs about what sort of things emotions are must have changed radically for Mozart to have even conceived of the possibility of music changing its expressive character so many times, and so quickly, in so small a musical space."[8]

Kivy, I believe, provides answers as to why the ensemble became an essential element of opera during the period under consideration. However, the question still remains as to whether such movements developed a significance for the power of their emotional representation or for their effectiveness as musical vehicles for dramatic action. Much concerning current conceptions of the ensemble stands in need of clarification if a true picture of its role in later 18th-century opera is to emerge.

Popular Dramatic Conceptions

It has long been traditional to divide ensembles into two main categories: active and static. The former, it is understood, comprise dramatic pieces embracing action important to the unfolding of an opera, while the latter are simply expressive, lyrical movements—"frozen" tableaux—in which the characters react to situations and events developed elsewhere. This antithesis is encountered in Edward Dent's study of ensembles from the early 18th-century Neapolitan repertory:

" ... we may expect to find two main types of ensemble movement, one making for the dramatization of the aria, the other heightening with music an already dramatic situation."[9]

Dent offers no precise explanation of what he means by the phrase "dramatization of the aria," although it becomes apparent that he is referring to a type of ensemble that furthers the action, a movement somehow developing from beginning to end, rather than representing an unchanging stage picture. Those ensembles "heightening with music an already dramatic situation" are the static type capitalizing on events previously defined in other musical forms (usually recitative). Charles Koch, following Dent's lead some 60 years later, establishes a much clearer antithesis through use of the contrasting terms "dramatic ensemble" and "expressive-reflective ensemble," defined thus:

"The dramatic ensemble is one in which the action of the play is continued ... in the expressive-reflective ensemble the characters of the opera merely give expression to their sentiments, or reflect, comment, or moralize upon the events of the play."[10]

Koch and others subscribe to the notion that "drama" is synonymous with "action," and that expressive ensembles, mere lyrical interruptions, do not develop the plot. But *are* these two words synonymous? "Action" is essentially a physical phenomenon: it signifies what characters do, either by themselves or in relation to others, and how their deeds and the consequences of these develop the events of the play. "Drama," on the other hand, is not simply physical; it relies just as much on what is said as on what is done, on the expression of the moods and mental attitudes of the various characters, and their reactions to the events they set in motion. "Action," therefore, is but one aspect of "drama," and "drama" may be defined as the sum total of the effect created by the interplay of different moods and events throughout a work. "Action" is of course dramatic—if we understand "dramatic" to mean enhancing and vivifying the presentation of the "drama"—but a stage work cannot be sustained by constant physical forward momentum. Moments of consolidation and reflection are also necessary; "drama" is thus a composite of energy and repose, tension and respite, translated in both physical and psychological terms.

Emotions, then, are as necessary to a drama—and as dramatically potent—as actions, conclusions running counter to the Aristotelian hierarchy of elements placing Plot above Character above Thought, but in line with thinkers such as Joseph Kerman who assert that character is the most important element of drama and not subsidiary to the action (*Opera as Drama*, 1956). Thus ensembles in which the characters "give expression to their sentiments, or reflect, comment, or moralize upon the events of the play" can have as much a dramatic function as do those embodying action.[11] In espousing the view that action alone is drama, previous commentators on the ensemble have sometimes failed to recognize the latter's full potential within the context of an operatic work. They have also certainly misapplied the term "dramatic ensemble," an over-generalized expression that is best avoided.

Another critical tendency frequently encountered is that of evaluating the effect and purpose of an ensemble in isolation, without considering how the movement forms part of a larger dramatic scenario. This results in too simplified a view of individual pieces, and largely explains why ensembles have hitherto been assessed according to their ability to generate action. To show that ensembles enhance musical drama and contribute to an effective unfolding of the plot in many other ways, their relation and relevance to previous and subsequent material, and the way in which they are blended into the overall design of a work, must be taken into account. However, investigating ensemble planning on a wider scale first requires an examination of the idea of dramatic contour and progression.

Ensembles Within the Framework: Dramatic Functions and Types

The unfolding of a stage work is a complicated, intricate procedure in which the pace is never constant. While the overall pattern is to build from the exposition and development to a final conclusion and dénouement, this is subject to several complications and enhanced by a number of smaller climaxes, each of which creates tension and requires an interim resolution. Thus the dramatic contour of a work varies in intensity according to the complexity and momentum of the plot: introduction, complication, acceleration, retraction, resolution, and so on. The dramatic effect of an individual lyrical movement should be judged in terms of its relevance to the given situation within the whole, and how successfully this is expressed in music. Is the ensemble well prepared and adroitly integrated? Does it grow naturally from previous situations and link effectively to the next? Does the character of the piece aptly reflect the stage situation? In applying these criteria to individual ensembles, certain types emerge, their characteristics applicable to the dramatic contour of any 18th-century work, and these may be identified as follows:

> *(i) Expository Ensembles.* This type of concerted movement sets the scene at the outset of an opera, or introduces new elements or characters within an act once the drama is under way. The first procedure becomes common in the *opéra-comique* of the period in question and allows ensembles to expand their function by assuming responsibility for communicating new information to audiences.
>
> *(ii) Tableau Ensembles.* These comprise movements in which the characters comment on previous events and voice their personal emotions and reactions. They act like a magnet

in drawing together the threads of previous occurrences, but in an unchanging stage picture, a tableau of simultaneous expression. This reinforces the drama ("heightening with music an already dramatic situation") and at the same time provides a measure of repose for the spectator. As such these have a universal application and can be sited at any juncture within the libretto.

(iii) Progressive Ensembles. This category of ensemble incorporates development important to the plot and consequently furthers the sequence of dramatic events. It includes action ensembles, a type increasingly cultivated in the *opéra-comique* during this period. However, since drama is psychological as well as physical, it also comprises movements in which an emotional progression is apparent: if, for example, characters experience a change of mood or mind through discussion with others. Some ensembles become "progressive" by adding new characters once the movement is underway, so that one ensemble runs into another: a duet, for example, may become a trio with the entrance of a third character. This feature has been described as the additive principle, or the principle of aggregation and acceleration.[12]

(iv) Climactic Ensembles. Ensembles belonging to this group are those which either build up to a dramatic high-point within a work, or which comprise the final climax itself. The ability of ensembles to telescope events and to concentrate expression makes their placement at such points in the drama particularly effective. Ensembles of perplexity, in which several characters express conflicting thoughts and emotions creating great tension and requiring resolution, are excellent examples of climactic ensembles. These were developed as the notion of concerted singing was popularized, thereby making such complex musico-dramatic pieces acceptable to audiences.

(v) Dénouement Ensembles. These ensembles are placed at the end of a work once all the complexities of the plot have been unravelled. They bring together the major characters, either to point a moral or, simply, to expatiate on their

happiness. They frequently have the character of a chorus since parts are distributed between voice types—soprano, alto, tenor, bass—rather than between individual characters; extra singers, if available, might join the solo cast in such movements.[13] In the *opéra-comique*, dénouement ensembles were often cast as vaudeville finales, although librettists and composers dispensed with tradition on several occasions to create more adventurous and innovative ensemble finales.

To what extent did these types of ensemble represent a new departure from tradition during the period 1758 to 1775? Expository ensembles were included rarely in the operatic repertory of the first half of the 18th century. They were exploited by *opéra-comique* librettists from the late 1750s onwards presumably because they offered greater freedom in the design of works and more scope for the inclusion of concerted movements. Progressive ensembles, also rare in earlier genres, were included ever more frequently in the *opéra-comique*, particularly action ensembles, and these enriched the stature of concerted writing considerably. Climactic ensembles were not a new phenomenon, yet with the inclusion of more concerted pieces they became a good deal more prevalent. Tableau ensembles and dénouement ensembles, the most traditional types of concerted movement in earlier 18th-century opera, remained standard features of the later *opéra-comique*.

What was also novel was the emergence of ensembles as an integral feature of operatic composition. This was reflected, for example, in the increasing frequency with which they were incorporated into the overall design of works, in the creation of movements for five, six, or more characters, in the fact that they often formed the major lyrical interest in individual scenes, occasionally followed one another in close proximity and, overall, aimed for an expressive musical translation of the situation they portrayed. It should not be concluded, however, that every ensemble from this period fitted easily into one or other of the categories described above. Some, indeed, served a dual dramatic purpose.[14] In balancing musical movements, whether solo *ariettes* or ensembles, with prose or verse dialogue, librettists and composers were working towards a composite musico-dramatic framework, continually experimenting with how and where to site lyrical movements to advantage and effect. Not all their efforts proved successful, and such examples are considered alongside their more positive achievements.

The Literary Collaborators of Duni, Monsigny, and Philidor

The path of the *opéra-comique* in the later decades of the 18th century was shaped by several librettists. Those who had started their careers during the transitional years of the mid-century (Anseaume, Marcouville, Poinsinet), or even before this (Favart), continued to expand their craft. Others emerged alongside the major musical figures of the period: Antoine-François Quétant, Pierre-René Lemonnier (not to be confused with Guillaume-Antoine Lemonnier, author of one *opéra-comique* libretto for Philidor)[15] and, most importantly, Michel-Jean Sedaine. Another crucial figure in the development of the *opéra-comique* at this time, although one less directly connected with the genre and for this reason often underestimated, was the philosopher Denis Diderot, whose ideas on theatrical reform circulated widely, and were supported and developed by many of the librettists cited above. Diderot's aesthetics must be considered in order to appreciate the achievements of artists working under his influence and, in particular, the developing character of the *opéra-comique* during his lifetime.

Denis Diderot

Diderot's criteria for theatrical reform were expressed in a number of literary and theoretical works, including his *Entretiens sur Le fils naturel, Le neveu de Rameau,* and the essay *De la poésie dramatique.*[16] His ideas mirrored innovations that had recently taken place on the English stage, particularly in the hands of the celebrated actor David Garrick, who made several trips to Paris during his lifetime. Garrick broke with tradition in creating a more realistic style of acting which replaced the stately, but artificial, practice of the past. His major achievements were to promote a more natural style of declamation, to incorporate gesture to dramatic effect, frequently elevating it to the level of speech, to make greater and more effective use of the stage as a whole, and to introduce costumes in keeping with the roles portrayed.[17]

One of Diderot's major aims, in emulation of Garrick, was to combat the lack of reality he perceived on the French stage. Roundly criticized was the style of "déclamation maniérée, symétrisée et si éloignée de la vérité"[18] that had been in vogue for many years. Diderot recommended that a more natural declamatory style be cultivated. In musical drama this meant that melody should be tailored closely to the accents of speech and faithfully translate the ideas inherent in the words. The music should serve and enhance the poetry rather than follow its own course; it should imitate nature and speak to the heart:

> "Il nous faut des exclamations, des interjections, des suspensions, des interruptions, des affirmations, des négations; nous appelons, nous invoquons, nous crions, nous gémissons, nous pleurons, nous rions franchement. Point d'esprit, point d'épigrammes; point de ces jolis pensées. Cela est trop loin de la simple nature ... Il nous le faut plus énergique, moins maniéré, plus vrai."[19]

In addition to a more natural style of declamation, Diderot argued for more realism in the physical conduct and action of those on stage. Gesture, he felt, should play an important role in the dramatic development of a work; indeed, "le geste doit s'écrire souvent à la place du discours."[20] Hence the verbal element is sometimes subordinated to the visual; as Kopp observes: "The most effective method of communicating a message to an audience, Diderot felt, was not to communicate the message, but rather suggest it by means of a memorable image."[21] On the same grounds Diderot advocated that stage decorations and costumes reflect the subjects they portrayed and thereby achieve greater naturalism: "ce qui montre surtout combien nous sommes encore loin du bon goût et de la vérité, c'est la pauvreté et la fausseté des décorations, et le luxe des habits."[22] These recommendations had already been put into practice, to a certain extent, by some establishments. In 1753, for example, Mme Favart had surprised audiences at the Comédie-Italienne by dressing in a simple peasant costume for performances of *Les amours de Bastien et Bastienne*. She later hired costumes from Constantinople for *Soliman II* (1761). Meanwhile Monnet, at the Opéra Comique, fresh from his sojourn in London and meetings with Garrick, was experimenting with realistic scenery and costumes. Rayner notes that Vadé's plays of the 1750s for this establishment contained several stage directions testifying to the use of detailed sets.[23]

Diderot's overall aim was to create not simply a more realistic type of drama, but one in which visual, aural, and literary aspects were closely co-ordinated. For this reason he felt that drama needed to be represented, not simply read, that it should come alive and reach as wide an audience as possible. This explains his view that the theater should become more social and less aristocratic in its orientation, and inspired his creation of the *drame bourgeois*, which influenced the style and subject-matter of the *opéra-comique* and eventually produced a musical equivalent, the *drame lyrique*. Both genres focused on characters drawn from the daily experiences of their middle- and lower-class audiences. They displayed a variety of virtues and vices, and served as effective mouthpieces for contemporary social, political, and religious issues. In this way Diderot achieved another important objective in enlightening and educating a wider public.

Diderot's influence radically altered the way in which stage works were conceived and represented, and this helps explain the reversal of the working relationship between poets and musicians in the *opéra-comique* of the later 18th century. But, as Kopp points out, the creative interchange between composers, their librettists, and a third party, the actors responsible for bringing their artistic labors to life, operated in a subtle and complex manner. The actor-singer renounced his right to improvisation, an important feature of the earlier *vaudeville-comédie*, and was further required to sacrifice his personality in pursuit of a more realistic style of acting: "C'est à l'acteur à convenir au rôle, et non pas au rôle à convenir à l'acteur."[24] However, given the increasing importance of stage directions and dramatic gesture, librettists and composers became more dependent on the performer to translate these intelligently and effectively to their audiences. Music, meanwhile, underwent "a remarkable change in function, from attractive melodies having little to do with characters or with the French language, to a true element of dramatic technique."[25] As a result, the librettist

"lost the control that, as *fredonneur*, he had held over the choice of *vaudeville* airs for his works. But the librettist who dared was able to control all visual and literary aspects of his work, including gesture, costume, setting, stage effects, and declamation."[26]

The extent to which these principles were applied to ensemble composition, and other ways in which librettists exercised their prerogatives over composers in this area, are aspects with which the rest of this chapter is concerned.

The Librettists

The early careers of Anseaume, Marcouville, and Poinsinet were outlined in the previous chapter: each made his debut at the beginning of the 1750s. Sedaine and Quétant appeared in 1756 and P.-R. Lemonnier in 1760. Those collaborating most frequently with the three main composers in question were Sedaine, Anseaume, and Favart who, between them, produced 24 of the 39 works examined in this chapter and the next (see Table VIII below, p. 116).

After having experimented with the *pasticcio opéra-comique* and worked closely with Laruette, Anseaume became Duni's principal collaborator. This partnership proved extremely successful: it resulted in nine works which, as will be shown, embodied many important developments in the *opéra-comique* during the late 1750s and 1760s.[27] Anseaume joined forces with Philidor on one occasion to produce *Le soldat magicien* (1760). He created, on average, one dramatic work each year up to 1766. In 1769 he collaborated for the first and only time with Grétry in *Le tableau parlant*, and his libretto to *L'yvrogne corrigé*, first set by Laruette in 1758, was used by Gluck in 1760 for a production in Vienna.

Following his successful collaboration with La Borde in *Gilles, garçon peintre* (1758), Poinsinet produced a succession of *opéras-comiques* for Philidor: *Sancho Pança* (1762), *Le sorcier* (1764), and *Tom Jones* (1765; revised the following year by Sedaine), as well as the *tragédie-lyrique Ernelinde* (1767; also revised by Sedaine, in 1773). In addition, he wrote one *opéra-comique* for Paul-César Gibert, *Apelle et Campaspe* (1763), had a second work produced at the Académie—a *pastorale, Théonis* (1767), with music by Pierre-Montan Berton and Jean-Claude Trial—and collaborated again with La Borde in 1769 on *Alix et Alexis*.

Favart, alongside Sedaine, was the only librettist to have collaborated with all three major composers of this period, in addition to others such as La Borde, Blaise, and Grétry. His most frequent partner during the late 1750s and 1760s was Duni, for whom he wrote five librettos. He collaborated twice with Monsigny (*Le nouveau monde*, 1763; *La belle Arsène*, 1773) and twice with Philidor (*Les fêtes de la paix*, 1763; *L'amant déguisé*, 1769).[28] For Grétry he provided *L'amitié à l'épreuve* in 1770.

Prominent among a new generation of literary figures were Quétant, P.-R. Lemonnier, and La Ribardière. Quétant's earliest years were his most productive: from the 1770s onwards his theatrical activities took second place to a successful administrative career. His first dramatic compositions were written towards the end of the transition period, and he thereafter collaborated with a number of composers although did not establish any lasting partnerships. Thus for Philidor he wrote *Le maréchal ferrant* (1761), for Gossec *Le tonnelier* (1765), for Kohaut *Le serrurier* (1765) and, later, for Martini, *L'amant sylphe* (1783). Brenner's *A Bibliographical List* gives details of 32 stage works, of which 16 form part of the *opéra-comique* repertory. Quétant was also one of the few librettists to theorize on the developing genre. His *Essai sur l'opéra-comique* (Paris, 1765) contains useful information concerning the design, content, and character of such works.[29]

Pierre-René Lemonnier enjoyed a successful career for two decades as a playwright in both comic and serious genres, and was particularly noted for the elegance of his style. He collaborated twice with Monsigny at the beginning of his career in *Le maître en droit* (1760) and *Le cadi dupé* (1761), and later with Trial and Pierre Vachon (*Renaud d'Ast*, 1765) and La Borde (*La meunière de Gentilly*, 1768). Brenner lists a number of other comic works written for more obscure or unidentified composers. In the following decade Lemonnier enjoyed a fruitful partnership with Etienne Joseph Floquet which resulted in three *ballet-héroïques* and one *tragédie-lyrique*, staged at Fontainebleau and at the Académie. La Ribardière produced librettos to four Parisian *opéras-comiques*. *Les aveux indiscrets* (1759), for Monsigny, was that composer's first stage work. A further two, *Les deux soeurs rivales* (1762) and *Les deux cousines* (1763), were for Desbrosses, and the last, *La réconciliation villageoise* (1765), was for Tarede. He also spent a brief period in Vienna where, Brenner notes, he had two plays staged, and assisted in the adaptation of *opéras-comiques* and other texts.

Other librettists include: Charles Collé, a prolific playwright and *chansonnier* who collaborated with Rameau, Blavet, and La Borde among others, and whose libretto to Monsigny's *L'isle sonnante* (1767) was typical of his "folle gaieté" and "bonhomie"; Roger-Timothée Régnard de Pleinchesne, author of many occasional pieces, whose best-known *opéra-comique* was Philidor's *Le jardinier de Sidon* (1768); Charles-George Fenouillot de Falbaire who, prior to collaborating with Philidor in *Zémire et Mélide* (1773), had written *Les deux avares* for Grétry (1770); Pierre Legier, who collaborated with Duni and Grétry; and Alexandre Guillaume Mouslier de Moissy, who appears to have written only one *opéra-comique*.[30] The last librettist to be considered, and certainly one of the most influential during the period, is Michel-Jean Sedaine.

Michel-Jean Sedaine

Sedaine came from a modest background. After his education at the Collège de Quatre Nations in Paris was curtailed by financial hardship, he began an apprenticeship as a stone-mason, gradually rising to become *constructeur-architecte* and then *garçon-piqueur*.[31] He made his mark as the author of occasional poems and *pièces fugitives* published during the early 1750s and, after having been persuaded by Monnet, wrote his first stage work in 1756. This was *Le diable à quatre* for the Foire Saint Laurent, a three-act *pasticcio* with music by Laruette and Philidor, still firmly conceived within the framework of earlier vaudeville models. The play was uninhibited in its literary content, but of a gay and vivid character throughout. The printed score (*c*1761) attests to the popularity of the work.

Sedaine's literary career developed rapidly after this date and by the Revolution he had become one of the most successful playwrights of his age:

> "hardly a year passed without the publication or performance of a new play by Sedaine. His dramatic writing ranges from gay, spirited farces for the theatres of the fairs to serious, polished works for the Comédie-Française, and includes numerous and various opéras-comiques for the Comédie-Italienne, as well as the libretti of several operas and plays for performance at private theatres."[32]

In the field of the *opéra-comique*, *Le diable à quatre* was followed by three collaborations with Philidor: *Blaise le savetier* (1759), *L'huître et les plaideurs* (1759), and *Le jardinier et son seigneur* (1761). All were of an abundantly comic spirit although the last introduced a social message openly criticizing the upper classes, "[qui] n'ont qu'un doigt pour faire du bien et qui en ont neuf dont ils peuvent faire du mal."[33] Sedaine continued to use the *opéra-comique* as a vehicle for expressing Enlightenment ideas when he joined forces with Monsigny, initially in 1761 for a short and purely comic work, *On ne s'avise jamais de tout*, and then for *Le roi et le fermier* (1762). In its choice of characters and dramatic substance this collaboration was a major departure from established traditions. Sedaine allowed working folk to mix freely on stage with royalty and the aristocracy, and focused on important social questions: equality between men, freedom of expression, personal liberty. The work was a comedy with serious overtones, designed to enlighten and instruct, and as such was very much in accordance with Diderot's recommendations.

During the 1760s Sedaine continued to work with Monsigny, and also with Duni, La Borde, and Philidor. He produced, in 1769, another innovative *opéra-comique* in conjunction with Monsigny: *Le déserteur*. Styled a *drame* rather than an *opéra-comique*, this work juxtaposed comic and serious elements far more pervasively than had *Le roi et le fermier*, and prepared the way for the *drame lyrique*. Sedaine again ventured onto new ground in the following decade when he began a long and successful collaboration with Grétry. In this, his third and final stylistic period, he continued to extend the scope of the *opéra-comique* by including historical, patriotic, medieval, legendary, and mythological subjects. He also furthered his experiments in the musico-dramatic design of his librettos.

One of the hallmarks of Sedaine's librettos was his instinct for the stage and his complete understanding of all aspects of the theater: how to capture a dramatic situation concisely, how to present and portray characters, their actions, and their reactions with effect and realism.[34] The result was a naturalness and spontaneity of style. However, Sedaine's greatest talent as a librettist was his ability to construct a text from the point of view of the composer. He readily conceded that music was necessary for the success of such works, the result being that "although many of his plays act extremely well, few make very satisfactory reading."[35] The sacrifices he made in this respect in fact allowed him to expand his craft to an unprecedented degree. In his extremely detailed stage directions concerning gesture, setting, costumes, and stage effects—ideas all derived from Diderot—he was frequently able to suggest new musical devices and directions to composers. Kopp rightly observes that such writing "thrust him into the composer's domain," and that Sedaine acquired as a consequence "a musical control far more elaborate than what the *fredonneur* had given up."[36]

Sources

Table VIII provides details of 39 works by Duni, Monsigny, and Philidor studied in this chapter and the next: 14 are by Duni, 11 by Monsigny, and 14 by Philidor. This corpus, which excludes *pasticcios*, collaborations, works outside the *opéra-comique* repertory or without extant sources, and (with the exception of Monsigny's *Félix*) works staged before 1775, represents nearly three-quarters of the output of the three composers in question. Printed or manuscript scores and librettos to all works listed survive.

TABLE VIII: Sources for Chapters III and IV

Date		Composer	Librettist	Title
16/7/57[1]	FSL	Duni	Anseaume	*Le peintre amoureux de son modèle* (2)
4/3/58	CI	Duni	Favart/Mme Favart/Santerre	*La fille mal gardée* (1)
9/9/58	FSL	Duni	(Richelet)	*Nina et Lindor* (2)
7/2/59	FSG	Monsigny	La Ribardière	*Les aveux indiscrets* (1)
9/3/59	FSG	Philidor	Sedaine	*Blaise le savetier* (1)
24/9/59	FSL	Duni	Anseaume (after Vadé)	*La veuve indécise* (1)
13/2/60[2]	FSG	Monsigny	P.-R. Lemonnier	*Le maître en droit* (2)
14/8/60	FSL	Philidor	Anseaume	*Le soldat magicien* (1)
29/12/60	CI	Duni	Anseaume/Marcouville	*L'isle des foux* (2)
4/2/61	FSG	Monsigny	P.-R. Lemonnier	*Le cadi dupé* (1)
18/2/61	FSG	Philidor	Sedaine	*Le jardinier et son seigneur* (1)
22/8/61	FSL	Philidor	Quétant	*Le maréchal ferrant* (2)
14/9/61	FSL	Monsigny	Sedaine	*On ne s'avise jamais de tout* (1)
24/9/61	CI	Duni	Anseaume	*Mazet* (2)
8/7/62	CI	Philidor	Poinsinet	*Sancho Pança dans son isle* (1)
22/11/62	CI	Monsigny	Sedaine	*Le roi et le fermier* (3)
29/12/62	Vers.	Duni	Anseaume	*Le milicien* (1)
28/2/63	CI	Philidor	Guichard/Castet	*Le bûcheron* (1)
23/7/63	CI	Duni	Anseaume	*Les deux chasseurs et la laitière* (1)
16/11/63	CI	Duni	Legier	*Le rendez-vous* (1)
2/1/64	CI	Philidor	Poinsinet	*Le sorcier* (2)
8/3/64	CI	Monsigny	Sedaine	*Rose et Colas* (1)
24/1/65	CI	Duni	Anseaume	*L'école de la jeunesse* (3)
27/2/65[3]	CI	Philidor	Poinsinet	*Tom Jones* (3)
26/10/65	Font.	Duni	Favart	*La fée Urgèle* (4)
24/7/66	CI	Duni	Anseaume	*La clochette* (1)
Aug. 67	priv.	Monsigny	Collé	*L'isle sonnante* (3)
27/1/68	CI	Duni	Favart	*Les moissonneurs* (3)
18/7/68	CI	Philidor	Pleinchesne	*Le jardinier de Sidon* (2)
26/10/68	CI	Duni	Sedaine	*Les sabots* (1)
6/3/69	CI	Monsigny	Sedaine	*Le déserteur* (3)
2/9/69	CI	Philidor	Favart/Voisenon	*L'amant déguisé* (1)
22/1/70	CI	Philidor	Mouslier de Moissy	*La nouvelle école des femmes* (3)
2/11/71	Font.	Monsigny	Sedaine	*Le faucon* (1)
11/1/73	CI	Philidor	G.-A. Lemonnier	*Le bon fils* (1)[4]
30/10/73	Font.	Philidor	Fenouillot de Falbaire	*Zémire et Mélide* (2)
6/11/73	Font.	Monsigny	Favart	*La belle Arsène* (4)[5]
20/3/75	CI	Philidor	Sedaine	*Les femmes vengées* (1)
10/11/77	Font.	Monsigny	Sedaine	*Félix, ou L'enfant trouvé* (3)

1. Revised by Anseaume for the Foire Saint Laurent (3/2/58), to include three extra ensembles (one trio, two quartets).
2. Some printed librettos bear the date 23/2/1760.
3. Revised by Sedaine, 30/1/66.
4. *Airs détachés* printed by Sr Huguet (Paris, c1773).
5. Printed libretto (Paris: Ballard, 1773) in three acts; printed score (c1776) in four. Performances at the Comédie-Italienne (14/8/75 onwards) were of the revised version.

Discrepancies between musical and literary sources are sometimes apparent. While these are considered in the following chapter, an explanation of why this occurs is offered at this point. Librettos were printed at various stages throughout the "career" of works given at the fair theaters and at the Comédie-Italienne: in advance of the first performance, in readiness for the opening night, or following a successful presentation.[37] If a work proved highly successful, librettos would be re-issued for subsequent revisions; thus, several editions of certain works may be available. Printed scores, on the other hand, were published after the date of their première, since composers often made modifications after seeing their work staged, particularly after gauging the audience's reactions to it. Some underwent a complete transformation: *Le peintre amoureux* and *Tom Jones* are obvious examples.[38] Available literary and musical sources may not, therefore, represent the same stage in the artistic development of a work. For these reasons discrepancies in sources occur; moreover, it was far from unknown for composers to depart from the recommendations of their poets.

The generic descriptions chosen by librettists and composers also differed considerably. This was because the *opéra-comique*, still largely unfettered by rules, continued to draw upon a wide range of descriptive terminology. Printed scores by Duni, Monsigny, and Philidor were termed variously: *opéra-comique*, *opéra bouffon*, *comédie*, *comédie mêlée d'ariettes*, *comédie lyrique*, *intermède*, *drame* or *pièce*. The librettos examined were more consistent in their use of either *opéra-comique* or *comédie mêlée d'ariettes*. Scores and librettos to only 18 of the 39 works agreed in their description of works. Up to 1761 it was common for the term *opéra bouffon* in scores to be matched by the inscription *opéra-comique* in librettos;[39] thereafter, scores favored the term *comédie* which was amplified in librettos to *comédie mêlée d'ariettes*. Some pieces eluded stylistic categorization: *Le peintre amoureux* was described variously as a parody, a *pièce* (play), and an *opéra-comique*.

Similarly, indication of ensembles in 18th-century librettos and scores was not always straightforward. Librettos were moderately consistent throughout the period in question in labelling concerted movements with terms such as *Duo, Trio, Quatuor* (75% of occurrences in those sources consulted). This was less often the case in scores, especially those from the late 1750s and early 1760s which frequently had no headings for ensembles; later works copied the example set in librettos and, overall, 60% of ensembles were named according to their type.

Alternative terminologies in both librettos and scores sometimes designated concerted movements either as *Ariette en Dialogue* (or *dialoguée*, or *en Duo*, or *en Trio* etc.), or as *Choeur*.[40]

The Librettists' Approach to Ensemble Movements

Alongside the usual decisions concerning which types of ensemble to include and where, which characters to combine and how frequently, librettists had now to design more complicated texts and consider whether these were to replace solo *ariettes*, the place of stage directions therein, and the dramatic function of the resulting ensemble both as an individual entity and within the overall context of the work. Some individual traits and preferences among librettists emerge.

Type and Frequency

Two complementary developments in concerted writing during the period of Duni, Monsigny, and Philidor were the increase in the number of ensembles per work, and the greater interest in the composition of larger ensembles. Overall, duets accounted for 56% of the concerted movements examined, trios for 20%, quartets for 15%, and other ensembles as follows: quintets 3%, sextets 2.5%, septets 3.5%. Compared with the original ensembles composed in works between 1756 and 1758 (see Table VII above, p. 77), the proportion of duets to other types of concerted movements is higher. However, it should be remembered that the corpus of works examined for the period 1758 to 1775 was much larger and that, in numerical terms, trios, quartets, and in particular quintets, sextets, and septets therefore featured more prominently. Table IX shows the frequency with which each librettist included the various types of ensemble in his dramatic works for comparison with the overall norm. In the case of those librettists who collaborated only once with the composers in question, a percentage breakdown may be unrepresentative; the number of ensembles this percentage represents in each category is thus noted.

TABLE IX: Proportion of Duets to Other Types of Ensemble

OVERALL	Duets 56%	Trios 20%	Quartets 15%	Quintets 3%	Sextets 2.5%	Septets 3.5%
SEDAINE (10 wks/47 ensembles)	49%	21%	17%	9%	2%	2%
ANSEAUME (9 wks/43 ensembles)	50%	19%	19%	4%	4%	4%
FAVART (5 wks/20 ensembles)	75%	15%	5%	—	5%	—
POINSINET (3 wks/20 ensembles)	70%	10%	15%	—	—	5%
P.-R. LEMONNIER (2 wks/18 ensembles)	67%	22%	11%	—	—	—
G.-A. LEMONNIER (1 wk/4 ensembles)	50% (2)	—	—	—	25% (1)	25% (1)
GUICHARD/CASTET (1 wk/5 ensembles)	20% (1)	20% (1)	40% (2)	—	—	20% (1)
COLLÉ (1 wk/9 ensembles)	56% (5)	22% (2)	11% (1)	—	—	11% (1)
QUÉTANT (1 wk/5 ensembles)	40% (2)	60% (3)	—	—	—	—
LA RIBARDIÈRE (1 wk/3 ensembles)	67% (2)	—	33% (1)	—	—	—
LEGIER (1 wk/4 ensembles)	50% (2)	25% (1)	25% (1)	—	—	—
PLEINCHESNE (1 wk/7 ensembles)	72% (5)	14% (1)	14% (1)	—	—	—
DE MOISSY (1 wk/9 ensembles)	67% (6)	22% (2)	11% (1)	—	—	—
DE FALBAIRE (1 wk/5 ensembles)	60% (3)	40% (2)	—	—	—	—
[RICHELET] (1 wk/3 ensembles)	67% (2)	—	33% (1)	—	—	—

Several interesting points emerge from these statistics. Sedaine, for example, included slightly fewer duets on average and was more adventurous in his use of the quintet, in works such as *Blaise le savetier* (1759), *Le jardinier et son seigneur* (1761), *On ne s'avise jamais de tout* (1761), *Rose et Colas* (1764), and *Le déserteur* (1769). His treatment of sextets and septets was less exploratory, although he was the first known librettist to create an *opéra-comique* septet. This was in *Le roi et le fermier* (1762) and predated that in *Le bûcheron* (Guichard/Castet) by three months. Anseaume should be noted for his emphasis on ensembles for five or more characters. The first sextet from the corpus examined occurs in one of his works (*L'isle des foux*, 1760) although this may have been at the suggestion of Marcouville, his collaborator who, as observed in the previous chapter, had been the first librettist to include quintets in the *opéra-comique*. However, Anseaume's subsequent libretto to *L'école de la jeunesse* was particularly innovative in containing one sextet and two septets, the highest concentration of larger ensembles in any work during the period in question. Favart adopted a more conservative approach by concentrating on smaller ensembles, as did Poinsinet, although the former (in collaboration with Voisenon) included a sextet in *L'amant déguisé* (1769), and the latter a septet in *Tom Jones* (1765). Most of the minor librettists showed a similar preference for duets, trios, and quartets, with the exception of G.-A. Lemonnier, whose sole *opéra-comique* libretto—*Le bon fils* (1773)— included one sextet and one septet.

The number of ensembles included in works by each librettist presents an extremely varied picture. Sedaine, for example, wrote nine ensembles in *Le roi et le fermier* (Monsigny, 1762), but included only three in *Le faucon* (Monsigny, 1771). Librettos by Anseaume and Favart contained between two and six concerted movements, and those by Poinsinet either six or seven. P.-R. Lemonnier was unusual, yet consistent, in incorporating ten and eight ensembles in his two collaborations with Monsigny. Those librettists collaborating only once with the composers in question, as Table IX shows, included as few as three and as many as nine concerted movements in their works.

There is little evidence to suggest that the number of acts in which individual works were cast influenced the frequency with which ensembles were incorporated. One-act compositions contained from two to eight such pieces, and two-act compositions from two to ten. *Le roi et le fermier*, one of the first *opéras-comiques* in three acts, included nine, as did *L'isle sonnante*, whereas *Les moissonneurs* had only two. *La belle Arsène*, the only work of the 39 in four acts, contained four ensembles, all concentrated within the last two acts (chorus movements having featured prominently in the opening act).

An assessment of the concentration of concerted movements in individual works is only complete, however, if the proportion of ensembles to solo *ariettes* is also taken into account. If one excludes movements based on traditional vaudevilles (which still featured in many works of the 1760s) and simply considers texts set to original music, the importance of the ensemble emerges. With the exception of one early work, *Nina et Lindor* (Duni/[Richelet], 1758), which is "archaic" in comprising a multitude of short *ariettes* and very few ensembles, concerted movements in the remainder constitute at least a quarter of the entire musical content, and in several cases this figure extends to almost one-half.

Sedaine's early works provide excellent illustrations. Seven of the 14 musical numbers in *Blaise le savetier* (50%), and seven of the 12 in *Le jardinier et son seigneur* (58%), are concerted movements. *Les femmes vengées* has, likewise, a high concentration of ensembles to solo *ariettes*: 47%. All three librettos were written for Philidor. Those set by Monsigny—with the exception of *Le roi et le fermier* (46%), originally intended for Philidor[41]—had a lower concentration ranging from 27% to 29%. Whether this was a conscious strategy by Sedaine cannot be corroborated by direct evidence, although Philidor was considered a superior technician and Monsigny renowned more for his melodic inspiration. However, the latter's concerted writing, as the following chapter will illustrate, certainly stands comparison with the former's, and in *Le roi et le fermier* Monsigny handled Sedaine's ensemble texts in an enterprising manner.

Anseaume's approach in this matter was more varied, ranging from 25% (*Mazet, L'école de la jeunesse*) to 43% (*La veuve indécise*). No consistent pattern is identifiable. With Favart, however, ensembles regularly accounted for around one-quarter of the overall musical design of librettos, the only exception being *L'amant déguisé* (written, significantly, for Philidor), in which the concentration of ensembles was 44%. Both Poinsinet and P.-R. Lemonnier gave concerted movements a high profile in their works. Figures for *Le maître en droit* and *Le cadi dupé* are 48% and 42% respectively; ensembles in *Sancho Pança* and *Le sorcier* likewise accounted for 45% and 43% of the musical content, although *Tom Jones* was lower with 32%. Calculations show that other librettists ranged between 29% and 39% in their provision of ensemble texts.

A study of the concentration of ensembles in one-, two-, three-, or four-act works offers no definite patterns. The prominence of ensembles in individual works still varied greatly. That they could, in the hands of some librettists, encompass up to half the musical content of an *opéra-comique* was, however, indicative of an increasing desire for such movements to form a vital part of the dramatic whole. This was the end to which French librettists and composers were working during the second half of the 18th century. Sedaine and Grétry, in *Richard Coeur-de-lion* (1784), made a significant advance in creating a final act devoid of individual solos.[42] Mozart's librettists displayed similar tendencies: Da Ponte opened *Così fan tutte*, for example, with three trios, and included only one solo aria in the first ten musical numbers. Another remarkable work was *Les deux journées* (J.N. Bouilly/Cherubini, 1800), whose three acts included only two solo numbers (both at the outset of the opera) and carried the drama by means of elaborate internal ensembles and extensive finale sequences mixing soloists and chorus. This, of course, was to be the complexion of many 19th-century operas: that the seeds of this process were sown quite early in the second half of the 18th century is a fact not generally appreciated.

Structure of Texts

As observed in the previous chapter, experiments altering the design of librettists' texts—in particular their presentation in parallel columns and as extended dialogues—had begun in the 1750s. These had important dramatic and stylistic repercussions, since they allowed divergent expression, simultaneous or alternate, to overrule the logic of literary expression. Of the texts examined from the period in question, 45% had a predominantly dialogue complexion and 36% used columns either partially or entirely. Solo or *unanime* expression was becoming an archaic feature of ensemble design, and irregularity the norm.

Dialogue texts had the advantage of progressing naturally from previous spoken dialogue and were increasingly conceived in place of the spoken word, enabling ensembles to "musicalize" events hitherto entrusted to speech. Some dialogue texts used in this way were extremely extensive, an excellent example being the duet/trio concluding Act I of *Le roi et le fermier* which stretches to almost three pages in the printed libretto. Like many dialogue texts it also included brief moments of ensemble singing.[43]

Ensemble texts written in parallel columns may be considered, to a certain extent, a development of the long-established technique of "interleaving." However, those from the *opéra-comique* during the period in question juxtaposed texts which were far more divergent and which were written for anything up to seven characters. Initially two columns only were used, either in duets or in quartets where the characters were ranged in pairs (i.e. the double duet formation). This design was gradually extended to include trios, as in this early example by Anseaume in *Le soldat magicien* (1760).

CRISPIN	BLONDINEAU	Mme ARGANT
revenant		
Ahi, Ahi, tout est perdu	Que dis tu?	Que dis tu?
C'est votre mari		Mon mari!
	Votre mari!	
	Je suis trahi.	
à Mme Argant		
Faut-il ouvrir?		Non, non.
	Où fuir?	
	Au cabinet?	
		S'il vous trouvoit
Il vous tueroit.		Il vous tueroit
	Il me tueroit!	
		Il frappe encor
		Plus fort.
Ah! je suis mort	Ah! je suis mort![44]	

Thereafter it occurred in quartets and quintets, including this example from *On ne s'avise jamais de tout* (1761) by Sedaine:

DORVAL	LISE	M. TUE	LE COMMISSAIRE	MARGARITA
La voilà, mais	Mon cher	Ah, ah! je vous	Messieurs	Quoi! vous
Ne me	Tuteur,	tiens-là.	De la douceur;	hésiteriez
trompez pas:	Mon Protecteur,	Ah! vous voilà?	En conscience	Vous douteriez,
Quoi, vous ne	Je suis à vos	Je ne veux pas.	Vous ne pouvez	Vous refuseriez
voulez pas?	genoux	C'est inutile,	Vous refuser	Leur amitié?
Je me moque	Ah! qu'il soit	Un mot en vaut	A l'alliance	Et quoique
de votre aveu,	Mon époux.	mille.	Qu'on vient	barbon,
Morbleu,		Je ne veux pas.	De proposer.	Vous dites non?
Je veux vous		Je ne veux pas	Ah! M. Tue,	Vous perdez
faire			Que cette vue.	donc le sens,
Voir beau jeu.				Sens?
Levez-vous,				Nul ressentiment
Levez-vous.				Pour le moment
				Je les unirois
				Je les marierois.[45]

and eventually in sextets and septets. The septet closing the second act of *Tom Jones*, comprising seven divergent columns, was the furthest point to which this technique was stretched during this period.

Columned texts, especially in larger ensembles, were particularly favored by Sedaine, and to a lesser extent by Anseaume (who had been among the first to introduce them into the *opéra-comique* during the late 1750s).[46] Other librettists tended to create ensembles using dialogue; their experiments with columns were less frequent and confined to smaller ensembles. Sedaine's practice was entirely in keeping with his desire to accommodate the composer as far as possible, since such texts sacrificed their literary value in order to allow a freer and more flexible musical treatment by the composer. On the same grounds they affirmed Diderot's ideal that works should be represented rather than read: texts such as those transcribed above needed a musical corollary to bring them to life.

In several ensembles librettists chose to blend different textual patterns: dialogue, parallel columns, solo or ensemble verses. The resulting texts emphasized how wide the choice available to them had become. One particularly complex example, by P.-R. Lemonnier, was the trio opening scene vii of *Le cadi dupé* which began with dialogue, was followed by a divergent duet (presented in columns), a short solo verse, and concluded with parallel columns in trio:

TRIO

L'AGA	Entrez donc.
OMAR	Non, non, non.
L'AGA	Entrez, allons;
	Que de façons!

LE CADI		OMAR
Allons, point de caprice;		Mais, mais, par quel caprice
Il faut qu'on obéisse.		Faut-il que j'obéisse.

OMAR
Laissez-moi m'en aller.
Qu'ai-je à démêler
Avec la justice?

ENSEMBLE

LE CADI	OMAR	L'AGA
Laissez-là ce garçon	Non, non, je n'irai pas, non, non,	Allons, marche, garçon.
Les discours sont hors de saison	Ah! Monseigneur, pardon, pardon:	Les discours sont hors de saison;
Je vais le mettre à la raison.	Non, non; c'est une trahison.	On va te mettre à la raison.[47]

The composer, Monsigny, was able to set this ensemble text in an extremely flexible manner, juxtaposing the different parts and repeating, transferring, and re-ordering lines and phrases at random. The manipulation of texts by composers, and this example in particular, is an aspect discussed in the following chapter.

Librettists included stage directions in ensemble texts with increasing frequency. These were explicitly intended to assist provincial actors (those far from the direct influence of the librettist) and encourage more careful thought about movement, in order to enhance the stage picture. Once again, Sedaine was at the forefront of these developments.

In the preface to *Blaise le savetier* (one of his earliest works) he addressed his general public, and the actors in particular, thus:

> "Si quelqu'un me reproche l'attention avec laquelle j'ai écrit la Pantomime de cette farce, qu'il fasse réflexion que le grand défaut de la plûpart des Ariettes au Théâtre, est de se voir dénuées d'action, soit que ce défaut vienne des paroles & de la situation théâtrale, soit que l'Acteur seulement musicien, ne sçache point les revêtir des gestes & du sentiment ... l'Acteur loin de tout conseil qui lui semble valable, en lisant la pantomime, se trouvera aidé de l'avis de l'Auteur; il peut en partant de-là, fixer ses mouvements, étendre son jeu, et arriver à ce point si difficile de rendre la nature sans la forcer."[48]

Stage directions underlined the increasing importance of the visual element in the developing *opéra-comique*, and once again emphasized the need for works to be staged rather than read as literature. In this respect ensembles proved a more effective vehicle for dramatic gesture than solo *ariettes*. The latter tended to be orientated introspectively and were more closely allied to verbal elements. Dramatic gesture could be used, but this was limited to substantiating psychological elements: the state of mind of a character and the emotions expressed. However, when several characters were brought together within the bounds of an ensemble, stage pantomime could be exploited to advantage by accentuating the interplay between the various participants and their immediate reactions to one another. Since, by their very nature, directions required movement, they allowed several ensembles to assume a more "progressive" character, combining physical action (the visual) with the verbal, allowing the former to vie in importance with the latter (as recommended by Diderot), thereby creating dynamic musical pieces which formed a vital part of the drama.

Although the *opéra-comique* of the first half of the 18th century was often improvisatory in character, librettos had included stage directions from the earliest days. Many of these, however, were limited to offering basic instructions as to whom characters should address, the mood or tone of voice they should adopt (*troublé*, *ironiquement*, etc.), and certain basic actions. Directions became more elaborate in the second half of the century and were aimed, initially, at enhancing the staged representation of an ensemble, then at controlling this performance and even the composer's musical setting of the text.

Some examples of the former type are found in the transitional decade of the 1750s: the duet in scene ii of *Gilles, garçon peintre*, whose text was reproduced in the previous chapter, suggested that the argument between the two characters be enhanced through humorous physical combat. During the following decade, directions became more elaborate, largely in the hands of Sedaine and Anseaume. On several occasions in *Blaise le savetier*, Sedaine issued instructions to his actors in careful footnotes, including this passage relating to the opening duet:

> "Comme dans le cours de ce Duo Blaise a moins à dire que Blaisine qui est agitée d'une plus grande passion, il faut que Blaise occupe la Scene en faisant une espece de toilette. Qu'il mette ses boutons de manche, son col noir. Qu'il ôte son bonnet, mette sa perruque, range sa table, &c."[49]

Sedaine appreciated early in his career one of the common pitfalls of the ensemble: that of leaving characters with nothing to do when they did not sing. Indeed, in *Mazet* (1761), Anseaume had been able to create a whole work relying on a non-singing participant: in a duet from Iiv the hero (Mazet) feigns loss of speech in order to win his way into the household of his beloved:

NUTO
C'est Madame qui viendra
Pour sçavoir ce qui passe:
Et puis elle te dira:
Mon enfant, dis moi, de grace,
Que fait Thérese?
(Mazet imite l'action de coudre.)
Bon cela.
Isabelle
Que fait-elle?
(Mazet imite avec ses doigts l'action de tricoter.)
C'est au mieux. Personne ici
N'est-il venu?
(Mazet désigne un Bailli, par la grande perruque,
le rabat & la démarche grave.)
Qui donc?
(Mazet recommence les mêmes lazzis.) . . .[50]

Many of the stage directions issued by librettists derived from the *lazzi* (stage pranks and acrobatics) of the *commedia dell'arte*. In the text above they were written in rather than left to the discretion of the performer. Other notable examples occurred in the opening scene of Anseaume's *Le soldat magicien*, which recorded several moves in a game of backgammon,[51] and in scene ix of Poinsinet's *Sancho Pança*, a duet depicting a duel in which both characters turned out to be cowards.

Stage directions necessary for the execution of an ensemble, rather than merely its enhancement, developed more intermittently during the same period. Anseaume again provided an excellent example in scene xvi of *La clochette*. This was a duet requiring one character to chase the other on and off the stage in supposed pursuit of one of the heroine's lost sheep:

> NICODEME
> Je l'entens encore.
> Où s'est-il fourré?
> *(Il entre dans la premiere coulisse à gauche.)*
> COLIN *entre sur le Théatre par la quatrieme à gauche.*
> Ah! pauvre pecore,
> Je t'attraperai.
> *(Il sort par la quatrieme à droite.)*
> NICODEME, *sortant de la premiere à gauche.*
> Petit agnelet,
> Petit moutonnet.
> *(Il passe derriere le bosquet.)*
> COLIN *au milieu du Théatre.*
> Pour nous divertir,
> Faisons-le courir.
> *(Il se sauve vers le fond du Théatre.)*
> NICODEME, *rentrant.*
> Il s'moque, je pense . . .[52]

Sedaine's later experiments with stage directions were even more far-reaching in their dramatic consequences, but since these were introduced in his librettos for Grétry, and since they were not always applied to the ensemble, a detailed examination lies outside the bounds of the present study. However, the extensive "rose scene" in Act II of *Le Magnifique* is worthy of mention as "a structural landmark," in which pantomime actually replaced the spoken word and served the composer as a fundamental element of musical composition.

Dramatic Treatment of Ensembles

In order to illustrate the ways in which librettists handled the different types of concerted movements introduced earlier (expository, tableau, progressive, climactic, and dénouement ensembles), individual examples from each category will be analyzed. First, however, it is useful to take a more general view of how concerted movements were incorporated into the overall planning of a work, as various patterns emerge that emphasize particular dramatic functions within the *opéra-comique* of this period.

One frequent procedure was for the pace of a work to relax after an expository ensemble, allowing subsequent stage business to unfold in the more traditional guise of solo *ariettes*. Further ensembles were included only after a series of individual movements, as in *Le soldat magicien*, *Tom Jones*, and *Le jardinier de Sidon*, although exceptions to this pattern occurred in *Blaise le savetier* and *Le jardinier et son seigneur*. In these works—both, as previously noted, with a high concentration of ensemble movements—the introductory duet was followed by a second ensemble after only one connecting *ariette*.

Another typical pattern was for concerted movements to form a sequence about two-thirds of the way through an opera. This was favored both within single-act works and in the final act of multi-act compositions. The effect was to increase momentum in the preparation of the climax, even though these movements were traditionally separated by spoken dialogue, since each ensemble grew in terms of the number of characters involved. Thus *Le maître en droit* included two duets and a trio prior to two solo *ariettes* leading into the quartet finale, while the sequence closing *Le bûcheron* comprised a duet followed by a trio, a quartet, and a septet before a final solo *ariette* and the closing vaudeville. An alternative to this pattern was for concerted movements to accumulate at the end of an opera in close succession, thereby constituting the final climax. An excellent example of this technique was built into the second act of *L'isle des foux*, which concluded with a quartet followed by a quintet and a duet leading into a sextet. *On ne s'avise jamais de tout* closed in a similar fashion with a quartet, a quintet, and a vaudeville finale. Allied with this emphasis on the ensemble as a dramatic high-point was the tendency for concerted movements to comprise entire scenes, a feature which further enhanced their prominence and impact in individual works.

How frequent and important were the five different categories of ensemble within the *opéra-comique* of this period? Moreover, can every ensemble be classified neatly into one of the five? Although each category is specific in its dramatic purpose, sometimes an overlap in function or effect is apparent. Tableau ensembles, for example, may be so intense and vivid in the picture they paint that they evoke a strong sense of climax within the scene in which they are placed. Progressive ensembles, in their forward momentum, may likewise contribute towards a climactic high-point. Some expository ensembles are also progressive in their quick generation of introductory events. The creation of categories can be justified in that they serve to clarify; but such practice creates problems

TABLE X: The Dramatic Functions of Ensembles

	Expository	Tableau	Progressive	Climactic	Dénouement
OVERALL	9%	44%	16%	17%	14%
Sedaine (10 wks)	5%	48%	17%	19%	11%
Anseaume (9 wks)	10%	27%	30%	14%	19%
Favart (5 wks)	12%	50%	25%	—	13%
Poinsinet (3 wks)	15%	45%	20%	10%	10%
P. Lemonnier (2 wks)	17%	55%	17%	—	11%

as well in delimiting the bounds and possibilities of each. The figures in Table X should therefore be treated with circumspection: they outline a general picture but should not be taken as conclusive in their implications.

Tableau ensembles were most commonly encountered, totalling 44% overall. The more innovative expository and progressive types constituted 9% and 16% respectively. Those leading up to, or constituting, a climax accounted for 17%, and dénouement ensembles made up the remaining 14%. Individual librettists had differing approaches which may be compared to the norm overall and summarized as follows. Sedaine included quite a high percentage of tableau ensembles and very few expository ensembles. Anseaume, in contrast, emphasized progressive ensembles at the expense of tableau movements. The former type also featured significantly in Favart's librettos, although these were mainly confined to an early work, *La fille mal gardée*, whose duet/trio, trio, and quartet all contained either psychological or physical development. Favart was thereafter far more cautious in pursuing this type. His use, however, of the expository ensemble was more pervasive, and this was also the case in works by Poinsinet and P.-R. Lemonnier (whose two librettos were included because they had a high concentration of concerted movements). The approach of other librettists is not considered since so few of their works were consulted in the present study.

(i) Expository Ensembles. When the exposition to a work is presented by a single character, either in speech or song, the situation may be perceived with relative ease and speed. To open, instead, with two or

more characters, particularly with a concerted number, creates a more vivid picture which immediately plunges the spectators into a complex scenario. They must establish, as quickly as possible, the identity of the characters and their relation to one another; and they must unravel the significance of what is sung in order to make sense of the stage picture. Simultaneous expression is more intense, and far less straightforward, than monologue. Diderot argued strongly for vivid expositions:

> " ... c'est le premier incident qui décidera de la couleur de l'ouvrage entier ... Si l'on débute par une situation forte, tout le reste sera de la même vigueur."[53]

Quétant voiced similar ideas: "l'intrigue doit s'expliquer dès la première Scene ou la seconde tout au plus, quand la Piece est longue."[54]

It is not surprising, therefore, that librettists began increasingly to include ensembles in the early scenes of their plays with the intention of intensifying the exposition. Neither is it surprising that these movements were, almost without exception, spirited interchanges in which the characters gave vent to strongly contrasting feelings. Ensembles opened seven of the 39 works examined, the earliest of which was *Le maître en droit* (Lemonnier/Monsigny, 1760).[55] These movements were all duets. Two further works contained ensembles—likewise duets—in their opening scenes, following on from spoken dialogue.[56] Seven more works included concerted movements in their second scene, among these Quétant's own *Le maréchal ferrant*. Four of the seven were duets and three were trios. Altogether, 17 of the 39 works included an ensemble in their first or second scene.

Ensembles were also used to introduce later acts: for example, duets in IIi of *Le roi et le fermier* (Sedaine/Monsigny, 1762) and in IIi of *Les moissonneurs* (Favart/Duni, 1768); the trio in IIi of *Mazet* (Anseaume/Duni, 1761); and the quartet opening the third act of *Tom Jones* (Poinsinet/Philidor, 1765), which featured four local drunkards for comic effect while the pace of the main drama was held in abeyance. Particularly unusual as expository ensembles were those placed in the interim stages of an act. P.-R. Lemonnier included one such example in *Le cadi dupé* (scene vii), a trio whose text was cited above (p. 124). It marks the entrance of Omar, a character vital to the development of the plot since it is his daughter Le Cadi seeks in marriage.

Expository ensembles accorded both prominence and importance to concerted movements: prominence in that the drama came immediately to focus on them, and importance in that they became responsible for conveying vital dramatic information. Offering ensembles this scope was an extremely significant advance implemented by librettists during the 1760s.

(ii) Tableau Ensembles. Ensembles reinforcing events previously communicated in dialogue or solo *ariettes* served the useful dramatic function of underlining and intensifying given emotions and situations. Their unique ability to telescope several dramatic ideas into one movement also made them an extremely economic form of expression. They provided the means for a vivid, yet concise, musical reinforcement of dramatic events, hence their frequent inclusion.

To understand how the ensemble portrayed a tableau, an outline of one particularly effective example is offered. This is taken from the final scene of *Les deux chasseurs et la laitière* (Anseaume/Duni, 1763) and paints a wonderfully comic situation. Colas and Guillot have been hunting a bear, unsuccessfully, for most of the opera and arguing incessantly as their misfortunes accumulate. Guillot, at the same time, has been attempting to win the favor of the young dairymaid, Perrette. The comedy reaches its climax as the bear lumbers onto the stage forcing Colas to climb on top of a tumbledown cottage. Perrette, meanwhile, has hidden behind this in order to escape from Guillot's attentions. Guillot then enters, enraged by both Colas and Perrette, and strikes the wall of the cottage, whereupon it collapses. Colas falls off, and the wall falls on top of Guillot; both believe themselves dead. They voice their predicament loudly in the trio while Perrette laughs away at the pair. The text—which is set in columns—illustrates how the ensemble reinforces the previous stage action swiftly and vividly:

COLAS	GUILLOT	PERRETTE
Je tombe,	La masure,	Quelle aventure!
Je tombe . . .	La masure,	La masure
Soutenez moi . . .	Tombe sur moi . . .	Est à bas. Ah!
Ahi, ahi, ahi, ahi,	Ahi, ahi, ahi, ahi,	ah! ah! ah!
Aidez-moi *(bis)*	Soutiens-moi *(bis)*	La masure est à bas.
Je suis fracassé		Il vouloit mourir
	J'ai le bras cassé! . . .	Et ne peut souffrir
Maudite chaumiere!	Maudite chaumiere!	Blessure légere.
		(Elle rit)
Je suis meurtri . . .	Je suis meurtri . . .	Hi, hi, hi, hi,
(Il pleure)		
Hi, hi, hi, hi.	Hi, hi, hi, hi.	Ah pauvres gens,

Quel triste sort!	Quel triste sort!	Je vous plains fort.[57]

Another fine example of a tableau ensemble is the trio opening Act III of *Le roi et le fermier*, which presents the three main female characters quietly occupied with various household tasks—spinning, stitching, lacework—as they await the return of Richard.

(iii) Progressive Ensembles. Two types of progressive ensemble were outlined earlier, one developing the drama in a predominantly physical way—commonly referred to by others as the "action ensemble"—and the other achieving the same effect through psychological means. The former were "outwardly" orientated in embodying tangible actions, incidents, and escapades; the latter were "inwardly" orientated, centering on alterations that took place within characters: a change of heart or mind, the making of an important decision, the admission of feelings not previously aired (for example, avowals of love). Around two-thirds (64%) of the progressive ensembles examined from the repertory of Duni, Monsigny, and Philidor were of the physical variety, this representing a distinct development from the previous decade during which the majority of progressive ensembles were psychological in complexion. Thus the idea of concerted movements portraying vivid, dynamic scenarios was one that took root quickly in the *opéra-comique* during the 1760s.

The trio "C'est peu de chose" in IIvii of *La nouvelle école des femmes* (Mouslier de Moissy/Philidor, 1770) may be regarded as a particularly striking example of a movement encompassing emotional development. Mme Saint Fard has taken the bold step of visiting her husband's latest *innamorata*, in order to discover how she may win back his love. Laure, unaware of her visitor's identity, is full of good advice, but Mme Saint Fard is forced into a closet with the sudden arrival of Saint Fard himself. After he has left, and Mme Saint Fard duly returned on stage, Laure announces that she intends to marry her suitor. The trio opens with Mme Saint Fard's shocked reaction to this disclosure, which consequently leads Laure and her maid to divine that their visitor is also in love with Saint Fard. After the ensemble it is quickly discovered that she is in fact his wife. Laure's sudden realization during the trio alters the course of the drama; it is a powerful psychological turning point, conveyed all the more vividly in a concerted movement than in dialogue or solo *ariette*.

An excellent example of an "action ensemble" is found in scene xvi of *La clochette* (Anseaume/Duni, 1766), whose text was reproduced in part above (p. 127) to illustrate the importance of stage directions in creating movements with a faster and more dynamic dramatic pace. It is a duet for Colin and Nicodeme, rivals for the hand of the shepherdess Colinette. Nicodeme has "stolen" one of Colinette's sheep so that he may win her favor by returning it to her; but he has been foiled in this ruse by Colin who, in the duet, goads his rival by running on and off stage with a bell taken from the sheep's neck. He is followed by Nicodeme who believes he is chasing the lost animal, and the duet ends with Colin successfully leading his rival into a convenient shed and locking him inside. As Nicodeme rages from within, Colin rubs his hands in glee. The staging of this ensemble not only lent great scope to physical movement and vital action, but must also have produced a great comic effect.

Progressive ensembles quite frequently involved larger groupings of characters: for example the quartet in scene xvii of *Sancho Pança* (Poinsinet/Philidor, 1762), in which the besieged hero (and coward at heart) decides to relinquish control of his island in favor of his daughter's lover; and the quintet closing Act I of *Mazet* (Anseaume/Duni, 1761), where Mazet furthers his plan to woo his beloved by gaining employment as her gardener. The quartet closing the second act of *Le roi et le fermier* (Sedaine/Monsigny, 1762) merits a closer analysis. "Avance, suis-moi, Charlot" combines two gamekeepers, Rustaut and Charlot, with two members of the king's entourage, Lurewel and Le Courtisan, who are lost in the forest. In an *Andante* section the two guards, believing their adversaries to be poachers, advance slowly as the lord and his companion sense their presence and prepare to defend themselves. A sudden change to *Presto* marks the entrance of five guards who seize Lurewel and Le Courtisan. The act is brought to a comic conclusion as the captives are marched unceremoniously offstage. Here, then, is vital action at a strategic point in the drama, concluding an interim act with a flourish and throwing expectation forward to the next. Although this is a fine example of an action finale, such movements were in fact uncommon in the *opéra-comique* of the period in question (although flourishing under Goldoni's pen in Italy). The majority of progressive ensembles of the physical type (86%) were placed internally within acts.

One further action ensemble is worth describing since it was unprecedented in juxtaposing contrasting stage events within a single movement. It is, moreover, a septet (although set by the composer as a sextet).[58] The finale to the second act of *L'école de la jeunesse* (Anseaume/Duni, 1765) takes time off from the main events of the drama to create a play within a play. Hortense, the *femme fatale* of the work, has gathered various entertainers in preparation for a sumptuous ball, and decides that they should rehearse for the company already gathered in her boudoir. The seven participants arrange themselves into three groups, the first of which consists of a single character, Le Chanteur. The second includes Hortense, her maid Finette, and her friend Mondor, while the third brings together three men: Cleon, Le Chevalier, and Le Baron, who become engrossed in a game of cards. The septet revolves around Le Chanteur's repetition of a song he has just performed to the satisfaction of the ladies, and is therefore unusual in being based on earlier musical material. As he repeats his *ariette*, broken into separate phrases, Hortense and her suite react with suitably appreciative comments, but from time to time upbraid the card players, who enact their own drama and are entirely oblivious of the singer's performance. They frequently break out into heated dialogue that impinges on, and interrupts, Le Chanteur's performance. The inspiration underlying the creation of this extremely complex scenario is at once innovative in its skilful handling of diverse factions, and unmatched by the later experiments of other librettists for several years.[59] The ensemble is also unique in that it is not only progressive in its dramatic function, but forms a tableau and a climax to the second act.[60]

One other style of progressive ensemble remains to be discussed: that which introduces a new character or characters once the movement is underway. This procedure, previously referred to as the additive principle (or aggregation) became a common feature during the period in question.[61] First apparent from as early as 1758 in a Favart libretto (*La fille mal gardée*), it was thereafter exploited most notably by Anseaume and Sedaine, but also by Poinsinet, Quétant, and Collé.

Favart's one—and, as far as it is known, only—example heralded a breakthrough in concerted writing, and has been described in detail by Smith:

> "In this piece, Le Magister, who wants to marry Nicolette, tries to pacify her by promising that she will be the boss in the future. The reluctant Nicolette doesn't place much faith in these promises, however, and instructs Le Magister to prove himself by asking her forgiveness, a humiliation to which he eventually consents ... Nicolette suddenly perceives Lindor, who wants to deliver a note to her secretly (mm. 44–49). In order that he may do this,

Nicolette contrives to humble Le Magister further by demanding that he bow down before her and kiss the ground. This permits Lindor to complete his mission and kiss Nicolette's hand (mm. 50–64). By the time Le Magister rises, Nicolette willingly feigns cooperation, and the music recapitulates the opening material, now sung as an amiable duet."[62]

The ensemble complex thus began as a duet, developed into a trio with the appearance and interjections of Lindor, and ended as a duet. In the process it encompassed three scenes and ran to 86 bars in length. Although this was not extensive by contemporary standards, the ensemble complex nonetheless attained a remarkable degree of musical continuity for its period, propelling the action forward in a manner then uncommon in concerted writing.

Anseaume was among the first librettists to follow Favart's lead, and one of his earliest attempts was also his most ambitious. This was in *L'isle des foux* (1760) where, in collaboration with Marcouville, he created a duet-trio-quartet complex that spanned 114 bars across scenes vi, vii, and viii in Act II.[63] The complex opens with a confrontation between the miserly Sordide and his ward, Nicette, who is kept under lock and key, and here upbraided for her wayward behaviour. She defends herself defiantly. Follette then enters and, mistaking their argument for an amorous *tête-à-tête*, accuses Sordide of inconstancy while he and Nicette continue their dispute. At this point, Anseaume wrote a short solo verse for Follette, a continuation of the sentiments she expressed in the trio. Duni, evidently believing that this would interrupt the momentum already achieved, chose to omit this, and his setting moved straight to the arrival of Fanfolin, precipitated by the heated trio. Eager to help his beloved Nicette, Fanfolin joins with the others to create a quartet in which all four characters continue to vent their separate grievances. The ensemble complex is well tailored to the action, the succession of duet, trio, and quartet dictating the dramatic pace and development, and representing an unprecedented achievement in the *opéra-comique*.

Other examples of the additive principle were almost always duets that developed into trios and produced concerted movements of similar length, although none spanned quite as many scenes as those from *La fille mal gardée* or *L'isle des foux*. In Anseaume's *Mazet* (1761) a duet closed IIix and led into a trio opening IIx. Act I of Sedaine's *Le roi et le fermier* (1762) and IIix of Quétant's *Le maréchal ferrant* (1761) both concluded with duets that developed into trios, as did IIx of Collé's *L'isle sonnante* (1767) and scene viii of Sedaine's *Les femmes vengées* (1775). Sometimes duets grew from solo *ariettes*, as in two librettos by Poinsinet: *Sancho Pança*, scene xiv (1762) and *Le sorcier*, Ii (1764). Occasionally the principle worked in reverse: in the third act of *La fée Urgèle* (Favart, 1765) two duets concluded with substantial solo singing. Favart attempted no further ensemble complexes comparable to that in *La fille mal gardée*, a reflection of his increasingly conservative approach with respect to ensembles in his later *opéra-comique* librettos.

The implications of aggregation for concerted writing were significant. On one level, the resulting concentration of ensemble movements increased their prominence within individual works. On another, it offered scope for the articulation of new dramatic devices within the confines of an ensemble: for example, changes in the attitudes of characters and ironic expansions of their relationships with one another.[64] In this respect and in others, aggregation was able to appropriate the function of spoken dialogue and the solo *ariette*, thereby assuming greater responsibility for both musical continuity and dramatic development.

(iv) Climactic Ensembles. Ensembles preparing or creating dramatic high-points in *opéras-comiques* from this period were generally movements for four or more characters, and this can be considered one of the primary dramatic functions of larger ensembles. Only one-third of the climactic ensembles examined were duets or trios, these creating interim points of tension within works. The remainder brought together large groups of characters in the latter stages of an act, and helped establish one of the most enduring types of ensemble in the history of opera: the ensemble of perplexity.

In order to maximize its dramatic effect, the ensemble of perplexity required adroit preparation by the librettist. The state of mind or predicament of each participant had first to be established, then intertwined with others, and all followed through to their inevitable juxtaposition, once the various passions could be contained no longer. Such ensembles are best appreciated in their overall dramatic context. However, they are also skilful and intricate musical movements in themselves: the more characters they bring together, the greater their dramatic and musical effect, and the greater the skill required by both librettist and composer.

Several quartets and quintets may be cited as examples of fine ensembles of perplexity: the quartet opening the final scene of *Les sabots*, the quintet in scene xvi of *Rose et Colas*, and a quartet and quintet in close proximity to one another in the closing stages of *On ne s'avise jamais de tout*, the former enhancing the dramatic effect of the latter. Ensembles of perplexity involving more than five characters were included regularly in the *opéra-comique* during the 1760s and, in this area, Anseaume proved one of the most gifted librettists. The two sextet finales to Acts I and II of *L'école de la jeunesse* (1765) offer evidence of this. In that closing the first act, Cléon, the main male character, has rejected his uncle's advice that he marry Sophie, seeking instead the company of Hortense, a rich young widow, and running considerably into debt. He muddles through the opening act in this manner, until the point is reached where the consequences of his actions can no longer be contained. Cléon is joined by five other characters, each inundating him with their own demands. Finette, Hortense's servant, informs him that her mistress is waiting to see him and is supported in this request by her friend Mondor. Dubois, Cléon's valet, looks on gravely and reminds him of what his uncle's reaction will be if Cléon is to visit the widow. Meanwhile, Damis, who is also in love with Sophie and had been confronting Cléon with this issue prior to their interruption, insists that their private discussion be continued; and Javard, Cléon's creditor, complicates matters further by demanding immediate payment of debts incurred. Cléon, in the midst of this, can only look on helplessly and attempt vainly to placate everyone. The general effect of the sextet is to bring together all the tensions of the first act and to emphasize Cléon's erring ways. It telescopes and exaggerates several individual strands; yet, clearly, the total effect is more significant than the sum of its different parts.

The sextet concluding the second act was described above as a progressive ensemble (in that it juxtaposed and developed three separate stage actions), a tableau ensemble (in presenting a play within a play), and a climactic ensemble. In this latter respect it serves as an impressive ensemble of perplexity, offsetting three groups with conflicting interests. Smith refers to "the ambitious character" of this finale and justly describes it as "one of the most vital ensemble passages in all of Duni's *opéras-comiques.*"[65]

Ensembles of perplexity involving seven characters were also common, being found in librettos by Sedaine (*Le roi et le fermier*, IIIxiv), Guichard and Castet (*Le bûcheron*, sc. xviii), Poinsinet (*Tom Jones*, Act II finale), Collé (*L'isle sonnante*, IIIxiv), and G.A. Lemonnier (*Le bon fils*, sc. vii). Musically and dramatically, these pieces represented the greatest challenge to the artists of the *opéra-comique*, whether they were librettists, composers or performers. Practice and experience in the handling of these complicated pieces doubtless did much to increase competence and to encourage further experimentation.

(*v*) *Dénouement Ensembles.* Concerted movements concluding *opéras-comiques* generally brought the whole cast together to express their reactions to the *lieto fine* and perhaps point to a latent moral. The most common type of conclusion was the vaudeville finale, which remained a traditional feature of the genre throughout its history. This comprised several verses sung in turn by different characters, with either an ensemble refrain interlaced or to conclude. Alternatives to this included chorus movements or ensembles for individual soloists. These latter ranged from duets to sextets. The wide range of finale movements in the *opéra-comique* is discussed more fully in the following chapter, since this is linked to a consideration of how composers deployed their soloists and available choral forces at such points in their scores. As far as the librettists were concerned, their texts were far less complex in structure than were those of internal ensembles, and almost always *unanime*. Their dramatic function was simply to round off the work in a satisfactory manner.

Dénouement ensembles, however, did not inevitably feature at the close of an opera. They might be placed at an intermediate point, with a bathetic effect in mind, as in the case of the duet concluding the second act of *Le déserteur*. This followed traumatic scenes between the hero and heroine and was written for two comic characters: Montauciel, the drunken dragoon, and the heroine's rather simple cousin, Bertrand. The basis of the ensemble was ingenious: two contrasting solo *chansons* sung separately and then juxtaposed. However, the shape this gave to the middle act and to the overall dramatic effect was unusual. The sudden transition to the comic sphere provided respite from the main action yet, at the same time, placed the severity of the drama in even sharper focus.

The technique of reducing tension at the close of an act (rather than building up to a climactic concerted finale) is apparent in another work by Monsigny, *L'isle sonnante*. A duet concluding the first act follows a quartet in which four main characters are brought into sharp conflict. Vivatché, the sultan of the island, has fallen in love with Célénie and, with the help of his magician, Presto, he tries to entice her to his palace. Célénie, however, remains faithful to Durbin, and the quartet represents a double duet in which the persecuted lovers are set against Vivatché and Presto. It creates a degree of tension that requires resolution, and the duet which follows after some spoken dialogue, and which closes the act, has the character of an anti-climax. It is not simply that the effect of a two-voiced ensemble is diluted after a powerful quartet, but that the subject-matter of the duet is inconsequential. Vivatché and Presto, the two characters left on stage, admit that they are not really in love (the former with Célénie, the latter with Henrietta) but nonetheless find it diverting that they should cause the two women discomfort.

As intimated earlier in the chapter, some ensembles were positioned less successfully than others with regard to dramatic effect. The quintet closing the first act of *Mazet* (Anseaume/Duni, 1761), although referred to earlier as a rare example of a progressive finale, is rendered less effective as a consequence of sketchy and somewhat improbable preparation. Smith has noted that the work as a whole is uneven in that the two male characters dominate the first act and the three female characters the second.[66] This imbalance takes its toll in the quintet finale to Act I. Mazet and Nuto, the gardener the hero wishes to replace, have spent several scenes deciding how to put their plan into operation. As a result, Nuto meets and consults with Madame Gertrude at a late stage in the act, and she has only a limited time in which to make her decision. After the briefest of musings (solo *ariette*) she hires Mazet as soon as she meets him, which is in the quintet itself. This important development in the plot is rushed because the ensemble must also introduce, for the first time, the two nieces of Madame Gertrude. The quintet suffers from having to present too much material in too short a time, problems that would have been alleviated if the female characters had been accommodated at an earlier stage within the act.

Character Groupings and Expressive Types of Ensemble

The more "realistic" portrayal of characters to which the *opéra-comique* now aspired meant that roles became much less stereotyped and that individual idiosyncrasies were projected more strongly. Emphasis on a more lifelike presentation of characters affected the dramatic situations in which they could be placed when singing ensembles. One finds, for example, characters grouped together while eating meals (*Le soldat magicien, Sancho Pança, Le bûcheron*), while fighting duels, reading letters or preparing to meet an invasion (*Sancho Pança*), while playing games (*L'école de la jeunesse, Le soldat magicien*), while fending off creditors (*Blaise le savetier, Le maréchal ferrant, Le bûcheron, L'école de la jeunesse*) or while drunk. Additionally, characters sing from inside locked cupboards (*Blaise le savetier*), from cellars (*Le maréchal ferrant*), from garden sheds (*La clochette*), in forests (*Le roi et le fermier*), in prisons (*Le déserteur*) or in palaces (*Le cadi dupé*).

Although concerted movements explored a wide variety of new physical surroundings, several traditional expressive types were still retained: lovers' reconciliations and misunderstandings, confrontation duets, rejection duets. However, these situations were exploited in a far more complex manner in librettos by Sedaine, Anseaume, and their contemporaries. In their emphasis on intrigue, subterfuge, and comedy they served as effective vehicles for ambiguity and dramatic irony. This, as noted earlier, was a feature ensembles were able to embrace more pervasively than other musical forms, since they allowed characters to interact, clash, and disagree with one another more spontaneously.

Le cadi dupé, Sancho Pança, and *L'amant déguisé* provide examples of these techniques at work in duets. Scene iv of the first contains an ensemble for Zelmire and Le Cadi which portrays the standard situation of a besieged heroine coping with a rejected suitor. However, Zelmire is far from virtuous, and has decided to wreak her own revenge; she therefore encourages Le Cadi to believe that his suit will prosper and the movement assumes the ironic guise of a playful lovers' duet. Scene v of *Sancho Pança* portrays a similar situation: Juliette feigns love for Sancho in order to make his final humiliation more complete. *L'amant déguisé* includes what appears to be a traditional avowal of love, in scene v, between Mme de Marsillane and her ardent suitor. The latter, however, is none other than Julie, *en travesti*, who is enjoying a ruse at the expense of Madame because she has refused to allow her daughter, Lucile, to marry the man she loves. Trios likewise offered ample scope for irony. In IIx of *L'isle sonnante* Célénie's confession of love for Durbin is comically misunderstood by Vivatché to apply to him; and in scene xi of *La fille mal gardée* the hero tricks Mme Bobinette into believing that he loves her, but asks that she bring Nicolette with her to add propriety to their elopement. These techniques contrast sharply with earlier practice in both the *tragédie en musique* and the *opera seria*, which tended to present straightforward and uncomplicated scenarios.

Lovers' duets still accounted for one-third (34%) of the duets examined from this period, although this is a lower proportion when compared to earlier practice. The range of nuance created within this traditional framework, and the more subtle painting of character and disposition of those involved, provided scope for the continued expansion of this expressive type of ensemble. *Opéra-comique* lovers were not always the *ingénues* of the earlier 18th century; many had spirit and guile in abundance and might already parade as husband and wife, or as duenna and elderly tutor, or as servants. The sentiments they expressed in their duets were varied. Misunderstandings, disagreements, reconciliations, and mutual avowals were all popular; playful banter and relaxed conversation were introduced, for example in *La nouvelle école des femmes* (Iviii) and *Le roi et le fermier* (IIIix); expressions of unhappiness were less common.

A further 24% of duets were for a male/female pairing, 16% of which involved the heroine with an unrequited suitor, again a traditional ensemble type. However, the reverse of this (the hero's rejection of an unwelcome lover) was a situation rarely exploited: only one example, in IIxii of Anseaume's *Mazet*, was encountered. Male/female pairings also explored family relationships, an emphasis recommended by Diderot in his pursuit of a reformed theater, and resulted in combinations such as brother and sister, or father and daughter.

Ensembles for either two male, or two female, characters accounted for 32% and 10% respectively of the total examined. The preference for such combinations embodied a distinct move away from traditional practice in other genres of grouping opposite sexes in duets, although the situations in which *opéra-comique* characters were placed were not new. Half of the duets for male singers were confrontations between rivals in love; the remainder comprised either general conversations (as in scene xi of *Rose et Colas* where two fathers discussed a match between their children), or playful banter (as in the dénouement duet for Montauciel and Bertrand closing Act II of *Le déserteur*, or in Le Docteur's reading of a letter to Sancho—amidst constant interruptions—in scene xiii of *Sancho Pança*). Duets for female singers were more adventurous in tending to avoid the traditional combination of heroine and confidante (in the *opéra-comique* a duenna or maid), instead favoring confrontation ensembles, a type presumably considered too undignified in earlier genres. Examples are found in IIvi of *Nina et Lindor* and in scene xiv of *Le jardinier et son seigneur*.

A good proportion of trios (42%) portrayed situations familiar from earlier genres in combining two lovers with either a sympathetic or dissenting third party. More innovative were the myriad permutations explored by a further one-third (36%). These included either the lovers with their tutors, governesses, servants or parents; or a husband and wife combination joined by various friends or acquaintances. In several cases these situations created small-scale ensembles of perplexity and introduced crises, as for example in scene xii of *Le soldat magicien*,[67] or in Iii of *Le maréchal ferrant*, where the trio was an expository ensemble introducing two new characters both involved in a heated argument. Trios for characters of the same sex accounted for 22% of the total examined and were more often for female characters (this representing a reversal of the practice favored in duets). Characters in these circumstances were generally in agreement, as in the two trios for Jenny, Betsy, and La Mère in IIIi and IIIv of *Le roi et le fermier*. However, that opening Iii of *Mazet*, in which Madame Gertrude and her two nieces discuss where the new gardener should live, contained some disagreement. Trios for male characters presented more lively situations and preserved less sense of unity. In IIix of *Le maître en droit*, Le Docteur is discovered in female attire and roundly mocked by two of his *écoliers*. (Part of this trio is reproduced as Example 4.5, pp. 173ff, and discussed in the following chapter.) The trio closing scene ix of *Le maréchal ferrant* presented a similarly comic picture of three men bumping around in a dark cellar. A third, and final, example occurred in scene vii of *Le cadi dupé* and was an expository ensemble.[68]

Quartets, by virtue of the frequency with which they were included in the *opéra-comique*, require special mention. Not surprisingly, they painted extremely diverse scenarios, the traditional double-duet pattern which combined two pairs of lovers accounting for only one-eighth of those examined. A large proportion (42%) combined the two main lovers with tutors, maids, governesses, parents or relatives, and portrayed characters either in conflict, or else reconciled (in which case the quartet featured at the close of a work). However, 38% involved a wide cross-section of individuals maintaining differing viewpoints, from which arose ensembles of perplexity. Such movements often resulted in an imbalance of male and female characters (the former tended to dominate), and examples are found in *Blaise le savetier* (sc. ii), *Le soldat magicien* (sc. xiv), *Sancho Pança* (sc. xvii), and *L'isle sonnante* (Iix). Quartets for characters of the same sex were rare. Only two, both for male voices alone, were encountered: the canonic drinking-ensemble opening the third act of *Tom Jones*, and the finale to the second act of *Le roi et le fermier*, described above (p. 133) as an interesting example of an action finale. It was also significant in mixing socially disparate individuals: members of the aristocracy with gamekeepers, a feature characterizing several other *opéra-comique* ensembles of the period.[69]

The greater the number of characters in an ensemble, the more diverse the scenario. It is therefore difficult to discuss quintets, sextets, and septets in general detail, other than to point to the tremendous variety of characters they brought together, and to the fact that they were all either ensembles of perplexity or dénouement ensembles. However, their very presence underlined the basic end towards which librettists of the period were aiming: this was to allow the ensemble to seek new and varied means of expression by introducing it at hitherto untested points in the drama, in the process creating increasingly unusual combinations of characters.

Librettists explored many different ways of emphasizing and expanding the scope of ensemble composition in the *opéra-comique* during the 1760s and early 1770s. Their works contained an extraordinarily high concentration of concerted movements, displayed a penchant for large ensembles accommodating anything up to seven characters, and introduced a new complexity in the design and length of texts. This could result either in ensemble complexes spanning successive scenes, or in whole scenes articulated primarily through concerted writing. That ensembles became a prominent feature of operatic composition was also made possible by a heightened awareness of their dramatic potential, an awareness resulting in the cultivation of expository, progressive, and climactic ensembles, while the more traditional tableau and dénouement types were maintained as well. Ensembles were encouraged to appropriate the function of spoken dialogue, a procedure that confirmed further their new-found dramatic credibility and flexibility. Librettists of this period made the ensemble an active and increasingly vital ingredient of the *opéra-comique*. How composers responded to this challenge, and how the musical language of the period was able to develop ensemble composition further, are matters with which the following chapter now deals.

Notes

1. The opening chapter examined the different musical reasons for the scarcity of ensembles in French and Italian opera during the first half of the 18th century. These musical preferences were, in France at least, accompanied by critical assumptions which are considered in Chapter V.

2. *Osmin's Rage: Philosophical Reflections on Opera, Drama, and Text* (Princeton, 1988).

3. *Ibid.*, inside front cover.

4. *Ibid.*, p. 193.

5. *Ibid.*, p. 188.

6. *Ibid.*, p. 182.

7. *Ibid.*, p. 222.

8. *Ibid.*, p. 245.

9. E. Dent: 'Ensembles and Finales in Eighteenth-century Italian Opera', *SIMG*, xi (1909–10), p. 543. The study is continued in *SIMG*, xii (1910–11).

10. C.E. Koch: 'The Dramatic Ensemble Finale in the Opéra Comique of the Eighteenth Century', *AcM*, xxxix/1–2 (1967), p. 72. Koch also identifies a type of ensemble half-way between the two, which he terms the "expressive-dramatic ensemble finale" (*Op. cit.*, p. 79 and p. 81).

11. This is a main contention in L.I. Wade: *The Dramatic Functions of the Ensemble in the Operas of Wolfgang Amadeus Mozart* (diss., Louisiana State U., 1969), which argues: "Unless such a proposition ... is accepted, many ensembles may simply be dismissed as having no dramatic function whatsoever," pp. 28–29. Kivy (*Op. cit.*) likewise argues the case for emotive expression as an essential operative element in the ensemble: "even where the ensembles are dramatic in the fullest sense, they also are, in the fullest sense, expressive of the emotions of the characters who take part," p. 234.

12. See Kivy, *Op. cit.*, pp. 234–235 and D. Charlton: '"L'art dramatico-musical": an Essay', *Music and Theatre: Essays in Honour of Winton Dean* (Cambridge, 1987), p. 250.

13. The role of the chorus is considered in the following chapter. (See below, pp. 163ff.)

14. See below, pp. 128–129.

15. *Le bon fils* (1773). Some sources err in attributing this work to Pierre-René Lemonnier. The *abbé* Guillaume-Antoine Lemonnier wrote under the pseudonym of Devaux.

16. These have been described as "the most coherent and closely argued consideration of dramatic theory published in eighteenth-century France." M. Cardy: 'The Literary Doctrines of Jean-François Marmontel', *Studies on Voltaire and the Eighteenth Century*, ccx (1982), p. 98.

17. See D. Heartz: 'From Garrick to Gluck: the Reform of Theatre and Opera in the Mid-Eighteenth Century', *PRMA*, xciv (1967–8), pp. 111–112.

18. F. Green, ed.: 'De la poésie dramatique' in *Diderot's Writings on the Theatre* (Cambridge, 1936), p. 201.

19. *Le neveu de Rameau*, ed. A. Adam (Paris, 1967), pp. 153–154 and p. 156. The first publication of this work was posthumous, and the ideas expressed therein could date from between c1762 and 1777.

20. 'De la poésie dramatique', p. 193.

21. J.B. Kopp: *The Drame Lyrique: a Study in the Esthetics of Opera-Comique, 1762–1791* (diss., U. of Pennsylvania, 1982), p. 125.

22. 'De la poésie dramatique', p. 188.

23. M.A. Rayner: *The Social and Literary Aspects of Sedaine's Dramatic Work* (diss., U. of London, 1960), p. 35. Monnet spoke warmly of Garrick in his memoirs; the actor apparently arranged a benefit concert for him prior to his return to Paris to assume the administration of the fair theaters. See his *Supplément au roman comique, ou Mémoires pour servir à la vie de Jean Monnet*, ii, (London, 1772), p. 55.

24. 'De la poésie dramatique', p. 174.

25. Kopp: *Op. cit.*, p. 114.

26. *Ibid.*, p. 326.

27. K.M. Smith, writing of Duni, has observed: "Many of his works, especially those with libretti by Anseaume, incorporate, and in some cases anticipate, innovations customarily assigned to the *opéras-comiques* of Philidor and Monsigny." *Egidio Duni and the Development of the Opéra-Comique from 1753 to 1770* (diss., Cornell U., 1980), pp. 220–221. One work of the nine, *L'isle des foux*, was written in collaboration with Anseaume's long-standing partner Marcouville. This was Marcouville's only contribution during the period in question.

28. Another Favart libretto, *La rosière de Salency*, was set by Monsigny and Philidor (in collaboration with other composers) in 1769.

29. Extracts from Quétant's essay are translated in D. Charlton: '"L'art dramatico-musical"', p. 236.

30. *La nouvelle école des femmes* (Philidor, 1770).

31. L.P. Arnoldson: *Sedaine et les musiciens de son temps* (Paris, 1934), p. 45.

32. Rayner: *Op. cit.*, p. 4.

33. Arnoldson: *Op. cit.*, p. 85.

34. One example of this was the use of peasant dialect in *Le jardinier et son seigneur*, which Sedaine found necessary to defend in the work's *Avertissement*. See Arnoldson: *Op. cit.*, p. 85.

35. Rayner: *Op. cit.*, p. 60. Contemporary critics were aware of this, Grimm for example remarking: "C'est dommage que M. Sedaine n'ait pas un peu plus de facilité dans le style. Il est souvent dur et raboteux. Ses vers surtout sont

faits de manière à faire mal à l'oreille quand on les lit. Tout cela disparaît au théâtre par la magie du jeu et de la musique, et par l'esprit, la verve, la vérité, et la naïveté, qui sont dans la chose. Encore une fois on ne peut avoir une idée de ses pièces par la lecture, et M. Sedaine est un homme dont je fais un cas infini." M. Tourneux, ed.: *Correspondance littéraire* (Paris, 1877–82), iv, p. 502.

36. Kopp: *Op. cit.*, p. 321 and p. 326. Many examples of Sedaine's "elaborate pantomime" dictating a specific response by the composer are discussed by Kopp (pp. 180–181, pp. 240ff.), although the most adventurous of these were carried out during the poet's final period of collaboration with Grétry.

37. A sample of librettos published during the late 1750s shows the following time-lags: the *approbation* for the libretto to *Le médecin de l'amour* (1/9/1758) was granted three weeks before the première (22/9/1758); that to *Gilles, garçon peintre* (27/2/1758) only a few days before (2/3/1758); that to *L'heureux déguisement* (14/8/1758) one week after (7/8/1758); and that to *La fille mal gardée* (8/5/1758) two months after (4/3/1758). Works with no extant librettos were either performed privately, remained unperformed, or were unsuccessful from the outset.

38. Charlton observes that "sometimes a printed score shows a reasonably definitive version of a work as acted in Paris, and sometimes only an outdated one," and warns that one should "guard against imagining that opéras-comiques in Paris possessed anything like the fixity that a printed score tends to suggest." *Grétry and the Growth of Opéra-Comique* (Cambridge, 1986), p. 18 and p. 42. Although these comments relate specifically to the later period of Grétry, there is no reason to assume that the situation was any different in the preceding decade. There are, for example, two different versions of the score to *L'isle des foux* (see Chapter IV below, p. 152).

39. For example: *Blaise le savetier*, *Le maître en droit*, *Le cadi dupé*, *Le jardinier et son seigneur*, and *On ne s'avise jamais de tout*.

40. Once again this raises the question of the role played by the chorus in *opéras-comiques* of the period and the distinction between chorus and solo ensemble (which is at times difficult to gauge). These matters are addressed in the following chapter.

41. Charlton notes: "Philidor's collaboration with Sedaine ended when he gave back the text of *Le Roi et le fermier*, saying that it was 'impracticable' (*infaisable*), a judgement that helps to explain the fulsome recognition in its eventual preface of Monsigny." '"L'art dramatico-musical"', pp. 242–243. (Sedaine assisted Philidor a few years later with revisions of *Tom Jones* and *Ernelinde*.) How far librettists designed texts with specific composers in mind, and how close was their creative interchange, is difficult to establish before the emergence of partnerships such as Sedaine/Grétry or Marmontel/Grétry. Sedaine left little autobiographical material, and his collaboration with Grétry is recorded in detail only in the composer's own writings. Anseaume, to the best of present knowledge, remained silent on this matter.

42. "Perhaps this was the only eighteenth-century opera without a straightforward aria in its last act." Charlton: *Grétry and the Growth of Opéra-Comique*, p. 242.

43. See p. 158 below for a more detailed analysis of this ensemble.

44. Printed libretto: Paris (Duchesne), 1760, p. 38 (sc. xii).

45. Printed libretto: Paris (Herissant), 1761, p. 40 (closing scene xix).

46. See Chapter II, p. 84.

47. Printed libretto: Paris (Duchesne), 1761, p. 21. Ensemble texts by Lemonnier in *Le cadi dupé* have been criticized by one recent author who writes: "one area in which Lemonnier may be faulted is his handling of duets, of which there are many in this opera. Nearly all of them contain sections in which the two characters' lines rhyme, but otherwise differ entirely in content." B.A. Brown: *Christoph Willibald Gluck and Opéra-Comique in Vienna, 1754–1764* (diss., U. of California, 1986), p. 693. Such texts, however, relate back to the practice discussed in earlier chapters of interleaving similar lines of poetry in order to establish an embryonic style of divergent expression. They prepared the ground for more complicated texts.

48. *Avertissement de l'auteur.* Printed libretto: Paris (Duchesne), 1759, p. 3.

49. *Ibid.*, p. 8. Charlton notes: "There are three interesting things about Sedaine's footnoted acting instructions. Firstly, they demand participation from both or all the actors on stage during the music; secondly, even in a solo an actor who is not required to sing may well be required to steal general attention by virtue of his mime; and thirdly, repeated sections of music (typically in an ABA aria form) are disguised or the effect of their repetition minimized by means of variety designated in the acting instructions." '"L'art dramatico-musical"', p. 242.

50. Printed libretto: Paris (Duchesne), 1771, p. 13.

51. These directions are included in the score, but not in the printed libretto: Paris (Duchesne), 1760, p. 4.

52. Printed libretto: Paris (Duchesne), 1771, pp. 32–33.

53. 'De la poésie dramatique', p. 159.

54. 'Essai sur l'opéra-comique', in *Le serrurier* (Paris, 1765), p. 44.

55. Precedents in earlier *opéras-comiques* should not be overlooked. While none of the original ensembles considered in the preceding chapter opened plays, a parody duet introduced the *pasticcio opéra-comique La bohémienne* (1754), following the design of its model, *La zingara*; and, in the earlier period, a duet opened Favart's *Le bal bourgeois* (1738). The remaining six works from the present period with introductory ensembles were: *Le soldat magicien* (Anseaume/Philidor, 1760); *Le milicien* (Anseaume/Duni, 1762); *Le rendez-vous* (Legier/Duni, 1763); *Tom Jones* (Poinsinet/Philidor, 1765); *Le jardinier de Sidon* (Pleinchesne/Philidor, 1768); and *L'amant déguisé* (Favart and Voisenon/Philidor, 1769).

56. *Blaise le savetier* (Sedaine, 1759) and *Le jardinier et son seigneur* (Sedaine, 1761). Additionally a duet in *Le sorcier* (Poinsinet, 1764) develops from a solo *ariette* opening the work. All three works were set by Philidor.

57. Printed libretto: Dresden (George Conrad Walther), n.d., p. 30.

58. Duni's manipulation of the text is described in Chapter IV below, p. 154.

59. Kopp notes that Sedaine "attempted a divided stage in *Les femmes vengées* [1775], in which action within two 'cabinets' is visible in addition to that in the central part of the stage," *Op. cit.*, p. 184.

60. As an ensemble of perplexity it is considered below, p. 137.

61. Charlton describes this tendency as "typical of the 1760s." "'L'art dramatico-musical,'" p. 250.

62. Smith: *Op. cit.*, pp. 123–124.

63. This positioning, however, differs in the two versions of the printed score. (See below, p. 152). It should also be noted that in his libretto Anseaume described the duet text as an 'Ariette', left the trio text unmarked, and headed the quartet text 'Quatuor'.

64. Charlton notes this technique at work in the *ariette*/duet opening *Le sorcier*: "The idea of simultaneity is ingeniously exploited as Agathe's undesired fiancé Blaise comes in unnoticed and sings his own words against those of her third strophe. In this way, with music as the means, the true face of each character is revealed before his/her interaction shows us a different side." "'L'art dramatico-musical,'" p. 245.

65. *Op. cit.*, pp. 265–267.

66. *Ibid.*, p. 214.

67. Text quoted above, p. 123.

68. Text quoted above, p. 124.

69. Other examples include the trio in scene vii of *Le jardinier et son seigneur*, in which the Seigneur sings with two of his tenants; and the septet in IIIxiv of *Le roi et le fermier*, which mixes a king and his courtiers with humble peasants.

Chapter IV

Musical Aspects of Ensemble Composition, 1758–1775

With the transition from the *pasticcio opéra-comique* to the *comédie mêlée d'ariettes*, the emergence of playwrights such as Sedaine and Anseaume, and moves towards far-reaching theatrical reform, there appeared three composers who were to steer the *comédie mêlée d'ariettes* through its first major phase of artistic expansion and establish the *opéra-comique* as a mainstream genre to be compared with the existing *tragédie-lyrique*. Egidio Duni (1708–75), Pierre-Alexandre Monsigny (1729–1817), and François-André Danican Philidor (1726–95) led a new generation of composers which also included: Paul-César Gibert (1717–87); Jean-Benjamin de La Borde (1734–94); Adolphe Benoît Blaise (*d*1772); Josef Kohaut (1738–?93); and François-Joseph Gossec (1734–1829). With these composers the *opéra-comique* developed from a light and essentially comic genre with sentimental overtones, to one relying increasingly on serious and more intense subject-matter. This progression, exemplified in works such as *Le roi et le fermier* (1762), *L'école de la jeunesse* (1765), *Tom Jones* (1765), and *Le déserteur* (1769), gave rise to the *drame lyrique* which embodied many of Diderot's philosophical precepts and which reached its apogee at the end of the century in works by composers of the Revolutionary era: Luigi Cherubini (1760–1842), Etienne-Nicolas Méhul (1763–1817), Nicolas-Marie Dalayrac (1753–1809), and Jean-François Le Sueur (1760–1837).

Duni was born in Matera, and was a contemporary of Vinci, Leo, and Pergolesi. He studied in Naples and had his first stage work—an *opera seria*, *Nerone*—performed in Rome in 1735. He travelled widely across Italy and Germany, also visiting London, and wrote several more *opere serie* before settling at the Parmesan court as *maestro di cappella*.

Working in a small Bourbon duchy evidently made Duni receptive to French tastes and prepared him for his future career in Paris, but there is little direct evidence to show that he began composing *opéras-comiques* while still at Parma.[1] He did, however, collaborate with Goldoni, who arrived at the court in 1756 and who, in 1762, followed Duni's earlier route to Paris.

Duni made his Parisian debut in 1757 with *Le peintre amoureux de son modèle* (initially disguised as a parody) and, before the emergence of Monsigny and Philidor in 1759, had presented a number of *opéras-comiques*. As a mark of recognition he was appointed music director at the Comédie-Italienne in 1761, and continued in this capacity after its amalgamation with the fair theaters the following year. He was acknowledged, not only for preparing the way for the *comédie mêlée d'ariettes*, but for synthesizing French and Italian musical styles in a manner that proved popular and enduring. For this he received fulsome praise from Diderot:

LUI
"J'ai été entendre cette musique de Douni et de nos autres jeunes faiseurs, qui m'a achevé.
MOI
Vous approuvez donc ce genre.
LUI
Sans doute.
MOI
Et vous trouvez de la beauté dans ces nouveaux chants?
LUI
Si j'y en trouve; pardieu, je vous en réponds. Comme cela est déclamé! Quelle vérité!
quelle expression!"[2]

Friedrich Melchior Grimm was, initially, another staunch supporter of Duni, remarking in his characteristically acerbic manner in connection with *Le procès* (1762): "on pourrait espérer de voir à la fin une école de musique en France."[3] Later, however, he felt that Duni's style became outdated, writing of *La clochette* (1766), for example:

"Notre bon papa Duni n'est plus jeune; les idées commencent à lui manquer."[4]

Monsigny left his birthplace in the Calais region at an early age to take up an administrative position in Paris. He soon made contacts in theatrical circles, and briefly studied composition before having his first work, *Les aveux indiscrets*, performed in 1759. Termed an *opéra-comique* (*intermède* in the score), this was a curious composition, originally comprising a French style of recitative intermingled with many short airs and relatively few ensembles, in the tradition of the *tragédie-lyrique*.[5] In later works, Monsigny was to adhere to the use of spoken dialogue and compose fewer, longer musical movements in closed forms. He is best remembered for his fruitful partnership with Sedaine, which lasted for nearly two decades and which was brought to a close only by the composer's failing health. (*Richard Coeur-de-lion* was originally intended for Monsigny and was subsequently offered to Grétry.) Partial loss of sight caused Monsigny to cease writing for the stage in the late 1770s. During the course of the early 19th century he received several marks of esteem, including the Légion d'honneur (1804) and admission to the Institut de France (1813).

Monsigny's major musical strength was as a melodist of unparalleled charm and spontaneity, which more than compensated for some limitations in motivic and rhythmic structure. His want of technique is often exaggerated, and Grimm's views should be treated with circumspection.[6] His concerted writing, as shall be illustrated, frequently belies these criticisms in terms of its contrapuntal daring and complexity, and the sensitivity with which so many of these pieces were shaped to dramatic exigencies.[7]

Philidor was a member of a famous musical family which had been in royal employ since the beginning of the 17th century. His early years were spent at the Versailles court, where he studied composition with Campra and also developed into a fine chess player. His musicianship was recognized early in his career by Rameau, after collaboration with Rousseau in *Les muses galantes*.[8] Shortly after this venture, however, he began a series of extensive travels and over the following decade established himself as one of Europe's leading chess players and an author of repute on this subject. On returning to Paris in the mid-1750s, he unsuccessfully sought employment at court: exposure to Italian music while abroad had had the effect of making his own style too italianate. Before long he had turned to the rising genre of the *opéra-comique*, and made his mark very shortly after Monsigny, with *Blaise le savetier* (1759). His long and fruitful career stretched over nearly four decades and included numerous comic compositions in addition to serious works such as *Ernelinde* (1767), *Persée* (1780), and *Thémistocle* (1785). One of his frequently-cited triumphs occurred in 1764 when, following performances of *Le sorcier*, he became the first composer to be acknowledged publicly on a French stage. Chess still continued to vie with his musical interests and eventually superseded these entirely.

Philidor was a composer with great technical capabilities. Grimm thought he cultivated harmony at the expense of melody,[9] but this opinion was later modified—"son style était lourd et pesant, il est devenu léger et plein de grâces"[10]—and Philidor quickly won the respect of others in the Encyclopedist camp. Diderot described him as "Le fondateur de la musique Italienne en France."[11] In the field of concerted writing, Philidor has generally been regarded as the most adventurous and experimental of the three composers in question, a view that should be tempered in the light of the discussion that follows.

From Libretto To Score:
Discrepancies in Ensemble Settings

The initial concern of this chapter is to discover how faithfully composers responded to the material with which their librettists presented them, and the extent to which modifications occurred in the process of setting ensemble texts to music. Generally, published librettos and scores match one another closely, even given the time-lag between the issue of each. Occasionally a given ensemble might be situated in different scenes of the libretto and printed score, this the result of composers either elongating or shortening the divisions established by the librettist. Thus, for example, the quintet "Vengez-nous" from *Le jardinier et son seigneur* featured in scene xvi of the libretto and scene xvii of the score. (The positioning of the ensuing duet was similarly affected.) More unusual were scenic discrepancies in the ensemble complexes of *L'isle des foux*. In the printed libretto the duet/trio/quartet aggregation comprised IIvi–viii. One version of the printed score appears to have followed this outline;[12] another, however, cast the complex within a single scene (IIvi).[13] The quintet (termed *Choeur*) following soon after ran from IIxii into IIxiii in the libretto, but was restricted in both scores to a single scene (IIx in the Paris: *l'auteur* version; IIxii in that engraved by Lefebvre and Ouvrard).

Score additions or omissions of complete ensemble texts found in libretto sources were comparatively rare. Duni included an extra trio (marked *Choeur*) to embellish the vaudeville closing *La clochette*, and

Monsigny a trio in IIIix of *La belle Arsène*. This latter materialized as the work was transformed from three to four acts. The several omissions in Duni's setting of *Le milicien* included a lovers' duet in scene vi and two texts involving a chorus (perhaps dispensed with through lack of effective chorus arrangements: see below, p. 163). The most significant omission, however, occurred in Philidor's *La nouvelle école des femmes*, whose final sequence in the libretto comprised a solo *ariette*, two duets (for two different pairs of lovers), and a quartet. The composer closed the opera using only the quartet text, creating a traditional dénouement ensemble and rejecting the opportunity to create a more adventurous large-scale ensemble finale.

Composers manipulated librettos more subtly by appropriating material surrounding the ensemble text, generally that which immediately preceded it. A duet by Duni in scene xvi of *La clochette,* for example, incorporated three lines from a previous section meant for recitative. Monsigny's quintet closing the first act of *Le déserteur* was more ambitious in integrating part of a solo *ariette* from the preceding scene with the ensemble text in that following, thus creating a substantial movement of 178 bars. In IIiv of *La nouvelle école des femmes* Philidor extended the content of ensemble texts in yet another way by building a single, substantial duet from two solo *ariettes* and a shorter duet text. Monsigny adopted a similar approach in IIx of *L'isle sonnante*, where a *duo dialogué* and a trio text were blended into one complete musical trio. Both are good examples of the "telescoping" principle in ensembles: the condensing of successive and disparate texts in order to throw characters into closer proximity and intensify the dramatic pace.

The same principles are seen at work in those librettists' texts transformed by the composer in order to accommodate more characters. Two of the most adventurous of these experiments were found in works by Monsigny: *L'isle sonnante* and *Le roi et le fermier*. In IIIxiv of the former, Collé included a *unanime* strophe for four characters followed by a trio text (in two columns) for three more, the whole rounded off with another verse for the original quartet. Instead of ranging one group of four against another of three in succession, Monsigny combined the three separate texts and the seven characters into one movement, the result being a complex septet and effective ensemble of perplexity. A still freer interpretation of the librettist's text at exactly the same point (IIIxiv) in *Le roi* also resulted in the creation of a septet. Sedaine had provided only five columns which were divided between eight characters: Le Roi, Lurewel,

Le Courtisan, Richard with Charlot and Rustaut, and Betsy with La Mère. This presentation could have suggested a five-part ensemble with various characters sharing the same musical line. Instead, Monsigny created seven musically distinct parts (Charlot and Rustaut sing together), the septet greatly enhancing the critical stage action at this point in the work: the recognition of the king. Sedaine discussed the dramatic and musical implications of this scene in the preface to his libretto of *Rose et Colas*. Here he described how, musically, the septet was able to prolong the recognition of the king, since the singers were able to enter in sequence and express their reactions simultaneously. Ordinary speech, he argued, would require an instantaneous, and therefore much briefer, reaction.

Similar experiments, though on a smaller scale, included the creation of a trio by Monsigny in IIIv of *L'isle sonnante* from a solo *ariette* with *à2* interjections, and the fashioning of a trio conclusion from two solo *ariettes* to scene ii of Philidor's *L'amant déguisé*. In these examples, as in those above, the purpose of the transformation was to economize and heighten the dramatic impact through ensemble singing. The reverse of this procedure might occur occasionally, but only one example was located from the 39 works examined. This was the second act finale to *L'école de la jeunesse*, marked *Choeur* in the libretto and designed for seven characters, but set as a sextet by Duni. (He dispensed with an ancillary character, La Marchande.) Since the ensemble nonetheless produced a fine dramatic climax, as described in the preceding chapter, the loss of one character had little effect.

That librettos and scores, with respect to ensembles, matched one another quite closely emphasizes the strong creative partnership forged between librettists and composers of the *opéra-comique* during the period in question. The changes implemented by composers were either quite minor, or were designed specifically to enhance particular aspects of a dramatic work. The extent to which the interchange between composer and librettist was a two-way process in partnerships such as Anseaume-Duni, Sedaine-Monsigny, and Poinsinet-Philidor (to say nothing of the many other poets with whom these three composers collaborated) remains, in the absence of comprehensive autobiographical sources, to be established.

The Musical Features of Ensembles

During the 1760s and beyond, Duni, Monsigny, and Philidor developed the character of ensemble composition through a variety of musical means. Chief among these were experiments with more complex and extensive formal structures and the development of more intricate vocal textures. A new autonomy in instrumental accompaniments also emerged, and more sensitivity in the choice of key and tempo is apparent. The sections that follow offer, first, an outline of general practice during the period in question and, where appropriate, focus on noticeable stylistic differences between the three composers. They then consider the extent to which these procedures and techniques were able to enhance the dramatic character of concerted writing.

Length and Form

One of the natural outcomes of developments in concerted writing during the 1760s was a substantial increase in the length of ensembles. Few (8%) were less than 50 bars long, and nearly half (49%) were over 100 bars. The average length of ensembles ranged between 75 and 150 bars, this accounting for almost two-thirds (63%) of the movements examined. However, 10% were between 150 and 200 bars long, four were over 200 bars long, and two were in excess of 300 bars. Philidor and Monsigny—the latter in particular—created the most extensive concerted movements of this period. Both the quintet (sc. iii) and closing duet in Philidor's *Blaise le savetier* were well in excess of 200 bars, as were trios by Monsigny in *Le roi et le fermier* (IIIi) and *Rose et Colas* (sc. ix). That in *Le déserteur* (IIxi) was 301 bars long, and the quintet in scene xvi of *Rose et Colas*, the most substantial of all the movements examined, stretched to a total of 384 bars. Significantly, only two of Duni's ensembles from the 14 works examined were longer than 150 bars.[14]

Binary and ternary forms accounted for nearly three-quarters (72%) of the concerted movements studied, but within these basic frameworks much variety was to be found. Bipartite ensembles, for example, had either AA[I] or AB designs, or experimented with two-tempo form. Some were elongated by codas. Tripartite ensembles were cast in ABA, ABA[I] or ABC patterns. The ABA[I] variety often followed a procedure whereby the voices cadenced in the dominant at the end of A and, after a bridge passage to B stressing the dominant, explored various secondary keys before returning to A^1 and recapitulating the opening section in the tonic. This harmonic design eventually formed the basis of the modern sonata form, and some ensembles approached this even more closely by exploring different themes in the A section, suggesting embryonic first and second subjects.[15] Ensembles cast in free or through-composed forms accounted for 18% of the total; the remaining 10% comprised several different types, of which rondo, chain, and single paragraph (for shorter movements) were the most common. Monsigny wrote a fugal trio in scene ix of *Rose et Colas* (again an innovative experiment by this musician), and Philidor a quartet in canon to open the final act of *Tom Jones*.

The approach of the three composers in question to matters of form and structure in ensemble composition varied considerably. Duni's concerted writing relied considerably on free forms, and over one-third of his ensembles displayed remarkable formal spontaneity. As Smith has recently pointed out with regard to this composer's lyrical movements in general:

> "Most of these are unique to the air in which they occur and seem to be organized as a series of tiny, conscientiously-declaimed musical phrases."[16]

Monsigny and Philidor favored closed forms to a much greater extent, the former showing a marked inclination for ternary patterns and the latter a preference for binary structures. Their experimentation with more open patterns was largely confined to duets and trios, this again contrasting with Duni's tendency to cast the majority of his larger ensembles in free forms.

How, then, were different formal structures used to theatrical effect, and what were the dramatic implications latent in each? Rudimentary sonata patterns allowed for more fluency and continuity in the musical structure of ensembles, since delineation of contrasting sections was achieved through continuous harmonic organization and modulatory patterns rather than through sectional punctuation by instrumental *ritournelles*. Musical expansion of this nature, and the emphasis on motivic contrast in particular, offered greater scope for contrasts of an emotional kind to be expressed, and this was in keeping with the emotive reality of associationist psychology.[17] The result was not merely the creation of longer and more substantial musical movements but also of longer texts exploring different psychological levels or embodying psychological development, which were hence progressive in character and far more significant in their dramatic function. The implications of the developing sonata form on the design of poetic texts were actually to reverse the usual pattern of the librettist's craft: no longer would poetry determine certain responses by the composer, as earlier in the century. Musical developments now obliged librettists to alter their approach, composer and playwright working from opposite ends of the spectrum to produce a final result in which all elements were satisfactorily blended.[18]

An idea of how sonata form principles worked to dramatic effect may be obtained through an analysis of the trio in scene vii of Philidor's *Le jardinier et son seigneur*. The main theme is introduced by the orchestra and then repeated by Le Seigneur, and is a lilting subject which expresses his appreciation of Fanchette, daughter of M. and Mme Simon, and which moves to the dominant. This key having been established at bar 33, Mme Simon starts with a more energetic line which is quickly taken up by her husband and fragmented between them. They are locked in argument, she worried by Le Seigneur's reaction to Fanchette, her husband encouraging his advances. Shortly afterwards Le Seigneur resumes his original theme, which is juxtaposed with that sung by the others. This progression cannot be construed entirely as a "second subject" section for several reasons: (i) it leads too rapidly on from the first, which is not sufficiently expansive to be considered a first subject; (ii) it does not contain a series of contrasting, interlocking "subjects," instead relying on the same theme for its duration; (iii) the main introductory theme continues throughout the whole of the first (i.e. A) section; and (iv) this main theme is lyrical and the second more vigorous, the opposite of later procedures within the sonata form pattern. However, the notion of thematic contrast within the A section, and within a precise harmonic pattern, is introduced and maintained. The second "part" of the A section remains in the dominant key (with brief excursions to the relative minor), and concludes with a six-bar bridge passage in the dominant which links to the next section.

The B section is short (22 bars) and offers harmonic contrast in the supertonic minor but little sense of thematic development. The argument between husband and wife continues. So, too, do Le Seigneur's amorous sentiments. The section ends with his protestations "C'est l'Amour," which blend skilfully into the recapitulation and give this a new dramatic urgency. M. Simon becomes even more ingratiating and his wife more adamant that the welfare of their daughter be protected. This is reflected in the music: Le Seigneur's opening theme is immediately juxtaposed with the second, rather than sung first as a solo, and the interplay between the three voices is accelerated to bring the trio to a resolute close. Thus the movement approaches the pattern of sonata form in its structural and harmonic plan, and it uses this framework to emphasize important dramatic points, although the style is as yet simple and lacking the much tighter degree of organisation found later in the Classical period.

Ensembles in free form, likewise relying for their coherence on wide-scale harmonic planning as well as on the interplay of successive rhythmic and melodic motives, provided another important means of achieving musical continuity and momentum. Open-ended structures facilitated in particular the creation of progressive ensembles, since the unfolding of these did not need to be geared to a specific musical time-scale or to considerations of sectional balance and symmetry. They were also well suited to ensembles of perplexity, in which the build-up of dramatic momentum was most effectively provided through a continuously evolving formal framework.

A study of ensembles written in free form shows that composers did not always use harmonic and thematic frameworks as a basis: they had recourse to several other compositional devices. In the duet/trio closing the first act of *Le roi et le fermier*—a fine and extremely substantial progressive ensemble 191 bars in length—the orchestra plays a vital role in ensuring musical coherence and continuity. Its atmospheric accompaniment paints a magnificent storm scene and the noise of a hunt in the background.[19] Interpolations of recitative, contrasting with sections composed in regular meters, allow the movement to build in substance, as does the later transition from duet to trio.

Sections in recitative serve as the basis for another lengthy through-composed progressive ensemble, in IIvii of *Le sorcier*. This is a duet which opens with solo recitative in C major and G major before developing into an *Andante* passage in E♭ major for the two singers, in which Julien conjures up demons to frighten his rival Blaise. In the ensuing *Presto* sections in B♭ major and F major, all punctuated with outbursts of recitative, Blaise is forced to relinquish his claim on Agathe, and Julien emerges as the victor. The duet totals 141 bars in all.

Le maître en droit provides another example of a progressive ensemble freely built from sections in contrasting tempos and meters. A duet in IIv begins *Andante* in $\frac{4}{4}$ time (including recitative in $\frac{3}{4}$) as Jacqueline, the governess aiding the two lovers, arrives on the scene and initially mistakes Le Docteur, the elder suitor, for Lindor. The music moves to a $\frac{2}{4}$ *Presto* as she realizes her mistake and arouses the suspicion of Le Docteur. In another brief section of recitative she quickly decides how to salvage the situation and the duet concludes with a return to $\frac{2}{4}$ *Presto* as she persuades Le Docteur to dress up in female costume. He acquiesces willingly, believing that Jacqueline is scheming on his behalf. (Quite why he is made to do this is a mystery that is solved only in subsequent scenes.)

Ensembles of perplexity cast effectively in free form include the quartet in scene xvii of *Sancho Pança*, in which the hero is suddenly beseiged by invading forces; and that closing Act I of *Le peintre amoureux*, which conveys a fine scene of confusion as the ageing painter is caught trying to win the favor of his young model. The sextet finale to *L'école de la jeunesse*, described in detail in the previous chapter, is likewise a vigorous ensemble with a freely-planned structure ensuring forward momentum.

Several ensembles in binary form, particularly the two-tempo AB (as opposed to the more repetitive AA^{I} variety), embodied apt translations of their dramatic setting, the change in musical style through use of contrasting speeds and meters mirroring sudden changes within the ensemble itself. The quartet closing Act II of *Le roi et le fermier* opens with the four characters prowling softly around a forest in $\frac{4}{4}$ *Andante*; with the entry of five guards (who, with the two gamekeepers, pounce on and capture the lord of the manor and his escort), the music changes to *Presto*, in ¢ time, and the finale concludes in a spirited manner. The duet for Colin and Nicodeme in scene xvi of *La clochette*, described in detail in the previous chapter, starts in g minor in $\frac{4}{4}$ time, and unfolds in a free recitative style as Colin leads his rival on and off the stage. When he succeeds in luring Nicodeme into the shed, the tempo changes to what is obviously a quicker $\frac{2}{4}$ in G major, and the piece closes with the captive's bitter complaints amidst Colin's unmitigated glee.

Two-tempo ensembles could also reflect psychological rather than physical change, for example the duet in scene iv of *Le rendez-vous* for an estranged husband and wife. In an opening dialogue, set in $\frac{2}{4}$ *Tempo comodo*, they wistfully recall the happier days of their marriage. A second, brisker section in $\frac{3}{8}$ returns the singers to the present and recalls their conflict. Another lovers' duet, in IIiii of *Le jardinier de Sidon*, begins in $\frac{2}{4}$ with Agénor misinterpreting his beloved's confusion as a sign of her waning love. She reassures him, and they are reconciled as the music moves to an *Adagio* in $\frac{6}{8}$ time.

Simple ternary forms were often the least conducive to dramatic continuity, and in some cases full-blown repetition of the opening section served to nullify the effect achieved in those preceding. The following critique of a duet by Monsigny, though focusing initially on the consequences of setting divergent sentiments to similar music, underlines the dramatic dilemma to which the repetition of complete sections at times gave rise:

> "Monsigny's preference for the lyrical over the dramatic often encourages him to set rhyming but contrasting points of view with the same or similar musical phrases ... the eventual result is that the two texts become unintelligible when delivered simultaneously ... When, however, a duet incorporates a change of heart or of opinion by one or both of the characters, Monsigny's decision to set rhyming texts with the same material sometimes proves stifling. In "Quittons, Lise, quittons ces lieux" (*On ne s'avise jamais de tout* scene 12), for example, both Dorval's initial proposition that they leave (mm. 7–12) and Lise's response "Non, restons, restons dans ces lieux" (mm. 13–18) are set to the same melody. Despite the lack of harmony of these two points of view, Monsigny concludes the first section of the duet with a conventional passage (mm. 21–26) in parallel tenths and thirteenths ... Having thus presented his material, Monsigny carries it through to the end of his duet, despite the lover's [sic] sudden decision to marry ... The lover's decision forces the recapitulation to express a unanimity of thought and purpose which had been absent in the exposition. The passage in tenths and thirteenths returns in the tonic with two nearly identical texts rather than two different points of view which had characterized the exposition. This characteristic ambivalence with respect to the matching of text and music can be annoying."[20]

The same criticism may be applied to other ensembles by Monsigny, for example the septet in IIIxiv of *Le roi et le fermier*, which opens with general astonishment following the revelation of the king's true identity (the passage is quoted in Example 4.9). As the ensemble progresses the participants recover their balance, but are made to reiterate their original feelings when the music repeats the opening section. This has the effect of diluting not only its impact but its credibility as well.[21]

Of the significant formal advances made during the period of Duni, Monsigny, and Philidor, the most important was that of increasingly tailoring the structure of ensembles to dramatic requirements. In terms of actual forms used, two important developments were the rise of a rudimentary "sonata" style and of free-form patterns, reflecting the wider harmonic scope of the early Classical period. Binary structures, common in both French and Italian opera of the earlier 18th century, were still favored, but composers had little recourse to the da capo form, although ABA patterns faithful to this principle were not uncommon.

The Structure of Finales

Linked to a discussion of form must be a consideration of the complexion of ensemble finales.[22] These divide into two categories: those concluding the entire work (hereafter called work finales) and those ending previous acts (hereafter referred to as internal finales). For convenience in the following discussion, "previous acts" will be referred to as internal acts. Of the 39 works examined, 19 were cast in two or more acts, and these afforded a total of 31 internal acts, 22 of which closed with ensembles.[23] The emphasis on concerted conclusions in *opéras-comiques* of this period emulated practice in the *intermezzi* and *opere buffe*, as suggested by the Parisian repertory of the Bouffons. It certainly contrasted with that in the *tragédie-lyrique*, whose acts generally terminated with lavish, large-scale *divertissements*.

Internal Finales: Two-thirds of the internal acts in question ended with either duets or trios.[24] Ensembles for four or more characters at such points in librettos were a particular speciality of Anseaume, who provided Duni with quartet texts closing the first acts of *Le peintre amoureux* and *Mazet*, and two sextet texts in *L'école de la jeunesse*. Sedaine wrote a quartet text for the second act finale to *Le roi*, and quintets to close the first acts of *Le déserteur* and *Félix*. Poinsinet created the largest internal finale of the period with the septet concluding Act II of *Tom Jones*.

Few of these act finales were particularly extensive. Half were under 100 bars long, and only one (the quintet closing Act I of *Félix*) extended beyond 200 bars. Monsigny created three of the most substantial movements: the duet/trio concluding Act I of *Le roi* (191 bars) and a quintet closing the first act of *Le déserteur* (178 bars), in addition to the aforementioned quintet from *Félix* (246 bars). (However, the second-act finales to all these works were much shorter: 61, 28, and 89 bars respectively.) Philidor was the most consistent of the three composers in that the majority of his internal finales were over 100 bars long.

All Duni's internal finales were through-composed, as were over half of those by Philidor. Monsigny, in contrast, cast such movements in either binary or ternary form, with the exception of the extensive duet/trio aggregation closing Act I of *Le roi*, which was through-composed. Their dramatic functions varied: most were designed either to create a climax or to emphasize a tableau. Less than one-fifth were progressive, whether embodying physical or psychological development. Add to this the fact that, with two-tempo exceptions by Monsigny ending Act I of *Félix* and Act II of *Le roi*, all the ensemble finales in question were cast in a single meter and tempo throughout, and it may be seen that the notion of the Goldonian chain finale (a movement comprising several contrasting sections and furthering the progress of the plot) had not yet found its way into the internal acts of the *opéra-comique*. Duni, Monsigny, and Philidor experimented to a certain extent with chain structures in ensembles within acts and, as will be illustrated presently, in finales closing works; but it was not until Grétry's *Le Magnifique* (1773) that interim act finales included more than a single change of meter, tempo, and key.[25]

Work Finales: Of the 39 works studied, 21 closed with a vaudeville finale. This was a far more common conclusion for one-act compositions than for multi-act works, accounting for two-thirds of endings in the former but only one-third in the latter. A vaudeville finale comprised several solo verses sung by individual characters in turn, and was interspersed with short ensemble (i.e. chorus) refrains and/or rounded off with a more substantial choral conclusion. Sedaine demonstrated a penchant for the vaudeville finale, seven of his ten librettos examined ending in this fashion.

Ensembles for individual soloists were also written to conclude works. One-quarter of the *opéras-comiques* examined ended in this fashion and these were just as often single-act, as multi-act, compositions. The most common type of ensemble in these circumstances was the quartet, which accounted for seven of the ten movements in question. (There was also one duet, one trio, and a duet developing into a sextet in *L'isle des foux*.) Additionally, quartets ran into vaudeville finales in *Les aveux indiscrets* and *La veuve indécise*.

These ensembles, with the exception of quartets by Duni in *Le peintre amoureux* and *Nina et Lindor*, were all in excess of 100 bars, the duet finale to *Blaise le savetier* being the most extensive (269 bars). Most were cast in binary, ternary or rondo structures. Two interesting exceptions were the duet/sextet in *L'isle des foux*, modelled upon a succession of contrasting sections in $\frac{3}{8}$ and $\frac{2}{4}$ *Allegro*, and the quartet in *Mazet*, which progressed from a $\frac{6}{8}$ *Allegro* in A major to an unspecified tempo in $\frac{3}{8}$ in the tonic minor before returning to the original key, tempo, and time signature. These therefore represented small steps towards the evolution of the chain finale in France although, like most of the other ensembles considered here, they were dénouement conclusions in which the characters sang of their happiness and extolled the power of love. The one progressive ensemble in this group was a through-composed quartet from *La fille mal gardée* which remained in the original key, meter, and tempo throughout.

Alongside work finales written as vaudevilles or for individual soloists were those experimenting with solo characters in more unusual combinations or in conjunction with an autonomous choral body. At this point, therefore, the complexion of the chorus in the early *opéra-comique* needs examining, as a number of intricate ensembles arising from the intermingling of solo and choral elements exist.

Librettos and scores of this period often apply the term "Choeur" (or "Choro"), especially at the close of works. Research using the *Régistres* of the Comédie-Italienne has established that until the middle of the 1770s, only a small number of extra singers were employed—and these on a very irregular basis—to form a chorus contingent.[26] Some might already have been part of the permanent company (Italian players or dancers); others could have been drawn from outside on a temporary basis (such artists were called *appointés*). Whatever the procedure, the chorus was variable in terms of size and the balance of voices. It was expected that the soloists themselves would form the backbone of the chorus in work finales.

For this reason, several concerted movements are designated "Choeur" by both librettists and composers when they are, in fact, genuine ensembles with each line taken by an individually named singer. For the purpose of the present study, such pieces are construed as quartets, quintets, sextets, and so on.[27] Problems of classification arise when soloists share lines, a procedure encountered in some work finales and, occasionally, in internal ensembles. *Mazet* ends with a quartet for five characters (two sopranos share a line), and *L'isle sonnante* concludes with a quartet whose four parts are distributed between seven characters. (The internal septet in Act III of *Le roi et le fermier* is scored for eight singers, two secondary charcters sharing a line.) If the sharing of parts is kept to a minimum (as in *Mazet* and *Le roi*), movements are still deemed solo ensembles and included in the present study. However, if most of the parts are duplicated, as in *L'isle sonnante*, the movement is deemed closer in design to a chorus, a decision justified by the fact that the vocal textures

Example 4.1 "Que voulez-vous?" *La fée Urgèle* IIiv (Duni, 1765)

164

Example 4.1 *(cont.)*

of such pieces are homophonic (i.e. choral) rather than built around the freer contrapuntal interplay found in solo ensembles. Inevitably, some pieces defy categorization: the internal ensemble in scene iv of *Sancho Pança* is a good case in point. This is for eight named participants who sing two to a part but have occasional solos. Only Sancho and Torillos, sharing the bass line, are principal characters; the rest (La Gouvernante, La Paysanne, Le Barbier, Le Tailleur, Le Procureur, and Le Paysan) may have been drawn from available chorus facilities. The vocal texture, when not dialogued, is predominantly homophonic, the movement therefore nearer in spirit to a chorus than to a solo ensemble.

Finales concluding works occasionally mixed soloists with an independent choral body to create mixed ensembles of the type first encountered in the opening chapter. *La fée Urgèle* closed with a duet superimposed over a chorus, the *Régistres* revealing that some five extra female singers and six extra male voices were paid for these performances.[28] (The work also included choruses in Acts I and III.) *La belle Arsène* also ended with a duet-chorus, the chorus having featured elsewhere in the work. The most ambitious mixed ensemble encountered was the finale to *Le déserteur*, which comprised an elaborate octet of principals and a four-part chorus. This was a substantial movement of 162 bars in which the soloists sang intermittently with the chorus, both factions either alternating, being superimposed, or blending with one another. Such mixed ensembles were rare in *opéras-comiques* of this period.[29]

Librettos by Favart (*La fée Urgèle, Les moissonneurs, La belle Arsène*) indicated the use of a separate chorus body most frequently, either for independent choruses or for mixed ensembles. Of the composers, credit should go initially to Philidor, and later to Monsigny, for extending its role.[30] It was only during the later 1770s and beyond that the size of the chorus at the Comédie-Italienne expanded sufficiently to allow composers to experiment freely with mixed ensembles and, consequently, create the substantial and elaborate large-scale finales that became the hallmark of later 18th- and 19th-century operas.

Vocal Textures

As Chapter II illustrated, the vocal textures of ensembles in the *opéra-comique* of the 1750s relied greatly on dialogue patterns established in Italian genres from the 1720s onwards, and had little recourse to the traditional homophonic style of writing cultivated in the contemporary *tragédie-lyrique*. This section examines, initially, the textures encountered in ensembles from the period of Duni, Monsigny, and Philidor, exploring in particular the ways in which these composers expanded the concept of dialogue in duets and larger ensembles by introducing more varied patterns and more contrapuntal elements. It then considers how vocal textures were increasingly designed with their dramatic effect in mind, illustrating with reference to individual ensembles how patterns were tailored to specific situations, thereby enhancing the ideas and events portrayed.

The Duet: Although homophony remained an important element of vocal texture, very few duets from this period sustained a note-against-note style throughout. The relatively few examples that were found used this texture for a deliberate dramatic effect and are therefore considered later.[31] One exception was the duet closing Act II of *Le déserteur*, whose homophonic style was the result of the imaginative juxtaposition of two separate songs.[32]

The dialogue duet, as described earlier, opened with long solos which were often imitative, the voices then alternating more frequently before merging at major cadences with sonorous intervals of thirds and

Example 4.2 "On la lui garde" *La veuve indécise* scene x (Duni, 1759)

sixths. During the 1750s this had become a common approach to duet composition in the *opéra-comique*. The pattern initially provided a structural framework, a means of attaining diversity within unity by allowing the voice parts to pursue different directions and yet blend coherently. Having served this purpose, the pattern was then modified by composers as they experimented with a less regular style weakening the framework. Thus the dialogue duet lost ground as a standard approach to duet composition and became simply one of a range of possibilities. By the late 1760s it represented a somewhat archaic style in comparison with other procedures because composers were increasingly tailoring textures to individual dramatic situations, the rigid framework of the dialogue duet often acting as an obstacle to this end.

Several examples of the orthodox dialogue duet are found in *opéras-comiques* of the period, particularly in works by Philidor, whose approach in this respect was often conservative. The five duets in *Sancho Pança* (1762) and four of the five in *Le sorcier* (1764) conform to a standard pattern, and similar examples are found in later works such as *Tom Jones* (closing Act I, IIIvi) and *Zémire et Mélide* (Iiv, Iv). The characteristics of basic dialogue texture are present in Example 4.1, the finale to Act II of Duni's *La fée Urgèle* (1765). After a six-bar orchestral introduction the voices enter, and although there are no extended opening solos, the two voices sing for much of the piece in strict alternation, as if a single melodic line were divided between them. Towards the end some overlapping takes place and the voices finally combine in sixths, two brief solo semiquaver interjections preparing the final concerted close, after which the movement is rounded off with an instrumental *ritournelle*. Dialogue duets of this nature were frequently cast in well defined forms (binary or ternary)—although this example is a single paragraph movement—and transcribed the librettist's text with little recourse to change or manipulation.

Example 4.2, reproduced complete from scene x of Duni's *La veuve indécise*, demonstrates how composers introduced a little more variety into traditional patterns and began to handle dialogue more spontaneously. Instead of the voices balancing in symmetrical answering phrases, the "conversation" between Mathurin and Colin, rivals in love, is rhythmically more sporadic. The parts soon overlap and join in thirds at an interim cadence. After a little more dialogue the voices combine again, this time rather unusually in unison. Another variation on the dialogue duet pattern occurs in Ivi of *Le déserteur*, where Jeannette leads Alexis to

Example 4.3 "Seroit-il vrai?", *Le déserteur* Ivi (Monsigny, 1769)

Example 4.3 *(cont.)*

believe that his beloved Louise is to marry someone else. The opening
part of this duet is quoted in Example 4.3. It begins in a standard fashion
with long imitative solos, after which the voices are immediately
juxtaposed (bars 24–9), this developing into a series of imitative responses
(bars 29–35). The pattern is repeated (bars 36–41 and 41–7) before the
opening solo material reappears in a new key to new text. After alternating
11-bar solos sung by Alexis and then Jeannette, the two parts are
juxtaposed, either in contrapuntal interplay or in cadential agreement, for
the remaining 48 bars of the duet. The movement is unusual in that it
extends to 133 bars without embracing a clear formal framework: it
eschews distinct sections with cadential climaxes punctuating the flow of
the music. While many ensembles in free form avoided the regular textural
contour characteristic of the dialogue duet, their textures generally,
however, remained indebted to the basic principle of this pattern in that
different sections began with solo statements and worked towards a
gradual blending of the voices.

On several occasions composers dispensed entirely with dialogue patterns and allowed other factors to shape duets. One example is the duet opening *Tom Jones*, in binary form. The first section comprises two lengthy, contrasting solos (one in $\frac{4}{4}$ and the other in $\frac{12}{8}$) which, in the second, are gradually blended. Segments of the two solos are sung in alternation, then overlap, and are finally juxtaposed in an extensive section bringing the duet to a close. The first section of a duet in ternary form opening *Le maître en droit*, Example 4.4, unfolds in an even more irregular manner. Its introductory solos suggest a dialogue framework, but from bar 14 onwards, after some interjections, this is entirely eschewed in favor of an unremitting juxtaposition of the two parts. The texture here is contrapuntal and independent, each voice following its own course; the cadential reconciliation at the close of the example is minimal. This style of duet is no isolated occurrence. Jacqueline and another character meet in Iv to sing another ensemble with a complex, differentiated texture.

Example 4.4 "Non, non, non, sortez" *Le maître en droit* Ii (Monsigny, 1760)

Example 4.4 *(cont.)*

Similar movements are found in IIiv of *Le roi et le fermier*, sung by two aristocrats as they attempt to find their way out of a forest at nightfall, and in IIix of *Tom Jones*, a confrontation between Sophie and her angry father.

At this point, the contrapuntal element in these ensembles should be distinguished from counterpoint as understood in its strictest sense: fugue, fugato, canon. The style of counterpoint most commonly cultivated in concerted writing of this period allowed the voices freedom to pursue independent lines which were not necessarily linked by identical or imitative themes. The vocal textures of only a very small number of ensembles were based on strict counterpoint: these were all larger ensembles and are therefore discussed presently. The term "counterpoint" and the adjective "contrapuntal" consequently refer here to a free style of juxtaposition in which the voices are blended in a spontaneous and irregular fashion, very often to conflicting texts, rather than to techniques

Example 4.5 "Ô Ciel!" *Le maître en droit* IIix (Monsigny, 1760)

Example 4.5 *(cont.)*

Note: The printed score (Paris *c*1760) notates the part of the 1er Écolier in the alto clef.

whereby the progression of the separate parts is dictated by set rules and procedures.

Trios and Quartets: Since trios and quartets were relatively few in number in earlier 18th-century French opera, their vocal textures had not evolved far beyond the bounds of homophony. During the 1750s these ensembles became regular features of the *opéra-comique* and the complexity of their vocal textures increased noticeably. Developments during the period of Duni, Monsigny, and Philidor continued the move away from note-against-note writing to the use of dialogue patterns and, eventually, of more complex and ambitious part-writing involving much counterpoint, both strict and free.

Example 4.6 "Est-ce lui?" *Sancho Pança* scene ii (Philidor, 1762)

Example 4.6 *(cont.)*

Trios and quartets, like early duets, were based initially on dialogue patterns. In its simplest form, a single melody was shared among the singers, the voices blending at major cadences: such was the contour, for example, of the trio in Ivii of *Le maître en droit*. Example 4.5 transcribes the first section of a more complex dialogue trio from IIix of the same work, in which Le Docteur is about to be discovered, in female attire, by his two *écoliers*. After eight bars of dialogue, the two upper parts briefly sing against the third before the dialogue resumes, and this is followed by a more pervasive juxtaposition of the three voices in preparation for the first major cadence. Thus, the overall contour of a dialogue framework is preserved, in that the texture of the trio progresses from the simple to the complex; but Monsigny has removed himself from the primary idea of a dialogue composition as a melody to be shared between three voices.

Several trios eschewed the conventions of dialogue structure and adopted other procedures. That in IIIi of *Le roi et le fermier* was a remarkable composition built around three extensive soprano solos which were slowly and effectively blended together in free counterpoint. Trios from *Rose et Colas* (sc. ix) and *Le déserteur* (IIxi), both by Monsigny, had fugal textures which were sustained throughout large sections of each movement.[33] Example 4.6, from scene ii of *Sancho Pança*, is a trio whose texture relies neither on dialogue contours nor on more formal

Example 4.7 "Découpez donc" *Le soldat magicien* scene xiv (Philidor, 1760)

contrapuntal structuring. After briefly alternating and overlapping through imitation, the two upper parts are combined, and when the third enters it is offset against the higher voices in more sustained imitative interplay, all three then being blended in preparation for the cadence in the dominant key closing the first section.

Since some 40% of the quartets studied were dénouement movements, many had recourse to homophonic textures. One example was that concluding *La nouvelle école des femmes*, whose predominantly *à4* texture was relieved only by some antiphonal duet writing and by moments of *à3* singing. Internal quartets were often based on dialogue patterns, and scene xiv of *Le soldat magicien* includes an excellent example of one conforming entirely to this principle. Its opening section is reproduced in Example 4.7. With the exception of an interim combining of voices in bars 18–20 and the concluding cadential homophony, the first section reads simply as one melody distributed among the four characters. The two subsequent sections of this quartet in ternary form are more complex and follow the dialogue principle of building up textural complexity during the different sections of a piece. In complete contrast to this is Example 4.8, an adventurous movement concluding Act II of *Le roi et le fermier* (described above, p. 159) in which the four parts are juxtaposed from the outset and retain this character throughout. Strict contrapuntal writing in quartets was attempted only once, by Philidor in *Tom Jones*: the quartet opening the third act was an unaccompanied canon for four voices.

Quintets, Sextets, and Septets: As there were virtually no precedents for ensembles of these dimensions in the *opéra-comique* of the 1750s, the development of textures for multi-voiced movements was largely the work of the three composers in question. Several of these were dénouement pieces concluding works and were therefore predominantly homophonic in texture. However, larger ensembles sited internally within works experimented from an early stage with dialogue and contrapuntal textures. To illustrate this point, Examples 4.9 and 4.10 transcribe the openings of two septets, the first from *Le roi et le fermier*, the second from *Tom Jones*. Whereas Monsigny's septet quickly combines all the voices in a fanfare-style opening, Philidor's introduces each more gradually and is more closely allied to dialogue principles. However, both develop into movements of contrapuntal complexity and have little recourse to choral, homophonic techniques.

Example 4.8 "Avance, suis-moi" *Le roi et le fermier* IIv (Monsigny, 1762)

Note: The printed score (Paris, 1763) notates the part of Le Courtisan in the alto clef.

Example 4.9 "Le Roi, Le Roi" *Le roi et le fermier* IIIxiv (Monsigny, 1762)

Example 4.9 *(cont.)*

Example 4.10 "C'est vous mon père" *Tom Jones* IIxi (Philidor, 1765)

Example 4.10 *(cont.)*

Oh je t'apprendrai ton de - voir, oh je t'apprendrai ton de - voir.

Generally, the more characters involved in ensembles, the more varied were the textural patterns to evolve. As well as dialogue and counterpoint, vocal duet, trio, quartet, or other combinations were possible, as was the offsetting of different character groupings. The quintet in scene xvi of *Rose et Colas* demonstrates this variety well. It occurs towards the end of the opera, at the point where the secret relationship of Rose and Colas is exposed to their prospective fathers by La Mère Bobi. The A section begins with dialogue, then balances Rose and Colas against their fathers before juxtaposing three lines in counterpoint. This gradually works up to a brief tutti cadence before the texture is reduced to a duet and builds up again to a dominant cadence. Subsequent sections variously combine the different factions as Colas prepares to make a dramatic exit, as Rose begs him not to leave, as the fathers realize their tormented states and La Mère Bobi the impact of what she has said and done. The ensemble is thus characterized by a varied combination of dialogue, contrapuntal, and homophonic elements.

With so many different types of ensemble and so many possible ways of combining voices, it is difficult to pinpoint precise chronological developments in vocal textures during this period. Neither is it possible to single out one composer as more innovative than another in this respect. Each played an active role in creating more unusual and enterprising textures. What was apparent, however, was a growing awareness of the need to shape vocal textures to dramatic requirements in concerted writing.

Ensemble textures could be designed for dramatic effect in two particular ways: either by differentiating individual lines in order to stress opposing moods and sentiments, thereby enhancing characterization; or by allowing the sum total of the parts (i.e. the overall effect) to reflect the spirit of the ensemble. Characterization through texture was but one means of rendering individuals more vivid through musical means. It proved most effective in smaller ensembles such as duets and trios, whose separate lines could be differentiated significantly and yet remain individually distinct. The tendency in larger ensembles was for groups, rather than particular characters, to be contrasted.

The duet opening *Le soldat magicien* introduces M. and Mme Argant occupied in a game of backgammon. Rapid, overlapping dialogue in this expository ensemble quickly portrays the testy, argumentative nature of the wife in comparison with her milder, but distinctly inattentive, husband. This is reinforced in the second section of the duet, where Mme Argant gives vent to a long tirade before abandoning her game and leaving the stage. Against this her husband can only offer timid interjections, and is finally left in a bemused state.[34]

In IIi of *La nouvelle école des femmes*, Finette, the maid, offers her mistress some unpalatable home truths. She has a lilting triplet line in the opening dialogue, which contrasts with the dotted rhythms sung by the ruffled Laure. These contrasting motives are juxtaposed at the end of the first section as the two women continue to hold opposing views. When Finette eventually decides to pander to her mistress the two are reconciled, and the duet ends with both singing in thirds. The texture of the trio in scene vii of *Le jardinier et son seigneur* also characterizes its participants well. The situation was explained in part earlier (see above, pp. 157–158): Le Seigneur, who has just arrived, is struck by the beauty of Fanchette, the daughter of M. and Mme Simon. Oblivious of his surroundings, he sings a steady, lyrical line throughout much of the ensemble, whereas husband and wife have more disjointed phrases. These enhance the portrayal of M. Simon grovelling to his lord while instructing his wife to behave, as she commands her daughter to remain by her side and berates her husband for his obsequiousness. The trio in the final scene of *Les deux chasseurs et la laitière* again contains some fine characterization through texture.[35] Perrette's reaction to the collapse of the cottage is one of amusement, captured in her quaver laughter on a single pitch in lilting $\frac{6}{8}$ time. Colas and Guillot are less amused: they embroider Perrette's line with slower complaints in dotted crotchets.

A quartet in scene ii of *Blaise le savetier* brings together husband, wife, and two bailiffs who are in the process of repossessing the couple's belongings. As Blaise and Blaisine continue their argument in rapid dialogue with rallying points, the two officials record the contents of the house to slow and pompous lines. Here the characterization is in pairs. In larger ensembles the pairs become groups. The septet in *Le roi et le fermier* (Example 4.9) offsets in separate textural patterns the astonished peasants—Betsy, La Mère, Richard, Rustaut, and Charlot—with two obsequious aristocrats, both groups contrasting with the regal figure of the recognized king who maintains a solo line.

Instances of textures chosen for a broader dramatic effect are found in two duets which deliberately opt for a homophonic style. The first of these, one of two duets in scene x of *La veuve indécise*, symbolizes the final reconciliation of two rival suitors. The second, in IIii of *Le jardinier de Sidon*, occurs at the point where the king Abdolonime, living as a gardener, decides to reveal his regal status so that his daughter may marry the man she loves. The note-against-note style in which much of the final section of the duet is set symbolizes acceptance of the change this decision will have on their lives.

Many complex contrapuntal textures serve the purpose of highlighting arguments and confusion. The trio in IIvii of *La nouvelle école des femmes*, for example, opens with dialogue as Mme Saint Fard attempts to contain her emotions.[36] When it is realized that she is Laure's rival, the texture develops so that contrasting motives are juxtaposed, reflecting conflicting interests and the confusion this revelation has caused. The quartet opening the final scene of *Les sabots* starts with the entrance of Mathurine, who is immediately regaled with three different versions of why the heroine's shoes were stolen and who was to blame. The texture includes much rapid dialogue and juxtaposition, and only snatches of agreement at cadence points. Indeed, such elaborate textures were the very essence of ensembles of perplexity, as in the sextet finale to the first act of *L'école de la jeunesse* and the septet in scene xviii of *Le bûcheron*, to cite but two examples from many.

One final point to consider is the role played by the standard dialogue duet and by the small number of ensembles written in strict counterpoint, both procedures dictating specific textural patterns. How effective were ensembles of this nature in portraying characters or specific dramatic situations? Some dialogue duets were able to accommodate given scenarios successfully within their pre-designed plan. That described above, in IIi of *La nouvelle école des femmes*, is a case in point. Another occurs at the close of the first act to *Tom Jones*, when Sophie tries to placate her aunt after having told her of her love for Jones. A fine musical contrast between the two voices is achieved: strident figures for one, a poignant chromatic line for the other. All this is articulated within the framework of the dialogue duet. There is, however, evidence of composers using this pattern indiscriminately on occasion. The duet opening Act II of *Les moissonneurs*, in which the heroine rejects an unwelcome suitor, is set in a straightforward dialogue that reflects neither the contentious dramatic situation nor the entirely divergent text provided by the librettist. (The text was not conceived in dialogue.) Similarly, two duets from *Le cadi dupé* (scenes ii and x) involved characters in conflict, but both ensembles conformed to a neat dialogue pattern. As discussed earlier, a noticeable tendency was to set arguments to increasingly contrapuntal and freer designs.

Whether strict counterpoint is antithetical to theatrical credibility is debatable. The few examples encountered in the concerted writing of Monsigny and Philidor may seem, to some, lacking in *vraisemblance* (a term explained fully in the following chapter), although their effect on the drama in wider terms is considerable, and as musical experiments they are certainly ingenious. The fugato style employed in the first section of the trio in IIxi of *Le déserteur* is perhaps the most successful example. It adds intensity to a remarkable point in the drama—the characters reacting to the news that Alexis is to be executed—but avoids sounding contrived because the movement is not a strict fugue. However, it may be argued that the fugal trio in scene ix of *Rose et Colas* presents the diverse emotions of the characers involved in too ordered and uniform a manner: Pierre and Mathurine are "staging" a vociferous argument which Rose observes in confusion. A final example, an unaccompanied drinking-quartet in canon from the third act of Philidor's *Tom Jones*, has been much acclaimed, one commentator writing:

"Its character fits the situation of the drama at this point. For it is only natural that four tipplers should sing without accompaniment, and should join in the song when the spirit moves them, a procedure that the canon adroitly suggests."[37]

Drinking songs in canon seem to have been traditional in England and Philidor, who knew London well, may deliberately have chosen to apply an English technique to an English subject. Indeed, in this quartet he achieves maximum *vraisemblance* in evoking the canonic aspect of the "English" catch.

Advances made in the design of vocal textures were among the most significant in ensemble composition of this period. Elaborate contrapuntal writing took root and flourished in movements with up to seven individual soloists. A great variety in the choice and design of vocal textures was established, as was the idea of delineating characters in concerted movements, or of emphasizing particular dramatic situations through texture. This responsibility was yet another breakthrough in ensemble composition, and one that contributed towards the enhanced status of such movements in operatic composition as a whole.

Text Manipulation

Earlier, this chapter described ways in which librettos were altered through the addition, omission or transformation of ensemble texts. This section concentrates more specifically on how the concerted texts used were treated by composers, and considers the devices they employed when setting ensemble texts to music.

Different portions of text were most commonly repeated, fragmented, and re-distributed among characters; the order of lines might be scrambled, some perhaps omitted, and short interjections occasionally interpolated. All these devices were used by Duni, Monsigny, and Philidor in their settings of ensemble texts. The difference, in this period, was that manipulation was carried out to a much greater extent than had previously been the case because the structure of librettists' texts was now so irregular. Whereas in the first half of the 18th century, in both French and Italian genres, the appearance of ensemble texts in librettos had frequently suggested certain approaches to composers, the use of columns and the disparate mix of these with varied dialogue patterns and solo verses gave composers a much freer hand in deciding how they were to be set. They were thus able to integrate the different voices of an ensemble in a far more

Example 4.11 "Entrès donc" *Le cadi dupé* scene vii (Monsigny, 1761)

Example 4.11 *(cont.)*

flexible manner, and this was a major reason for the emergence of intricate vocal textures during this period.

The degree of text manipulation varied from ensemble to ensemble: procedures were dictated by the structure of individual texts and by musical/dramatic requirements. Extensive texts were generally subjected to little manipulation since they had so many words to run through, one case in point being the duet/trio closing Act I of *Le roi et le fermier* which, as noted in the previous chapter, ran to three pages in the libretto. Short texts, on the other hand, were prime targets for manipulation in order to create musically substantial movements. This was frequently achieved through extensive repetition, as in the duet in scene v of *Blaise le savetier*, which comprised four lines divided between the two characters and extended to 115 bars in length.[38]

Dialogue texts offered opportunities for extensive manipulation since composers contrived that voices should combine in the concerted cadences ending individual sections. Thus lines sung by different characters were often juxtaposed. Indeed, not only dialogue texts, but more irregular structures were subjected to similar treatment so that the musical texture of an ensemble was able to progress from simple to complicated patterns and conclude with a concerted climax.

Text manipulation at its most pervasive is best illustrated through analysis of individual ensembles. Example 4.11 transcribes the trio in scene vii of *Le cadi dupé*, the text of which (a disparate blend of solo verses, dialogue, and parallel columns) was cited in the previous chapter (see above, p. 124). The opening four lines for L'Aga and Omar are first set in dialogue for these two characters and then juxtaposed; Le Cadi then appropriates lines 3 and 4 (originally sung by L'Aga) and these are blended with a repeat of Omar's line "Non, non, non." Different lines from two divergent couplets for Le Cadi and Omar are then set in dialogue before L'Aga joins with Le Cadi to sing against Omar in a brief moment of homophony. After Omar's solo has been heard once, the musical setting returns to the opening four lines of dialogue which are distributed among all three characters. The final part of the text (the three parallel columns) is set in homophony, each character confining himself to his own text but repeating this substantially (which has the effect of emphasizing each individual stance). Thus, in his musical setting, Monsigny draws on nearly every possible device of text manipulation—juxtaposition, transference, re-ordering, extensive repetition—to create an ensemble whose texture follows no set pattern and is well shaped to dramatic requirements.

Orchestral Accompaniments

The majority of accompaniments in ensembles by Duni, Monsigny, and Philidor retained the string textures established in concerted writing during the first half of the century. Instrumental accompaniments by Monsigny and Philidor were commonly in four parts, and those by Duni in either three or four parts (most often the former, with either the two violin parts, or the viola and bass lines, playing in unison).

Woodwind instruments (flutes, oboes, bassoons, horns) were added to enhance basic string textures. Duni frequently included oboes and, in concerted finales, oboes and horns. Monsigny's combinations of woodwind instruments were more varied: flutes paired with oboes, oboes with bassoons, bassoons with horns. Unlike Duni, he did not always reserve fuller orchestral textures for finales. Several internal ensembles in later works were accompanied by substantial forces: for example, four-part strings, oboes, horns, and bassoons in *Rose et Colas*, *L'isle sonnante*, *Le déserteur*, and *Le faucon*. Instrumentation in Philidor's ensembles followed similar patterns, regularly enhancing four-part string textures with horns and oboes; oboe and flute parts were sometimes combined and bassoons, on occasion, were added.

The main role of the orchestra was to support the voices, discreetly enhancing their lines, substantiating cadences, and filling in between sections. Gradually, however, a more autonomous character evolved. This led to the rise of expressive accompaniments and descriptive orchestral writing, features distinguishing ensembles in the *opéra-comique* of this period from those written earlier in the century.

Such instrumental writing might be designed with either specific or general effects in mind. Specific effects are found in the duet in IIii of *L'isle des foux*, where the palpitations of the lovers' hearts are represented by dotted semiquaver figurations (♪. ♪♪. ♪). A lovers' disagreement in scene ii of *Les aveux indiscrets* is enhanced by tremolo semiquaver motives and wide leaps in the string accompaniment. The backgammon duet in the first scene of *Le soldat magicien* includes several quick, catchy dotted figures depicting the movement of the dice. This pictorial effect was so striking that one contemporary observer wrote:

> "... il n'y a pas un coup de dez dans le cornet, sous la main & dessus la table, qui ne soit rendu, & où, jusqu'au genre de mesure, tout est analogue au mouvement de l'action, ou à l'expression des paroles."[39]

Another ensemble by Philidor containing striking pictorial effects is the trio finale to Act I of *Le maréchal ferrant*, in which the blacksmith's sister is harangued by two local workers regaling her with their animals' problems. Donkeys' brays are highlighted by leaps of two octaves in the violins, and the clip-clop of horses' hooves is portrayed in dotted rhythms.

Accompaniments aiming to paint a general picture sustained their effects throughout an ensemble. The duet/trio closing Act I of *Le roi et le fermier*, mentioned earlier, was particularly striking in this respect. A growing storm is first painted in the music by chromatic motives, tremolos, careful dynamic markings including frequent crescendos and diminuendos, and by swelling semiquaver scales. The sounds of a distant hunt are then introduced with horns playing cross-rhythms in $\frac{6}{8}$ against the normal $\mathbf{C}$ tempo, and the passing of huntsmen echoed in this figure:

Such detailed effects in accompaniment motives were also used to advantage in the depiction of character. Composers experimented with contrasting orchestral colors in order to highlight differences in mood or personality, as for example in the duet in scene xii of *Sancho Pança*: bassoons accompany the hero's excited quaver line while Le Docteur sings with violins in slow, pompous minims. In a trio from *La belle Arsène* (IIIix), the hero's lament is set against pizzicato strings while interjections from his beloved (remaining aloof) are accompanied by flutes and bassoons. Duni's ambitious septet in IIv of *L'école de la jeunesse* has Le Chanteur singing his *chanson* to gentle running semiquavers on the harp and harpsichord, only to be interrupted by violent exchanges at the card table accompanied by strident string writing.

The trend during the period in question was towards more individually shaped and expressive orchestral accompaniments in ensembles (as, too, in solo *ariettes*). Many more descriptive musical details might be cited. Such devices were most actively exploited by Philidor, but were also present in works by Monsigny and Duni; they provided a further means of introducing more realism and intensity into the *opéra-comique*.

Keys, Tempos and Time Signatures

In their choice of keys, tempos, and time signatures all three composers displayed strong individual preferences. Duni cast some 80% of his ensembles in major keys, favoring bright tonalities such as G, D, and A, whereas Monsigny and Philidor wrote a higher proportion (around 40%) of concerted movements in the minor and generally explored a wider range of keys. Philidor showed a preference for flat keys in both the major and minor; Monsigny, like Duni, favored sharp keys.

Two-thirds of the ensembles studied were written in quick tempos (Duni 66%, Monsigny 75%, Philidor 60%). *Allegro* proved the most popular designation (*Presto* and *Prestissimo* in ensembles by Monsigny), although French equivalents such as *vite*, *vivement*, and *gayement* were still used. In several cases where an indication of speed was absent, the character of the vocal lines and the orchestral accompaniment suggested a brisk pace. Duni's scores are more frequently wanting in this respect than those by Monsigny or Philidor.

Duni's indication of slower tempos was extremely varied: *Andante*, *Gracioso*, *Amoroso*, *Tendrement*, *Grave*, and *Lent* (one example of each being encountered). Thus, while such terms all denoted a more sedate style of ensemble, there was no consistency in how these were employed. Monsigny favored *Andante* and *Amoroso* markings (a few movements were labelled *Moderato*). For one ensemble, an expressive trio in IIIix of *La belle Arsène*, the term *Andanté poco lamentabilé* was used, showing the beginning of a concern that tempos should indicate not simply speed, but mood as well. Concerted movements in comic works increasingly reflected poignant situations as well as the usual gay, lively scenarios, and with Philidor this tendency is very pronounced. His scores contain the lowest proportion of ensembles with *Allegro* (or similar) markings.

Duni used either $\frac{2}{4}$, $\frac{3}{8}$ or $\frac{6}{8}$ time signatures, sometimes $\frac{4}{4}$ but never $\frac{3}{4}$ in his ensembles. Monsigny preferred $\mathsf{C}\!\!\!\!/$, $\frac{2}{4}$ or $\frac{4}{4}$. He wrote a small proportion of ensembles in triple time but, in contrast to Duni, avoided compound time. Philidor's choice of time signatures was the most varied: $\mathsf{C}\!\!\!\!/$, $\frac{4}{4}$, $\frac{2}{4}$, $\frac{3}{4}$, $\frac{6}{8}$, and $\frac{3}{8}$ were all commonly encountered.

It is also important to consider changes of key, time, and tempo within ensembles. These were limited to a small proportion of movements (approximately 14%), the majority of which were cast in two-tempo form, i.e. containing only one change in key, time, and/or tempo. The remainder comprised three contrasting sections, although quite often the third was a recapitulation of the first. Two exceptions to this pattern are found in Philidor's *Zémire et Mélide*. The duet in Iv opened in A major ($\frac{4}{4}$ *Poco Lento*) and progressed to the tonic minor ($\frac{3}{8}$ *Andante*) before returning to the major ($\frac{3}{8}$ *Allegro*). A second duet closing IIii began in Eb major ($\frac{4}{4}$ *Larghetto*), moved to f minor ($\frac{2}{4}$ with no tempo indication), and concluded in Eb major (¢ *Allegro assai*). These ensembles, alongside the finale to *L'isle sonnante* (E minor, ¢ *Allegretto*, followed by four sections alternating between $\frac{4}{4}$ *Grave* and ¢ *Allegro*, all in the tonic major), represented the only serious attempts at chain constructions in concerted movements during the period in question.

What was apparent in this small group of ensembles, however, was the tendency to tailor such changes to dramatic effect so that they actively enhanced the mood or situation of the piece. Many two-tempo structures depicted developments in the stage action or psychological changes within ensembles, as discussed above: for example, duets in scene xvi of *La clochette*, in scene iv of *Le rendez-vous*, and in IIiii of *Le jardinier de Sidon* (this ensemble also oscillating between the tonic major and minor to underline the anxious discourse of the two lovers, their questionings, and their misunderstandings).[40] Other examples may be cited: the duelling-duet in scene ix of *Sancho Pança* which begins with both characters feigning bravery in a *Moderato* section, only to abandon their swords and resort to the safer medium of fists in the ensuing *Allegro* section. In IIxi of *Le déserteur* all three components are altered: Louise rushes back to her lover, having discovered that he is to be executed, and is joined by her father in an opening ¢ *Prestissimo* section in c minor. As all three resign themselves to the inevitable the music moves to $\frac{3}{4}$ *Lento Amoroso* in the tonic major, a poignant reflection of their unhappy situation. One of the most innovative experiments in this area was undoubtedly that carried out by Philidor in the opening duet of *Tom Jones*, a much-cited ensemble. Here the heroine, Sophie, sings in $\frac{4}{4}$ while her maid, Honora, sings in $\frac{12}{8}$, these conflicting time signatures resulting in an adventurous juxtaposition of very different themes and figurations.

Changing and contrasting keys, tempos, and time signatures for dramatic effect in ensembles were, therefore, another important development during this period. The tendency in earlier concerted writing—with exceptions in the field of the *intermezzo* and the *opera buffa*, discussed in the opening chapter—was for changes to be more arbitrary in function. Indeed, in the *tragédie en musique* changes in meter (to accommodate the demands of French prosody) were virtually the only type encountered: tempo and tonality were rarely altered during the course of an ensemble. That the *opéra-comique* should adopt a far more flexible approach was in keeping with one of its main aims: that of creating a more dramatic and dynamic style of theatrical representation.

Vocal Groupings

This section considers the vocal ranges of characters grouped together in ensembles and the overall blend of voices in duets, trios, quartets, and larger movements. Before such observations are recorded, however, various anomalies should be noted. Firstly, some scores did not consistently notate a character's part in the same clef. The roles of Colin in *Le rendez-vous*, and of Charlot in *Le roi et le fermier*, used both tenor and bass clefs. This links to a second anomaly, in that the clefs used did not necessarily reflect the character's voice type or range. For example, roles notated in the bass clef frequently extend up to f^1 or g^1. In the present century such a tessitura would indicate a baritone voice, a type yet to be recognized during the period in question.[41] Conversely, several roles notated in the alto clef fall within what is now considered a tenor range and may therefore have been sung by high tenors rather than by *haute-contres*. The interchangeability of tenor and alto clefs is evident in Example 4.5, where the role of the first *écolier*, with a range spanning *d* to g^1, is notated in the alto clef whereas that of Le Docteur, whose range is one tone less, *d* to f^1, appears in the tenor clef. To confuse matters further, some scores maintained the earlier 18th-century Italian practice of writing male roles in the soprano clef (*Nina et Lindor* and *La fille mal gardée*, both by Duni, followed this practice); and the opposite could prevail, the role of Mme Bobinette in *La fille mal gardée* (sung by one "Me. Champville") being notated in the bass clef.

Combinations of singers in concerted movements are most usefully analyzed, therefore, in terms of the overall balance they achieve between male and female voices. The clefs chosen by composers indicate, to a certain extent, the spread of voice types within an ensemble, but do not necessarily dictate the tessitura of each. In particular it should be noted that, in ensembles using two or more sopranos, tenors or basses, the voices are not necessarily equal in range.

In their use of clefs in concerted movements, the three composers studied differed in one significant respect: Monsigny retained the alto clef whereas Duni and Philidor made use of it only rarely.[42] Duets for male/female pairings by these two composers favored combinations of soprano/tenor or soprano/bass, the former more popular than the latter. Monsigny continued to write duets in soprano and alto clefs as well. Duets for two female singers were always for sopranos; the majority of those for male singers were for tenor/bass combinations, or for two basses, occasionally for two tenors. Combinations in Monsigny's operas used alto clefs in conjunction with tenor and bass clefs as well.

Trios involved various permutations of soprano, tenor, and bass voices, although those by Monsigny were more diverse since they also included singers whose parts were notated in the alto clef. Those written for characters of the same sex grouped together either soprano voices or combinations of tenors and basses.[43] Quartets tended to balance male and female voices in clef combinations of SSTT, SSTB, SSBB or, in the case of Monsigny, SSAT and SSAB. Ensembles by Philidor, however, often favored bottom-heavy combinations in which male voices outnumbered female voices: STTT, STTB, STBB. The now-familiar SATB distribution of clefs remained to be established as a regular pattern in internal ensembles and was restricted to dénouement movements, which were often general choruses. In quintets SSATB was a popular combination. Ensembles for six or more voices were frequently dominated by tenors and basses: STTTTB in sextets (but also SSSTTB) and SSTTTTB, SSSTTBB, and SSSTTTB in septets.

Characterization

Characterization in ensembles was an idea new to French opera in the second half of the 18th century. By this is meant the delineation and emphasis of individual moods, temperaments, and personalities. The statuesque style of the *tragédie en musique* had not lent itself to this practice and serious characters, as stressed in the opening chapter, were presented less as individuals than as projections of different emotional states. Earlier sections in the present chapter have dealt with the ways in which characterization could be emphasized in ensemble composition: through certain formal structures, through patterns of vocal texture, through instrumental writing and orchestral effects, and through careful contrasts of tonalities, meters, and tempos. It remains to point out that characterization could be heightened through recourse to more general musical means such as rhythm and melody, many individual examples of which are easily discernible in the ensembles studied.

Why should ensembles prove such an effective vehicle for characterization? In combining different individuals within the same movement and allowing singers to interact in close proximity, they allowed contrasts to be more vivid and much more immediate. Certain techniques—conflicting vocal textures, contrasting time signatures or tonalities, for example—were not possible in solo *ariettes*: they could only follow on in successive sections or be elaborated in the orchestral writing. The idea presented at the beginning of Chapter III was that one of the unique features of the ensemble was its ability to juxtapose characters for a variety of dramatic purposes. The various sections of the present chapter have illustrated how this was made possible, and how techniques were expanded, in the *opéra-comique* of the 1760s and early 1770s.

Duni, Monsigny, and Philidor, representing the first major generation of *opéra-comique* composers, succeeded in introducing vital new elements into ensemble composition in conjunction with their many literary collaborators. Working from infinitely more complex texts, they experimented with wider-ranging formal structures and with more intricate patterns of vocal textures; they also created expressive accompaniments and showed sensitivity in their choice of keys and meters. The most striking development of this period, however, remains the frequency with which many different types of ensemble were introduced into individual works, and their much greater dramatic significance within these. The impact of the Bouffons' repertory on concerted writing in the *opéra-comique* of the 1750s was considerable; but developments in subsequent decades were (with the obvious exception of Duni) the inspiration and innovation of native artists who came to the genre just as the transition to the *comédie mêlée d'ariettes* had been effected. Their experiments and achievements expanded on earlier 18th-century styles of Italian comic concerted writing considerably and, most significantly, engendered a "basic belief in the ensemble as a modern resource, promoting musico-dramatic realism."[44]

To conclude, the *opéras-comiques* of other composers should be taken into account, although only a brief synopsis of ensemble composition in some dozen works is undertaken here. Some of the most notable contemporaries of Duni, Monsigny, and Philidor were mentioned at the start of the chapter: La Borde, Gossec, Kohaut, Blaise: others were Charles-Guillaume Alexandre (*c*1735–87/8), and Pierre Gaviniès (1728–1800). These composers wrote few large ensembles, restricting themselves to quartets and quintets, and concentrated mainly on duets and trios. Their librettists—Favart, Harny de Guerville, Quétant, P.-R. Lemonnier—made provision for fewer concerted movements in each work (on average four or five), *Le prétendu* (Riccoboni/Gaviniès, 1760) being exceptional in containing nine ensembles within its three acts. (It is, significantly, the only surviving *opéra-comique* written by this composer.) Several works opened with duets, emphasizing the importance of the expository ensemble. Many of the remainder were tableau ensembles. Very few progressive pieces were written, but one of the most adventurous in this respect was a trio finale closing the second act of *Le prétendu*. This was also a substantial chain construction in five contrasting sections (a minor $\frac{4}{4}$ *Moderato*, F major $\frac{3}{4}$ *Adagio*, d minor $\frac{4}{4}$ *Allegro moderato*, a minor $\frac{4}{4}$ *Allegro staccato*, b minor $\frac{4}{4}$ *Presto*), although the length of the last (217 bars) was disproportionate to the rest and the dramatic development of the whole ensemble confined to two of the characters successfully persuading the third to accept the fact that they were lovers. Another progressive ensemble was a quintet from the closing scene of *La meunière de Gentilly* (Lemonnier/La Borde, 1768), an extensive movement of 223 bars but cast in a single tempo throughout.

The composers in question experimented with a variety of musical forms, binary structures accounting for 40% of the ensembles studied (few examples of two-tempo form were found), and simple ternary patterns for a further 20%. The remainder were either through-composed, set in verse structures (where an ensemble stanza followed two solo verses), or were cast in rondo, chain or single paragraph form. The italianate dal segno, a type uncommon in ensembles by Duni, Monsigny, and Philidor, was encountered on occasion: for example in *Georget et Georgette* (Alexandre, 1761) and *Isabelle et Gertrude* (Blaise, 1765). Vocal textures mirrored practices described previously: dialogue and contrapuntal juxtaposition were used extensively. In the field of orchestral writing Gossec's achievements should be noted. His accompaniments, in both *ariettes* and ensembles, revealed an incomparable richness of harmonic language, with unusual prominence being given to woodwinds and lower strings. One of his most remarkable achievements was a storm scene linking the first and second acts of *Toinon et Toinette* (1767).

It is worthwhile considering, as part of a wider conclusion, the effect of developments in *opéra-comique* ensembles on those in the *tragédie-lyrique* which was still, during the period in question, considered the main operatic genre in France. Some 33 new French works were

performed at the Académie Royale de Musique between the premières of
La serva padrona and Gluck's *Iphigénie en Aulide* in April 1774,
representing an average of only one or two new pieces each year.[45] This
contrasted with the speed with which fresh productions were mounted at
the Comédie-Italienne and, prior to their amalgamation with this
establishment in 1762, the fair theaters. The relatively few *créations* at the
Académie were bolstered, as earlier in the century, by numerous revivals,
these numbering between four and five each year. Works by Rameau were
restaged on over 30 different occasions, and several *tragédies* by Lully
continued to enjoy considerable popularity almost one century after they
were first written. The fundamental character of the *tragédie* did not
therefore undergo any substantial change. Works by the most successful
contemporary composers (the Rebel/Francoeur team, Dauvergne,
Mondonville) showed few traces of experimentation, and novelty was
suppressed, or at least frowned upon, as reviews of Monsigny's
ballet-héroïque, Aline, reine de Golconde testified:

> "Cet Opéra est d'un genre assez nouveau sur ce Théâtre, & toute innovation,
> même avantageuse, est ordinairement contredite."[46]

The character of concerted writing in French serious opera
therefore continued substantially unchanged from patterns established in
the first half of the 18th century. The number of ensembles in each work
remained low, and duets continued to predominate. Trios and quartets
accounted for less than 10% of the total encountered, many of these being
confined to unusual works such as *La coquette trompée*—a one-act
comédie (studied in Chapter II) later interpolated as an *entrée* in
Dauvergne's *ballet, Les fêtes d'Euterpe* (1758)—and Philidor's
tragédie-lyrique, Ernelinde (1767; revised 1769 and 1773), considered
presently. There was little experimentation in terms of character groupings
and expressive types of ensembles: two-thirds of the duets united lovers
and the remainder, with few exceptions, were vengeance duets,
confrontation duets or duets of rejection, all well-established types. That
concerted movements should contribute actively to the unfolding of the
plot and serve a variety of effective dramatic functions, were objectives
towards which the *tragédie-lyrique* of this period did not aspire.

The majority of ensemble texts were still *unanime* quatrains which
were set to predominantly homophonic textures. Great importance
continued to be attached to the clear expression of the poetic text. Few
texts were divergent in character, and the underlying unanimity of the

sentiments expressed offered little scope for contrapuntal writing. Librettists likewise experimented only rarely with dialogue patterns, with the result that dialogue textures were uncommon but not untried. Duets by Dauvergne in Iv of *Enée et Lavinie* (1758) and by La Borde closing Act I of *Ismène et Isménias* (1763), for example, included dialogue singing. Significantly, both composers were versed in the comic idiom. The binary form in which so many ensembles from the earlier half of the century had been cast still proved popular, accounting for around 50% of the movements studied. Ternary, rondo, and single paragraph structures were also common; through-composed and chain forms explored in the *opéra-comique* were rare.

A brief overview of Rameau's concerted writing beyond 1752 largely corroborates the above observations, although certain ensembles in *Les Paladins* (1760) are distinctively unusual. Its four duets and two trios embraced a wide variety of dramatic situations and the majority experimented freely with contrapuntal textures. The confrontation between Atis and Orcan, rivals for the hand of Argie, in Iv, results in a fine divergent duet sustaining a contrapuntal texture throughout. None of Rameau's ensembles from this period displayed any italianate influences derived from imported comic genres.

If, however, the serious works of composers who also wrote *opéras-comiques* during this period are considered, some interesting patterns come to light, particularly in the case of Philidor's *Ernelinde*, which consistently transferred techniques of concerted writing developed in the comic genre to serious compositions. *Ernelinde* was also innovative in other respects, one contemporary review noting that:

> "Les sentiments [du public] ... sont encore tellement partagés, sur-tout quant à la musique en général & au genre de nouveauté qu'elle renferme."[47]

The history of this *tragédie-lyrique* is complicated. Initially given 18 performances at the Académie in 1767, it was restaged as *Sandomir, prince de Dannemarck* in 1769 when public response was more favorable. Poinsinet's libretto then went to Sedaine, who changed the structure of the work from three to five acts. This revision was given a flamboyant staging at Versailles in 1773, and returned to the Académie in 1777 where it met with sustained public acclaim.

Librettos to all four versions, the printed score pertaining to the first revision in 1769, and a manuscript score (*F-Po*) of the 1777 version all testify to numerous changes in the choice and distribution of ensembles.[48]

The most innovative ensembles were those from Acts I and II of the 1767 and 1769 versions. The opening duet was expository in function, a device inherited from the *opéra-comique* but as yet untried in the *tragédie-lyrique*, a confrontation between the heroine and her father. Poinsinet's text was cast in strict dialogue, around which Philidor created a texture based on dialogue principles. Each section opened with contrasting solos previously introduced in the initial *ritournelle*. These solos were gradually juxtaposed, the voices then merging for the cadence concluding the first section. This progression is illustrated in Example 4.12. The second section (the duet is in binary form) followed a similar pattern. Text, texture, dramatic function, the sentiments expressed (sharply divergent), and the combination of father and daughter (unprecedented, as far as it is known, in the *tragédie-lyrique*) were uncharacteristic features of concerted composition in the serious genre: they were all directly lifted from contemporary practice in the *opéra-comique*.

The duet following shortly afterwards in Ivi (IIi/ii in the five-act versions) was another innovative movement. Structured around a divergent text, it had a dialogue texture and was sited at the end of the first act (1769), thus serving (in Poinsinet's libretto) as a climactic ensemble. The combination of two rivals for the hand of Ernelinde, making this a male confrontation duet, was an expressive type previously used in the *tragédie-lyrique*, but its novel musical style resulting from its dialogue character was strongly felt and was described in the *Mercure* as:

> "d'un goût peu connu jusqu'ici sur le théâtre de l'opéra, mais du plus grand effet."[49]

The quartet from IIviii of the 1767 and 1769 versions was an intricate ensemble of perplexity, perhaps one of the first to feature in a *tragédie-lyrique* and, therefore, a bold experiment. It combined the plighted lovers, Ernelinde and Sandomir, with Rodoald, the sympathetic father, and the raging Ricimer. As the heroine voices her misfortune, she is comforted by Sandomir who also threatens his rival. Meanwhile, Rodoald upbraids his deserting troops (including Ricimer in his general invective) and expresses concern for his daughter. To complete this picture, Ricimer instigates his revenge with brutal commands to his soldiers. Not surprisingly, the ensemble was based on an intricate text by Poinsinet. The texture was modelled around dialogue patterns in which two musical sections built up from simple solos to complicated

Example 4.12 "Quoy vous m'abandonnés mon Pere" *Ernelinde* Ii (Philidor, 1767)

Example 4.12 *(cont.)*

juxtaposition. The result was a highly dramatic number creating a fine climax in the penultimate scene of the second act.

The three remaining ensembles in the 1769 score were less obviously modelled on practice in the comic sphere although each was unusual in various ways. The trio moved from IIIv (1767) to IIIiii (1769)—subsequently IViv—was a reflective tableau ensemble for the two lovers and a sympathetic third party, an expressive type found in earlier *tragédies*. However, although the sentiments of the three characters stemmed from a common denominator (all were united in their desire for retribution), each was given a different nuance so that three distinct personalities and emotional predicaments emerged. Ernelinde gives herself over to complete despair, having been forced to choose between saving the life of her father and that of her lover. Rodoald shows more optimism in preparing to launch one final attack against his enemy, and is supported in this cause by Sandomir. The vocal texture of this trio was not, in contrast with the three previous ensembles, structured around dialogue patterns, and instead involved much solo singing for Rodoald with occasional *à2* interjections from the lovers; however, the final stages of the ensemble built up through imitative points to a concerted conclusion.

With the departure of Rodoald, the lovers give vent to their anguish in a traditional duet which, significantly, was the shortest ensemble (45 bars) in the 1769 score. However, Philidor embraced modern practice in creating a dialogue texture, albeit a very straightforward one: the two sections in which the duet was cast progressed quickly from alternating solos to cadential homophony and avoided complicated vocal interplay.

The last ensemble, the trio finale, was also brief (five bars longer than the duet) and predominantly homophonic in texture, as befitted a dénouement ensemble. The two lovers were joined by Ernelinde's father, a benevolent third party, in a common combination and expressive type of ensemble during the 18th century.

The three new ensembles in the 1777 manuscript (two introduced in the 1773 five-act version and a third added to the 1777 revival) were also less adventurous in style. The trio added in IIIvii replaced a solo aria for Rodoald, but since it was extremely short (29 bars) and retained much solo singing for that character (with brief *à2* interjections from Ernelinde and Ricimer) it largely preserved the character of the original solo. The replacement quartet, now sited in IIIviii, was a poor substitute less than half the length of the original and with a much simpler vocal texture. Moreover, the sentiments of the four participants were greatly simplified, the quartet thereby losing its impact as an intricate ensemble of perplexity. The new quartet in the 1777 version was more perceptively shaped, although in contrast with the finales it replaced was not sited at the end of the work: it was a fine climactic ensemble leading into recitative in which the crisis was finally resolved. Such continuity was in itself an unusual feature. The vocal texture, too, was more complex, although involving only three of the four characters for much of the movement, Ricimer's contribution being limited to a short interjection halfway through. Each line was introduced with imitative entries leading up to a brief cadence and to Ricimer's rejection of defeat. Thereafter Ernelinde, Sandomir, and Rodoald were pitched in juxtaposition as they persuaded their rival to cede magnanimously, their final cadence leading directly into the recitative in which the usurper capitulated. The situation portrayed by this ensemble was thus forceful, and an unusual expressive type to encounter in a *tragédie-lyrique*.

Philidor's notable innovations, apparent in the majority of ensembles in the different versions of *Ernelinde*, were recognized as novel in their day, but were not consistently emulated by his immediate contemporaries. With the advent of Gluck, Piccinni, and Sacchini, the *tragédie-lyrique* entered a new stylistic period in which the French traditions that had been upheld for over a century gave way to new ideas, in particular those from Austria and Italy. To understand the approach towards concerted writing of this new generation of composers would first require that the many developments in ensemble composition in Italian genres after 1750 be studied, and that Gluck's output, including his

Viennese *opéras-comiques* and his Parisian reform operas, also be investigated in detail from this point of view.

Notes

1. Smith has concluded that Duni wrote an *opéra-comique* entitled *Le retour au village*, "an extensive reworking of Favart's *Ninette à la cour*," between 1755 and 1758. *Egidio Duni and the Development of the Opéra-Comique from 1753 to 1770* (diss., Cornell U., 1980), p. 87.

2. *Le neveu de Rameau*, ed. A. Adam (Paris, 1967), pp. 139–140.

3. M. Tourneux, ed.: *Correspondance littéraire, philosophique et critique par Grimm, Diderot, Raynal, Meister, etc.* (Paris, 1877–82), v, p. 97.

4. *Ibid.*, vii, p. 106. Smith calls this work "derivative," relying on subject-matter similar to that in *Les deux chasseurs* (1763). (*Op. cit.*, p. 282.)

5. In their *Avertissement* to the printed libretto (Paris: Lambert, 1759) the authors wrote: "Cet Ouvrage a été fait en vers, & mis en Musique il y a quatre ans; on a été obligé, pour le donner au Public, de substituer de la prose à la place du Récitatif. L'Auteur de la Musique a cru devoir le faire graver en grande partition, & laisser substituer les Récitatifs tels qu'ils avoient été faits."

6. Commenting on *Le roi et le fermier* in the *Correspondance littéraire* (v, p. 191) for example, Grimm wrote: "M. de Monsigny n'est pas musicien; ses partitions sont remplies de fautes et de choses de mauvais goût; mais il a des chants agréables."

7. One recent view is that "contrapuntal part-writing of any sophistication was simply beyond him [Monsigny], even where his material cried out for it." B.A. Brown: *Christoph Willibald Gluck and Opéra-Comique in Vienna, 1754–1764* (diss., U. of California, 1986), p. 694. Later, however, Brown refers to the trio for three sopranos opening the third act of *Le roi et le fermier* as "a brilliant piece of naturalism, in the way their phrases mingle and join after the songs have been heard separately"; and he comments favorably on the septet from the same work, concluding: "The fact that Sedaine and Monsigny had dared so much in this opera meant that it would be easier in the future for them and others to explore ensemble writing in *opéra-comique*." (pp. 785–786).

8. Rousseau recalls Rameau's reaction to this work thus: "il m'apostropha avec une brutalité qui scandalisa tout le monde, soutenant qu'une partie de ce qu'il venait d'entendre était d'un homme consommé dans l'art, et le reste d'un ignorant qui ne savait pas même la musique." *Les confessions*, ed. J. Voisine (Paris, 1964), p. 392.

9. "M. Philidor a fait grande dépense en harmonie et en bruit, fort peu en chant et en idées musicales." *Correspondance littéraire*, v, p. 130, in reference to *Sancho Pança*.

10. *Ibid.*, viii, p. 145.

11. Letter to Charles Burney dated 15 May 1771. See D. Heartz: 'Diderot et le Théâtre lyrique: "le nouveau stile" proposé par *Le neveu de Rameau*', *RdM*, lxiv (1978), p. 247.

12. This was the Paris: *l'auteur* (c1761) version with 136 pages, giving the date of the première as 20 December 1760. Although this score does not indicate the progression of scenes within the complex (i.e. the beginning of IIvii or IIviii) the scene immediately following the duet/trio/quartet is numbered IIix.

13. This score (c1761) bears the inscription: "Le 1er acte gravé par Mme Lefebvre le 2e acte gravé par Mme Cousineau de Ouvrard [sic]." It is 13 pages longer than the version described above and each act is separately paginated (pp. 85 and pp. 64 respectively). It gives a different date for the première: 29 September 1760. The existence of different scores is unusual for *opéras-comiques* of this period.

14. These were the septet in *L'école de la jeunesse* (174 bars) and a duet in scene ix of *Les sabots* (152 bars).

15. See, for example, the trio (sc. vii) and quintet (sc. xvii) in Philidor's *Le jardinier et son seigneur*. The former is discussed on pp. 157–158.

16. *Op. cit.*, pp. 195–196. He also cites Otto Jahn (*W.A. Mozart*): "Zum grossen Teil berührt die Wirkung von Dunis Kunst auf seiner erstaunlichen Vielseitigkeit und Bewiglichkeit der Form, die ebenfalls die italienische Schule verrät. Er kennt nicht nur alle Formen von der einfachen, zweiteiligen Chanson an bis zur Dacapo-Arie und der grösseren, zusammengesetzen Formen, sondern er macht sie auch in sinnvoller Weise der dramatischen Situation dienstbar."

17. Peter Kivy considers sonata form "provides opportunity, within either a small or a large framework, for many different and perhaps contrasting expressive moods, rapidly giving place to one another ... sonata form is a continuous emotive discourse." *Osmin's Rage* (Princeton, 1988), pp. 226ff.

18. For further discussion of this subject, see D. Charlton: "'L'art dramatico-musical": an Essay', *Music and Theatre: Essays in Honour of Winton Dean* (Cambridge, 1987), pp. 258ff.

19. These pictorial effects are considered in a later section dealing with orchestral accompaniments. (See pp. 191ff.)

20. Smith: *Op. cit.*, p. 177.

21. It was noted in the preceding chapter how Sedaine attempted to overcome this dramatic problem—particularly in *Blaise le savetier*—by focusing on stage action.

22. Koch's article, aspects of which were considered in Chapter III, is the most frequently cited research in this field. However, the criteria on which his study is based are questionable and the results do not present an accurate or representative picture.

23. The rest closed with solo *ariettes*, with dialogue (Acts I and III of *La belle Arsène*), with choruses (*Les moissonneurs*, Act II; *La belle Arsène*, Act IV) or, in the case of the third act of *La fée Urgèle*, with a *divertissement*. It is significant that these three works were all written by Favart. Only three of their eight internal acts ended with an ensemble, and this again emphasizes Favart's

more traditional approach to the *opéra-comique* during the later stages of his career.

24. The figure includes the first act of *L'isle des foux* which ended with an elaborate duet/chorus, and the first act of *Le roi et le fermier* which concluded with a duet/trio aggregation.

25. With regard to Grétry's experiment Charlton writes: "it did not fit readily into *opéra-comique*. Above all, the French disliked its dramatic artifice; moreover, their tradition of the final vaudeville was not only strong, but susceptible of integration with higher musical forms of development." *Grétry and the Growth of Opéra-Comique* (Cambridge, 1986), pp. 116–117.

26. D. Charlton: 'Orchestra and Chorus at the Comédie-Italienne (Opéra Comique), 1755–1799', *Slavonic and Western Music: Essays for Gerald Abraham* (Oxford, 1985).

27. The sextet finales in Acts I and II of *L'école de la jeunesse*, for example, were both termed "Choeur" in Anseaume's libretto and Duni's score. A quintet by the same collaborators in scene x of *L'isle des foux* was styled "Choeur des Foux."

28. See Charlton: 'Orchestra and Chorus', p. 97.

29. Mixed ensembles sited within internal acts include a duet-chorus closing the first act to *L'isle des foux*, and a sextet-chorus opening IIiii of *Le sorcier*, for which Charlton notes that three extra female singers and four male singers were paid. *Ibid.*, p. 97.

30. "Tentative beginnings were made in choral music, principally by Philidor, which led towards Monsigny's *Le Déserteur* (1769) wherein the four-part chorus played a climactic part in both the musical and the dramatic structure." *Ibid.*, p. 97.

31. See below, p. 185.

32. This ensemble was described above, p. 138.

33. Both were extensive ensembles, 213 and 301 bars long respectively.

34. The opening part of this duet is reproduced as Example 6.1 below, p. 269.

35. The situation of this trio was described in the preceding chapter (see above, pp. 131–132).

36. As pointed out in the previous chapter (above, pp. 132–132), Mme Saint-Fard has just heard of Laure's intention to marry her own husband.

37. C.M. Carroll: *François-André Danican Philidor: his Life and Dramatic Art* (diss., Florida State U., 1960), pp. 376–377.

38. In this work, due to the skill of the librettist, Sedaine, "the discrepancy between brevity of text and length of setting was bridged by the histrionic dimension. Its quintet No. 5, with thirty short lines of text, some two words long, gave rise to 246 bars of music. Four bare lines of text were provided for the duet No. 8; nine lines of text in the final duet produced 268 bars of music." D. Charlton: '"L'art dramatico-musical"', p. 255.

39. L. Garcin: *Traité du mélodrame* (Paris, 1772), pp. 10–11. Garcin's views on this ensemble, and others, are analyzed in closer detail in Chapter VI. (The ensemble in question, from *Le soldat magicien*, is reproduced as Example 6.1, p. 269.)

40. See above, p. 159.

41. See Charlton: *Grétry and the Growth of Opéra-Comique*, pp. 14–15.

42. Only two ensembles in the works by Duni and Philidor examined notated parts in the alto clef: the quintet ("Choeur des Foux") in IIx of *L'isle des foux*, and the quintet in scene xv of *Le soldat magicien*.

43. Two trios for male characters in Monsigny's operas were written using ATT and ATB clefs.

44. Charlton: "'L'art dramatico-musical'", p. 246.

45. This figure is derived from the manuscript *Journal de l'Opéra* housed at *F-Po*. Theodore de Lajarte's *Bibliothèque musicale du théâtre de l'Opéra* (Paris, 1878/R1971) lists only 31 (omitting Mondonville's *Thésée*, staged in 1767, and *Endymion de Jestras*, 1773). In some years (1758, 1766, 1773) three new works were given; in others (1754, 1764, 1765) none.

46. *L'Avant-coureur* (1766), p. 256.

47. *Mercure de France*, January, i (1768), p. 240.

48. The original version contained eight concerted movements (five duets, one trio, and two quartets), two of which—both *divertissement* duets—were omitted in the 1769 revision which, since it ended with the suicide of the usurping prince, also substituted a trio in place of a quartet embodying the *lieto fine* of the original version. The printed score (Paris, 1769) thus contains three duets, two trios, and a quartet. In the 1773 revision, Sedaine inserted an extra trio and replaced the quartet previously in IIviii with a new one in IIIviii. Both changes were preserved in the final 1777 version, which ended with a *lieto fine* and thus replaced the concluding trio with a new quartet. It has sometimes been assumed that the 1773 and 1777 versions were identical (see, for example, Carroll: *Op. cit., p. 187*).

49. January, i (1768), p. 222.

Chapter V

Eighteenth-Century Theories on the Duet and Ensemble

Our investigation now turns away from scores and librettos to writings on music and on opera in contemporary literature. The aim of this chapter is to show that during the course of the 18th century specific theories concerning the duet and larger ensembles were formulated, which dealt with their role and scope in operatic composition, how they should be approached by librettists and composers, and the main features of their musical style. The diverse sources from which information has been drawn highlight the great inclination of the French during the 18th century for critical discourse. These sources include treatises, letters, dictionaries and encyclopedias, music histories, autobiographical writings, journals, and periodicals. Most of the opinions expressed concerning the ensemble were articulated by men of letters rather than by professional musicians.[1] Where such authors occupy themselves in detail on this subject, an outline of their general critical position with regard to opera is provided in order to clarify the stance they adopted vis-à-vis concerted writing.

First, the background against which these ideas were formulated must be introduced. The emergence of operatic criticism in France is first apparent towards the end of the 17th century, and its subsequent development during the 18th century, particularly from the mid-point onwards, is a testimony to the acceptance of continuously-sung drama in critical circles.

Operatic Criticism

The Early 18th Century: Les salons and les beaux esprits

French cultivated society of the period in question was greatly preoccupied with matters of taste. Educated people were able to express their views on a variety of issues, and for this purpose many *salons* were established. Here coteries of intellectuals and would-be intellectuals from the leisured classes would gather to exchange the most fashionable ideas and opinions.[2] The men and women who frequented these *salons* were known as *connaisseurs* or as *les beaux esprits*. They had refined tastes and a good general culture; many proved competent judges of the issues to which they addressed themselves.

18th-century *beaux esprits* held drama—and opera in particular—in the highest esteem. The *tragédie en musique* was an expensive, luxurious spectacle, an important social activity, and the very epitome of aristocratic life. For this reason it was seized upon as a fertile field for discussion and, as the many musical controversies of the century attest, occupied the *connaisseurs* to a considerable extent. The disagreement between Le Cerf de la Viéville and the *abbé* Raguenet in the early 1700s concerned the relative merits of French and Italian opera. This was followed some decades later by disputes between supporters of Lully (*lullistes*) and Rameau (*ramistes*), by the Querelle des Bouffons of 1752–4 and, finally, by the Gluck/Piccinni controversy of the 1770s.

That these arguments all focused on opera emphasizes the fact that during the 18th century, in France, music was understood by the majority to refer to the music of the theater. The development of operatic criticism thus substantially embodied the rise of musical criticism during this century. The basis upon which operatic criticism was originally established reflected the fact that its protagonists, *les beaux esprits*, although competent judges, were musical amateurs. Their impressions were based almost entirely on personal taste rather than on a professional and theoretical knowledge of music or the stage. Consequently, the early character of operatic criticism was concerned with general issues: comparative discussions of French and Italian works (in which individual preferences were very much in evidence); historical accounts of the opera (including a marked interest in the musical drama of the Ancients); and effusive—but general—outlines of *tragédies* written by the first master of the genre, Lully.

The Encyclopedists

Around the middle of the 18th century there emerged a powerful body of *littérateurs* known as the Encyclopedists, and with them a new aesthetic spirit, that of the Enlightenment. Heralded by the publication of the *Encyclopédie, ou Dictionnnaire raisonné des sciences, arts et métiers* from 1751 onwards under the joint editorship of Denis Diderot (1713–84) and Jean le Rond D'Alembert (1717–83), the Enlightenment sought to elucidate and educate the public, and to establish man's right to question the established order of the universe.[3] Although, like earlier *connaisseurs*, none of the Encyclopedist critics had received much formal training in music, their treatment of this subject in their writings, particularly those concerning the opera, displayed insight and awareness. Diderot's theatrical reforms were discussed in Chapter III. D'Alembert simplified Rameau's complex theoretical writings for the benefit of the general public.[4] Jean-Jacques Rousseau (1712–78) and Baron Friedrich Melchior Grimm (1723–1807) significantly altered the course of French musical drama by their advocacy of Italian opera.[5] Jean-François Marmontel (1723–99) was a prominent and influential librettist during the second half of the 18th century, collaborating with composers such as Rameau, Dauvergne, Grétry, and Piccinni. Louis de Cahusac (1706–59), who also collaborated with Rameau, was renowned for his knowledge of the ballet, which remained an integral part of French serious opera. Other Encyclopedists included Paul Heinrich, Baron d'Holbach (1723–89) and Louis, Chevalier de Jaucourt (1704–79).[6]

The Encyclopedists may not have thought as a corporate body—indeed, hostilities soon arose within their ranks—but they shared a fund of common opinions. Ideas were many and discourse was plentiful; they acted as "arbitres de goût et directeurs de conscience artistique du public."[7] Their contributions to the development of operatic criticism were many, and especially helped to sharpen ideas that had gained currency during the earlier part of the century. One of these was the growing recognition of music—at the expense of poetry—as a fundamental aspect of operatic composition; another was an increasing concern for *vraisemblance* (verisimilitude in composition and performance). The impact of both was significant for the development of ensemble theories.

In the first place, the enhanced status of music meant that individual features of operatic composition began to receive greater critical attention; thus from the early 1740s onwards the vocal ensemble was considered as a separate entity more and more frequently in source materials. Secondly, the insistence on *vraisemblance*, one of the most important critical concepts of the period, provided the framework around which theories concerning concerted writing were structured.

Major Trends in 18th-Century Operatic Criticism

The increasing significance of music

As emphasized in the opening chapter, French opera in its formative years was regarded as another form of tragedy, but inferior to the spoken drama. It was judged and criticized as literature. Music had no significance beyond its relation to the words; it simply enhanced the text and combined with the ballet, the machines, the décor, and costumes to create a magnificent and imposing spectacle. As the *tragédie en musique* developed into a legitimate and independent genre, critics came to realize that it required a completely new set of rules and conventions, and that literary and operatic dramaturgy could not be subject to the same criteria. Oliver records that Charles Perrault, in the late 17th century, was:

> "the first to see that music, aside from its sensual appeal, was a determining factor in the development of opera, not merely a lyrical appendage ... song was more than an ornament; it was a major dramatic discovery."[8]

One important concession granted to the *tragédie en musique* was recognition of Quinault's librettos, previously criticized for being based on a limited vocabulary, as admirably and skilfully adapted to meet the needs of the composer. Another was the acceptance of continuous lyrical declamation, of entirely sung drama, and a third the sanctioning of the *merveilleux* (the use of spectacular and complicated stage machinery, and the integration of deities and mythological characters alongside ordinary mortals to produce fantastic operatic tableaux). But while concessions were granted, actual guidelines and procedures for musical composition were slow to emerge. Mably, as late as 1741, observed:

"Après le succès constant que l'Opera a eu en France ... il est étonnant
qu'aucun Ecrivain ne se soit avisé de chercher les régles de ce Spectacle."[9]

Oliver has discussed how this situation was remedied to a
considerable extent by the advent of the Encyclopedists who, guided by
their preference for Italian works, recommended that opera should become
more "musical" and less "literary" in its orientation.[10] In adopting this
stance, a much greater attention than ever before was accorded to the
musical components of the opera: "Air," "Ballet," "Choeur,"
"Divertissement," "Duo," "Entr'acte," "Ouverture," "Récitatif" were but
some of the articles appearing in the *Encyclopédie* that attest to this, to say
nothing of the many individual works that incorporated discussions on
such subjects. The interest shown by the Encyclopedists in music, the
detail in which they discussed its role in French and Italian operatic genres,
and the recommendations they made, are nowhere better reflected than in
the fact that some of the first concrete theories about the ensemble are to
be found in their writings.

The Concept of Vraisemblance

The notion of *vraisemblance* was seminal to the rationalistic spirit
of the French, to their love of order, logic, and clarity. In the early years
of the 18th century Jean-Baptiste Dubos defined *vraisemblance* in music
as a true and apt imitation of nature:

"Un fait vraisemblable est un fait possible dans les circonstances où on le fait
arriver. Ce qui est impossible en ces circonstances ne sçauroit paroître
vraisemblable."[11]

When applied to opera, however, *vraisemblance* ceased to refer
necessarily to what could be deemed true and believable. This was because
it became irrevocably intertwined with another fundamental operatic
concept, that of illusion.[12]

Operatic illusion was initially a product of continuous lyrical
declamation and of the *merveilleux*. It created a magical atmosphere in
which surprise and bedazzlement were key objectives, the result designed
to delight and appeal to the senses, rather than to the intellect.[13]
Vraisemblance was clearly absent and, at this stage, sharply opposed to
illusion.

Hobson, however, points out that although *vraisemblance* and
illusion were seemingly in conflict with one another they were not directly

antithetical, since they operated within different parameters. *Vraisemblance* "says nothing of the consumer's state, but speaks only of the work: it does not specify the consumer's experience."[14] Thus, in the complex relation and interaction of the "consumer" and the work of art, and in the changing reactions to operatic works, a growing rapprochement between *vraisemblance* and illusion can be discerned during the course of the 18th century.

The spectator responded to operatic illusion in two ways. He could, on the one hand, be conscious of it (as was Saint-Evremond) and place himself outside its power and magnetism: "to be conscious of appearance is to be a spectator of appearance."[15] In such circumstances the opera spoke to the intelligence and failed to enthrall on that very count. On the other hand, the spectator might allow himself to be seduced by the illusion. Since this implied a certain resistance, an overpowering of the senses, it may be assumed that, while responding to the illusion, the spectator also recognized it as such. However, awareness of the artifice did not dilute the surprise and rapture first inspired by the experience; rather it enhanced and strengthened these feelings.[16] In other words, the spectator suspended his disbelief, and illusion infiltrated the province of *vraisemblance*.

It was the very unreality of the *tragédie en musique* that made it a vital and living experience for the theater-goer. By offering a marvellous, spectacular world peopled by exalted heroes and mythological characters, it invited spectators to leave their usual domain and enter the universe of their own imagination:

> "la musique nous fait pénétrer dans un univers spécifiquement différent. Le chant ininterrompu, l'union continuelle de la musique à la parole opèrent une rupture avec le quotidien—et c'est au coeur de cette invraisemblance que s'établit l'opéra."[17]

Contemporary writers made frequent reference to the power of illusion. Maillet-Duclairon declared: "Le Théâtre est le temple de l'illusion, on n'y va même que pour en éprouver tous les charmes."[18] Mably regarded it as a fundamental prerequisite of opera: "L'illusion est absolument nécessaire pour former un Spectacle raisonnable & intéressante."[19] Others willingly sacrificed *vraisemblance* to illusion: "Qu'on nous tourne la tête avec un peu de merveilleux, nous dispensons de cette *vraisemblance*, qui nous est si chere."[20] Likewise Jacques Lacombe:

"Nos Tragédies destinées à être mises en Musique diffèrent essentiellement de celles qui doivent être déclamées. On cherche ici à faire plus illusion aux sens qu'à l'esprit, & l'on veut plutôt produire un spectacle enchanteur qu'une action où la *vraisemblance* soit exactement observée."[21]

Illusion did not in fact replace *vraisemblance* during the course of the 18th century; it simply swallowed it up in its own developmental process (or, strictly speaking, in the spectator's changing appreciation of the opera). *Vraisemblance*, as Hobson remarks, eventually came to be "a precondition for illusion rather than to be opposed to it."[22] Thus, almost paradoxically, the two concepts eventually referred to the same theatrical sensation, a point stressed by Marmontel:

"Il est deux espèces de *vraisemblance*, l'une de réflexion et de raisonnement, l'autre de sentiment et d'illusion."[23]

To summarize, therefore, *vraisemblance* and illusion were initially sharply contrasting entities. As the notion of unreality (or, rather, acceptable reality) in opera gained ground, so the latter gradually became an admissible feature, incorporating, and finally subsuming, the former. The two concepts were first separate and then were twins; eventually they fused into one. That two initially contradictory entities could be reconciled thus was symptomatic of the overall character of French aesthetics during the 18th century. At the heart of this lay a fundamental dualism and tension of ideas. Whether seeking to reconcile reason with sentiment, subjective beauty with empirical knowledge, or rules with spontaneity, the underlying philosophical urge was to grapple with radically different entities, to put them in touch with one another, and to achieve a satisfactory synthesis so that the initial antithesis was transformed into a single, unified concept.[24] As Ernst Cassirer explains:

"It is as if logic and aesthetics, as if pure knowledge and artistic intuition had to be tested in terms of one another before either of them could find its own inner standard and understand itself in the light of its own relational complex."[25]

The development of ensemble theories ran along similar lines. On the one hand, ideas were formed in strict accordance with notions of *vraisemblance*. On the other, more progressive theorists introduced opinions questioning established principles. Both lines of thought, by the late 18th century, were gradually blended into a single acceptable dogma. The result was that, throughout the period in question, the ensemble was increasingly regarded as a natural and acceptable mode of expression in operatic composition.

Early Views on the Ensemble

Very few concrete statements were made about vocal ensembles in the late 17th century, since critical attention focused primarily on the translation of the poetic text, on the *merveilleux* and the use of machines, or on the novelty of continuous lyrical declamation. Other than recitative, individual musical elements were rarely submitted to a close scrutiny.

Then, in 1704, Jean Laurent Le Cerf de la Viéville (1674–1707) published a detailed critique of the *tragédie en musique* entitled *Comparaison de la musique italienne et de la musique françoise*. In this work he considered not only current controversies, but also many of the individual musical characteristics of opera, including duets and trios. Since his treatise was conceived as a defense of French opera in response to the *Paralèle des italiens et des françois en ce qui regarde la musique et les opéra*, written by the *abbé* François Raguenet (*c*1660–1722) in 1702, his views on these ensembles were based primarily on a comparison of French and Italian examples.

Le Cerf, taking general comments by Raguenet on "les Pieces à plusieurs parties" as his cue, assumed that by this his opponent referred to both vocal and instrumental compositions. Thus his discussion of the trio actually compared two different types: the Italian instrumental trio sonata and vocal pieces from Lully's *tragédies*.[26] The latter, predictably, were deemed superior, and various examples were singled out for praise, Le Cerf adding:

> "Lulli nous ait donné je ne sçai combien de *Trio* tres touchans & tres flatteurs … il est toujours aisé & naturel dans cette fécondité-là. Ils ne paye pas seulement de science, comme vos Italiens: la nature lui fornit, lui dicte toûjours ses chants, qui sont toûjours liés & suivis."[27]

Of importance here is Le Cerf's opinion that Lully's vocal trios were of a very natural character, translating credible and lifelike situations. Italian compositions were considered too complex and *travaillé*; French models found favor because of their simple, unaffected, and more direct style. This view epitomized the controversy between partisans of Italian music and supporters of French style at the turn of the century.

Le Cerf then turned his attention to the duet, remarking, as with the trio, that many beautiful examples were to be found in Lully's works.[28] Among those cited were "Nous ressentons les mêmes douleurs" (*Persée*, IVii) and "Les plus belles chaînes" (*Thésée*, Vv). In both these duets the two main lovers were united, whether to express joy or sadness, in a musically *unanime* and homophonic fashion. Le Cerf then made the following observation:

> "L'avantage des *Duo* va plus loin que celui des *Trio* ... car il est vrai-semblable & ordinaire qu'il y ait plus de *Duo* que de *Trio*."[29]

This seemingly represents one of the first attempts to link ensemble composition to notions of *vraisemblance* in critical writings. Although Le Cerf did not expand on this statement, its implications are that pieces for three voices could be countenanced, but those for only two singers were more natural and therefore more credible. Additionally, from the specific examples cited by Le Cerf, the musical characteristics that made these duets popular are apparent: homogeneous sentiments set to homophonic textures ("une Musique douce & unie" rather than "sçavante & travaillée.")[30] The style of concerted writing Le Cerf advocated was exactly that perpetuated in the *tragédie en musique* during the first half of the 18th century (and, indeed, beyond).

In the decades following the publication of this work, no known critical sources followed Le Cerf's lead either in analyzing the musical characteristics of ensembles or in addressing the question of their *vraisemblance* more profoundly. However, an amusing verse in a parody of Rameau's *Hippolyte et Aricie* (written by Giovanni Romagnesi and Antonio Riccoboni and produced at the Comédie-Italienne in 1733) offers an interesting insight into attitudes towards the ensemble—and the performance of such movements at the Académie Royale de Musique—one-third of the way through the century. The verse is found towards the end of the work (in scene xx) as Diane unites the two happy lovers. Hippolyte observes that here, traditionally, he and Aricie should sing together: "Mais nous sommes obligés de chanter encor un duo." Aricie responds thus:

> "Chanter à deux n'a rien qui m'interésse.
> A l'Opera, c'est le moment d'ennuie.
> Les duos y vont aujourd'hui
> Comme deux seaux font dans un puits:
> L'un hausse et l'autre baisse.

L'un apres l'autre il vaut mieux raisonner;
Nous serons moins sujets tous deux à détonner."[31]

This verse has attracted comment from a number of 20th-century writers. Masson regards it as a wry attack on the *invraisemblance* of "des duos simultanés et continus," that is, on the traditional style of concerted writing in the *tragédie*.[32] Noiray likewise suggests that the parody sought to expose the unnatural character of contemporary duet composition: "Ce qui est en cause ici est donc le mouvement convenu des voix dans un type de morceau considéré comme exagérément artificiel."[33] Sadler interprets the verse as a criticism of "passages in which the two singers declaim different texts, a feature that offended the reason of certain opera-goers."[34] What the verse most certainly advocated was a move away from the juxtaposition of voices (captured in the imagery of two buckets swinging up and down in a well) and the use, instead, of dialogue ("L'un apres l'autre il vaut mieux raisonner.") It implied that ensembles structured in this manner were a more natural form of expression than simultaneous song, and that they were less likely to run the risk of being poorly performed by the singers involved.[35]

This recommendation in fact reflected current practice at the Comédie-Italienne and the fair theaters during the first half of the 18th century, as the dialogue vaudevilles studied in Chapter I illustrate. Practice in the *tragédie en musique* during the same period steered a separate course, structuring ensembles around *unanime* texts and homophonic textures, and since the first major theories pertaining to ensemble composition, formulated in the early 1740s shortly after this parody, were guided by practice in the then dominant serious genre, they sought to justify simultaneous expression and made no reference to dialogue principles. The wisdom of Aricie's parody verse was grasped only from the middle of the century onwards, when the Italian dialogue duet began to gain currency in France. From this date onwards changes in direction in ensemble theories become apparent. Writers begin to extol the advantages of dialogue textures and argue that simultaneous song be avoided, thus repeating exactly what the authors of the alternative *Hippolyte et Aricie* had recommended some two decades previously.

At this point theories relating to the ensemble must be separated into two strands. The first charts the development of critical thought vis-à-vis the duet, the most popular type of concerted movement throughout the century. The second investigates ideas pertaining to trios, to quartets, and to larger ensembles, which emerged more tentatively, and at a later date, than those concerning the duet.

The Duet

The 1740s: Mably and Saint-Mard

In 1741 two important works considering the opera appeared in print, the *Réflexions sur l'opéra* of Toussaint Rémond de Saint-Mard and Gabriel Bonnot de Mably's *Lettres à Madame la marquise de P... sur l'opéra*. The former was published in La Haye and had left the presses in time to be reviewed in the May issue of the *Mercure*.[36] The latter appeared shortly afterwards, although the *Avertissement de l'éditeur* informed the reader that the four letters had been written some years prior to their publication and had already been read by "plusieurs personnes de goût."[37] Both works contained interesting and quite similar views on the duet. While Mably's ideas may well have predated those of Saint-Mard, there is little point in trying to ascertain which of the two was the first to express such opinions, since both were undoubtedly reporting notions then current among *les beaux esprits*.

Saint-Mard (1682–1757) and Mably (1709–85) represented the typical 18th-century *beau esprit*. The former was the son of a *fermier général du roi* and his wealth and social position allowed him to pursue his artistic interests freely. He was primarily a literary critic, but a strong supporter of the opera as well. Musical drama for him, as for the leisured class he represented, signified entertainment and diversion; he therefore readily defended the tenets upon which it was based.[38] He did, however, bemoan the new complexities of recent French opera (for which he held Rameau responsible), and the fact that many of his contemporaries had grown to admire the difficult, the unusual, and the extraordinary at the expense of the beautiful, the simple, and the natural.[39] He sought to correct certain traits of operatic composition in order to create a spectacle "sinon, le plus touchant, du moins le plus magnifique & le plus propre à s'amuser & à plaire."[40] His ideas concerning the duet reflect this concern.

Mably also came from a titled family, but concerned himself more with diplomatic and political administration (as well as with theology and history) than with *les beaux arts*. His *Lettres*, published anonymously, in fact represented his only venture into this field. Their main purpose was to establish for the opera "ses rêgles, sa justesse, ses proportions et sa *vraisemblance.*"[41] Like Saint-Mard, Mably's treatment of the *tragédie en musique* was sympathetic but his comments, at least on the duet, were a good deal more penetrating.

Although Saint-Mard did not wish to exclude the duet from the opera, he saw it as "une beauté dont je souhaiterois qu'on fût un peu plus avare, & qui d'ailleurs est assez souvent mal employée."[42] In elaborating on this view, his position becomes clear:

> "Il nous est difficile d'entendre, sans être un peu blessés, parler deux personnes ensemble, d'entendre par exemple dire à l'une, qu'*il faut aimer*, à l'autre, qu'*il faut changer toujours* ... il y a là quelque chose de risible qui va mal avec le sérieux de l'Opéra, & qui par-là devient ridicule."[43]

Thus divergent duets, in which the characters contradicted one another by singing conflicting texts, were considered both improper to the dignified character of the *tragédie* ("risible") and a hard trial for the listener. Saint-Mard recommended that composers refrain from writing duets of this nature. On the other hand, those in which the singers expressed the same sentiments were considerered perfectly acceptable. Duets combining joyful lovers fell very appropriately into this category:

> "Je ne dis rien aux Amans, ils ont les mêmes choses à se dire; ils ont à se jurer qu'ils s'aiment, qu'ils s'aimeront toujoûrs; il est dans la Nature qu'ils se le jurent ensemble."[44]

Saint-Mard thus advocated that the characters of a duet express the same sentiments at carefully prepared moments in the opera, so as to preserve the intelligibility of the text and the plausibility of the situation. Those portraying more improbable events and violating the sense of propriety so important to the *tragédie* were to be avoided. His emphasis on natural expression can be traced back to Le Cerf.

Mably's discussion of the duet opened with a reference to the controversy surrounding the subject, and this would imply that it had recently formed the basis of conversations in Parisian *salons*:

> "Les *Duo* ... ont fait naître de grandes contestations. Madame de S... veut les conserver, & N... qui ne goûte de plaisir que quand sa raison est satisfaite, veut impitoyablement les renvoyer aux Fêtes."[45]

Underlying this statement is an implication echoing Saint-Mard's opinion that the duet was not always a sufficiently rational phenomenon. Mably's next statement affirms this, but it is at this point that his ideas may be distinguished from Saint-Mard's, since his grounds for including duets in operatic works were more cautious and depended on a variety of other factors. One of the most important of these was the length of individual pieces:

> "Je sçais bien qu'un Duo ne paroît guére naturel, & que dès qu'il renferme plus d'un Vers ou deux, il y a quelque chose de trop concerté où l'on découvre un art qui déplaît."[46]

However, Mably acknowledged the fact that the opera should be entitled to its own rules and conventions, and his subsequent comments show that the contemporary trend towards a more sympathetic and expanded view of *vraisemblance* was filtering through to duet theories:

> "il y auroit trop de rigueur à ne vouloir pas souffrir que dans certaines circonstances un Spectacle ne s'élévât pas de quelques degrés au-dessus du naturel; & comme on s'est fait une raison sur les Monologues & les *à parte*, ne pourroit-on pas passer aussi les Duo en faveur du plaisir qu'ils donnent dans de certaines occasions . . .?"[47]

The rest of Mably's comments, which consider specific examples from Lully's operas, were designed to elaborate this important point. The type of duet he considered acceptable in the *tragédie en musique* and those which he felt transgressed the bounds of *vraisemblance* are thereby made clear. "Il ne faut plus nous voir" in Viv of *Alceste* was a duet for the two main lovers (strictly speaking, a succession of duet fragments interrupted by a third character) in which identical sentiments were voiced in a mostly simultaneous fashion (there was some imitative writing and a few alternating phrases). Mably's opinion of this ensemble was favorable, and this was very probably due to the brevity of the ensemble utterances. He reiterated Saint-Mard's view that in such a situation it was natural, and indeed to be expected, that two such characters should sing in this manner:

> "il me semble qu'Alceste & qu'Admete en se parlant ainsi à la fois, font une impression bien plus vive sur mon coeur, que si Quinault avoit suivi la méthode ordinaire du Dialogue. Il est même assez naturel que deux Amans dans un pareil moment, où ils ne sentent que leur malheur & ne sont pleins que de leur passion, soient emportés par le sentiment sans songer aux bienséances. Il n'est point surprenant que deux Coeurs unis par l'Amour ayent la même pensée, & qu'ils employent même les mêmes expressions."[48]

However, with reference to the quartet in Vii of *Atys*, which was in fact a double duet and which he described as a *duo*, Mably was more critical. This ensemble was an extensive movement of 62 bars grouping the lovers Sangaride and Atys against their persecutors Cybèle and Célénus. The former sang one set of words, the latter another, both pairs alternating musically and each singing in homophony. Mably found this movement far too contrived:

> "on y perd patience. Quand Célénus ne manqueroit pas de respect à Cybéle en parlant en même tems qu'elle, il n'y a point de hazard assez singulier pour combiner les choses de façon, que ces deux Personnages se servent précisément, & pendant si long-tems, des mêmes expressions pour exprimer les mêmes pensées. C'est aussi un vrai prodige qu'Atys & Sangaride semblent s'être donné le mot pour faire constamment les mêmes réponses. L'art dans tout cela se montre d'une maniere trop évidente; il déplaît, il lasse, & je n'ai vû personne qui n'en fût choqué."[49]

It is interesting that the closing sentence in this quotation ("L'art dans tout cela se montre d'une maniere trop évidente") repeats one of Mably's first criticisms of ensembles ("dès qu'il renferme plus d'un Vers ou deux, il y a quelque chose de trop concerté où l'on découvre un art qui déplaît.") Mably found this ensemble contrived because it was too long and, consequently, too complex and repetitive. The artifice of the whole design lacked *vraisemblance*. For this reason Mably could not consider the quartet an apt translation of dramatic events.

Mably's criteria for *vraisemblance* in duets mirrored that of Saint-Mard to a certain extent. Both argued for duets to be incorporated carefully, yet sparingly, into operatic works; both found lovers' duets pleasing and natural; and both were against the inclusion of complicated divergent pieces. Saint-Mard's approach, however, was more general in that he simply advocated *unanime*, as opposed to divergent, expression as necessary for *vraisemblance* in duets. Mably, in contrast, argued on a more local basis, carefully judging the length and musical style of individual movements and their impact on the drama. He favored the short ensemble utterances typical of Lully's *tragédies* because these grew naturally from the dramatic situation. Concerted singing on a larger scale was more difficult to countenance because this often had the effect of sounding artificial and, therefore, contrived. This basic attitude was to underpin ensemble theories for a considerable time. Concerted singing was deemed a natural phenomenon by Mably and Saint-Mard only if it was limited to certain occasions, representing a logical dramatic outcome, and only if the characters clearly voiced the same sentiments at the same time. Any other style was considered "hors de nature," a term frequently encountered in the writings of subsequent theorists.

The 1750s: Grimm and Rousseau

Just as Mably and Saint-Mard had voiced their views on the duet at approximately the same time, so, too, did the next succession of theorists, the Encyclopedists Grimm and Rousseau. Whereas it is not yet known whether Mably and Saint-Mard moved in the same circles, there can be no doubt that Grimm and Rousseau were thoroughly acquainted with one another. In *Les confessions* Rousseau recalled that they became intimate as friends and thinkers around 1750.[50] Their exchange of ideas was mirrored in the theories each formed concerning the duet. Rousseau was the first to articulate new directions in this field; Grimm followed suit some years later, after having previously subscribed to ideas originally advocated by Mably and Saint-Mard.

This initially traditional approach was expressed in the Lettre de M. Grimm sur *Omphale* which, criticizing the revival of Destouches' *tragédie* at the Académie Royale de Musique in January 1752, dated from the early part of that year. Rousseau followed with the *Lettre sur la musique françoise* published in November 1753. He also wrote the extensive article 'Duo' for volume v of the *Encyclopédie* which appeared in 1755 (although the original draft was submitted to the editors well in advance of this date). Grimm's article 'Poème lyrique,' which also contained references to the duet, would likewise have been written well before 1765, the year in which it appeared in volume xii of the *Encyclopédie*. The exact chronology of these four sources is difficult to establish because of the lapse in time between the writing of the two *Encyclopédie* articles and their subsequent publication. It is a matter that requires attention, and which is addressed presently, because there is cause to question dates that have previously been suggested.

The *Lettre sur Omphale* began by restating an idea familiar from the previous decade: "Les Duo en général ont déja l'inconvénient d'être hors de nature."[51] Grimm argued, like others before him, that the concept of concerted singing was essentially unnatural, but that within the context of operatic reality some exceptions might be made. Music could beguile and charm, and thus create its own laws: pleasure led to credibility:

> "Il n'y a que l'agrément extrême de ces morceaux & l'enchantement que la Musique y sçait répandre ... qui puissent me faire oublier ce défaut de vraisemblance."[52]

After extolling the duet sung by Omphale and Isis in Viii, a *unanime* movement with a predominantly homophonic texture, as "simple, naturel, d'un chant agréable & chanté juste," he then repeated the established belief that duets best satisfied notions of *vraisemblance* when sung by two tender lovers:

> "J'écoute avec plaisir deux Amans tendres (pourvu que la Musique le soit aussi) se jurer réciproquement une constance éternelle. Leurs plaintes, leurs malheurs me touchent &, si le Musicien le veut ou le peut, ils me percent l'ame."[53]

However, Grimm then went on the offensive in emphasizing, like his predecessors, the idea that violent altercations were far less suitable contexts for duets. In *Omphale* there were two such pieces, both for Alcide (Hercule) and Argine: "Amour, quelle furie" (IIiv) and "Je sens triompher dans mon coeur" (IIIvi). Grimm, in the following passage, was doubtless referring to the latter, a semi-divergent duet set in a fast tempo with persistent quaver figurations and imitative entries causing significant displacement of text. A mere 18 bars long, it was repeated in full after six bars of recitative (but even with this, Grimm's reckoning of "un quart d'heure" should be regarded as an exaggeration):

> "Mais voir Alcide & Argine se quereller, se menacer pendant un quart-d'heure, par les mêmes paroles, & quand le Poëte enfin m'en délivre, & les fait partir, les voir revenir sur leurs pas, parce que le Musicien ne peut pas oublier sitôt le beau morceau qu'il croit avoir fait, les voir recommencer à se dire les mêmes injures en mesure, c'est voir le comble de l'extravagance & du mauvais goût."[54]

These comments affirmed Mably's stance towards certain duets: that too much art and artifice broke with *vraisemblance* and led to unrealistic concerted writing. Grimm concluded his comments on this duet with the claim that it would have found its true character had it been intended as a parody, facetiously wondering whether Destouches had not been suspected by his librettist, La Motte, of working for the Comédie-Italienne (rather than for the Académie), a remark evidently intended to disparage.[55]

Whereas Grimm's observations simply reaffirmed established tenets and did not advance theories then current concerning the duet, Rousseau's article 'Duo' for the *Encyclopédie* advocated several new and important ideas. It is here that problems of dating arise. Jansen has indicated that Rousseau worked on his *Encyclopédie* commission during 1748 and 1749, the evidence being documented by Rousseau himself in a letter dated 27 January 1749.[56] Oliver records that all the articles on music were ready by the summer of 1749 and given to Diderot in 1750.[57] Rousseau again affirms this in the preface to his *Dictionnaire de musique* (1768), where he also emphasizes that his contributions were written very much in haste: "au bout de trois mois mon manuscrit entier fut écrit, mis au mot & livré; je ne l'ai pas revu depuis."[58] That Rousseau lost all track of his manuscript is untrue. A letter to D'Alembert dated 26 June 1751 reveals that he had been given the opportunity to revise several articles in the proof-reading process. (The same letter indicated, moreover, that certain comments antagonistic to Rameau in the original drafts had been edited out by D'Alembert.)[59] There is further evidence to suggest that the 'Duo' article was revised in proof some time after the arrival of the Bouffons in August 1752.

Some of the evidence is circumstantial, for example the fact that the two duets Rousseau included in his *intermède Le devin du village*, written in the spring of 1752, did not entirely coincide with the theories he subsequently advocated so ardently.[60] Also hypothetical is the fact that if Rousseau sent the revised articles 'C' ('Cadence,' 'Canon,' 'Cantate,' 'Cantatille,' 'Chant' for volume ii; 'Chiffrer,' 'Choeur,' 'Composition' for volume iii; 'Consonance' for volume iv) to D'Alembert in June 1751, it is probable that he would, at a later stage, have checked over the 'Duo' article which appeared in the fifth volume in 1755. A third relevant point is the sudden change in opinion Rousseau experienced at some stage in the early 1750s regarding the merits of French opera. The sentiments expressed in his *Lettre sur la musique françoise*, one of the most vitriolic pamphlets of the Querelle des Bouffons, to the effect that the French nation could never hope to find a successful musical style of its own, should be compared with opinions he supposedly transmitted to Grimm in a letter dating from 1750, shortly after he would have completed his initial drafts for the *Encyclopédie*:

> "quoi qu'on dise, une belle musique française est très capable de plaire, même aux étrangers … la musique italienne a son genre particulier, et la française le sien … la différence qui s'y trouve n'admettant pas de comparaison, elles doivent passer pour également bonnes chacune dans leur genre."[61]

The most incontrovertible evidence, however, may be found towards the end of the *Lettre sur la musique françoise*, where Rousseau refers to Pergolesi's *intermezzo, La serva padrona*, as "connu de tout le monde." Since this was given only four performances when premièred in

Paris in 1746, and was not a popular success until 1752, his comment implies that the 'Duo' article was reworked between the later months of that year and November 1753, when the *Lettre sur la musique françoise* was published, since the pages dealing with the duet in this epistle reproduce, almost verbatim, the contents of his *Encyclopédie* article.

Rousseau's attitudes towards music in general greatly colored the opinions he expressed concerning the duet, and these must therefore be considered in detail. His fundamental belief was that melody, not harmony, should form the basis of musical composition, that this should flow in an uninterrupted fashion, free from impediment, and that music must sing in order to move and please the listener: "La Musique doit donc nécessairement chanter pour toucher."[62] His belief in the supremacy of melody stemmed partly from personal deficiencies as a composer and performer, but also from the quasi-philosophical belief that the earliest languages, in being highly inflected, had taken melody as their basis.[63] He therefore denied any central role to harmony in musical composition and, with this, all Rameau's discoveries, a stance which accounted for much of his animosity towards this composer. He held contrapuntal writing in distaste and felt that it was impossible for the ear to concentrate on more than one melody at a time: "Les fugues en général servent plus à faire du bruit qu'à produire de beaux chants."[64]

Musical composition was thus subordinated to the principle of "l'unité de mélodie" which Rousseau explained thus in his *Dictionnaire*:

> "L'*Unité de Mélodie* exige bien qu'on n'entende jamais deux Mélodies à la fois, mais non pas que la Mélodie ne passe jamais d'une Partie à l'autre; au contraire, il y a souvent de l'élégance & du goût à ménager à propos ce passage …"[65]

The main force of Rousseau's duet theories revolved around this notion. Primacy of melody was achieved through the voices singing one after another, in other words, in dialogue. Rousseau was thus the first writer to introduce the idea of dialogue into theories of duet composition, and this was to serve as their basis for many years. His recommendations also involved a considerable simplification of musical texture, the avoidance of contrapuntal complexities, and a "harassing insistence on *vraisemblance*."[66] Only if a certain situation exactly mirrored nature could it be structured into an ensemble movement without undermining *vraisemblance*. As will eventually become clear, these stipulations gave

Rousseau's theories an extremely narrow outlook, and offered duets only a very restricted scope within the dramatic framework of an opera.

Rousseau began his article 'Duo' with a general discussion on two-part writing, and then voiced the familiar complaint against the *invraisemblance* of ensemble singing:

> "rien est moins naturel que de voir deux personnes se parler à la fois durant un certain tems, soit pour dire la même chose, soit pour se contredire, sans jamais s'écouter, ni se répondre."[67]

To this he added that in serious opera such practice was particularly lamentable since the dignity and bearing of the characters ought to preclude their being placed in such circumstances.

The notion that the duet should be treated as far as possible in dialogue, that is as a musical conversation, afforded a way around the problem of *vraisemblance*. Rousseau first reminded the librettist of his responsibility in providing the composer with a suitable text, "distribué de telle sorte que chacun des interlocuteurs parlent alternativement ... [qui] passe dans son progrès d'une partie à l'autre, sans cesser d'être une [mélodie] et sans enjamber." With regard to the musical style of the duet, the composer was advised in very specific terms how to proceed. Rousseau's first stipulation was designed to preserve the notion of "l'unité de mélodie":

> "Quand on joint ensemble les deux parties, ce qui doit se faire rarement et durer peu, il faut trouver un chant susceptible d'une marche par tierces ou par sixtes, dans lequel la seconde partie fasse son effet sans distraire l'oreille de la premiere."

His second, containing advice on harmony and dissonance, accorded with his wider views on this subject:

> "Il faut garder la dureté des dissonances, les sons perçans et renforcés ... pour des instans de desordre et de transport, où les acteurs semblent s'oublier eux-mêmes, portent leur égarement dans l'âme de tout spectateur sensible, et lui font éprouver le pouvoir de l'harmonie sobrement ménagée. Mais ces instans doivent êtres rares et amenés avec art."

A third recommendation was once again geared to the notion of "l'unité de mélodie" in asserting the primacy of beautiful melody in duet composition:

> "Il faut pour une musique douce et affectueuse avoir déjà disposé l'oreille et le coeur à l'émotion ... car quand l'agitation est trop forte, elle ne sauroit durer; et tout ce qui est au-delà de la nature ne touche pas."

In laying down such detailed guidelines for the composer—careful and circumspect integration of the voices in sonorous intervals of thirds and sixths, similar caution in harmonic language and, above all, attention to well-regulated and touching melody—Rousseau defined a rigorous prescriptive doctrine for the composition of operatic duets. He created a foundation on which much subsequent theorizing was based. To conclude his account, he stated that in outlining the measures composers and librettists should take, he had simply described the approach of those writing Italian opera, and cited the duet "Lo conosco a quegl'occhietti" from *La serva padrona* ("connu de tout le monde," it will be recalled) as an example of duet composition at its finest: "un modèle de chante, d'unité de mélodie, de dialogue et de goût." The advocacy of Italian methods was fundamental to Rousseau's quest for *vraisemblance* in duet composition.

As Rousseau's article 'Duo' for the *Encyclopédie* was not published until 1755, it was to these comments as they had been incorporated into the *Lettre sur la musique françoise* that subsequent writers replied. This pamphlet produced around 25 responses continuing the literary dispute known now as the Querelle des Bouffons. Only a few contained reactions to Rousseau's views on the duet. From these we may discern three separate lines along which later theories developed: the first an immediate contradiction of Rousseau's stance by staunch supporters of French music; the second a complete and unquestioning assimilation of his philosophy; and the third a reaffirmation of his fundamental ideas, but in substantially modified and expanded form.

Opposition to Rousseau's Theories

Two months after the publication of Rousseau's *Lettre sur la musique françoise*, the *abbé* Marc-Antoine Laugier (1713–69) responded with a detailed pamphlet, 78 pages long, entitled *Apologie de la musique françoise contre M. Rousseau*. A man of wide cultural interests, Laugier was an advocate of French music and showed an informed appreciation of works by Lully, Campra, Lalande, and others. Although he took exception to Rousseau's sweeping statement that the French were incapable of musical composition, he did not defend his preferences blindly, and argued instead that both French and Italian styles had their merits and failings.[68]

Laugier challenged the very heart of Rousseau's theories, his exclusive preference for the dialogue duet. He offered detailed justification for the composition of movements in which the characters sang simultaneously, including those where the sentiments expressed by each party differed. Like previous writers, he was careful to seek precedents for his ideas in nature (in other words, to ensure that they met the demands of *vraisemblance*). His thoughts on this subject are worth quoting extensively.

After recalling Rousseau's criticism of situations where two characters sang at the same time, whether in agreement or not, Laugier addressed his target thus:

> "je lui demande, s'il est contre nature que deux personnes éprouvent un sentiment uniforme, ou un sentiment contraire dans le même tems. Il me semble que rien n'est plus naturel & plus ordinaire. Or dès qu'il est possible qu'elles l'éprouvent, il est convenable qu'elles l'expriment. Alors ce ne seront plus deux personnes qui se parlent à la fois; mais deux personnes qui à la fois manifestent la situation particulière de leur coeur; dispensées par conséquent, & même absolument hors d'état de s'écouter & de se répondre."[69]

The conclusions he draws are interesting:

> "Concluons de-là que le *duo* n'est point du tout arbitraire; qu'il n'est légitime que lorsque deux personnes agitées du même mouvement, ou d'un mouvement contraire, sont autorisées par la nature à l'exprimer séparément, quoique tout à la fois; & qu'alors le *duo* bien loin d'être choquant produit une satisfaction des plus vives. Il n'est donc pas nécessaire de décomposer toûjours nos *duo* pour les traiter en simple dialogue, comme le voudroit M. Rousseau. Il est encore moins nécessaire, quand on joint ensemble les deux parties, de s'attacher exclusivement, comme il le prescrit, à un chant susceptible d'une marche par tierces ou par sixtes, dans lequel la seconde partie fasse son effet, sans distraire l'oreille de la première. Un pareil chant seroit contre nature dans la situation de deux personnes qui éprouvent à la fois deux sentimens contraires: & lors même que c'est un sentiment uniforme qui les occupe, il est assez naturel que chacune aye sa manière différente de sentir relativement à la diversité du caractère; il n'est donc pas hors de propos que chacune conserve dans l'expression cette manière différente, & alors la double mélodie, bien loin d'être contre nature, en rend plus exactement les diversités."[70]

Laugier's interpretation of *vraisemblance* in concerted singing was directly antithetical to Rousseau's, and underlined a fundamental flaw in the earlier theorist's thinking. He quite rightly pointed out that emotions felt simultaneously in response to a given impulse or event were only prevented from being expressed in this manner by the constraints of verbal discourse. Opera, however, had established its own rules and was predicated on the artifice of singing, not of speech. Duets, therefore, might legitimately express the imitation of private emotions felt simultaneously, without having to be composed in dialogue or blending the voices in sonorous intervals at certain stages within a movement. Indeed, Laugier considered this approach "contre nature" in many situations. Rousseau, on the other hand, could only maintain that listening to two melodies at the same time was like trying to understand the conversation of two people speaking at once. The result, as Oliver has pointed out, was that he "carried his definition of melody as musical discourse to the ridiculous extreme of suppressing the word musical entirely," which showed "a deplorable lack of appreciation of music."[71]

Laugier's stance was reaffirmed shortly afterwards by the *abbé* Jean-Louis Aubert (1732–c1810) in the *Réfutation suivie et détaillée des principes de M. Rousseau.* Aubert was a man of letters (a writer, dramatist, and editor of several journals) and, like Laugier, an admirer of French composers such as Rameau, Leclair, and Mondonville. His *Réfutation* was even more extensive than the *Apologie*, spanning 98 pages, and frequently witty and sarcastic in tone. However, Aubert's views on the duet were less incisive than those expounded by Laugier; he was concerned not so much with problems of *vraisemblance* as with the fact that Rousseau's views allowed musicians little freedom in their composition of duet movements:

> "Vous ne demandez à présent que des *Duo en Dialogue*, quoique traités autrement ils enchantent, & que ce soit le triomphe de la Musique de faire accorder parfaitement deux voix … à quoi donc prétendez-vous réduire tout le travail de nos Musiciens?"[72]

Aubert argued, as did Laugier, that since musical and verbal discourse were modelled around different precepts, the operatic duet was no more unnatural a phenomenon than other extraordinary, yet acceptable, aspects of theater such as the monologue or the *à parte*.[73] He saw in duet composition, moreover, "une occasion favorable de déployer les plus belles richesses de l'Harmonie. Et c'est une excellente raison pour en faire aimer l'usage dans les Opéra, encore plus que celui des Monologues, des à parte, &c. dans les autres espéces de Drames."[74] This view certainly opposed Rousseau's revered principle of "l'unité de mélodie." It also implied that duets could be justified on musical grounds alone, a modification to *vraisemblance* that was to be articulated more persistently in subsequent decades.

Assimilation of Rousseau's Theories

Laugier and Aubert, in arguing for a style of duet that allowed characters to express a diverse range of emotions simultaneously, found little support for such radically alternative theories among their immediate contemporaries. Subsequent writers sided very much with the principles laid down by Rousseau. The *Examen de la lettre de M. Rousseau sur la musique françoise*, written by Charles Bâton *le jeune* in late 1753, was heavily critical of Rousseau's unconciliatory stance towards French music in general. It is therefore surprising to find that Bâton concurred entirely with the pro-italianate duet theories expounded by Rousseau, repeating his observations almost word for word:

> "Il est dans la nature que deux personnes parlent ensemble dans un excès de joie ou de tristesse, mais cela ne doit pas durer plus de tems que la passion le demande, & un *Duo* traité en dialogue peut la développer insensiblement, & ménager le moyen de joindre les deux parties pour donner à cette passion le dernier degré d'expression, qui lui est nécessaire."[75]

Bâton, about whom little is known, was a minor composer and a virtuoso on the *vielle* (hurdy-gurdy). Zaslaw has pointed out that he was a solid writer with a firm grasp and understanding of the major issues surrounding the Querelle des Bouffons.[76] His ideas concerning the duet, however, offered no new insights.

D'Alembert, writing during the early 1750s, likewise reiterated the stance of his fellow Encyclopedists. His comparison of French and Italian duets emphasized the extent to which italianate ideas had influenced the several writers on this subject:

> "Je désirerois que les duos fussent plus en dialogue; on pourroit prendre pour modèles ceux de la *Serva padrona*. Je remarqueray à cette occasion que dans les duos qui vont ensemble, c'est un défaut que de vouloir y mettre trop d'harmonie: la mélodie la plus simple y suffit; le chant à la tierce y est le plus propre, et je ne connois guères de duos qui aient réussi où l'accord ne soit à la tierce."[77]

Jacques Lacombe (1724–1801) then followed suit in a treatise entitled *Le spectacle des beaux-arts*, which was published in 1758. Lacombe, previously encountered as a librettist of comic works during the 1750s, was a lawyer by profession. He was also a prolific writer on *les beaux-arts* and edited various journals including the *Mercure de France* and *L'Avant-coureur*. His views on the duet reiterated those already in circulation:

"Le Duo est propre pour le Dialogue; c'est pourquoi l'on doit ordinairement
y entendre une partie qui interoge avec une autre qui répond & qui se réunit à
la première dans des intervalles trés-courts; car de faire continuellement
marcher ensemble deux voix qui disent la même chose, & qui forment la même
expression, ce n'est point mettre de différence entre les voix & les instrumens;
c'est en abuser, & les faire sortir de leur genre; en un mot, c'est blesser toute
vraisemblance. Est-il naturel que deux personnes se devinent pour dire, &
retourner sans cesse les mêmes paroles?"[78]

A fourth writer to espouse Rousseau's ideas, underlining once
again their popularity, was Grimm, whose article 'Poème lyrique'—
published in volume xii of the *Encyclopédie* (1765) but probably drafted
well in advance of this date—represented a change in the opinions he had
expressed in the earlier *Lettre sur Omphale.* In this essay, Grimm offered
a concise definition of the dialogue duet, the wording of which effectively
implied that only duets composed in such a style were admissible in an
operatic work:

"Le duo ou *duetto* est donc un air dialogué, chanté par deux personnes animées
de la même passion ou de passions opposées. Au moment le plus pathétique
de l'air, leurs accents peuvent se confondre; cela est dans la nature; une
exclamation, une plainte peut les réunir; mais le reste de l'air doit être en
dialogue."[79]

Grimm took the opportunity, in this article, to criticize once again
the complicated vengeance duets of the *tragédie en musique*, this time
selecting an example from Lully's *Armide* ("Poursuivons jusqu'au trépas"
in Iiv). In contrast to the orderly dialogue singing by characters in Italian
duets, this example displaced a *unanime* text so that the characters sang
different words at the same time (as had been the case in "Je sens triompher
dans mon coeur" in *Omphale*). It was this feature, alongside extensive
repetition of the text and a forceful musical style, that aroused Grimm's
displeasure and resulted in accusations of *invraisemblance*:

"Il ne peut jamais être naturel qu'Armide & Hidraot, pour s'animer à la
vengeance, chantent en couplet:
            Poursuivons jusqu'au trépas . . .
Ils recommenceroient ce couplet dix fois de suite avec un bruit & des
mouvemens de forcenés, qu'un homme de goût n'y trouveroit que la même
déclamation fausse fastidieusement répétée."[80]

In contrast to his *Lettre sur Omphale*, Grimm made no reference in
the 'Poème lyrique' to the typical lovers' duet of the *tragédie*, where the
characters expressed identical sentiments with a good deal more clarity
than in vengeance duets. Examples in this style from *Omphale* had

previously received high praise and had also been advocated in the writings of Mably and Saint-Mard. This omission reflected the break that Rousseau, with his notions of dialogue and "l'unité de mélodie," had made with earlier theories. Newer ideas, which took as their basis Italian models and which were not relevant to the course of duet composition in the *tragédie en musique* during the second half of the century, simply displaced those previously in circulation.

Expansion of Rousseau's Theories

The writers cited above affirmed, but did not develop, the theories first outlined by Rousseau in the early 1750s. It was not until the appearance of a further work by this author, the *Dictionnaire de musique*, that the introduction of new ideas and, with this, a more accommodating stance in theories concerning the composition of duets, may be perceived.

Since the *Dictionnaire* was in essence a revision of the articles on music that had appeared in the *Encyclopédie*, it presents similar problems of dating. It has been suggested that Rousseau had the revised versions substantially in his portfolio before "retiring" to the Ermitage in 1756, evidence in a letter dated 3 January 1755 to Marc-Michel Rey corroborating this hypothesis: "Je prépare mon Dictionnaire de Musique pour le mettre sous presse l'Eté prochain."[81] It did not in fact reach the presses until 1767 (although it is dated 1768).[82] Rousseau recalled the preparation of the dictionary at various points in *Les confessions*: since his object in publishing the work was entirely financial, he occupied himself with it intermittently and as his needs dictated.[83] It may be assumed, therefore, that Rousseau developed his original ideas some time during the mid-1750s, and perhaps revised these further during the subsequent decade. Whatever the creative process, the result did not circulate in print until the late 1760s.

The article 'Duo' in the *Dictionnaire* firstly repeated the familiar notion that the duet was "hors de nature," that nothing was more unnatural than to hear two people singing at once, and reaffirmed Rousseau's stance with regard to the importance of "l'unité de mélodie":

> "le *Duo* est de toutes les sortes de Musique celle qui demande le plus de goût, de choix, & la plus difficile à traiter sans sortir de l'unité de Mélodie."[84]

Rousseau then expanded on existing theories by outlining other dramatic situations in which he felt duets might successfully be inserted, that is, without impairing the *vraisemblance*. Climactic moments ("des situations vives & touchantes") in which both the singers and the spectators became so carried away by their emotions that they were oblivious to all notions of "les bienséances théatrales" were considered especially appropriate, as were a variety of poignant occasions:

> "L'instant d'une séparation, celui où l'un des deux Amans va à la mort ou dans les bras d'un autre, le retour sincere d'un infidele, le touchant combat d'une mere & d'un fils voulant mourir l'un pour l'autre; tous ces momens d'affliction où l'on ne laisse pas de verser les larmes délicieuses: voilà les vrais sujets qu'il faut traiter en *Duo* avec cette simplicité de paroles qui convient au langage du coeur."

Thus did Rousseau admit more latitude into the dramatic character of duet movements; yet it is interesting to note that the situations he outlined were all particularly well suited to traditional mellifluous melodic treatment. He recommended that librettists and composers avoid setting more dramatic and turbulent texts, since violent passions almost always resulted in the expression of conflicting emotions, a feature best avoided:

> "La fureur, l'emportement marchent trop vîte; on ne distingue rien, on n'entend qu'un aboiement confus, & le *Duo* ne fait point d'effet. D'ailleurs, ce retour perpétual d'injures, d'insultes conviendroit mieux à des Bouviers qu'à des Héros."

Rousseau targetted another aspect of musical style in duets. His recommendations that such pieces be composed in dialogue form, that they avoid dissonance and harmonic complexity wherever possible, and that the voices combine only in sonorous intervals all stemmed from the idea that melody should serve as the basis of musical composition; so, too, did his view that duets should ideally be composed for two equal voices:

> "Les *Duo* qui font le plus d'effet sont ceux des voix égales, parce que l'Harmonie en est plus rapprochée; & entre les voix égales, celles qui font le plus d'effet sont les Dessus, parce que leur Diapason plus aigu se rend plus distinct, & que le Son en est plus touchant."

In other words, a melody distributed between equal voices gave less impression of being segmented, and sharpened the sense of musical unity. This was especially distinct in the combination of soprano voices, and Rousseau was quick to point out that this was a pairing greatly favored by Italian composers.[85] However, he made one significant concession after recommending the use of equal voices:

"Mais quoiqu'il doive y avoir égalité entre les Voix, & unité dans la Mélodie, ce n'est pas à dire que les deux Parties doivent être exactement semblables dans leur tour de chant: car outre la diversité des styles qui leur convient, il est très-rare que la situation des deux Acteurs soit si parfaitement la même qu'ils doivent exprimer leurs sentimens de la même maniére: ainsi le Musicien doit varier leur accent & donner à chacun des deux le caractère qui peint le mieux l'état de son ame."

This concession may perhaps have been a response to Laugier's criticisms which, as noted earlier, had argued that it was natural for characters to express themselves in an individual manner, no matter how similar their sentiments. However, Rousseau still refused to acknowledge the dramatic credibility of divergent duets, whose opposing texts and contrasting vocal lines he believed destroyed all sense of a unified melody, as well as poetic intelligibility.

The article closed with an analysis of a dialogue duet by Metastasio, "Mia vita ... addio" from *L'olimpiade*, as set to music by Pergolesi. In praising "l'unité de Dessein par laquelle le Musicien en réunit toutes les Parties, selon l'intention du Poëte," Rousseau once again drew attention to the vital role played by the librettist in furnishing the composer with suitable material. In the comic sphere, "Lo conosco a quegl'occhietti" (from *La serva padrona*) remained the classic example.

In 1769 Pierre Nougaret (1742–1823) published a treatise in two volumes entitled *De l'art du théâtre en général*. This work was a detailed study of the *opéra-comique* (or the *opéra bouffon*, as it was termed), an area of great interest to its author as witnessed by the many *comédies*, *parodies*, and *pastorales* he wrote for several theatrical establishments during the 1760s and 1770s, including the Foire Saint Germain and the Ambigu-Comique.[86] *De l'art du théâtre* is considered by some as a satirical attack on the genre;[87] but given Nougaret's active interest and participation in this field, it seems more probable that he aimed at a humorously ambiguous attitude rather than at unremitting satire throughout. Whatever his intent, his chameleon outlook would account for the rather curious stance he adopted with regard to the duet.

Nougaret began by paraphrasing comments from Rousseau's *Dictionnaire* which had advocated duets for tender lovers and argued for dialogue composition with little blending of the two voices. In relating these theories to practice in the *opéra-comique*, however, Nougaret found little relation between the two:

"La plus-part des Compositeurs, de la nouvelle musique sur-tout, observent-ils toujours ces règles judicieuses, puisées dans la Nature?"[88]

One particular transgression he noted was the use of violent passions and turbulent dramatic situations as the basis of duets, a feature Rousseau had ardently proscribed:

"C'est pourtant presque toujours dans de telles circonstances que les Auteurs de la Comédie-mêlée-d'Ariettes placent le Duo; je crois qu'ils n'ont pas tout-à-fait tort."[89]

A little later he explained why:

"Il est pourtant vrai que les duo sont supportables dans les Poèmes du nouveau genre. La gravité des personnages que l'on y fait agir, ne les empêche pas de s'écrier tous à la fois; c'est même la coutume des gens du petit peuple, lorsqu'ils sont échauffés, de parler tous ensemble, en confusion & sans presque s'entendre."[90]

Nougaret's stance remains curious because of its ambivalence. In extensively paraphrasing Rousseau's logic he implied a tacit approval of these precepts; yet instead of criticizing the violation of these in duet composition, he seemingly argued in favor of contemporary practice. He felt, for example, that highly passionate situations, in which the participants sang in a disordered and contradictory fashion, remained true to notions of *vraisemblance*, because certain people often acted in this manner in real life. If Nougaret meant those sections in which he discussed the duet (and other ensembles) to be satirical in their intent, it is possible that his satire was aimed primarily at Rousseau's painstakingly elaborate theories, rather than at the librettists and composers who all too completely disregarded these. The short comments noting such transgressions after several sentences of paraphrasing have a markedly bathetic effect, suggesting that this may be the case.

Whatever the intention of Nougaret's treatise, one tendency is clear: the emergence of a more flexible attitude towards the duet, as evidenced by a more liberal interpretation of the concept of *vraisemblance*, and by an acceptance of the increasing disparity between theoretical recommendations and compositional procedures. This attitude is also found in duet theories that were articulated in the years immediately following the publication of Nougaret's work.

In the 'Essai sur l'opéra' published in 1772 as the first volume of his *Théâtre lyrique*, V. de La Jonchère transferred Nougaret's more liberal ideas concerning the duet to the sphere of serious opera.[91] He first praised duets written for two lovers, which he felt had scaled great heights in terms of beauty and expression—"Que l'on observe la nature dans ces moments délicieux"[92]—but then asked why they were employed so sparingly and always to accentuate the same dramatic tableau:

> "Pourquoi ne les employoit-on ordinairement qu'à la fin de l'action? pourquoi ne servoient-ils qu'à exprimer l'unanimité de deux amants dont les voeux sont comblés?"[93]

La Jonchère, although willing to expand the scope of duet writing, still worked within the limits of *vraisemblance*. He argued, analogously to Nougaret, that nature provided the source not only for lovers' duets, but for those in which two people, experiencing a certain degree of anger and therefore often in discord, were moved to express their feelings simultaneously:

> "Ces sortes de Duo ne sont guere en usage à l'Opéra. Et cependant ils y feroient autant d'effet, que ceux qui servent à exprimer le bonheur des Amants. L'unanimité & l'opposition de sentiments peuvent également fournir matiere aux Duo ... Quand les interlocuteurs parlent ensemble, il n'est pas toujours nécessaire qu'ils disent les mêmes choses. S'ils sont en opposition de sentimens, cela n'est pas possible; & quand ils sont d'accord, il n'est pas toujours naturel que leurs expressions s'accordent parfaitement."[94]

In this passage La Jonchère argued for a more complex style of dialogue duet, inspired possibly by those he may have heard in Philidor's *Ernelinde* (which incorporated sentiments of a more divergent nature).[95] He certainly distanced himself from the idea that the poetic text should be rendered clearly—"Quand les interlocuteurs parlent ensemble, il n'est pas toujours nécessaire qu'ils disent les mêmes choses"—which developed earlier concessions made by Rousseau in his *Dictionnaire*, at the same time mirroring the opinions voiced by Laugier some two decades previously.

La Jonchère suggested a more turbulent style of dialogue duet because he felt its impact could have several advantages within an opera:

> "Il est beaucoup d'occasions où l'on pourroit les employer avec succès, pour interrompre le dialogue, varier le chant, & donner de la chaleur à l'action."[96]

These comments represented another new direction in duet theories by recognizing a wider dramatic function for such compositions: that of increasing momentum and excitement, and of intensifying the action. Earlier thinking had conceived duets not in terms of "action", or their wider effect on an opera, but as static, more isolated encounters between characters. La Jonchère's approach could well have stemmed from moves to invest the serious opera with more realism in the second half of the 18th century. Certainly, his ideas embody this tendency in recommending that the duet shed its conventional character and incorporate greater stylistic diversity, the aim being to enhance the action ("donner de la chaleur à l'action" must allude to the possibility of "developmental" ensembles), and to allow this type of ensemble to be integrated more freely, and to greater effect, in serious opera.

The *Traité du mélodrame* (1772) by the *littérateur* Laurent Garcin (*fl* 1770s) also expanded current theory on the duet, but from an entirely different angle. Like Nougaret's *De l'art du théâtre*, it dealt primarily with the *opéra-comique*. Despite showing an informed appreciation of the subject, with careful attention to detail and to musical examples, it was criticized severely (and unjustly) by Grimm.[97]

Garcin's opening comments on the duet suggest, initially, a conservative approach in denying such movements any *vraisemblance*: "Il ne faut pas être habile Observateur pour s'appercevoir que les Duos ne sont point dans la nature."[98] He agreed, moreover, with several ideas fashioned by Rousseau in arguing that duets be placed in moving, vivid situations where the agitation of the singers might naturally cause them to sing briefly alongside one another, and that they be composed in dialogue: "les Duos en dialogue, soit phrasé, soit coupé, sont ceux qu'il [Rousseau] admettra le plus volontiers, comme ayant une marche plus naturelle."[99]

Garcin's ideas, for one who regarded duets as "point dans la nature," then took a seemingly unusual turn, although on closer examination it becomes apparent that he in fact used this as the very basis for new theories. In contrast to La Jonchère, whose aim had been to extend the dramatic context of the duet within the bounds of conventional *vraisemblance*, Garcin suggested that the actual musical style of duets be taken into consideration. In other words, *vraisemblance* was to relate not solely to what was deemed dramatically plausible, but to what could also be considered musically effective.

To this end, Garcin suggested that composers should cease to rely exclusively on the dialogue duet and should instead experiment with fugal patterns:

"Il y a qu'on peut disposer en forme du fugue, & ceux-ci sont encore d'un plus grand effet ... le Duo fugué donne beaucoup de liberté à l'action du corps, au lieu que le Duo symétrique [the dialogue duet] oblige les Chanteurs à se tenir droits comme des statues. Un Duo bien fait en ce genre, ne pourra manquer d'exciter l'admiration des Musiciens, ainsi que le plaisir des Spectateurs."[100]

One of Garcin's reasons for advocating fugal duets lay in the fact that he perceived them, somehow, to liberate the actors physically.[101] In the years before actors were required to consider their stage movements more carefully, they had often ceased to maintain their role whenever they did not sing. How quickly new ideas had been put into practice by Garcin's time is still unclear, but the above statement implies that acting methods, at least in duets, still left much to be desired. He therefore argued that contrapuntal vocal textures allowed characters to act and interact in a more theatrically spontaneous manner than when they alternated in dialogue, since they were both required to sing throughout the entire movement. Much evidence remains to be brought to light on acting styles at the Comédie-Italienne and the Académie during the third quarter of the 18th century before Garcin's criticisms—"droits comme des statues"—may be corroborated, and before the manner in which fugal (and other contrapuntal) duets opened the way for "beaucoup de liberté à l'action du corps" may be understood fully. What is clear at this stage, however, is that more realism in acting techniques paved the way for new definitions of *vraisemblance* which, in turn, allowed a greater degree of musical artifice and elaboration. Garcin's ideas reflected this tendency, and his acceptance of a contrapuntal style in duet composition, an aspect explored by other theorists later on in the same decade, was an extremely important development. Previously, musical artifice in ensemble composition could only be perceived as unnatural, as will be recalled from Mably's criticisms of the quartet in Lully's *Atys*.

In 1776, volumes i and ii of the *Supplément de l'Encyclopédie* were published. The second volume included two articles on the duet: 'Duo (Poésie Lyrique)' by Marmontel, and 'Duo (Musique),' a collaboration between Rousseau and Castillon *fils*. Exactly when these articles were compiled is unknown, but that they were commissioned in order to augment Rousseau's original article in the *Encyclopédie* was an indication of how far theories had developed within the space of 25 years.

Marmontel's entry was conventional in tone, echoing several of Rousseau's earlier notions rather than taking into account the more progressive ideas of later theorists. It may first have been drafted during the 1760s. His *Éléments de littérature* (1787), which reproduced the article in its entirety, remarked that since it had been written the author had provided many ensemble texts of the nature he described for composers working at the Académie and the Comédie Italienne. By 1776, the date the article first appeared in print, Marmontel had already collaborated with Rameau, Dauvergne, La Borde, Kohaut, and Grétry.

Marmontel enjoyed a varied career as a dramatist, poet, critic, editor, historian, academic, and government official. It is from his point of view as a librettist that his opinions concerning the duet were conceived. Rousseau, in the *Encyclopédie* and in his *Dictionnaire*, had noted that the construction of duet texts required sensitivity and skill on the part of the poet. Marmontel reiterated the onus under which the librettist was placed and his obligations towards the musician:

> "Le talent de faciliter pour le musicien la marche du *duo*, sur des mouvemens analogues & sur un motif continu, ne laisse pas d'avoir ses difficultés; il suppose dans le poëte une oreille sensible au nombre, & beaucoup d'habitude à manier la langue & à la plier à son gré."[102]

He then praised Metastasio for the manner in which he had structured his dialogue and had reserved concerted sections for the most dramatically poignant moments, an approach considered "la plus naturelle de toutes":

> "Metastase est encore pour nous le modele le plus parfait dans l'art d'écrire le *duo*; il s'y est attaché sur-tout à donner aux repliques correspondantes une égalité symmétrique; & ce qui est encore plus essentiel, il a choisi pour le *duo* le moment le plus intéressant & le plus vif du dialogue, & il y a ménagé les gradations de maniere que la chaleur va toujours en croissant. Cette forme de chant, la plus naturelle de toutes, est aussi la plus animée, & celle d'où l'on peut tirer les effets les plus surprenans."

The rest of Marmontel's article adhered to traditional interpretations of *vraisemblance*—"plus le *duo* se rapproche de la nature, plus il est susceptible d'expression, d'agrément & de variété; & qu'à mesure qu'il s'en éloigne, il perd de ses avantages"—and voiced, as a consequence, a preference for the Italian models which were felt to embody this ideal, rather than for the French models, "tel qu'on [les] a fait jusqu'à présent." Marmontel did not stipulate whether, in his criticism below, he was referring to duets from the repertory of the Académie or from that of the Comédie-Italienne, but the findings of previous chapters would suggest that his criticisms were aimed at the complex dialogue and contrapuntal duets heard at the latter establishment:

> "c'est-là ce qu'il y a de plus éloigné de la vérité, & en même tems de moins agréable. Ce n'est qu'un bruit confus & monotone qui se perd dans le cahos

des accompagnemens, & dont tout l'agrément se réduit à quelques accords qui
ne vont point à l'ame, parce qu'ils manquent d'expression."

Marmontel's only concession to more progressive views on
vraisemblance was a remark to the effect that when the two voices in an
Italian dialogue duet, overcome by passion, merged in ensemble, musical
matters overtook dramatic concerns: "Ici l'art prend quelque licence."
This had, however, long been accepted as a feature of such duets:
Marmontel was reluctant to allow "art" to impinge on conventional
vraisemblance in any more elaborate manner.

As if parodying the subject of its own consideration, the second
article, 'Duo (Musique),' was set out as a dialogue between its two authors.
Rousseau's contributions, taken directly from his *Dictionnaire*,
represented an older critical position which was repeatedly challenged by
the responses of Castillon *fils*.[103]

Rousseau's opening words outlined the difficulties involved in
maintaining unity of melody in the "duo dramatique." Castillon replied
(with material from the *Dictionnaire*) that in order to combat accusations
of *invraisemblance*, duets should be placed carefully so as to arise
naturally out of "des situations vives et touchantes." Rousseau then
restated his ideas on dialogue textures and the situations he felt appropriate
("celles qui sont susceptibles de la mélodie douce et un peu contrastée")
and inappropriate ("la fureur, l'emportement") for duet settings.

Castillon then allowed the even tenor of the article to change by
questioning Rousseau's idea that the expression of violent passions should
be suppressed:

> "M. Rousseau me permettra de remarquer que, si dans les *duo* d'emportement
> on ne distingue rien, on n'entend qu'un aboiement confus, c'est la faute du
> compositeur ou de l'acteur, & peut-être de tous deux. Graun (qui est sans
> contredit un des premiers musiciens qui ait jamais existé, quoiqu'il ne soit pas
> autant connu qu'il le mérite), Graun, dis-je, a composé deux *duo*
> d'emportement où tout est distinct, & qui expriment autant qu'il est possible
> les paroles qui sont détestables."[104]

The two duets to which Castillon referred were "Segui pur giovane
audace" in *Ifigenia in Aulide* (1749) and "Tralaseia [Tralascia] un vano
amore" in *Fetonte* (1750). Both were classic Italian dialogue duets, cast
in a five-part da capo structure in which each section progressed from
alternating singing and juxtaposition to cadential agreement.[105] As such,
Graun's treatment of "les duo d'emportement" contained no novel
features, but the point Castillon was making was that if the composer

arranged the musical lines carefully and the singers made sure to enunciate these clearly, then the clarity of both text and music could be preserved. If musical balance and order were maintained, there could be no reason for regarding duets of this nature as unnatural. The desire to expand existing theories in this respect was, like the arguments of Nougaret, La Jonchère, and Garcin, important since it encouraged librettists and composers to create duets from more diverse subject-matter and thus integrate them more freely into their operas.

After allowing Rousseau to reiterate his views on duets for "des voix égales," Castillon, ever anxious to expand the composer's licence, quickly capitalized on the admission that the two voices of a duet need not be entirely similar. In searching for ways in which a musician could produce two vocal lines which, though different, did not injure the unity of the melody and could interact freely while still comprising a coherent expression, Castillon maintained that the answer lay in counterpoint. In this opinion, which was sharply opposed to Rousseau's principle of "l'unité de mélodie," he followed on directly from Garcin:

> "En étudiant avec soin le contre-point double, l'imitation & la fugue, ces parties si essentielles de la composition, & négligées au point, que de cinq compositeurs, quatre ne savent pas ce que c'est; je le répete et le répéterai tant que l'occasion s'en présentera, il est honteux à un artiste d'ignorer les ressources de son art, sur-tout quand la paresse seule est la cause de son ignorance."[106]

Like Garcin, Castillon made reference only to strict counterpoint rather than to freer contrapuntal devices. Unlike Garcin, there was no attempt to reconcile these purely musical elements with *vraisemblance* in acting, although Castillon's reference to "les ressources de son art" implied that dramatic plausibility was beginning to take second place to the effect of ingeniously composed music. In arguing that it was natural and permissible for duets to exploit musical artifice, Castillon's theories emphasized once again how much the concept of *vraisemblance* had been transformed under the pressure of changing tastes. *Vraisemblance* applied to duet theories became less insistently rationalistic (i.e. seeking direct precedents in immediate nature) and more prone to accept illusion (i.e. aligned to musical artifice). As such, the change mirrored general developments during the period in question. The result liberated composers from the shadow of Rousseau's doctrines and invited them to develop their art more freely and eloquently than before.

To summarize: the earliest theorists, Mably and Saint-Mard, associated *vraisemblance* in the duet with fairly brief simultaneous singing by certain characters (ideally lovers) in certain situations (ideally those expressing agreement). Divergent texts were considered undignified in the *tragédie en musique*, as they undermined the integrity and clarity of the poetic text. These theories were superseded quite rapidly by new ideas when Italian opera finally gained a foothold in France in the early 1750s. Spearheaded by Rousseau, these interpreted *vraisemblance* primarily in terms of dialogue. A few contemporaries, notably Laugier and Aubert, continued to advocate simultaneous singing, though from a more expanded point of view than Mably and Saint-Mard, in that they also deemed contradictory expression, and more divergent contexts for duets, *vraisemblable*. However, the majority of Rousseau's ideas held their ground for nearly two decades.[107] Thereafter theories of *vraisemblance* in duets began to move away from purely rational concerns to explore the idea of a musically satisfactory artifice. This was reflected in the admission of divergent expression, of contrapuntal elements, and of greater dramatic diversity in subject-matter.

The same progression may be charted in theories relating to larger ensembles, even though these are less well documented. Writers addressed the matter of trios, quartets, and other ensembles in operatic composition at a much later stage in the 18th century, and were generally more cautious in what they wrote since the ground was less tested than in the case of duets. Their theories expanded the concept of *vraisemblance* more slowly than those relating to the duet, since it proved more difficult to justify large groupings of characters in rational terms and to resolve the problems resulting from this, in particular the unintelligibility of the poetic text and the issue of turbulent dramatic contexts. An examination of attitudes towards *vraisemblance* in larger ensembles, and the theories these engendered, forms the final part of this chapter.

Larger Ensembles

As early as 1704, Le Cerf de la Viéville had commented to the effect that duets were more *vraisemblable* than trios, and this was a notion that took root strongly in France. Duets were certainly composed far more frequently than any other type of ensemble, and remained popular for the

first half of the 18th century. Only one further source before 1750 is known
to contain more than a passing reference to larger ensembles. This was a
work published in 1743 by Gautier de Montdorge (d1768) entitled
Réflexions d'un peintre sur l'opéra. Although he may have styled himself
as such, Montdorge was not a painter by profession but, like his
contemporaries Mably and Saint-Mard, a *connaisseur* whose private
wealth allowed him to pursue his interest in the arts. As he remarked in
the opening pages of his work: "si tout le monde se mêle aujourd'hui
d'écrire sur l'Opera; pourquoi n'écrirois-je pas?"[108]

Montdorge's comments concerned the quartet, and are interesting
since they were among the first to draw attention to the poet's
responsibility to provide suitable verses for several characters to sing.
Having made reference to a supposed librettist of his acquaintance,
Montdorge reported a letter sent to this friend by a composer with whom
he was collaborating. This letter concerned the text of a quartet:

> "On me conseille de finir le troisième Acte par un Quatuor; il me faut des
> paroles: mais il ne faut pas qu'aucun vers tienne à l'autre, pour que je fasse
> fuger mes quatre parties. Un de mes amis m'a fait ce Quatuor, en quatre vers,
> que je trouve excellens; je m'en servirai, si vous ne pouvés pas m'en faire
> d'aussi bons.

> > Oui je vous aime.
> > Quel bien suprême!
> > Comblés mes voeux.
> > Je suis heureux.

> Remarqués que ces paroles sont faites comme il faudroit tous les Choeurs des
> Opera. Quand une partie dit, *oui je vous aime,* l'autre peut dire, *comblés mes
> voeux,* l'autre, *quel bien suprême,* l'autre, *je suis heureux.* Le sens est toujours
> tiré au clair, sans confusion. Voilà les bons. Et je ne sçai si vous sentés que
> dans ces quatre vers, on est maître de commencer par le premier, le second, le
> troisiéme, ou le quatriéme, la parole est toujours également bonne."[109]

This passage underlined the fact that ensemble texts of this nature
required careful preparation, that the librettist needed to be fully aware of
the musical potential of his verse and its possible manipulation by the
composer. That concerted movements for several voices demanded even
more skill than those for only two singers was a fact acknowledged by
theorists in subsequent decades. As Montdorge recalled, the end results
were not always successful:

> "Le Quatuor qui, aparemment, allongeoit trop l'Acte, ou dont la Musique ne
> valoit rien, fut suprimé."[110]

It is possible that Montdorge, in recounting this story, was speaking from personal experience and using his librettist "acquaintance" as a fictitious cover (just as he did the designation "peintre" in the title of his work). In 1739 he had collaborated with Rameau in the *opéra-ballet Les fêtes d'Hébé*. Neither the libretto nor the original score of this work indicates the omission of a quartet. However, it is possible that the quartet referred to was tried out and then cut during the rehearsal period, or even at an earlier stage in the creative process (assuming that Montdorge was indeed recounting a personal experience).

While critical writing on the duet flourished in the 1740s and 1750s, little of significance appeared in print concerning larger ensembles.[111] Most surprising is Rousseau's relative silence on the subject (given his interest in the duet), but this could be explained by his aversion to music comprising several parts. He did provide the article 'Trio' for the *Encyclopédie*—it appeared in volume xvi (1765)—but in this he was concerned with technical, not dramatic, aspects of three-part writing. Volume xiii, published earlier in the same year, contained articles also by Rousseau on the quartet and quintet, described briefly as pieces for four or five "parties récitantes." His *Dictionnaire* contained no new views on the trio, but did expand the *Encyclopédie* entries on the quartet and quintet, if in a somewhat negative fashion:

> "Il n'y a point de vrais *Quatuor*, ou ils ne valent rien. Il faut que dans un bon *Quatuor* les Parties soient presque toujours alternatives, parce que dans tout accord il n'y a que deux Parties tout au plus qui fassent chant et que l'oreille puisse distinguer à la fois; les deux autres ne sont qu'un pur remplissage, & l'on ne doit point mettre de remplissage dans un *Quatuor*."[112]

Of the quintet he was even more dismissive:

> "Puisqu'il n'y a pas de vrai *Quatuor*, à plus forte raison n'y a-t-il pas de véritable *Quinque*."[113]

Predictably, Rousseau expected larger ensembles to conform, like duets, to his notions of "l'unité de mélodie" through the use of dialogue. Since the maximum number of voices he would tolerate singing at the same time was two, any more, he maintained, were superfluous since their function was merely to fill out the musical texture. Four autonomous parts he would not countenance. These comments represented Rousseau's final words on the matter; although he contributed several articles to the *Supplément*, he was not asked to write those dealing with the trio, quartet or quintet.[114]

It was only with the publication of Nougaret's *De l'art du théâtre* in 1769 that critical thought began to focus more penetratingly on larger ensembles. This author's considerations extended not simply to trios and quartets, but to the larger sextets and septets as well. Remarks on all these ensembles are scattered across several sections in the two volumes of the work.

With reference, initially, to the spoken theater, Nougaret related how ancient philosophers such as Horace had restricted the number of actors in individual scenes to four: too many people on stage at once caused confusion and restricted the flow of the action. Nougaret observed, however, that the strict application of this principle to the *opéra-comique* would deprive the genre of one of its most beautiful attractions: "le nouveau Spectacle perdrait son plus bel ornement."[115]

Nougaret recognized that writing of this nature was open to criticism:

> "Il est alors à supposer que ses personnages ne doivent plus se faire entendre; car parlant tous à la fois, il est presque impossible de démêler dans cette confusion un seul mot de ce qu'ils disent."[116]

In justifying the inclusion of such pieces in the *opéra-comique*, he first and foremost defended their *vraisemblance* on musical grounds— "un morceau de Musique fait oublier bien des fautes"—admitting elsewhere that such writing was "délicieux pour les oreilles." He also justified the *vraisemblance* of larger ensembles in accordance with the more conventional precepts that had been established in duet theories:

> "Les trio, quatuor & quinqué n'ont, ainsi que le duo, un air de *vraisemblance* qu'en arrivant tout-à-coup lorsqu'un violent sujet de colère, de joye ou de surprise, viendra s'emparer des Acteurs. S'ils sont placés dans d'autres situations, j'ôse affirmer qu'ils feront peu d'effet."[117]

and, in a later section:

> "le Spectacle moderne est èxcusable d'adopter une telle absurdité. Le quatuor ou le quinqué est un éxcellent moyen de peindre une grande rumeur, & les cris d'une foule de gens qui se disputent ou se réjouissent."[118]

After having settled the problem of *vraisemblance*, Nougaret made several recommendations concerning the poetic and musical style of large ensembles. He suggested that their texts comprise as few words as possible and that the composer distribute the different lines with regard for intelligibility and clarity, "avec tant d'art que l'une n'empêchat pas d'entendre l'autre."[119] He also felt that dialogue was too artificial in the context of such complex ensemble movements:

> "Ils évitent encore un dialogue qui traînerait en longueur, puisqu'ils font èxprimer à plusieurs personnages tout-à-la fois, ce qu'il faudrait leur faire dire à chacun séparément."[120]

Nougaret suggested, finally, that the stage be cleared at the end of such pieces, thus effectively establishing their primary dramatic function as climactic ensembles: "Après le *quinqué* ou le *septuor*, il faut au moins faire ensorte que la plus grande partie des Acteurs se retirent."[121] He noted that few composers in the *opéra-comique* actually heeded this advice but, in the light of findings in Chapter IV which established that several larger ensembles were act finales, this comment can be identified as satirical exaggeration.

Nougaret's detailed theories and advice, which blended an objective approach to *vraisemblance* (i.e. establishing convincing parallels for large ensembles in nature) with the more progressive notion of succumbing to the sheer musical experience, were considerably ahead of their time. Subsequent writers reverted to voicing familiar reservations about larger ensembles. In his *Traité du mélodrame*, for example, Garcin wrote: "Si les Duos ne sont point dans la nature, que sera ce d'un Trio, d'un Quatuor, d'un Quinqué, &c?," and continued:

> "Je demande à tout Spectateur, qui ne vient pas au Théâtre pour la Musique seulement, si ces morceaux-là ne l'impatientent pas un peu, s'ils ne refroidissent pas son attention à la Scène. Je voudrois donc: 1°. Qu'on les admît plus rarement dans un Drame. 2°. Qu'on se bornât à les accompagner d'une simple basse, & non de tout ce fracas symphonique, qui, quoique les Acteurs se tient à crier, n'en absorbe pas moins les paroles qu'ils chantent."[122]

Garcin was far less able than Nougaret to reconcile complex concerted numbers to the demands of *vraisemblance*. He could not accept them for their musical value alone, but he did not deny that they might occasionally have their role to play in opera.

Other writers simply applied Rousseau's ideas on the duet to larger ensembles in insisting on dialogue as a criterion for *vraisemblance*. Charles de Villiers, in his *Dialogues sur la musique* (1774), observed:

> "Je voudrais que les *Duo, Trio, Quatuor*, &c. se rapprochassent davantage de la Nature, qu'ils fussent toujours dialogués. Il n'est pas de la bienséance que plusieurs personnes parlent à la fois, parce qu'elles ne s'entendent pas entr'elles; il semble qu'elles ne parlent que pour les auditeurs qui ne les entendent pas mieux. En dialoguant, comme je propose, les *Duo, Trio*,

> *Quatuor,* &c. on se parle, on s'entend, & la Musique peut donner à chaque
> Partie l'expression qui lui est propre. Mais si différents personnes exposent à
> la fois des sentimens contraires, il est impossible que l'accompagnement les
> exprime distinctement; il n'en résulte qu'un bruit confus et inintelligible."[123]

Marmontel, in the *Supplément* (Article 'Duo'), likewise advocated the use of dialogue, but pointed out that in the heat of the moment the voices might merge briefly:

> "Il arrive aussi quelquefois que deux, trois, quatre personnes, *&c.* dans la
> vivacité parlent toutes ensemble; que les repliques du dialogue, en se pressant,
> se croisent, se confondent, ou que le mouvement de l'ame des interlocuteurs
> étant le même, ils disent tous le même chose: c'en est assez pour établir le
> *vraisemblance* du *duo,* du trio, du quatuor, *&c.*"[124]

Thus the views of both Marmontel and de Villiers were more conservative than Nougaret's, because they closely related procedures for the composition of large vocal ensembles to those already defined for the duet. Generally, 18th-century theorists, with the exception of Nougaret, did not consider that, as more characters were integrated into concerted movements, so the compositional approach should be re-assessed, and the dramatic conceptions surrounding each type of ensemble modified. That the *vraisemblance* of ensembles for several voices proved hard for many to justify was reflected in the *Supplément* of the *Encyclopédie*, which lacked an entry on the trio, and whose articles on the quartet and the quintet did not consider such pieces from a dramatic point of view in any great detail.

Both these entries were written by Castillon *fils,* whose progressive views concerning the duet were outlined earlier. These were not transferred to the field of the larger ensemble. Like Garcin, de Villiers, and Marmontel, Castillon worked from the established belief that if duets and trios were unnatural aspects of operatic composition, then the quartet was even more so. He observed that the problems of both librettist and composer grew in direct proportion to the number of parts with which they had to deal:

> "Le *quatuor* demande encore plus d'attention ... que le trio & le duo, parce
> qu'il paroît bien plus hors de nature que quatre personnes chantent ensemble
> sans s'écouter que deux ou trois."[125]

In developing this theme Castillon suggested (as had Nougaret) that quartets were most effective when integrated into highly charged dramatic moments expressing "un degré de passion de plus qu'au trio," but he allowed quartets no more scope than this. His subsequent recommendations were quite restrictive: that only the four principal characters perform in quartets ("car un personnage subalterne ne ressent aucune passion assez forte pour un *quatuor*,") and that the sentiments expressed by the singers should not conflict, but merely paint different modifications of the same feeling:

> "Si le poëte trouve le moyen de faire avec raison chanter à quatre personnes les mêmes paroles, il est clair que c'est au fond une même passion modifiée différemment qu'il veut exprimer. Le musicien modélera sa mélodie principale sur cette passion, & les différens degrés de hauteur & de gravité des voix joints à quelques autres nuances, composerent les modifications de cette passion."[126]

Castillon's article also included a more technical paragraph describing how four parts of a composition could blend in a harmonically acceptable manner. His approach in the article 'Quinqué' was identical. Here, he described such movements as one step removed from the quartet: "Le *quinqué* vocal exige encore plus de passion que le *quatuor*; il est plus difficile à faire, tant pour le poëte que pour le musicien."[127] The remainder of his observations centred around an explanation of five-part harmony.

Critical thought with regard to larger ensembles in the third quarter of the 18th century was, therefore, mostly cautious in its outlook and recommendations. Concerted singing had, still, to divest itself of the scepticism that continuous lyrical declamation had faced almost a century previously, namely that it was a bizarre and unnatural form of expression. Theorists, alongside librettists and composers, were, however, gradually breaking down these barriers. Of the few writers who broached the subject of larger ensembles, most took established duet theories as their starting point and formulated a similar aesthetic for trios, quartets, and quintets. Thus *vraisemblance* became a "graded" concept. For example, if the duet was unnatural (although it was surmounting such accusations), then the trio was a little more unnatural and the quartet even more so. Similarly, when characters combined in song, they were more impassioned in trios than in duets, became greatly carried away in quartets and quintets, and so on. Nougaret was the only theorist studied to address the question of ensembles for more than five voices. He was also the most progressive of writers in that he sought a different basis for *vraisemblance* in its application to larger ensembles. This was founded partly upon the justification of new dramatic contexts for such movements, and partly upon an appreciation of their especial musical value and effect.

The very theoretical and rational manner in which writers approched the question of the operatic ensemble during the 18th century epitomized the spirit of the French Enlightenment, which sought to classify, to order, and to categorize. The underlying belief of the age was that in order to explain a concept, it had to be encased in a set of rules and conventions. As one contemporary writer observed:

> "tous les Arts ont leurs limites; quand ils passent au-delà, ils tombent dans des compositions bisarres qui choquent la Nature dont ils sont les imitations; & c'est un grand service à leur rendre que de fixer les bornes dans lesquelles ils doivent se renfermer."[128]

The relevance of theoretical rules and judgements, whether simple or elaborate, can only be understood fully in assessing their relation to practice. Did theory influence practice through composers and librettists conforming to the intellectual ideals of the *littérateurs*? Or did they set their own standards, so that practice stood in advance of theory? And what was the role, if any, of the public? How far did their tastes and expectations shape the approaches of *littérateurs*, librettists, and composers? In order to draw these disparate threads together, and bring the present survey of the ensemble in 18th-century French opera to a close, the final chapter will attempt to answer these points, and inspect some of the complexities inherent in the relations between evolving theory, theater practice, and the public.

Notes

1. The role of the musical *savant* is considered by W. Weber in: 'Learned and General Musical Taste in Eighteenth-Century France', *Past and Present*, xcix (1980).

2. "Le bel esprit est si fort en vogue à Paris depuis quelques temps que la maison du plus petit financier est remplie d'académiciens ou d'aspirants à l'être." M. Tourneux, ed.: *Correspondance littéraire, philosophique et critique par Grimm, Diderot, Raynal, Meister, etc.*, (Paris, 1877–82), i, p. 97. (Undated entry: late September 1747.)

3. Diderot, for example, saw his role in two lights: "L'un d'augmenter la masse de connaissances par les découvertes ... l'autre de rapprocher des découvertes et de les ordonner entre elles, afin que plus d'hommes soient éclairés, et que chacun participe, selon sa portée, à la lumière de son siècle." Quoted in D. Heartz: 'Les lumières: Voltaire and Metastasio; Goldoni, Favart and Diderot', *IMSCR*, xii: *Berkeley 1977*, p. 235. Grimm expressed similar sentiments in his *Lettre sur Omphale*: "L'autorité & le crédit des gens de Lettres avanceront sans doute ce terme si glorieux pour la France. C'est à eux, comme Professeurs de leur Nation & de l'Univers, d'éclairer la multitude par leurs lumieres & de la guider par leurs préceptes." (p. 36.)

4. See his *Éléments de musique théorique et pratique suivant les principes de M. Rameau* (Paris, 1752).

5. See the discussion on pp. 225ff.

6. Literature concentrating on the Encyclopedists and their musical stance includes: A. Jullien: *La musique et les philosophes au xviiie siècle* (Paris, 1873); A.R. Oliver: *The Encyclopedists as Critics of Music* (New York, 1947); E. Fubini: *Les philosophes et la musique* (Paris, 1983); B. Didier: *La musique des lumières* (Paris, 1985). Several books and articles deal with individual figures: A. Jansen: *Jean-Jacques Rousseau als Musiker* (Berlin, 1884); P.-M. Masson: 'Les idées de Rousseau sur la musique', *BSIM*, viii (1912); J.F. Strauss: 'Jean Jacques Rousseau: Musician', *MQ*, lxiv (1978); S. Baud-Bovy: *Jean-Jacques Rousseau et la musique*, ed. J.J. Eigeldinger (Neuchâtel, 1988); J. Carlez: *Grimm et la musique de son temps* (Caen, 1872); J.-G. Prodhomme: 'Diderot et la musique', *ZIMG*, xv (1913–14); P.H. Lang: 'Diderot as Musician', *Diderot Studies*, x (1968); J.-M. Bardez: *Diderot et la musique* (Paris, 1975).

7. D. Launay: 'La Querelle des Bouffons et ses incidences sur la musique', *IMSCR*, xii: *Berkeley 1977*, p. 232.

8. Oliver: *Op. cit.*, p. 13.

9. G. Bonnot de Mably: *Lettres à Madame la marquise de P... sur l'opéra* (Paris, 1741), pp. xiv–xv.

10. *Op. cit.*, p. 56. See also Didier: *Op. cit.*, p. 225. However, K. Pendle, in *'Les philosophes* and *opéra comique*: the Case of Grétry's *Lucile*', *MR*, xxxviii

(1977), argues to the contrary: "musical criticism in this period [the 1760s and 70s] was more often than not written by literary critics who reinforced the traditional French concern with the quality of the libretto while at the same time making few concrete statements about the music." (p. 186.) This follows the line taken by G. Bonnet earlier in the century: "Les Encyclopédistes ... ne considèrent pas la musique comme étant par soi-même un langage ayant sa puissance expressive et sa signification propres, mais comme un accessoire. La musique ne consiste, pour eux, que dans une traduction littérale de la parole." *Philidor et l'évolution de la musique française* (Paris, 1921), p. 86.

11. J.-B. Dubos: *Réflexions critiques sur la poésie et sur la peinture* (Paris, 1719), i, p. 226.

12. For a detailed study of theories of illusion in 18th-century France, see M. Hobson: *The Object of Art* (Cambridge, 1982). The following discussion quotes extensively from this work. On the subject of illusion, Fubini also writes: "Ce concept ... revêt une signification plutôt ambiguë, particulièrement lorsqu'il est appliqué à la musique, art asématique, auquel les notions d'imitation, de nature, de *vraisemblance*, s'applique difficilement." *Op. cit.*, p. 85.

13. This was precisely why critics such as Saint-Evremond were opposed to the opera: "mon Ame, d'intelligence avec mon Esprit plus qu'avec mes Sens, forme une résistance secrete aux impressions qu'elle peut recevoir, ou pour le moins elle manque d'y prêter un consentement agréable." *Oeuvres mêlées* (London, 1709), ii, p. 215.

14. Hobson: *Op. cit.*, p. 37.

15. *Ibid.*, p. 26.

16. *Ibid.*, p. 143.

17. G. Snyders: *Le goût musical en France aux xviie et xviiie siècles* (Paris, 1968), p. 56.

18. A. Maillet-Duclairon: *Essai sur la connoissance des théâtres françois* (Paris, 1751), p. 5.

19. Mably: *Op. cit.*, p. 20.

20. T. Rémond de Saint-Mard: *Réflexions sur l'opéra* (La Haye, 1741). He continues: "du moins est-il sûr que nous souffrons peu de ne la pas trouver; pourvu qu'on nous dédommage de son absence," pp. 13–14.

21. J. Lacombe: *Le spectacle des beaux-arts* (Paris, 1758), pp. 144–145.

22. *Op. cit.*, p. 42.'

23. J. Marmontel: 'Dénouement', *Encyclopédie*, iv, (Paris, 1754).

24. On a musical level this was embodied in attempts to synthesize French and Italian opera, to reconcile melody with harmony, and to establish a rapport between *vraisemblance* and illusion.

25. E. Cassirer: *The Philosophy of the Enlightenment* (Princeton, 1951), pp. 276–277.

26. These included the "Trio des Parques" (*Isis*, IVviii) and "Gardons nous bien d'avoir envie" (*Cadmus*, IIIi). Both compositions contained *unanime* expression and were written in a predominantly homophonic texture.

27. *Comparaison*, pp. 66–67.

28. "nous avons de lui quantité de *Duo* d'un goût exquis," *Ibid.*, p. 68.

29. *Ibid.*, p. 68. Of quartets he wrote: "Nous en avons peu, & ce ne sont proprement que des *Duo* doublés." (p. 70.)

30. *Ibid.*, p. 69.

31. The manuscript libretto from which this extract is taken is housed at *F-Pn* [Musique] (Th^B 2083).

32. P.-M. Masson: *L'opéra de Rameau* (Paris, 1930), pp. 264–265.

33. M. Noiray: '*Hippolyte* et *Castor* travestis: Rameau à l'Opéra-comique', *Jean-Philippe Rameau: Dijon 1983*, pp. 117–118.

34. G. Sadler: 'Rameau, Pellegrin and the Opéra: the Revisions of "Hippolyte et Aricie" during its First Season', *MT*, cxxiv (1983), p. 533.

35. Whether this criticism accurately reflected performance standards in ensemble singing at the Académie, or whether it was a satirical exaggeration, remains to be established. From reviews in the *Mercure de France* it is apparent that some performers were skilled in ensemble singing. In December 1735, for example, it was reported that a difficult divergent duet for two disconsolate lovers in IIIii of *Scanderberg* (Rebel and Francoeur) "ne laisse rien à desirer ni du côté de la composition, ni du côté de l'exécution." (p. 2704.) However, the same periodical noted in February 1737, with regard to a duet in IVii of Lully's *Persée*: "il fait un fort grand effet quand il est bien exécuté." (p. 359.)

36. See the *Mercure* (May 1741), pp. 953–955.

37. The date of publication is provided by P.F. Desfontaines in *Observations sur les écrits modernes*, xxvi (Paris, 1741), pp. 3–24 (Letter ccclxxvi, dated 23 September 1741). Mably's quotation is taken from p. xii of his *Avertissement*.

38. His attitudes towards *vraisemblance* and illusion were quoted above (p. 216). For a detailed biographical study of Saint-Mard see R. L. Myers: 'Rémond de Saint-Mard: a Study of his Major Works', *Studies on Voltaire and the Eighteenth Century*, lxxiv (1970), pp. 11–198.

39. "Je veux, quand le chant est beau, qu'on me laisse un peu goûter; & pour cela je serois bien-aise qu'on ne l'étouffât pas à force d'harmonie." *Op. cit.*, p. 48.

40. Quoted in the *Mercure* (May 1741), p. 935.

41. *Lettres à Madame la marquise*, p. 7. (See also above, pp. 214–215.)

42. *Réflexions*, pp. 51–52.

43. *Ibid.*, pp. 52–53. The ensemble text quoted in this passage refers to a duet sung in Iiv of Lully's *Alceste*.

44. *Ibid.*, pp. 52–53.

45. *Lettres à Madame la marquise*, pp. 157–158. By "renvoyer aux Fêtes" the speaker intends that duets be relegated to *divertissement* scenes only, where their irrational impact on the drama would be minimal.

46. *Ibid.*, p. 158.

47. *Ibid.*, p. 158.

48. *Ibid.*, pp. 159–160.

49. *Ibid.*, p. 162.

50. By the mid-1750s, however, the relationship between the two had cooled considerably. It later became extremely hostile when Rousseau broke with the Encyclopedist camp. See *Les confessions*, ed. J. Voisine (Paris, 1964), p. 453, p. 457, p. 488, and pp. 555–557.

51. F.M. Grimm: *Lettre de M. Grimm sur Omphale* (Paris, 1752), p. 23.

52. *Ibid.*, p. 23.

53. *Ibid.*, pp. 23–24. Such comments illustrate that Grimm's letter was not a wholesale criticism of the *tragédie en musique*.

54. *Ibid.*, p. 24.

55. *Ibid.*, p. 25.

56. See Jansen: *Op. cit.*, p. 481, and R.A. Leigh: *Correspondance complète de Jean Jacques Rousseau* (Geneva, 1965–), ii, pp. 112–115 (Letter 146).

57. *Op. cit.*, p. 90.

58. *Dictionnaire de musique* (Paris, 1768), p. iv. Judging from the preceding evidence, however, Rousseau evidently had more than three months in which to prepare his articles.

59. See Leigh: *Op. cit.*, ii, pp. 159–160 (Letter 162): "Je vous renvoie, Monsieur, la lettre C ... j'approuve les changemens que vous avez jugé à propos de faire; j'ai pourtant rétabli un ou deux morceaux que vous aviez supprimés ... Cependant, je veux que vous soyez absolument le maître, et je soumets le tout à votre équité et à vos lumières." I am grateful to Dr. P.E.J. Robinson for drawing the existence of this letter, and others in Leigh, to my attention.

60. See Chapter II above, pp. 87–89, for a discussion of these duets.

61. Quoted in Jansen: *Op. cit.*, pp. 459–460. Samuel Baud-Bovy argues, however, that Rousseau's letter was written several years before this date, and suggests that it was intended for Gabriel Bonnot de Mably. See "Jean-Jacques Rousseau et la musique française", in *Jean-Jacques Rousseau et la musique* (Neuchâtel, 1988), pp. 47ff.

62. 'Unité de mélodie', *Dictionnaire de musique*.

63. "Les premiers discours furent les premières chansons." Quoted from the *Essai sur l'origine des langues* in Hobson: *Op. cit.*, p. 295. Rousseau documented the difficulties he experienced as a musician on several occasions in *Les confessions*, for example: "Rien ne m'a plus coûté dans l'exercice de la musique que de sauter aussi légèrement d'une partie à l'autre, et d'avoir l'oeil à la fois sur toute une partition" (p. 244); and "La musique était pour moi une autre passion, moins fougueuse, mais non moins consumante par l'ardeur avec laquelle

je m'y livrais, par l'étude opiniâtre des obscurs livres de Rameau, par mon invincible obstination à vouloir en charger ma mémoire, qui s'y refusait toujours, par mes courses continuelles, par les compilations immenses que j'entassais, passant très souvent à copier les nuits entières" (p. 253).

64. See P.E.J. Robinson: *Jean-Jacques Rousseau's Doctrine of the Arts* (Bern, 1984), p. 32. Hobson also discusses Rousseau's reasons for rejecting Rameau's discoveries (*Op. cit.*, pp. 266–267).

65. 'Unité de mélodie', *Dictionnaire de musique*.

66. Hobson: *Op. cit.*, p. 258.

67. This quotation, and those following, are all taken from the article 'Duo', *Encyclopédie*, v, (Paris, 1755).

68. The Querelle des Bouffons subsequent to Rousseau's *Lettre* focused largely on how French prosody could be adapted to music, and a major part of Laugier's work deals with the extent to which language conditioned the character of a nation's music. His essay also embraces such subjects as church music, the embryonic *opéra-comique*, and individual aspects of operatic composition, including a criticism of Rousseau's views on the duet.

69. *Apologie de la musique françoise contre M. Rousseau* (Paris, 1754), pp. 56–57.

70. *Ibid.*, pp. 57–58.

71. *Op. cit.*, p. 66.

72. *Réfutation suivie et détaillée des principes de M. Rousseau* (Paris, 1754), pp. 66–67.

73. This particular view may well derive from Mably. See above, p. 223.

74. *Op. cit.*, p. 66.

75. *Examen de la lettre de M. Rousseau sur la musique françoise* (Paris, 1753), p. 31.

76. See 'Bâton, Charles *le jeune*', *The New Grove Dictionary of Music and Musicians*, ed. S. Sadie (London, 1980), in which Zaslaw recounts how this article was once thought to have been written by Diderot.

77. J. D'Alembert: 'Fragment sur la musique en général et sur la notre en particulier', *Oeuvres et correspondance inédites de D'Alembert*, ed. C. Henry (Paris, 1887), p. 181. This source is dated only "vers 1752".

78. *Le spectacle des beaux-arts* (Paris, 1758), p. 325. Lacombe equates musical and verbal discourse in the same way as Rousseau.

79. 'Poème lyrique', *Encyclopédie*.

80. *Ibid.*

81. See Leigh: *Op. cit.*, ii, pp. 85–87 (Letter 269).

82. See P.E.J. Robinson: *Op. cit.*, p. 250. The publication was reviewed by Grimm in the *Correspondance littéraire* in November 1767.

83. "C'était un travail de manoeuvre, qui pouvait se faire en tout temps, et qui n'avait pour objet qu'un produit pécunaire. Je me réservai de l'abandonner,

ou de l'achever à mon aise, selon que mes autres ressources rassemblées me rendraient celle-là nécessaire ou superflue." *Les confessions*, p. 608.

84. 'Duo', *Dictionnaire*, p. 179. Subsequent quotations are from the same article.

85. Vocal groupings in duets from 18th-century Italian operas were discussed in Chapter I above, p. 32.

86. Details of these are given in C.D. Brenner: *A Bibliographical List of Plays in the French Language, 1700–1789* (Berkeley, 1947, rev. 2/1979). One *pastorale*, *La bergère des Alpes* (after Marmontel), was set to music by Léopold-Bastien Desormery (*c*1740–*c*1810) and was performed in Lyons in 1763.

87. Hobson (*Op. cit.*, p. 157) draws attention to a comment on p. xx of Nougaret's preface: "Le lecteur se souviendra donc que la plupart des louanges que je donne à l'Opéra Bouffon ne doivent point être prises à la lettre."

88. *De l'art du théâtre*, ii, p. 331.

89. *Ibid.*, ii, p. 330.

90. *Ibid.*, ii, p. 336.

91. Little biographical information is available concerning this author. He described himself as "un Poëte Lyri-dramatique" in the preface to his work, and stated that his views on serious opera were "de simple réflexions."

92. 'Essai sur l'opéra', *Théâtre lyrique*, i, (Paris, 1772), p. 49.

93. *Ibid.*, p. 49.

94. *Ibid.*, p. 48.

95. See Chapter IV above, pp. 200ff.

96. *Op. cit.*, p. 50.

97. "Cet homme ne sait ni louer ni critiquer; il ne m'est même pas démontré qu'il sache bien précisément ce qu'il veut dire. Ce livre n'a aucun succès et n'est pas fait pour en avoir." *Correspondance littéraire*, ix, p. 398. Grimm's opinion is not representative of contemporary or current opinion. Garcin's views on individual ensembles are considered in detail in the following chapter.

98. *Traité du mélodrame* (Paris, 1772), p. 212.

99. *Ibid.*, p. 213.

100. *Ibid.*, p. 214. No duets from the *opéra-comique* repertory were actually written in strict fugue at this time. It is possible, however, that Garcin was referring to the freer type of counterpoint discussed in Chapter IV (see p. 172), rather than to the strict counterpoint his terminology in this passage suggests.

101. Other reasons are outlined in Chapter VI below, p. 272 and p. 274.

102. 'Duo (Poesie Lyrique)', *Supplément de l'Encyclopédie*, ii (Amsterdam, 1776). Subsequent quotations are from the same article.

103. Little is known of Castillon *fils*. Michaud's *Biographie universelle* includes an entry for one Jean-François-Mauro-Melchior-Salvemini de Castiglione, and suggests that he was Castillon *père*. Born in Italy in 1709, Castiglione became renowned as a mathematician and philosopher. He held several professorships at European universities, and died in Berlin in 1791.

104. 'Duo (Musique)', *Supplément*, ii.

105. Both duets were reprinted in *Duetti, terzetti, quintetti, sestetti ed alcuni chori delle opere del signore Carlo Enrico Graun* (Berlin & Königsberg, 1773–4).

106. 'Duo (Musique).' Compare these remarks with those of the German theorist Johann Mattheson in note 111 below.

107. They were even reiterated by some early 19th-century theorists, for example J.-D. Martine: "Les duos doivent être, autant que possible, dialogués. On sent combien il est inconvenant que deux personnes parlent ensemble; il en résulte *invraisemblance* et confusion surtout quand elles disent des choses différentes. Ce n'est que dans les moments d'une passion violente, d'une expansion soudaine ... que le duo peut être simultané." *De la musique dramatique en France* (Paris, 1813), pp. 41–42.

108. *Réflexions d'un peintre sur l'opéra* (La Haye, 1743), p. 3.

109. *Ibid.*, pp. 23–24.

110. *Ibid.*, p. 27.

111. Reference should be made at this stage to the opinions expressed by Johann Mattheson (1681–1764) in *Der vollkommene Capellmeister* (Hamburg, 1739), even though it is doubtful that they circulated in France during the period in question. He observed that melodic and harmonic clarity were essential in the composition of vocal ensembles, and one comment in particular could be translated aptly to the sphere of concerted writing in contemporary French opera: " ... we must not make a shield for ignorance from these observations. Many do such who are not like to venture past two and one-half voices and yet have problem enough bringing these out clearly and gracefully." E.C. Harriss: *Johann Mattheson's 'Der vollkommene Capellmeister': a Revised Translation with Critical Commentary* (Ann Arbor, 1981), pp. 684–685.

112. 'Quatuor', *Dictionnaire de musique*.

113. 'Quinque', *Ibid.*

114. These were written instead by Castillon *fils* and are discussed presently (pp. 250ff).

115. *De l'art du théâtre en général*, i, pp. 254–255.

116. *Ibid.*, i, p. 255.

117. *Ibid.*, ii, p. 331.

118. *Ibid.*, ii, p. 337. Nougaret voiced similar sentiments in his theories concerning the duet (see above, p. 238).

119. *Ibid.*, ii, p. 332.

120. *Ibid.*, ii, p. 337.

121. *Ibid.*, i, p. 255.

122. *Traité du mélodrame*, pp. 235–236.

123. *Dialogues sur la musique* (Paris, 1774), pp. 56–57.

124. 'Duo (Poésie Lyrique)', *Supplément*.

125. 'Quatuor', *Supplément*.

126. *Ibid.*

127. 'Quinqué', *Supplément.*

128. Anon: *Suite des lettres sur la musique françoise en reponse à celle de Jean-Jacques Rousseau* (Geneva, 1754), p. 35.

Chapter VI

Theory, Practice, and the Public

The final chapter in this study of the 18th-century duet and ensemble compares the theoretical views outlined in the preceding chapter with the practical achievements of librettists and composers working in the *opéra-comique* and the *tragédie-lyrique* during the third quarter of the century. It aims to discover whether the guidelines established by writers on these matters were adopted, or whether creative artists explored a different course. It also considers the reaction of audiences and the contemporary press, analyzing comments on individual ensembles and discussing the implication of these in terms of their relation to practice and to prevailing theoretical ideas.

Theory and Practice: the Approach of Librettists and Composers

Early views on the duet, expressed by Mably and Saint-Mard in the 1740s and by Grimm in the early 1750s, were influenced by, and based upon, the style of concerted writing cultivated at that time in the *tragédie-lyrique*. While these writers voiced reservations about certain types of ensembles and concern as to their over-use, they did not suggest any basic alterations to a practice that had been in operation for over half a century.

With Rousseau this situation altered considerably, because the genre upon which his opinions were formed was not the French *tragédie-lyrique*, but the pre-Classical Italian *opera seria*. This genre, as Chapter I illustrated, had evolved a very different style of ensemble composition. Duets were composed mainly in dialogue, the voices blending at the end of each section in intervals of thirds or sixths; they were reserved for climactic moments in the opera and were almost always written for the two main lovers, who expressed similar viewpoints. Many works included only one such ensemble in the course of the drama. This was exactly the approach Rousseau recommended; it is inconsistent, therefore, that the model he cited, "Lo conosco a quegli occhietti," was from an *intermezzo*, *La serva padrona*. The general style of comic concerted writing differed greatly from that of the *opera seria*: dialogue textures, for example, were often broken as voices overlapped and merged more freely. Furthermore, characters were often in opposition, and were certainly brought together more frequently in concerted movements.

Opposing views shared by Laugier and Aubert, namely that the characters of a duet might sing at the same time and voice contrasting sentiments if desired, can still be linked to the traditional style of ensemble composition in the *tragédie-lyrique*, a genre these writers supported. When Rousseau expanded his earlier opinions in the *Dictionnaire de musique* of 1768, he continued to advocate Italian practice, with new recommendations that duets be written for equal voices, in emulation of the castrato soprano/soprano combination common in Italy. Other theorists of the 1760s and 1770s, most notably Nougaret and Garcin, used the *opéra-comique* as their starting point. Their attitude towards the progressive approach of librettists and composers working in this genre was an enlightened one, particularly in their tolerance of larger concerted movements and of contrapuntal textures. That theorists used different operatic genres as the basis for their opinions explains the contrasting nature of the conclusions they reached and suggests, moreover, that these had limited relevance for the librettists and composers working in each field.

The Opéra-Comique after 1758

The interaction of theory and practice in ensemble composition in the *opéra-comique* from the end of the 1750s onwards can be viewed from two perspectives: by considering firstly how closely composers' scores reflected the musical procedures recommended by *littérateurs*, and secondly the extent to which dramatic *vraisemblance* shaped the character of concerted movements.

On a musical level, very few points of similarity exist. The widespread use of dialogue textures links practice to prevalent theories to a degree, but Rousseau's conception of dialogue as a melody distributed equally between the voices (these combining only at heightened moments) was a pattern adopted in only a small number of ensembles. Indeed, the concept of dialogue was so quickly developed in *opéra-comique* concerted writing as soon to bear little relation to Rousseau's original ideas. In other respects, ensembles in this genre were composed and integrated into works in a manner that took no account of this theorist's views. The relatively limited use of duets combined with the profusion of trios, quartets, and larger pieces; complex dramatic scenarios integrating a wide variety of characters and frequently depicting volatile situations (in particular ensembles of perplexity); extremely divergent texts giving rise to the expression of sharply conflicting emotions; contrapuntal vocal textures; and vivid, picturesque orchestral accompaniments. All these were characteristics greatly at variance with procedures favored by Rousseau.

As Chapter IV illustrated, however, these musical devices contributed considerably to greater realism in concerted writing. Form, texture, accompaniments, contrasting keys, meters, and tempos were designed with particular effects in mind and to accentuate a given dramatic situation. The application of new musical techniques led to an expansion of definitions of *vraisemblance*. Having been defined initially around one set of dramatic criteria, that established in the *tragédie-lyrique*, and articulated in theories by Mably and Saint-Mard, *vraisemblance* was then modified in the light of new musical approaches in the *opéra-comique* (the *tragédie-lyrique* retaining its traditional characteristics). Writers adapting Rousseau's strictures in the late 1760s and early 1770s strove to articulate ideas that more nearly matched the style of ensemble composition in the *opéra-comique* at this time, Nougaret, Garcin, and Castillon *fils* championing variously the composition of larger, more complicated ensembles and the use of contrapuntal vocal textures, divergent expression, and varied dramatic situations. The pattern this indicates, therefore, is of practice leading theory on both a musical and dramatic level. This is in keeping with several observations made by Nougaret to the effect that contemporary thought did not keep pace with musical ideas and that artists readily explored new directions in concerted writing of their own accord.[1]

The Tragédie-Lyrique

The musical style of concerted writing in serious genres during the third quarter of the 18th century coincided, in certain respects, with prevailing theoretical recommendations: duets were composed rarely, and the majority were written to *unanime* texts for lovers in "des situations vives et touchantes," embodying "une musique douce et affectueuse." Vocal pairings of soprano and *haute-contre* approached the recommendation that duets be composed for equal or nearly equal voices. These similarities, however, were purely coincidental because the style of ensemble in the *tragédie-lyrique* after 1750 merely continued long-established traditions. On both a musical and dramatic level, practice did not keep pace with the new impetus given to ensemble theories by Rousseau (and others thereafter). This is particularly evident in the continued use of homophonic textures, which allowed for little or no use of the dialogue patterns so ardently advocated, characters continuing to sing simultaneously rather than in alternation. It is also evident from the fact that on only a few occasions (such as in *Ernelinde*) did ensembles aim for *vraisemblance* through the use of idiosyncratic and more experimental musical devices. The tendency was, still, to project emotional "states", and to rely on well-established expressive types of ensemble such as the lovers' reunion or the vengeance duet.

Composers and librettists would certainly have been aware of the ideas articulated by their literary counterparts, and those emanating from the Encyclopedists' camp, in particular, circulated widely. However, operas were undoubtedly shaped first and foremost by the theatrical experiences of their creators. There were points of contact between practical and theoretical spheres, but the overall relationship was for concerted writing in the *opéra-comique* to be inspired by practical innovation and thus lead theoretical thought to new ground, while in the *tragédie-lyrique* practice remained traditional and simply coincided with some aspects of contemporary thought.

Critical and Popular Response to Ensembles

Theorists operated in one sphere, composers and librettists in another. The general public comprised a third party. How far did contemporary audiences support the practical achievements of composers and their librettists, and did they subscribe at all to the views prevalent among theorists? Answers to these questions are found by examining reviews of contemporary operas in leading journals, and opinions expressed in other literary sources. In collating reactions to individual ensembles, we detect some general patterns of response, but an investigation of this nature presents certain difficulties.

The first of these lies in judging how representative the evidence contained in source materials can be. Posterity does not preserve every detail and aspect of contemporary thought, and this is particularly true of the comments located regarding ensembles (many of which are of a complimentary rather than critical nature). It would be incorrect to assume that the various styles of concerted writing discussed met with unqualified approval; however, we can only interpret the available range of views and opinions and draw conclusions from these in the absence of alternatives. By consulting a cross-section of sources, and by clarifying the stance and individual preferences of the authors concerned, the limitations of historical evidence may, as far as it is possible, be overcome.

Secondly, it is important to remain aware of the critical standards operating during the period in question and to understand trends in contemporary taste (unaffected by a knowledge of later musical styles). Applying these considerations to the subject in question shows that the criteria used to describe and evaluate ensemble composition in the earlier chapters of this study were not necessarily those that would have been in force during the 18th century. Audiences of this time were presumably less interested in the vocal texture and musical form of ensembles, or the structure and manipulation of libretto texts, than in the standard of performance (which our modern age can never recreate), the quality of the poetic text, the suitable expression of this in music, and the piquancy and clarity of the dramatic situation: in other words, the contextual musical and dramatic effect of ensembles. An awareness of critical standards and prevailing tastes must also be accompanied by an appreciation of how language was used, in the 18th century, to convey ideas and opinions. Meanings and nuances change over the years, making the precise connotations of certain words and phrases sometimes difficult to establish. The extant musical evidence of the ensembles may serve, however, as a guide towards understanding what writers were intending to convey.

The Opéra-Comique

During the experimental years of the 1750s few detailed comments concerning ensembles are to be found in contemporary source materials. Contant d'Orville offered musical synopses of several works dating from this decade in his *Histoire de l'opéra bouffon* (1768), these containing mostly passing opinions on ensembles. D'Orville found the *opéra-comique* "un monstre agréable" and was of the opinion that it would never be "un genre, mais peut devenir un rien fort agréable."[2] This critical position was held by several commentators of the period, who accepted the popularity of the new form but felt that it did not compare with the *tragédie-lyrique* in terms of artistic merit and dignity.

Nevertheless, d'Orville's references to ensembles are favorable. The duet "Une dame vous enflâme," in *Ninette à la cour* (Favart, 1755), was described as "un duo dialogué à l'Italienne, dont le contraste toujours soutenu, finit vivement le second acte."[3] This was a parody duet whose music was modelled on "Sei compito e sei bellino" from Selletti's *Il cinese rimpatriato*. D'Orville's approval of this movement underlined the popular appeal of Italian ensembles, in particular their dialogue textures; the contrast mentioned reflected the fact that the duet portrayed a heated argument between the two lovers and therefore incorporated contrasting musical ideas. The lively conclusion it provided to the second act also indicated that ensembles with a spirited subject-matter were as popular with audiences as the more traditional and mellifluous lovers' duets. This is corroborated by d'Orville's opinion of the fine action quartet concluding *Les troqueurs*, analyzed in Chapter II: "Rien de plus vif & de plus brillant que ce quatuor."[4] It was likewise written in dialogue and included spirited interchanges between the four characters.

From the late 1750s onwards more tangible responses towards ensembles in the *opéra-comique* emerge. Contemporary commentators concentrated on two aspects in particular. One concerned the association of words and music: the translation of the librettist's text by the composer and the apt and natural musical expression achieved. The other considered the increasing contrapuntal complexity of concerted writing. These are discussed under the headings of "Dramaturgy" and "Contrapuntal Writing" below.

Dramaturgy: As Chapter IV pointed out, a strong characteristic of concerted writing at this time was its ability to paint characters and situations aptly through a variety of musical means. Contemporary recognition of this is found in the *Mercure de France*, the leading critical journal of the time. Each monthly issue reported on productions at the major Parisian theaters, some more extensively than others, the length of reviews for individual works staged at the Comédie-Italienne varying from one to four pages. Much of the *Mercure's* writing was of a complimentary nature and was concerned to vaunt the prowess of national music and the achievements of French artists. Some reviews passed only general comments: in 1763 concerted movements from Philidor's *Le bûcheron* were grouped together in one general eulogy:

> "le *Quatuor* des Créanciers, &c. le *Trio* des Consultations, le *Septuor* de la fin, Morceau détaillé sans la moindre confusion, & les airs de Suzette et de Colin, tout cet ensemble saisit & frappe par la vérité des caractères de chaque Interlocuteur établis dans cette Musique pittoresque."[5]

If the style of the ensembles cited in this passage is considered, it will be seen that each is very different. The quartet (in scene viii) paints a complex scenario which is enhanced by a fugato texture. The trio (in scene xiv) substantiates previous dialogue and is written in dialogue. The septet (scene xviii) brings the drama to a climax and is likewise set in dialogue. Linking the *Mercure's* praise to specific musical and dramatic characteristics, given such a brief quotation, is impractical. Neither would an analytical approach necessarily reflect what contemporary audiences would have admired, for what the review in fact praises is the immediate and overall effect of the ensembles (and other movements) it describes. These proved popular because of their charming musical style and, more importantly, because they embodied an expressive and realistic translation of character and dramatic situation: the term *vérité*, encountered frequently in sources, is best translated in modern terms in this manner.

Individual treatises, particularly Garcin's *Traité du mélodrame*, discussed ensembles in much greater depth than reviews in periodical publications.[6] This author's extensive study of the *opéra-comique* was penetrating, at times critical, but generally supportive of the developing genre. As he remarked in the introduction to his study:

"presque toutes nos notions les plus générales en Musique sont autant de préjugés ... j'ai essayé ... de ramener les choses au vrai, citant toujours l'oreille, & même l'esprit, au tribunal du sentiment, comme à leur premier Juge."[7]

Garcin's comments were cited extensively in the previous chapter. We may recall, for example his opinion of the duet opening *Le soldat magicien* (Philidor, 1760):

"le Duo du jeu de trictrac, dans lequel on peut dire qu'il n'y a pas un coup de dez dans le cornet, sous le main & dessus la table, qui ne soit rendu, & où, jusqu'au genre de mesure, tout est analogue au mouvement de l'action, ou à l'expression des paroles."[8]

The printed score to *Le soldat magicien* indicates several detailed stage directions during the course of this duet, and the picture is greatly enhanced in Philidor's music, hence Garcin's observation that "tout est analogue au mouvement de l'action, ou à l'expression des paroles." Example 6.1 transcribes bars 21–35 of this movement, which contain many clever vocal and instrumental figurations. The throwing of the dice is depicted in bar 21 by a rising demisemiquaver motif; the more deliberate orchestral figures from bar 22 onwards (the bass-line marking time on each main beat while the upper strings fill in with semiquavers) suggest the players momentarily concentrating on their moves; repeated semiquavers towards the end of the example paint M. Argant's laughter; and the clever contrast of forte and piano dynamic markings in bars 31 to 34—imitating the orchestral introduction to the duet which had contained 13 changes of dynamics in 14 bars— symbolizes the volatility of the game.

Garcin wrote at much greater length on the ensembles in Philidor's later opera, *Tom Jones* (1765). The duet for Sophie and Mme Western closing Act I caught his interest because of the manner in which the music painted the dramatic situation, emphasized character, and was used to support and mirror the poetic text:

"je crois reconnoître la marche & le ton de la nature dans celui que chante Madame Western & Sophie. Celle-là s'y exhale en reproches conformes à son caractère, celle-ci y fait entendre les accens supplians de la douleur. On trouvera néanmoins quelque chose de bien déplacé dans le chant de Sophie: ce sont ces tenues au mot *calmer*, & au mot *colère*. Une voix altérée par l'émotion de l'ame ne donne point de durée à ses tons: dans cet état, les poumons se resserrent, les oscillations de l'air dans la poitrine, sont pressées

Example 6.1 "Quatre et cinq" *Le soldat magicien* scene i (Philidor, 1760)

& contraintes, l'haleine est courte, le souffle manque, & ce sont ces phénomènes que l'Art doit saisir, sans quoi la Musique donne le change à la Poësie."[9]

"Que les devoirs que tu m'imposes" was satisfactory in that the contrasting characters of the two ladies were skilfully reflected in the design of the music, but Garcin implies that the line sung by Sophie did not wholly correspond with her agitated state. In effect he argues that the music would have translated the poetic text with more fidelity had Sophie's long notes to words such as *calmer* and *colère* been replaced by shorter and more broken figures. By extension, this critique might also be interpreted as an argument, not simply for more naturalism in declamation,

Example 6.2 "A la fête du village" *La clochette* scene viii (Duni, 1766)

but for greater realism in acting as well. If so, when Garcin speaks of "ces phénomènes que l'Art doit saisir," he speaks just as much to singers recreating the music as to composers.

Several features of the duet sung by Sophie and her father in IIix, "A ton père," were praised by Garcin for their dramatic poignancy:

> "le but de Sophie dans ce Duo, c'est d'attendrir son pere; le chant doit donc être plus pathétique que pittoresque. Plusieurs traits sont de ce caractère; on n'y trouve ni remplissage, ni confusion, ni longueurs. La colère de M. Western est d'un caractère plus violent que celle de sa soeur; elle est aussi plus fortement exprimée, par l'emploi que le Musicien a sçu faire des contre-basses. Cependant il semble que cette passion se modère par intervalles; suspension délicate dans laquelle se peint la tendresse paternelle!"[10]

In pointing to the well-designed character of Sophie's line and the effective contrast produced by her father's more violent emotions (these tempered by moments of compassion), Garcin's critique reflects the extent to which ensembles were judged in terms of the empathy between music and the emotive content of the poetry. This, in conjunction with acted realism, was imperative in order to achieve a naturalistic translation of the dramatic situation. Through such means *vérité* in ensemble composition could be achieved.

Garcin also had unqualified praise for the duet closing scene viii of *La clochette* (Duni, 1766), "A la fête du village"—see Example 6.2 for the opening of this—where, once again, the music was felt to capture the poetic text and dramatic situation perfectly:

> "Quoi de plus naturel encore … Ne semble-t-il pas que les paroles aient été composées pour la Musique?"[11]

These comments may be interpreted in a very basic sense as referring to the treatment of certain words—note in bar 8 the way *mépris* coincides with a c♮—but it is more likely that Garcin felt the general spirit of the text admirably captured in the cheerful melody, the bright major key, and the lilting rhythms, especially between bars 13–20.

Contant d'Orville also commented on the apt and natural expression in the duet "Non, non, vous ne m'avez jamais traitée ainsi" from Ivi of *Le roi et le fermier* (Monsigny, 1762):

> "Ce duo est charmant & bien caracterisé. Tout y peint avec une *vérité* singuliere & les pleurs de *Betsy* & l'impatience de Richard."[12]

Example 6.3 transcribes the opening bars of this movement to illustrate how *vérité* was achieved through well-chosen musical means. Richard has

Example 6.3 "Non, non, vous ne m'avez jamais" *Le roi et le fermier* Ivi (Monsigny, 1762)

treated his sister brusquely because he is worried about Jenny, his lover, who has not yet returned home. This has upset Betsy. Monsigny paints her emotions through his use of broken, plaintive figurations, contrasts these with Richard's sterner and more strident line, and then juxtaposes the two parts to accentuate these conflicting emotions.

Contrapuntal Writing: Experimentation with more contrapuntal textures was an important feature of concerted writing during the third quarter of the 18th century, but one that met with mixed reactions from contemporary commentators. A work occasioning much reaction in this respect was Monsigny's *Le roi et le fermier* (1762), which contained four duets, one duet/trio, two trios, a quartet, a septet, and a closing chorus. The first duet, "Non, non, vous ne m'avez jamais traitée ainsi," was considered by Garcin an excellent example of "un Duo fugué":

> "Un Duo bien fait en ce genre, ne pourra manquer d'exciter l'admiration des Musiciens, ainsi que le plaisir des Spectateurs; & sur la foi des uns & des autres, je proposerai hardiment le Duo de Richard & de Betsy, dans *le Roi & son Fermier* [sic], comme un modèle, dont toute la mélodie italienne n'approchera jamais."[13]

Garcin was prepared to vaunt contrapuntal devices at the expense of melody if such techniques were introduced with skill by the composer and proved dramatically effective. D'Orville held similar views, as his praise for the trio introducing the third act of the same opera testified. This was the ensemble in which Jenny, Betsy, and their mother each sang separate solos, these then being skilfully interwoven:

"Elles chantent toutes trois, chacune un air différent qui forment un Trio d'un genre neuf & dont la précision satisfait les oreilles les mieux organisées."[14]

Another review likewise supported this novel venture but noted that it was not instantly successful, due to performance difficulties:

"La Scène, où en attendant RICHARD, la MERE, BETSI & JENNI chantent chacune des choses différentes, est un tableau très-bien rendu, & dont l'effet agréable n'avoit pû être aussi-bien senti à la premiere Représentation, attendu la difficulté de l'extrême précision qu'il éxige dans l'exécution."[15]

Similar problems were reported in a third source, the periodical *L'Avant-coureur*, which referred in the context of wider criticisms to:

" ... la réunion en trio des trois chansons des travailleuses, que tout le monde soupçonne devoir produire le plus brillant effet quand il s'exécutera d'accord, mais qui jamais ne sera exécuté."[16]

L'Avant-coureur, edited at this time by Jacques Lacombe (whose theoretical views on the ensemble were outlined in the previous chapter), was a more critical journal than the *Mercure*, as the tone of the above passage suggests. Indeed, it was not averse to heavy criticisms, and to quote in full the passage from which the above comments were extracted is to emphasize the extent of the opposition to Monsigny's adventurous ensembles in *Le roi et le fermier*. The review initially condemns the "cacophonie dans les duo, trio, &c," and continues thus:

" ... quand le poëte & le musicien se seront déterminés à quelques petits sacrifices, ils verront la chaleur faire généralement l'ame de leur ouvrage; l'esprit des paroles, le goût charmant & fin de presque tous les morceaux de chant, tout sortira, & sortira avec avantage. Si, par exemple, l'on sacrifioit la moitié du duo de Betsy & Richard, le morceau de guerre que chante le roi dans le moment trop déplacé, la réunion en trio des trois chansons des travailleuses, que tout le monde soupçonne devoir produire le plus brillant effet quand il s'exécutera d'accord, mais qui jamais ne sera exécuté; ainsi si l'on sacrifioit les deux tiers du quatuor de la fin du second acte, les amateurs verront avec plaisir cette soumission, faite par des auteurs qui ne doivent pas regarder le public comme leur tyran, puisqu'il les a plus habitués aux applaudissements qu'aux corrections."[17]

It is interesting to note that this critique focuses on three ensembles with highly contrapuntal ("cacophonous") textures. The modifications, suggested in order to increase "la chaleur" and ostensibly reach to the "soul" of the drama, echo a complaint familiar from the preceding chapter: namely that too much artifice and complexity in ensemble composition inevitably resulted in a lack of *vérité*. ("Chaleur," in this context, could be interpreted as vibrancy or spirit, and as such becomes an important constituent of *vérité*.) The critique suggested initially that half the duet (in Ivi) be cut, a movement that Garcin, in contrast, had praised as a model "duo fugué." It also recommended that the trio opening the third act omit the *à3* portion combining the songs of the three ladies, especially since its performance left much to be desired. Finally, it argued that two-thirds of the quartet finale to Act II be dispensed with. This ensemble, it will be remembered, was a comic action finale in which the sentiments of the characters concerned were juxtaposed skilfully and to great expressive effect.[18] Contrapuntal writing, partly because of its complexity and partly because of the demands it placed on the performers, was often considered an artificial ploy, and as such an unnatural portrayal of character and dramatic situation.

Whether this review was written by the editor, Lacombe, cannot be ascertained. However, the view of the ensembles in question as "cacophonous" and the criticism of contrapuntal techniques suggests that the writer's preference was for concerted movements of a more conservative nature, for example those composed in dialogue, a procedure to which Lacombe had subscribed in *Le spectacle des beaux-arts* (1758).

Having warmly praised one "duo fugué" from *Le roi et le fermier*, Garcin adopted a more circumspect tone when discussing ensembles with similar characteristics in Monsigny's later work, *Rose et Colas* (1764). Initially, his remarks were of a complimentary—and typically searching—nature, approving of the contrapuntal techniques employed and criticizing Italian composers for their all too infrequent use of such methods. Of the first duet, "Ah! comme il y viendra" in scene ix, he wrote:

"Le Scène des deux peres est un chef-d'oeuvre de dialogue, & le Duo un chef-d'oeuvre d'harmonie. C'est à l'harmonie à décorer des airs faits pour des Vieillards, comme c'est à la mélodie à embellir les chants d'un Amant & d'une Maîtresse, attention que les Italiens négligent toujours, parce qu'ils ne se doutent pas de la régle. Ils ne travaillent jamais note contre note, ils ne font point usage des Duos fugués, qu'ils renvoyent sans nécessité au chant Ecclésiastique."[19]

However, the trio following this duet, written in a strict fugal style, was considered a less successful musical translation of the dramatic situation. Garcin preluded his criticisms with this passage:

> "Je ne m'étendrai pas sur la fugue qui se chante entre Rose, Mathurine & Pierre le Roux. Quiconque connoît la difficulté de semblables Piéces de Musique, quiconque a vu beaucoup de Maîtres Italiens, fort applaudis au Théâtre, échouer dans cette partie, quiconque sçait que la fugue est l'*ultimum* du Théoricien, & le désespoir du Compositeur, n'aura pas de peine à évaluer le mérite de celle-ci. Il verra sur-tout combien ce genre de Musique est propre à des Scènes de caractères, au mouvement des passions, à l'*imbroglio* des Scènes: si de tels morceaux sont rares dans nos Opéras, la raison en est aisée à comprendre, c'est que le génie y est encore plus nécessaire que la science."[20]

and then continued:

> "Tandis que Rose demande pardon, Pierre le Roux envoie Mathurin à tous les Diables, & Mathurin menace Pierre le Roux de l'assommer: de-là naît une confusion qui étourdit l'Auditeur, & qui fait que l'intérêt se perd dans le tumulte. Je demande à tout Spectateur, qui ne vient pas au Théâtre pour la Musique seulement, si ces morceaux-là ne l'impatientent pas un peu, s'ils ne refroidissent pas son attention à la Scène."[21]

In criticizing the contrapuntal texture of the quintet towards the end of *Rose et Colas*, an ensemble of perplexity, Garcin indicates why he approved of such textures in certain concerted movements, but not in others:

> "Le quinque suivant seroit le plus beau morceau de la piéce, s'il n'avoit pas le défaut dont j'ai parlé tout-à-l'heure. Les phrases, il est vrai, sont plus détachées, plus distinctes, mais cet avantage est perdu par la rapidité du mouvement, qui confond le langage de tous les Interlocuteurs, de façon qu'on n'entend plus qu'une grande noise [sic] entre quatre ou cinq personnes."[22]

His comments first of all imply that the speed of a movement could cause confusion, and then that the more characters involved in contrapuntal ensembles, the greater the risk of marring the intelligibility of the text and, consequently, dramatic *vérité*, since the result was to dampen ("refroidir") the experience for listeners (unless they were interested in the music alone). Such a stance would explain why Garcin sanctioned the introduction of smaller contrapuntal ensembles—"duos fugués"—in certain circumstances (always with the proviso that they represented text and dramatic situation effectively), and why he was reluctant to transfer these techniques to larger ensembles. To substantiate this hypothesis, Garcin's lengthy critique of Philidor's innovative duet from the opening scene of *Tom Jones*, which juxtaposed different time signatures, is quoted below. Here he noted the potentially confusing effect of such a design on the listener, but stressed that the ploy was simple enough to be perceived quickly, presumably because there were only two contrasting musical lines to isolate and distinguish from one another. That the composer resorted to such "artifice" in the construction of this duet was deemed a triumph for the matching of poetic text and music. It allowed the opposing sentiments of the two characters to be contrasted in a clear and vivid manner and thus translated the dramatic situation aptly, at the same time producing an intriguing and novel musical result:

> "Le premier Duo me paroît d'une exécution heureuse, & sur-tout d'une excellente invention. Comment faire chanter en même temps deux personnes dont l'une n'a que des idées sérieuses, & l'autre que les idées folles, comment, dis-je, les faire chanter ensemble, sans jetter de la disparate dans l'Air, & sans parler à l'oreille un langage obscur ou barbare? ... Au premier jugement de l'oreille, le chant de ce Duo paroît un peu bisarre en effet ... Il semble que l'Air d'Honora est d'un autre mouvement & d'un genre plus gai que celui de Sophie: mais avec de l'attention, l'oreille se détrompe, & reconnoissant l'artifice du Musicien, jouit à la fois de sa sensation & de sa surprise. Cet artifice consiste simplement à donner à la partie d'Honora un mouvement de $\frac{12}{8}$, qui, comme on sçait, peut se résoudre dans la mesure à quatre temps ... Ajoutez à cela, que les *legate* d'une partie sont des *staccate*, ou notes syllabiques dans l'autre, ce qui contribue à rendre le chant de l'une plus traînant, & par conséquent plus triste, celui de l'autre plus rapide, & par conséquent plus gai. Ainsi toutes les loix du Mélo-Drame se trouvent remplies dans ce Duo; l'Auteur y donne à la Poësie tout ce que la raison peut exiger, & à la Musique tout ce que l'oreille a droit de prétendre."[23]

Public opinion at large, as reflected in the more general critiques of leading periodicals, supported new techniques such as contrapuntal complexity in ensemble composition. The *Mercure* noted that the duet closing Act II of *Le déserteur* (1769), in which a drinking-song for Montauciel was superimposed over a simple *chanson* sung by the rustic Bertrand, was "aussi ingénieux que singulier" and one of the most applauded pieces in the entire work.[24] The contrast underlying this duet is comparable to Phildor's experiment with dual time signatures in *Tom Jones*, and would suggest the general acceptance of such experiments in ensemble composition.

The nine ensembles in Monsigny's *L'isle sonnante* (1767), which frequently introduced complex vocal textures, were similarly praised in *L'Avant-coureur*:

"Il y a dans la piéce des Duo animés, des Ariettes agréables, des tours de chant neuf & expressif, des Trio & des Quatuor d'une harmonie pleine & imposante."[25]

This stance contrasts with earlier criticisms levelled at contrapuntal ensembles in *Le roi et le fermier* by the same periodical. It is possible that, between 1762 and 1768, its editorship had changed, or that, because such ensembles had become more common in the *opéra-comique*, they proved more acceptable. The latter explanation is more likely since, in 1764, the same periodical had marked out for particular comment a contrapuntal quartet in IIx of Philidor's *Le sorcier* ("Ah! mon frère!") with the words "cette piquante invention dont le public est si avide de nos jours," a comment that indicates the enthusiastic public acceptance of a contrapuntal style in concerted writing.[26]

The Tragédie-Lyrique

Opinions expressed in 18th-century literature on ensemble composition in serious genres range from short statements to more detailed analyses of individual ensembles. A traditional approach continued to prove popular, in spite of the new and more progressive approaches being developed in the *opéra-comique*, but those ensembles composed in other styles (for example dialogue, divergent, and contrapuntal movements) were also praised. The sections that follow consider the reactions of audiences and critics to three different categories of ensemble: those with homophonic textures and *unanime* texts; those composed in dialogue; and those based on divergent expression.

Homophonic Ensembles: Mondonville's *pastorale héroïque Titon et l'Aurore*, first performed at the Académie in January 1753, proved a triumph for supporters of the *coin du roi* in the Querelle des Bouffons.[27] Of the three duets contained in this work, that for the lovers in Iii, "Règne Amour dans nos âmes," was a great success. Its style, as Example 6.4 indicates, was entirely traditional: it was based on a *unanime* quatrain, was written for soprano and *haute-contre* in a homophonic texture throughout, had characteristic coloratura to words such as "lance" and "règne", and a discreet two-part string accompaniment. The *Mercure* remarked that this number was "fort applaudi";[28] and Cazotte, in his pro-French pamphlet *La guerre de l'opera*, described it as "un duo qui ne laisse rien à desirer."[29]

Example 6.4 "Règne Amour" *Titon et l'Aurore* Iii (Mondonville, 1753)

Another duet by Mondonville in this style, "Je n'auray jamay trop de lezé" in IIIvi of the *pastorale languedocienne Daphnis et Alcimadure*, proved successful when first performed at Fontainebleau at the end of 1754. The *Mercure* reported that "on chanta deux fois le duo du dernier acte, ainsi que la Cour avoit paru le desirer."[30] When the work was revived at the Académie in a new French version 14 years later, the ensemble was praised more extensively in the same periodical as a "vrai chef-d'oeuvre de goût & d'art, soit pour la coupe des paroles, soit pour la belle mélodie, soit pour la beauté de l'accompagnement & le brillant de la musique."[31] This duet was based upon a quatrain text, repeated three times to form a ternary structure. Example 6.5 reproduces the opening section (which is similar in character to the two that follow). In praising "la coupe des paroles," the review probably referred to the way in which the text was

Example 6.5 "Je n'auray jamay" *Daphnis et Alcimadure* IIIvi (Mondonville, 1754)

Example 6.5 *(cont.)*

Example 6.5 *(cont.)*

segmented between bars 12 and 14, and again between bars 16 and 18. Its admiration of "la beauté de l'accompagnement" was not misplaced. The singers were supported at first by a simple continuo line; from bar 20 onwards soft, sustained chordal figurations were added in the upper string parts and a delicate, rocking quaver motion for tutti bass instruments introduced, the intensity of this accompaniment increasing as the section approached its conclusion. The beautiful melody also mentioned in the review requires no qualification; "le brillant de la musique" no doubt referred to the overall impact of the ensemble. Another important feature, although one that receives no comment in the *Mercure*, is the harmonic organization of the duet and the classical tendencies this displays: the tonic pedal upon which the first 11 bars are based; the Alberti-like movement of the bass-line between bars 20 and 35; and the cadential progression concluding the first section. In addition, the accompaniment is more

Example 6.6 "Formons des chaînes éternelles" *Hylas et Zélie* scene vi (Bury, 1762)

Example 6.6 *(cont.)*

elaborate than had previously been the case in this and the preceding period.

Other ensembles from the *tragédie-lyrique* repertory displayed similar harmonic tendencies and, while still set to *unanime* texts and with homophonic textures, therefore earned the distinction of forging a new musical style. For example, an anonymous pro-French pamphlet published during the Querelle des Bouffons, entitled *Reponse du coin du roi au coin de la reine*, described "Règne Amour" (Example 6.4) in warm terms as written "dans un genre neuf."[32] This example illustrates the tonic-dominant patterns around which the movement was organized, the first section concluding in the dominant key. A duet from Bury's *pastorale Hylas et Zélie* (1762), transcribed in part in Example 6.6, likewise displays modern harmonic tendencies, especially in the sonata-like polarization of tonic and dominant keys and the use of pedal points (bars 9–11 and bars 19–24). It was described in the *Mercure* as "agréablement travaillé dans le goût moderne."[33]

Dialogue Ensembles: Ensembles composed in dialogue were, like those written in traditional homophonic style, also well received, and this is shown by the *Mercure*'s praise for the duet "Je veux me venger d'un Rival qui m'outrage" in scene iii (not ii, as indicated in the quoted passage) of *La coquette trompée*, the *entrée* closing Dauvergne's ballet *Les fêtes d'Euterpe* (1758):

> "On ne laisse pas de retrouver dans les airs, & surtout dans le duo dialogué, qui termine la second scene, le même genie qui a produit la musique des *Troqueurs*."[34]

This ensemble combined two quarrelling lovers, Damon and Clarice, the former having suddenly appeared on stage accusing his betrothed of infidelity. As Example 6.7 illustrates, it consisted of rapid and irregular exchanges, a pattern unlike that of the standard dialogue duet described elsewhere, although it adhered to the principle of "l'unité de mélodie." The choice of the word "genie" was presumably an acknowledgement of the energetic style of the duet, its pace, and its brilliant accompaniment.

Two other dialogue duets were singled out for attention by the *Mercure*. The first, a vigorous lovers' misunderstanding from Iv of Dauvergne's *comédie-ballet La Vénitienne* (1768), set in a lively rondo, was described quite simply as "un duo contrasté dont la musique est d'un très-bel effet."[35] The second, from IIv of *L'Union de l'Amour et des Arts* (Floquet, 1773) was alluded to in even more general terms, alongside references to other high-points of the opera and without reference to any particular musical characteristics: "On admire son duo & sa belle chaconne du second acte ... comparables aux plus beaux morceaux de ce genre."[36] This, too, was a disagreement between the two main lovers involving the expression of conflicting sentiments and a rapid exchange of views. Given the very general nature of comments in the *Mercure*, it is unlikely that the ensembles in question received praise simply because of their dialogue textures. As already noted, reviews were concerned primarily with the overall impact and dramatic effect of individual movements.

In their *tragédie-lyrique Ernelinde*, Philidor and Poinsinet introduced dialogue ensembles modelled upon Italian patterns.[37] These inspired interesting reactions from the sources reviewing this controversial work. The first duet (the heated dispute between Ernelinde and her father) was described by the *Mercure* as "aussi saillant que conforme à leur situation,"[38] the word "saillant" presumably chosen to acknowledge the duet's vigorous style and the unusually powerful emotions it expressed. Another source emphasized the strong effect the

Example 6.7 *(cont.)*

Rend vo-tre coeur lé - ger.   vous a - vés pu chan-

moi?   moi?

- ger?   vous,   per - fi - de,   vo - la - ge, vo-tre coeur est un Pa-pil-

Votre Es

- lon   Qui vole   ou le plai-sir   le   fla - te d'avan-ta - ge

- prit   est un tourbil-lon   qui   tour - - - - ne et

Example 6.7 *(cont.)*

duet exercised on contemporary audiences, the result of the rigorous contrast between Ernelinde's line and that sung by her father:

> " … j'ai pleuré comme un milicien au premier duo … Que je plains les malheureux si durement organisés, qui refusent à ce morceau tout le *mélos* & le patétique d'un chant qui s'empare de l'ame & la fait voler entre une fille désolée & un pere en fureur, qui s'arrache effectivement de ses foibles bras pour courir au danger de la mort."[39]

Attitudes towards the second duet, "J'excuse ton jeune courage," closing Act I of the 1769 version, were also complimentary, the *Mercure* describing it as "une querelle des plus vive, & très-vivement exprimée dans un *duo* d'un goût peu connu jusqu'ici sur le théâtre de l'opéra, mais du plus grand effet."[40] The novelty of this duet, it will be remembered, lay as much in its uncommon pairing of male characters (*haute-contre* and bass) in passionate circumstances, as in its italianate dialogue texture and strongly divergent text. Another commentator observed that the musical result had powerful dramatic consequences:

> "La scene sixieme est d'une chaleur & d'une *vérité* démontrée par le suffrage *unanime* de tous les coeurs, & le duo qui la termine est d'une énergie dont on sentiroit encore plus l'effet s'il en faisoit moins, parce que les battemens de mains engloutissent ce beau morceau dans les acclamations publiques."[41]

The substance of such reviews, as with those highlighting harmonic developments in earlier pieces, indicates that novelty in ensemble composition in the serious genre, although carried out to a lesser extent than in the *opéra-comique*, was appreciated just as much. Critical and public opinion may consequently be regarded as forming a bridge between innovations in practice and the incorporation of these procedures into subsequent ensemble theories.

Divergent Ensembles: Only a small number of ensembles from the *tragédie-lyrique* of the third quarter of the 18th century were based on contrapuntal vocal textures and expressed conflicting sentiments. As a result, only one review (in the *Mercure*) contains relevant comments, this of Rameau's *comédie-ballet Les Paladins* (1760), which included two divergent duets and a divergent trio.

Both duets were confrontations between the ancillary characters Nerine and Orcan, in Iiii and IIvii respectively. The first was described as "un *Duo*, de la plus grand beauté" and the second as "un Duo *fort* agréable."[42] The trio in IIIiii was also found "fort agréable & très-bien éxécuté."[43] Lack of further detail makes it impossible to establish why these ensembles should have been considered "beautiful" or "agreeable": whether, for example, this was because of their vocal textures or for other musical or dramatic reasons.

The commentaries analyzed in this chapter represent only a cross-section of the opinions expressed on this subject during the period in question, but they nonetheless indicate the general nature of public taste and show how audiences of the time responded on occasion to concerted movements. What is apparent is that many different expressive types and musical styles of ensemble from both the *opéra-comique* and the *tragédie-lyrique* proved popular. Our final conclusions attempt to clarify more precisely the standards by which contemporary audiences judged ensembles, what they valued, and what they considered important.

Attitudes towards ensemble composition in the *opéra-comique* mirrored the approach of contemporary composers in that the specific musical procedures recommended by theorists (and by Rousseau in particular) were not generally considered relevant. Musical characteristics alone did not govern popular and critical responses to concerted movements. The dramatic impact of individual ensembles was of vital importance: musical achievements were expected to match dramatic intentions.

Dramaturgical effect was determined in close accordance with prevailing views on *vraisemblance*. Thus in the passages cited many references are made to *vérité*, to *chaleur*, and to *le naturel* ("le ton de la nature," etc.); to the fact that the music should not "betray" the poetry ("donne le change à la Poësie,") but that the two should correspond ("tout est analogue.") In short, ensembles were expected to embody an expressive and realistic portrayal of both character and the particular dramatic situation.

Ensembles in the *tragédie-lyrique*, at least from the substance of the opinions encountered, do not appear to have been judged in the same way. This may have been because the preconceptions attached to the serious genre and to its constituent parts, having been established over several decades, were more entrenched than those pertaining to the newer *opéra-comique* genre. Thus, while the poetic text and its clear presentation were deemed important, it would appear that musical aspects (melody, harmonic novelty, accompaniments) more than dramaturgical concerns (painting of character, apt and expressive translation of text) received primary attention. In other words, ensembles were judged more particularly in terms of the musical impression they created. These contrasting approaches in fact serve to underline the fundamental difference between the comic and serious genres. The *tragédie-lyrique* ensemble aimed at an idealized or "classical" mode of presentation (with exceptions such as *Ernelinde*), whereas the *opéra-comique* produced ensembles of a vivid and realistic character.

Inherent in this generalized distinction is a tension between musical and dramatic values, a tension characterizing opera since its inception. It parallels the tension between artifice and *vraisemblance*, that between theory and practice, and between the many other concepts that were in conflict during the Enlightenment.[44] As ever, this tension was eased through the process of balancing opposites and finding a point of synthesis, although this process was complicated by the fact that the opposites in question were very often in a state of evolution and flux.

The case of ensembles in fact brought the tension between "artifice" and "*vraisemblance*" to an insoluble pitch: the "truer" ensembles became (i.e. the more *vérité* they were felt to emanate) the more "artifice" they required on the part of both librettist and composer. The musical scope of the ensemble increased considerably during the third quarter of the 18th century. Individual concerted movements admitted more and more characters, introduced contrapuntal textures to enhance the representation of contrasting sentiments, experimented with more elaborate instrumental accompaniments, and explored new techniques of formal construction. These increasingly complex designs placed greater demands on singers and orchestral players, as well as on audiences who, if Garcin is typical, perhaps felt challenged by the speed, technique, and diversity of several concerted movements. Successful renditions of such pieces were, as many of the opinions cited above emphasize, well-received and highly acclaimed for their *vérité*. At times, however, performance difficulties would obtrude; this exposed the artifice and, as a result, *vraisemblance* was sacrificed. The balance between experimentation (artifice) and success (*vraisemblance*) was often extremely fine.

How, then, may the interaction between theory, practice, and the public be summarized in broad terms? From the middle of the 18th century onwards, a new aesthetic outlook caused a complete reversal of the relation between theory and practice. Stereotyped Baroque patterns, canonized by theory, were replaced by examples from a lower-class theater (the *opéra-comique*) that suddenly set theory to nought and left many writers searching for the means to express their ideas. Nougaret voiced this dilemma by asking rhetorical questions such as:

> "La plus-part des Compositeurs, de la nouvelle musique sur-tout, observent-ils toujours ces règles judicieuses, puisées dans la Nature?"[45]

Even after 1762 and the development of the genre under royal patronage, the repertory of the Comédie-Italienne, because of its accessibility and its emphasis on realism and everyday life, was destined to replace older ideas. It was directed at a new and more mixed "public", whose tastes and expectations were very different from those of the more aristocratic audiences which had patronized established theaters during the first half of the century. As Charlton points out:

> "The old guard ... was becoming adulterated by bourgeois elements, for in that same period Parisian bankers, merchants and others rose to supremacy. With an estimated 40,000 members, five times as numerous as the nobility, this class was financing major architectural and industrial programmes. Of course, they demanded entertainment."[46]

The *opéra-comique* thus heralded the emergence of new musical and dramatic standards at the Comédie-Italienne. These were opposed by traditionalists, but the Enlightenment spirit gained momentum during the later decades of the 18th century. It first of all replaced Baroque traditions with elements constituting the Classical style; the free-thinking and individualism it encouraged thereafter led to the Revolution of 1789, and ultimately gave birth to the ideology of Romanticism.

Notes

1. See above, pp. 237–238.
2. A. Contant d'Orville: *Histoire de l'opéra bouffon* (Paris, 1768), i, p. 4 and p. 12.
3. *Ibid.*, p. 55.
4. *Ibid.*, p. 17. For an analysis of this quartet, see above, p. 82.
5. *Mercure de France*, April, i (1763), p. 200.
6. Journals examined, in addition to the *Mercure*, included *L'Avant-coureur, Annonces, affiches et avis divers*, and *Les spectacles de Paris*.
7. L. Garcin: *Traité du mélodrame* (Paris, 1772), pp. vii–viii.
8. *Ibid.*, pp. 10–11.
9. *Ibid.*, pp. 214–215.
10. *Ibid.*, p. 215.
11. *Ibid.*, p. 204.
12. *Op. cit.*, i, p. 259.
13. *Op. cit.*, p. 214.
14. *Op. cit.*, i, p. 261.
15. *Mercure de France*, January, i (1763), p. 182.
16. *L'Avant-coureur* (1762), pp. 767–768.
17. *Ibid.*
18. See above, p. 133 and p. 159.
19. *Op. cit.*, p. 234.
20. *Ibid.*, pp. 234–235.
21. *Ibid.*, pp. 235–236.
22. *Ibid.*, p. 238.
23. *Ibid.*, pp. 205–207.
24. *Mercure de France*, May (1769), p. 156.
25. *L'Avant-coureur* (1768), p. 29.
26. *Ibid.* (1764), p. 46.
27. Supporters of French opera in the Querelle des Bouffons gathered under this name while advocates of Italian opera were collectively known as the *coin de la reine*.
28. *Mercure de France*, February (1753), p. 180.
29. J. Cazotte: *La guerre de l'opera* (Paris, 1753), p. 13.
30. *Mercure de France*, December, ii (1754), p. 211.
31. *Ibid.*, July, i (1768), p. 140.
32. *Reponse du coin du roi au coin de la reine* (Paris, 1753), p. 6. This was refuted in an anonymous pro-Italian pamphlet published shortly afterwards: "Accordons au jeune homme que le *Duo* est agréable; mais non qu'il soit dans un genre neuf." *Arrêt rendu a l'amphithéatre de l'opera, sur la plainte du milieu du parterre intervenant dans la querelle des deux coins* (Paris, 1753), p. 10.

33. *Mercure de France*, July, ii (1762), p. 131.

34. *Ibid.*, September (1758), p. 190.

35. *Ibid.*, June (1768), p. 178.

36. *Ibid.*, October, i (1773), p. 142.

37. See above, p. 200.

38. *Mercure de France*, January, i (1768), p. 216.

39. *Lettre à M. le Chevalier de *** à l'occasion du nouvel opéra* (Paris, 1768), p. 7.

40. *Mercure de France*, January, i (1768), p. 222.

41. *Lettre à M. le Chevalier*, p. 8.

42. *Mercure de France*, March (1760), p. 173 and p. 176 respectively.

43. *Ibid.*, p. 179.

44. This point was stressed by Cassirer: see above, p. 217.

45. Quoted originally on p. 238.

46. D. Charlton: *Grétry and the Growth of Opéra-Comique* (Cambridge, 1986), p. 11.

Conclusion

The 18th century witnessed a significant transformation of the operatic ensemble in terms of musical language, dramatic substance, and general status. In the early part of the century the concept of the ensemble, that is of characters combining simultaneously in song, was not such as to encourage the frequent inclusion of such pieces in operatic works. An aesthetic establishing the *vraisemblance* of concerted movements had to be defined, the musical and dramatic approaches of composers and librettists articulated, and the results accepted by audiences, *connaisseurs*, and critics. The gradual process by which this was achieved in one country has been described in the chapters of this book, through reference in particular to the *opéra-comique*. By the 1770s the ensemble had become an important component of opera, one still ripe for further development, but established and accepted as a form of expression.

The characteristics of ensemble composition in French serious genres were established in the late 17th century and continued in this manner, with some notable departures from conventional practice, for several decades. Concerted movements were written mainly for two characters, designed upon *unanime* texts, and composed in predominantly homophonic textures. The dignified tone of these genres largely denied such movements a dramatically varied or dynamic role, and their primary function was to reinforce sentiments previously introduced in recitative or solo *airs*.

The *opéra-comique*, whose rapid development after 1750 was influenced by elements of Italian *buffa* style, was much less hidebound by rules and conventions. Consequently, a more experimental approach to concerted writing was adopted. This resulted, firstly, in the creation of more intricate and extensive ensemble texts, gradually admitting up to seven clearly individual characters. Thereafter, the musical complexion of concerted movements aimed for a much closer empathy with the poetic text. This accompanied a more realistic, integrated representation of concerted movements on stage. Finally, much greater attention was focused on ensembles in the wider planning of stage works, and as a result their unique dramatic potential came to be recognized and exploited. They were able to appropriate and convey aspects of a stage work previously entrusted to solo song, recitative or spoken dialogue. Where to place such movements became a crucial concern rather than an arbitrary matter.

How innovative and influential these achievements were may only be understood fully by studying the progression of concerted writing in other genres. To what extent, for example, did ideas implemented in the *opéra-comique* match developments in the *opera buffa* and *opera seria* during the second half of the 18th century, particularly in the hands of librettists such as Goldoni, and composers including Jommelli, Galuppi, Traetta, Piccinni, Sacchini, and Paisiello? What techniques did Gluck appropriate in his reworkings of *opéra-comique* librettos for the Viennese court during the 1750s and 1760s, and how many of these ideas were carried over to his serious operas in later decades, in particular those performed in Paris from 1774 onwards? To what extent did Grétry, his collaborators, and their contemporaries continue, during the 1770s and 1780s, the experimental work of their predecessors in the *opéra-comique*? How, eventually, did Mozart synthesize these different strands of ensemble composition in his varied dramatic works?

What has been presented thus far in relation to the 18th-century operatic ensemble is a starting point to be developed and expanded in several ways. That the ensemble played an important role in the *opéra-comique* during the third quarter of the 18th century has been shown. That the *opéra-comique*, in turn, exerted a considerable influence in the evolution of a Classical operatic style during the same period should also be stressed.[1] A taste for French culture had spread across Europe. Many foreign courts adopted the French language and customs; the political and philosophical free-thinking of the Enlightenment also found many supporters.

The *opéra-comique* was exported to Austria, Germany, Russia, England, and Central Europe.[2] Mozart based his early opera *Bastien und Bastienne* (1768) on a French work, Favart's *Les amours de Bastien et Bastienne*. The origins of *Die Entführung aus dem Serail* (1782) may also be traced back to an earlier French source: *Les pèlerins de la Mecque*, written by Le Sage, Fuzelier, and d'Orneval for the Foire Saint Laurent in 1726. This work had, in the meantime, been used by Gluck in his Viennese setting of *La rencontre imprévue* (1764); and Brown has recently drawn attention to other links between this stage of Gluck's career and Mozart:

"At Mozart's death it was neither the *tragédies lyriques* nor the pantomime ballets of Gluck, but the French comic operas that were represented in his library by manuscript scores to *Le Diable à quatre* and *L'Arbre enchanté*— which, one would like to think, were presents from their composer."[3]

Grétry's influence on Mozart has also been documented, Charlton pointing to the latter's possession of a score of *Zémire et Azor*, which:

"can be compared to *Die Zauberflöte* both in detail (e.g. the magic meal conjured in act I) and in its general panoply of effects and qualities: the wide formal range of solo and ensemble music; experimental orchestration; the importance of the passage of time and changes of place; the testing and the triumph of virtue."[4]

The diffusion of the *opéra-comique* during the second half of the 18th century was, therefore, considerable, and its influence even on the masters of the Classical period remains to be examined further. One of the most significant features of the genre's rapid development was the importance attached to ensemble composition. Mozart, in creating concerted movements of considerable complexity and extending the boundaries yet further, drew on models that had not only secured a unique dramatic identity within the overall framework of operatic composition, but had also attained a remarkable degree of musical sophistication in terms of duration, formal and harmonic structuring, vocal and orchestral interplay, and expressive effect.

Notes

1. See B.A. Brown: 'La diffusion et l'influence de l'opéra-comique en Europe au xviiie siècle', *L'Opéra-comique en France au xviiie siècle*, ed. P. Vendrix (Liège, 1992).

2. See A. Iacuzzi: *The European Vogue of Favart: the Diffusion of the Opéra-Comique* (New York, 1932); and M. Robinson: 'Two London Versions of *The Deserter*', *IMSCR*, xii: *Berkeley 1977*.

3. B.A. Brown: *Christoph Willibald Gluck and Opéra-Comique in Vienna, 1754–1764* (diss., U. of California, 1986), pp. 861–862.

4. D. Charlton: *Grétry and the Growth of Opéra-Comique* (Cambridge, 1986), p. 100. More direct use of Grétry's material by Mozart occurs with the quotation from the women's chorus closing the first act of *Les mariages samnites* in the piano variations KV 352/374c (Charlton, *Op. cit.*, p. 145); with almost identical musical material in comparable dramatic situations in *L'amant jaloux* and *Le nozze di Figaro* (p. 169); and with the use of material by another *opéra-comique* composer, Dezède (*Julie*), in a set of variations KV264/315d (p. 281).

Appendix I

Works performed, but not necessarily premièred, at the Académie Royale de Musique, 1673–1751. See T. de Lajarte: *Bibliothèque musicale du théâtre de l'Opéra* (Paris, 1878/R1971) for a more comprehensive listing. Daily performances were recorded in the *Journal de l'Opéra* (MS: *F-Po*) for many of the years in question.

Lully

1673	Cadmus et Hermione	Quinault	tragédie en musique
1674	Alceste	Quinault	tragédie en musique
1675	Thésée	Quinault	tragédie en musique
1676	Atys	Quinault	tragédie en musique
1677	Isis	Quinault	tragédie en musique
1678	Psyché	Corneille	tragédie en musique
1679	Bellérophon	Corneille & Fontenelle	tragédie en musique
1680	Proserpine	Quinault	tragédie en musique
1682	Persée	Quinault	tragédie en musique
1683	Phaëton	Quinault	tragédie en musique
1684	Amadis	Quinault	tragédie en musique
1685	Roland	Quinault	tragédie en musique
1686	Armide	Quinault	tragédie en musique
1686	Acis et Galatée	Campistron	pastorale

Préramistes

1687	Achille et Polyxène	Collasse / Campistron	tragédie en musique
1689	Thétis et Pélée	Collasse / Fontenelle	tragédie en musique
1690	Enée et Lavinie	Collasse / Fontenelle	tragédie en musique
1693	Médée	Charpentier / Corneille	tragédie en musique
1694	Circé	Desmarets / Saintonge	tragédie en musique
1695	Théagène et Cariclée	Desmarets / Duché de Vancy	tragédie en musique
1695	Ballet des saisons	Collasse / Pic	opéra-ballet
1695	Les amours de Momus	Desmarets / Duché de Vancy	ballet
1696	La naissance de Vénus	Collasse / Pic	opéra
1696	Ariane et Bacchus	Marais / Saint-Jean	tragédie en musique

1697	Issé	Destouches / Lamotte	pastorale-héroïque
1697	L'Europe galante	Campra / Lamotte	opéra-ballet
1697	Vénus et Adonis	Desmarets / Rousseau	tragédie en musique
1697	Aricie	Lacoste / Pic	opéra-ballet
1698	Les festes galantes	Desmarets / Duché de Vancy	ballet
1699	Le carnaval de Venise	Campra / Regnard	comédie lyrique
1699	Amadis de Grèce	Destouches / Lamotte	tragédie en musique
1699	Marthésie	Destouches / Lamotte	tragédie en musique
1700	Hésione	Campra / Danchet	tragédie en musique
1700	Le triomphe des arts	Labarre / Lamotte	opéra-ballet
1701	Aréthuse	Campra / Danchet	ballet
1701	Omphale	Destouches / Lamotte	tragédie en musique
1702	Tancrède	Campra / Danchet	tragédie en musique
1703	Les muses	Campra / Danchet	opéra-ballet
1704	Le Carnaval et la Folie	Destouches / Lamotte	comédie-ballet
1704	Iphigénie en Tauride	Desmarets & Campra / Duché de Vancy & Danchet	tragédie en musique
1705	Alcine	Campra / Danchet	tragédie en musique
1705	Philomèle	Lacoste / Roy	tragédie en musique
1706	Cassandre	Bertin & Bouvard / Lagrange-Chancel	tragédie en musique
1706	Alcyone	Marais / Lamotte	tragédie en musique
1707	Bradamante	Lacoste / Roy	tragédie en musique
1708	Hippodamie	Campra / Roy	tragédie en musique
1709	Sémélé	Marais / Lamotte	tragédie en musique
1710	Diomède	Bertin / La Serre	tragédie en musique
1710	Les fêtes vénitiennes	Campra / Danchet	opéra-ballet
1712	Callirhoé	Destouches / Roy	tragédie en musique
1712	Creuse	Lacoste / Roy	tragédie en musique
1712	Idomenée	Campra / Danchet	tragédie en musique
1713	Télèphe	Campra / Danchet	tragédie en musique
1713	Médée et Jason	Salomon / Pellegrin	tragédie en musique
1713	Les amours déguisés	Bourgeois / Fuzelier	opéra-ballet
1714	Les fêtes, ou Le triomphe de Thalie	Mouret / La Font	opéra-ballet
1714	Télémaque et Calypso	Destouches / Pellegrin	tragédie en musique
1715	Les plaisirs de la paix	Bourgeois / Menesson	opéra-ballet
1715	Théonoé	Salomon / Pellegrin	tragédie en musique
1716	Ajax	Bertin / Menesson	tragédie en musique
1716	Hypermnestre	Gervais / La Font	tragédie en musique
1716	Les festes de l'été	Montéclair / Pellegrin	opéra-ballet
1717	Ariane	Mouret / Roy & Lagrange-Chancel	tragédie-lyrique
1718	Sémiramis	Destouches / Roy	tragédie en musique
1718	Le jugement de Pâris	Bertin / Barbier & Pellegrin	pastorale-héroïque
1719	Les plaisirs de la campagne	Bertin / Barbier & Pellegrin	opéra-ballet
1721	Les élémens	Destouches / Roy	opéra-ballet

1723	Les festes grecques et romaines	Collin de Blamont / Fuzelier	ballet-héroïque
1723	Pirithous	Mouret / La Serre	tragédie-lyrique
1725	Télégone	Lacoste / Pellegrin	tragédie en musique
1726	Pirame et Thisbé	Rebel & Francoeur / La Serre	tragédie en musique
1726	Les stratagèmes de l'amour	Destouches / Roy	ballet-héroïque
1727	Les amours des dieux	Mouret / Fuzelier	ballet-héroïque
1728	Tarsis et Zélie	Rebel & Francoeur / La Serre	tragédie en musique
1728	Orion	Lacoste / Pellegrin & La Font	tragédie en musique
1728	La princesse d'Elide	Villeneuve / Pellegrin	ballet-héroïque
1730	Pyrrhus	Royer / Fermelhuis	tragédie en musique
1732	Biblis	Lacoste / Fleury	tragédie en musique
1732	Jephté	Montéclair / Pellegrin	tragédie en musique
1732	Le triomphe de sens	Mouret / Roy	ballet-héroïque

Rameau

1733	Hippolyte et Aricie	Pellegrin	tragédie
1735	Les Indes galantes	Fuzelier	opéra-ballet
1737	Castor et Pollux	Bernard	tragédie
1739	Les fêtes d'Hébé	Montdorge	opéra-ballet
1739	Dardanus (i)	Le Clerc de la Bruère	tragédie
1744	Dardanus (ii)	Le Clerc de la Bruère	tragédie
1745	La princesse de Navarre	Voltaire	comédie-ballet
1745	Platée	Le Valois d'Orville	comédie lyrique
1745	Les fêtes de Polymnie	Cahusac	opéra-ballet
1745	Le temple de la Gloire	Voltaire	opéra-ballet
1747	Les fêtes de l'Hymen et de l'Amour	Cahusac	opéra-ballet
1748	Zaïs	Cahusac	pastorale-héroïque
1748	Pigmalion	Ballot de Sauvot	acte de ballet
1748	Les surprises de l'Amour	Bernard	opéra-ballet
1749	Naïs	Cahusac	pastorale-héroïque
1749	Zoroastre	Cahusac	tragédie en musique
1751	La guirlande	Marmontel	acte de ballet
1751	Acante et Céphise	Marmontel	pastorale-héroïque

Rameau's Contemporaries

1734	Les fêtes nouvelles	Duplessis / Massip	opéra-ballet
1735	Achille et Déidamie	Campra / Danchet	tragédie
1735	Les grâces	Mouret / Roy	ballet-héroïque
1735	Scanderberg	Rebel & Francoeur / Lamotte & La Serre	tragédie
1736	Les voyages de l'Amour	Boismortier / Le Clerc de la Bruère	ballet

1736	Les romans	Niel / Bonneval	ballet-héroïque
1736	Les génies	Duval / Fleury	ballet
1737	Le triomphe de l'harmonie	Grenet / Lefranc de Pompignan	ballet-héroïque
1738	Les caractères de l'Amour	Collin de Blamont / Pellegrin	ballet-héroïque
1738	Le ballet de la Paix	Rebel & Francoeur/ Roy	ballet-héroïque
1739	Zaïde, reine de Grenade	Royer / La Marre	ballet-héroïque
1740	Les nopces de Vénus	Campra / Danchet	divertissement
1741	Nitétis	Mion / La Serre	tragédie-lyrique
1741	Le temple de Gnide	Mouret / Bellis & Roy	divertissement
1742	Les amours de Ragonde	Mouret / Néricault-Destouches	comédie-lyrique
1742	Isbé	Mondonville / La Rivière	pastorale-héroïque
1743	Don Quichote chez la duchesse	Boismortier / Favart	ballet-comique
1743	Le pouvoir de l'Amour	Royer / Le Fevre de Saint-Marc	ballet-héroïque
1743	Les caractères de la Folie	Bury / Duclos	opéra-ballet
1744	L'école des amants	Niel / Fuzelier	opéra-ballet
1744	Les Augustales	Rebel & Francoeur / Roy	divertissement
1745	Zélindor	Rebel & Francoeur / Moncrif	divertissement
1746	Scylla et Glaucus	Leclair / D'Albaret	tragédie
1747	L'année galante	Mion / Roy	opéra-ballet
1747	Daphnis et Chloé	Boismortier / Laujon	opéra
1749	Le carnaval du Parnasse	Mondonville / Fuzelier	ballet-héroïque
1750	Léandre et Héro	de Brassac / Le Franc de Pompignan	tragédie-lyrique
1750	Almasis	Royer / Moncrif	acte de ballet
1750	Ismène	Rebel & Francouer / Moncrif	pastorale-héroïque
1751	Titon et l'Aurore	Bury / La Marre & Lamotte	pastorale-héroïque
1751	Aeglé	La Garde / Laujon	pastorale-héroïque

Appendix II

Sample of Italian operas performed between 1690 and 1754 (dates denote either year or Carnival of performance). The right hand column provides details of modern editions (where published) or of manuscript sources.

1690–1720

1690	Scarlatti	La Statira	Ottoboni	Cambridge MA, 1985
1690	Scarlatti	La Rosaura	Lucini	*GB-Lbl*
1694	Bononcini	Xerse	Stampiglia	*GB-Lbl*
1694	Scarlatti	Massimo Puppieno	Aureli	Cambridge MA, 1979
1694	Albinoni	Zenobia	Marchi	New York, 1979
1696	Bononcini	Il trionfo di Camilla	Stampiglia	*GB-Lbl*
1696	Pollarolo	Gli inganni felici	Zeno	New York, 1979
1697	Scarlatti	La caduta de' Decemviri	Stampiglia	Cambridge MA, 1980
1698	Scarlatti	Il prigioniero fortunato	Paglia	*GB-Lbl*
1700	Scarlatti	L'Eraclea	Stampiglia	Cambridge MA, 1974
1701	Ariosti	La fede ne' tradimenti	after Gigli	*GB-Lbl*
1702	Bononcini	Cefalo	Guidi	*GB-Lbl*
1702	Bononcini	Polifemo	Ariosti	Berlin, 1938
1705	Mancini	Gl'amanti generosi	Candi	New York, 1978
1707	Bononcini	Turno Aricino	Stampiglia	*GB-Lbl*
1707	Scarlatti	Il Mitridate Eupatore	Frigimelica Roberti	Milan, 1953
1708	Albinoni	Pimpinone	Pariati	Madison WI, 1983
1710	Scarlatti	La principessa fedele	A. Piovene	Cambridge MA, 1977
1711	Fago	La Cassandra indovina	Giuvo	*GB-Lbl*
1711	Porpora	Flavio Anicio Olibrio	Zeno & Pariati	*GB-Lbl*(Acts 1 & 2)
1713	Lotti	Porsenna	Piovene	*GB-Lbl*
1714	Scarlatti	Scipione nelle Spagne	Zeno & Serino	*GB-Lbl*
1714	Scarlatti	L'amor generoso	Papis & Stampiglia	*GB-Lbl*
1715	Scarlatti	Il Tigrane	Lalli	*GB-Lbl*
1717	Lotti	Alessandro Severo	Zeno	New York, 1977
1718	Sarro	Arsace	Salvi	New York, 1978
1718	Scarlatti	Telemaco	Capece	New York, 1978

1718	Orlandini	Antigona	Pasqualigo	*GB-Lbl*
1718	Scarlatti	Il trionfo dell'onore	Tullio	*GB-Lbl*
1719	Caldara	Dafne	Biavi	Vienna, 1955
1719	Scarlatti	Marco Attilio Regolo	?	Cambridge MA, 1975
1719	Orlandini	Il marito giocatore[1]	Salvi	New York, 1984
1719	Conti	Don Chisciotte	Zeno & Pariati	New York, 1982

1720–1750: *opere serie*

1720	Bononcini	Astarto[2]	Rolli	London, 1721
1722	Sarro	Partenope	after Stampiglia	*GB-Lbl*
1725	Vinci	Elpidia[3]	Zeno	*GB-Lbl*
1725	Porpora	Didone abbandonata	Metastasio	*GB-Lbl* (Acts 2 & 3)
1725	Porpora	Siface	Metastasio	*GB-Lbl* (Acts 1 & 3)
1726	Porpora	Meride e Selinunte	Zeno	*GB-Lbl*
1726	Porsile	Spartaco	Pasquini	New York, 1979
1726	Vinci	Didone abbandonata	Metastasio	New York, 1977
1726	Vinci	Siroe, re di Persia	Metastasio	*GB-Lam*
1726	Vinci	L'Ernelinda	Silvani	*GB-Lcm*
1728	Vinci	Catone in Utica	Metastasio	*GB-Lcm* (Acts 1 & 2)
1728	Vinci	Medo	Frugoni	*F-Pc*
1728	Leo	Argene	Lalli	*GB-Lam*
1728	Porpora	Ezio	Metastasio	*GB-Lam*
1729	Orlandini	Adelaide	Salvi	*GB-Lam*
1729	Giacomelli	Lucio Papirio dittatore	Zeno & Frugoni	*GB-Lam*
1729	Porpora	Semiramide riconosciuta	Metastasio	New York, 1977
1729	Leo	Catone in Utica	Metastasio	New York, 1983
1729	Vinci	Semiramide riconosciuta	Metastasio	*GB-Lcm* (Act 1)
1730	Vinci	Alessandro nell' Indie	Metastasio	*GB-Lbl*
1730	Feo	Andromaca	Zeno	New York, 1977
1730	Vinci	Artaserse	Metastasio	*GB-Lbl*
1730	Hasse	Artaserse	Metastasio	*GB-Lbl*
1732	Pergolesi	Salustia	?Morelli	Milan, 1941
1732	Hasse	Cajo Fabricio	after Zeno	*F-Pc*
1732	Hasse	Euristeo	Lalli	*F-Pc*
1733	Hasse	Siroe, re di Persia	Metastasio	New York, 1977
1733	Pergolesi	Il prigioniero superbo	after Silvani	Milan, 1942
1733	Porpora	Arianna in Nasso	Rolli	*GB-Lbl*
1733	Caldara	L'olimpiade	Metastasio	New York, 1979
1734	Pergolesi	Adriano in Siria	Metastasio	Milan, 1942

1. Revision of the 1715 version.
2. Revision of the 1715 version.
3. A pasticcio composition with contributions from other composers.

1734	Leo	Il castello d'Atlante	Mariani	*GB-Lbl*
1734	Porpora	Enea nel Lazio	Rolli	*GB-Lbl*
1735	Porpora	Ifigenia in Aulide	Rolli	*GB-Lbl*
1735	Pergolesi	L'olimpiade	Metastasio	Milan, 1942
1735	Leo	Demofoonte	Metastasio	*GB-Lbl*
1735	Vivaldi	Griselda	Zeno, rev. Goldoni	New York, 1978
1735	Porpora	Polifemo	Rolli	*GB-Lbl*
1735	Leo	Lucio Papirio	Salvi	*GB-Lbl*
1736	Porpora	Mitridate	Cibber	*GB-Lbl* (Acts 2 & 3 only)
1736	Porpora	La festa d'Imeneo	Rolli	*GB-Lbl*
1736	Hasse	Alessandro nell' Indie[4]	Metastasio	*GB-Lbl*
1736	Leo	Farnace	Lalli	*F-Pc*
1737	Leo	L'olimpiade	Metastasio	New York, 1978
1738	Pescetti	La conquista del velo d'oro	Cori	*GB-Lbl*
1738	Hasse	Cleofide[5]	after Metastasio	*F-Pc*
1739	di Capua	Volegeso	Luccarelli	New York, 1977
1739	Leo	Il Ciro riconosciuto	Metastasio	*F-Pc*
1741	Jommelli	Astianatte	Salvi	*GB-Lbl*
1741	Jommelli	Ezio	Metastasio	*GB-Lbl* (1st version)
1741	Leo	Il Demetrio	Metastasio	*F-Pc*
1741	Jommelli	Merope	Zeno	*GB-Lbl*
1741	Jommelli	Semiramide riconosciuta	Metastasio	*GB-Lbl* (1st version)
1742	Porpora	La Rosmene	?	*GB-Lbl* (with omissions)
1742	Jommelli	Eumene	Zeno	*GB-Lbl* (1st version)
1742	Leo	L'Andromaca	Salvi	New York, 1979
1742	Jommelli	Tito Manlio	Roccaforte	*GB-Lbl* (1st version)
1743	Jommelli	Demofoonte	Metastasio	*F-Pc* (1st version)
1743	Hasse	Antigono	Metastasio	*GB-Lbl*
1743	Graun	Artaserse	Metastasio	New York, 1978
1744	Jommelli	Ciro riconosciuto[6]	Metastasio	*GB-Lbl*
1744	Galuppi	Ricimero	Silvani	*F-Pc* (1st version)
1745	Wagenseil	Ariodante	Salvi	New York, 1981
1745	Hasse	Arminio	Pasquini	Mainz, 1957–66
1745	Hasse	Tigrane[7]	Palella	*GB-Lam*
1746	Sellitto	Orazio Curiazio	?	*GB-Lcm*
1746	Jommelli	Caio Mario	Roccaforte	*GB-Lbl*
1747	Hasse	Semiramide riconosciuta[8]	Metastasio	*GB-Lbl*
1747	Galuppi	L'olimpiade	Metastasio	New York, 1978
1747	Hasse	La spartana generosa	Pasquini	*F-Pc*

---

4. A revision of Cleofide 1731.
5. The original version of this work was performed in 1731.
6. A revision of the 1743 original.
7. A revision of the 1729 version.
8. Originally performed in Naples, 1744.

1747	Hasse	Demetrio[9]	Metastasio	*F-Pc*
1748	Gluck	La Semiramide riconosciuta	Metastasio	New York, 1982
1748	Galuppi	Demetrio	Metastasio	*F-Pc* (1st version)
1748	Perez	Artaserse	Metastasio	*GB-Lcm*
1749	Jommelli	Artaserse	Metastasio	*GB-Lbl*
1749	Jommelli	Didone abbandonata	Metastasio	*F-Pc* (2nd version)
1749	Galuppi	Semiramide riconosciuta	Metastasio	*F-Pc*
1749	Galuppi	Artaserse	Metastasio	*F-Pc*
1750	Perez	Semiramide	Metastasio	*GB-Lcm*

1720–1754: *opere buffe*

1722	Vinci	Li zite 'ngalera	Saddumene	New York, 1979
1732	Pergolesi	Lo frate 'nnamorato	Federico	Milan, 1939
1735	Pergolesi	Il Flaminio	Federico	Milan, 1941
1735	Latilla	Angelica ed Orlando	Tullio	*GB-Lbl*
1738	Latilla	La finta cameriera[10]	Barlocci	New York, 1979
1739	Leo	Amor vuol sofferenze	Federico	Bari, 1962
1742	Leo	L'ambizione delusa	Canicà	*F-Pc*
1747	Logroscino	Il governatore	Canicà	New York, 1979
1750	Galuppi	Il mondo della luna	Goldoni	*F-Pc*
1750	Galuppi	Il mondo alla roversa	Goldoni	Leipzig, 1758
1752	Galuppi	La calamità de' cuori	Goldoni	*F-Pc*
1754	Cocchi	Li matti per amore	Goldoni	New York, 1982
1754	Galuppi	Il filosofo di campagna	Goldoni	Milan, *c*1970

1720–1750: *intermezzi*

1725	Telemann	Pimpinone	Praetorius	Mainz, 1936
1726	Hasse	Larinda e Vanesio	Salvi &/or Carasale	Madison, 1979
1727	Hasse	Grilletta e Porsugnacco	after Molière	*GB-Lcm*
1728	Hasse	Scintilla e Don Tabarano	Saddumene	*F-Pc*
1730	Hasse	Lucilla e Pandolfo	?	*GB-Lcm*
1733	Pergolesi	La serva padrona	Federico	Milan, 1941
1734	Pergolesi	La contadina astuta	Mariani	Milan, 1941
1742	Jommelli	Don Chichibio	?	*GB-Lbl*
1749	Jommelli	Don Trastullo	?	*GB-Lbl*
1750	Jommelli	L'uccellatrice	?	Milan, 1954

---

9.   Originally performed in 1732.
10. Originally performed as Gismondo in Naples, 1737.

Select Bibliography

Pre-1800 sources

Annonces, affiches et avis divers.

L'Avant-coureur, feuille hebdomadaire.

G. Bonnot de Mably: *Lettres à Madame la marquise de P... sur l'opéra* (Paris, 1741).

C. Burney: *Memoirs of the Life and Writings of the Abate Metastasio* (London, 1796).

F.A. Chevrier: *Observations sur le théâtre* (Paris, 1755).

A. Contant d'Orville: *Histoire de l'opéra bouffon* (Paris, 1768)

J. D'Alembert and D. Diderot, eds.: *Encyclopédie, ou Dictionnaire raisonné des sciences, arts et métiers* (Paris and Neuchâtel, 1751–65; suppls Amsterdam, 1776–7).

J. D'Alembert: 'Fragment sur la musique en général et sur la notre en particulier', *Oeuvres et correspondance inédites de D'Alembert*, ed. C. Henry (Paris, 1887).

D. Diderot: *Le neveu de Rameau*, ed. A. Adam (Paris, 1967).

J.-B. Dubos: *Réflexions critiques sur la poésie et sur la peinture* (Paris, 1719).

A.-P.-C. Favart, ed.: *Mémoires et correspondances littéraires, dramatiques et anecdotiques de C.S. Favart* (Paris, 1808).

L. Garcin: *Traité du mélodrame* (Paris, 1772).

A. Gautier de Montdorge: *Réflexions d'un peintre sur l'opéra* (La Haye, 1743).

Journal de l'Opéra (MS: F-Po).

J. Lacombe: *Le spectacle des beaux-arts* (Paris, 1758).

V. de La Jonchère: 'Essai sur l'opéra', *Théâtre lyrique*, i, (Paris, 1772).

J.L. Le Cerf de la Viéville: *Comparaison de la musique italienne et de la musique françoise* (Brussels, 1704–6).

*Lettre à M. le Chevalier de *** à l'occasion du nouvel opéra* (Paris, 1768).

A. Maillet-Duclairon: *Essai sur la connoissance des théâtres françois* (Paris, 1751).

Mercure de France

J. Monnet: *Supplément au roman comique, ou Mémoires pour servir à la vie de Jean Monnet* (London, 1772).

P. Nougaret: *De l'art du théâtre en général* (Paris, 1769).

F. Parfaict and C. Parfaict: *Mémoires pour servir à l'histoire des spectacles de la foire* (Paris, 1743).

A.-F. Quétant: 'Essai sur l'opéra-comique', in *Le serrurier* (Paris, 1765).

F. Raguenet: *Paralèle des italiens et des françois en ce qui regarde la musique et les opéra* (Paris, 1702).

T. Rémond de Saint-Mard: *Réflexions sur l'opéra* (La Haye, 1741).

J.-J. Rousseau: *Les confessions*, ed. J. Voisine (Paris, 1964).

———: *Dictionnaire de musique* (Paris, 1768).

C. de Saint-Evremond: 'Sur les opera à Monsieur le Duc de Buckingham', *Oeuvres mêlées*, ii, (London, 1709).

C. de Villiers: *Dialogues sur la musique* (Paris, 1774).

Post-1800 sources

J.R. Anthony: *The Opera-Ballets of André Campra: a Study of the First Period French Opera-Ballet* (diss., U. of South Carolina, 1964).

———: *French Baroque Music from Beaujoyeulx to Rameau* (London, 1973, rev. 2/1978).

L.P. Arnoldson: *Sedaine et les musiciens de son temps* (Paris, 1934).

J.-M. Bardez: *Diderot et la musique: valeur de la contribution d'un mélomane* (Paris, 1975).

G. Barksdale: *The Chorus in French Baroque Opera* (diss., U. of Utah, 1973).

C. Barnes: *The Théâtre de la Foire (Paris, 1697–1762): its Music and Composers* (diss., U. of Southern California, 1965).

S. Baud-Bovy: *Jean-Jacques Rousseau et la musique*, ed. J.-J. Eigeldinger (Neuchâtel, 1988).

H. Becker: 'Das Duett in der Oper', *Musik, Edition, Interpretation: Gedenkschrift Günter Henle* (Munich, 1980).

G. Bonnet: *Philidor et l'évolution de la musique française* (Paris, 1921).

C.D. Brenner: *A Bibliographical List of Plays in the French Language, 1700–1789* (Berkeley, 1947, rev. 2/1979).

———: *The Théâtre Italien: its Repertory 1716–1793* (Berkeley, 1961).

O.G. Brockett: 'The Fair Theatres of Paris in the Eighteenth Century: the Undermining of the Classical Ideal', *Classical Drama and its Influence: Essays Presented to H.D.F. Kitto* (London, 1965).

B.A. Brown: *Christoph Willibald Gluck and Opéra-Comique in Vienna, 1754–1764* (diss., U. of California, 1986).

——: *Gluck and the French Theatre in Vienna* (Oxford, 1991)

——: 'La diffusion et l'influence de l'opéra-comique en Europe au xviiie siècle', *L'Opéra-comique en France au xviiie siècle*, ed. P. Vendrix (Liège, 1992).

L.E. Brown: *The Tragédie-Lyrique of André Campra and his Contemporaries* (diss., U. of North Carolina, 1978).

——: 'Departures from the Lullian Convention in the *tragédie-lyrique* of the *préramiste* Period', *RMFC*, xxii (1984).

E. Campardon: *Les spectacles de la foire* (Paris, 1877).

M. Cardy: 'The Literary Doctrines of Jean-François Marmontel', *Studies on Voltaire and the Eighteenth Century*, ccx (1982).

F. Carmody: 'Le répertoire de l'opéra-comique en vaudevilles de 1708 à 1764', *University of California Publications in Modern Philology*, xvi (1933).

H. Carrington-Lancaster: 'The Comédie Française, 1701–1774', *Transactions of the American Philosophical Society*, xli (1951).

C.M. Carroll: *François-André Danican Philidor: his Life and Dramatic Art* (diss., Florida State U., 1960).

E. Cassirer: *The Philosophy of the Enlightenment* (Princeton, 1951).

D. Charlton: 'Orchestra and Chorus at the Comédie-Italienne (Opéra-Comique), 1755–1799', *Slavonic and Western Music: Essays for Gerald Abraham* (Oxford, 1985).

——: *Grétry and the Growth of Opéra-Comique* (Cambridge, 1986).

——: '"L'art dramatico-musical": an Essay', *Music and Theatre: Essays in Honour of Winton Dean* (Cambridge, 1987).

G. Cucuel: 'Sources et documents pour servir à l'histoire de l'opéra-comique en France', *L'année musicale*, iii (1913).

——: 'Notes sur la Comédie-Italienne de 1717 à 1789', *SIMG*, xv (1913–14).

——: *Les créateurs de l'opéra-comique français* (Paris, 1914).

C. Dahlhaus: 'What is a musical drama?', *COJ*, i (1989).

W. Dean: *Handel and the Opera Seria* (Berkeley, 1969).

W. Dean and J. Merrill Knapp: *Handel's Operas, 1704–1726* (Oxford, 1987).

E. Dent: *Alessandro Scarlatti: his Life and Works* (London, 1905).

——: 'Ensembles and Finales in Eighteenth-century Italian Opera', *SIMG*, xi (1909–10); xii (1910–11).

B. Didier: *La musique des lumières* (Paris, 1985).

E.O. Downes: *The Operas of Johann Christian Bach as a Reflection of the Dominant Trends in Opera Seria 1750–1780* (diss., Harvard U., 1958).

R. Fajon: *L'opéra à Paris du Roi Soleil à Louis le Bien-Aimé* (Paris and Geneva, 1984).

A. Font: *Favart, l'opéra-comique et la comédie-vaudeville aux xviie et xviiie siècles* (Paris, 1894/R1970).

R. Freeman: *Opera Without Drama: Currents of Change in Italian Opera, 1675–1725* (Ann Arbor, 1981).

E. Fubini: *Les philosophes et la musique* (Paris, 1983).

C. Girdlestone: *La tragédie en musique (1673–1750) considérée comme genre littéraire* (Geneva, 1972).

V.B. Grannis: *Dramatic Parody in the Eighteenth Century* (New York, 1931).

F. Green, ed.: *Diderot's Writings on the Theatre* (Cambridge, 1936).

D.J. Grout: *The Origins of the Opéra-Comique* (diss., Harvard U., 1939).

———: 'The *Opéra Comique* and the *Théâtre Italien* from 1715 to 1762', *Miscelánea en homenaje a Monseñor Higinio Anglés*, i (Barcelona, 1958).

———: *Alessandro Scarlatti: an Introduction to his Operas* (Berkeley, 1979).

G. Hardie: *Leonardo Leo (1694–1744) and his Comic Operas 'Amor vuol sofferenza' and 'Alidoro'* (diss., Cornell U., 1973).

D. Heartz: 'From Garrick to Gluck: the Reform of Theatre and Opera in the Mid-Eighteenth Century', *PRMA*, xciv (1967–8).

———: 'Les lumières: Voltaire and Metastasio; Goldoni, Favart and Diderot', *IMSCR*, xii: *Berkeley 1977*.

———: 'The Creation of the Buffo Finale in Italian Opera', *PRMA*, civ (1977–8).

———: 'Diderot et le Théâtre lyrique: "le nouveau stile" proposé par *Le Neveu de Rameau*', *RdM*, lxiv (1978).

———: 'Hasse, Galuppi and Metastasio', *Venezia e il melodramma nel settecento: Studi di musica veneta*, vi (Florence, 1978).

———: '*Vis comica*: Goldoni, Galuppi and *L'Arcadia in Brenta*', *Venezia e il melodramme nel settecento: Studi di musica veneta*, vii (Florence, 1981).

———: 'The Poet as Stage Director: Metastasio, Goldoni, and Da Ponte', *Mozart's Operas*, ed. T. Bauman (Berkeley, 1990).

S. Henze-Döhring: *Opera seria, opera buffa und Mozarts Don Giovanni*, *AnMc*, no. 24 (1986) [whole issue].

M. Hobson: *The Object of Art* (Cambridge, 1982).

A. Iacuzzi: *The European Vogue of Favart: the Diffusion of the Opéra-Comique* (New York, 1932).

R. Isherwood: *Music in the Service of the King* (Ithaca and London, 1973).

——: *Farce and Fantasy: Popular Entertainment in Eighteenth-Century Paris* (Oxford, 1986).

A. Jullien: *La musique et les philosophes au xviiie siècle* (Paris, 1873).

P. Kivy: *Osmin's Rage: Philosophical Reflections on Opera, Drama, and Text* (Princeton, 1988).

C.E. Koch: 'The Dramatic Ensemble Finale in the Opéra Comique of the Eighteenth Century', *AcM*, xxxix/1–2 (1967).

J.B. Kopp: *The Drame Lyrique: a Study in the Esthetics of Opéra-Comique, 1762–1791* (diss., U. of Pennsylvania, 1982).

T. de Lajarte: *Bibliothèque musicale du théâtre de l'Opéra* (Paris, 1878/R1971).

L. de La Laurencie: 'La grande saison italienne de 1752: les Bouffons', *BSIM*, viii (1912).

——: 'Deux imitateurs français des Bouffons: Blavet et Dauvergne', *L'année musicale*, ii (1912).

P.H. Lang: 'Diderot as Musician', *Diderot Studies*, x (1968).

D. Launay, ed.: *La Querelle des Bouffons* (Geneva, 1973) [facs. of 61 pamphlets pubd 1752–4].

——: 'La Querelle des Bouffons et ses incidences sur la musique', *IMSCR*, xii: *Berkeley 1977*.

G. Lazarevich: *The Role of the Neapolitan Intermezzo in the Evolution of Eighteenth-Century Musical Style* (diss., Columbia U., 1970).

R.A. Leigh: *Correspondance complète de Jean Jacques Rousseau* (Geneva, 1965–).

P. Letailleur: 'Jean-Louis Laruette, chanteur et compositeur: sa vie et son oeuvre', *RMFC*, viii (1968); ix (1969); x (1970).

D. Libby: 'Italy: Two Opera Centres', *Man and Music: the Classical Era*, ed. N. Zaslaw (London, 1989).

H. Lühning: *'Titus'-Vertonungen im 18. Jahrhundert: Untersuchungen zur Tradition der Opera Seria von Hasse bis Mozart*, *AnMc*, no. 20 (1983) [whole issue].

P.-M. Masson: 'Les idées de Rousseau sur la musique', *BSIM*, viii (1912).

——: *L'opéra de Rameau* (Paris, 1930).

——: 'La Lettre sur Omphale (1752)', *RdM*, xxvii (1945).

M. McClymonds: *Niccolò Jommelli: the Last Years 1769–1774* (Ann Arbor, 1978).

L. Michaud, ed.: *Biographie universelle* (Paris, 1843–65).

F. Millner: *The Operas of Johann Adolf Hasse* (Ann Arbor, 1979).

R.L. Myers: 'Rémond de Saint-Mard: a Study of his Major Works', *Studies on Voltaire and the Eighteenth Century*, lxxiv (1970).

M. Noiray: '*Hippolyte* et *Castor* travestis: Rameau à l'opéra-comique', *Jean-Philippe Rameau: Dijon 1983*.

A.R. Oliver: *The Encyclopedists as Critics of Music* (New York, 1947).

K. Pendle: '*Les philosophes* and *opéra-comique*: the Case of Grétry's *Lucile*', *MR*, xxxviii (1977).

J.S. Powell: 'The Musical Sources of the Bibliothèque-Musée de la Comédie-Française', *CMc*, xli (1986).

J.-G. Prodhomme: 'Diderot et la musique', *ZIMG*, xv (1913–14).

M.A. Rayner: *The Social and Literary Aspects of Sedaine's Dramatic Work* (diss., U. of London, 1960).

M. Robinson: 'Porpora's Operas for London, 1733–1736', *Soundings*, ii (1971–72).

———: *Naples and Neapolitan Opera* (Oxford, 1972).

P.E.J. Robinson: *Jean-Jacques Rousseau's Doctrine of the Arts* (Bern, 1984).

J. Rushton: 'Philidor and the Tragédie Lyrique', *MT*, cxvii (1976).

S. Sadie, ed.: *The New Grove Dictionary of Opera* (London, 1992).

G. Sadler: 'Rameau, Piron and the Parisian Fair Theatres', *Soundings*, iv (1974).

———: 'The Role of the Keyboard Continuo in French Opera, 1673–1776', *Early Music*, viii (1980).

———: 'Rameau, Pellegrin and the Opéra: the Revisions of "Hippolyte et Aricie" during its First Season', *MT*, cxxiv (1983).

K.M. Smith: *Egidio Duni and the Development of the Opéra-Comique from 1753 to 1770* (diss., Cornell U., 1980).

G. Snyders: *Le goût musical en France aux xviie et xviiie siècles* (Paris, 1968).

O. Sonneck: 'Ciampi's "Bertoldo, Bertoldino e Cacasenno" and Favart's "Ninette à la cour": a Contribution to the History of the Pasticcio', *SIMG*, xii (1910–11).

M. Tourneux, ed.: *Correspondance littéraire, philosophique et critique par Grimm, Diderot, Raynal, Meister, etc.* (Paris, 1877–82).

C. Troy: *The Comic Intermezzo* (Ann Arbor, 1979).

L.I. Wade: *The Dramatic Functions of the Ensemble in the Operas of Wolfgang Amadeus Mozart* (diss., Louisiana State U., 1969).

W. Weber: 'Learned and General Musical Taste in Eighteenth-Century France', *Past and Present*, xcix (1980).

H.C. Wolff: 'Italian Opera 1700–1750', *Opera and Church Music, 1630–1750, NOHM, v (London, 1975)*.

Index